Copyright © 2024 L
All rights rese.

This is a work of fiction. Unless otherwise indicated, all the names, characters, businesses, places, events and incidents in this book are either the product of the author's imagination or used in a fictitious manner. Any resemblance to actual persons, living or dead, or actual events is purely coincidental.

ONE

The sky dimmed from a bright eggshell blue to the clearest coral in a margin along the horizon. An incandescent line spanning the full width, flat Suffolk countryside for as far as the eye could see. The atmosphere sparkled in the cold, sharp January afternoon, two hours before a dusk that would come quickly.

The brambles around the perimeter of the garden did not yield easily to their progress and, even in the depths of winter, with a raw frost still on their dark green leaves, they were quick to bite at exposed skin with the thorns that had grown woody since Summer.

"Can we go through there?"

"Of course we can."

"I thought it was an airfield."

He laughed, "it hasn't been an airfield for 30 years!"

"But the fence is still there."

"Yes, here it is but look, twenty yards along theres nothing. You can step in right off the ploughed field. Anyway, its hardly an airfield."

She followed him as he parted the brambles and stepped over the forlorn chain link fencing. Rusted now and diminished to a couple of feet off the ground from its original eight foot barrier.

She cocked a leg over the fence and stood beside her brother in the long unkempt grass. It *was* hardly an airfield. The site was open and flat and spanned into the distance. To their left were ploughed fields, cultivated land now. To their right a coppice of spindly trees and a couple of grey

stone buildings, somewhat in disrepair. The site having been crudely bulldozed and cleared; now left, Mother Nature had once again begun to wrap her green fingers around its contours.
She drew a long breath of the sharp air, the low winter sun right in from of her making her squint.
"What are they going to build?"
"It was a warehouse – a distribution centre. They cleared the site a few years ago. Then the developer pulled out."
"So, it might still be developed?"
He shrugged. "May be. Been like this for years."
"Come on." He nodded, "Lets go and have a look over here."

The caravan was cold. It was always cold. Except in the summer if it was blisteringly hot outside. Then the caravan was too hot. But today, with the air outside as brittle and sharp as the thin layer of ice on the pond at the far end of the airfield the caravan was cold. The stove was hot and the soup was hot. He had poured the can of soup into the saucepan, waited for it to heat while he watched it then poured the contents of the saucepan into a bowl while he wondered if there was a way to heat the soup directly in the can, then eat the soup directly out of the can. Save washing up, save hot water. Was there something like that in the army – he vaguely recalled he may have read it somewhere. Self heating tins? It was an idea. Maybe somewhere on this airfield there was a whole stash of them – just like the alleged buried vehicles and the jettisoned bombs in the ponds. If there was, he surely would have found them by now – he knew nearly every last inch of this place. At least he liked to think he did – all except that very last inch.
It would be dark soon – lucky it had been a bright day or it would be dark already. Still, he left the curtains open to allow the last of the winter light to come in for a long as he could.
Then he heard voices. He stopped and listened, held his breath. Yes, he heard voices outside. People talking, one male, one female. Instantly he stood up and set the soup down. Without hesitation he went to the door and pushed it outwards into the icy air. It was late in the day, if this was the final knock on his door which would signify his tenuous residence here was finally over then it was an inconvenient time on such a cold day.
"Hey!" He called, hanging in the doorway.
They weren't even looking at the caravan, they weren't even taking any notice of it being there. Maybe he could have stayed in the warm. They did not look like a threat.

They both turned, slightly surprised. The tall, lanky guy probably near his own age – good clothes, good haircut. Not from round these parts he surmised.

"Hey – are you lost. Its getting dark, maybe you should be heading home ..." he ameliorated his initial stance.

The woman, reddish brown hair, pale skin – big eyes. A slight smile on her face. Athletic – he thought – athletic but probably nearer 30 than he was. Looked like she had bought the clothes she was wearing just to walk across the airfield.

"Hi." The guy said, and they started forward. "No, we're not lost – just looking over here. We're from the house over there ..." he nodded. "It was our Uncle's – we have been fortunate to inherit it."

Poking around he thought. Newcomers. Probably trouble without being 'trouble'.

"Your uncle?" He asked. "Which house?"

"Valspar" He turned and pointed. "Needs some updating ... I don't think its changed since I was there last which must be 30 years ago!"

"Valspar." He said. "Dick Saint? Your uncle?"

"Yes ..." he seemed a little astonished and stepped a stride closer.

The caravan was getting colder with the door open, and he was now into a conversation he couldn't be bothered with. He backed in a little.

"Nice house, trust its warmer than in here so if you'll excuse me..." he nodded. "Take care stumbling around here as its getting dark. There are open shafts ..."

He closed the door and left them standing there looking at it before they looked at each other briefly.

He sat down inside. The soup was getting cold.

The power went off. There was a click then she was plunged into the absolute darkness of a mid-winter Suffolk night – one where the stars and moon had decided to grace somewhere else with their presence. For a few seconds she sat there, not scared, not panicking – not really hurrying to do anything in the vain hope that in ten seconds it would click again, the lights would come on and she could continue watching her guilty pleasure on the television. There was no click and thirty seconds later she was still sitting there.

She sighed and stood up. Amazed at how silence could become so complete in that split second and how every tiny noise you wouldn't normally notice she now missed! The room was still in some disarray – boxes here and there, stuff left for another day, but she negotiated to the window without injury and peered out. From the few properties she could see there appeared to be a total blackout, nothing. Then a torch haphazardly sweeping about in the house to the left. She didn't have a torch – or at least know where on was. So, she stood for a few moments, pressing her face to the glass – waiting for light and life to resume around her. Then it did, the lights popped on as quick as they had popped off and the windows were once again filled to their edges with a pale yellow light – at least in the house to the left but not in this one. She looked behind herself as if hoping to see the lights return on her command, but they did not. The silence remained.

So. what now. Why hadn't these lights come on?

The wiring was old. It had probably knocked some kind of trip out in the huge old fusebox over the back door in the kitchen. With careful hands in the house she was not entirely used to being in, she made her way through the room without gaining bruises from items placed where she had forgotten. The kitchen was no lighter. In fact, the corner where the fuse box was even darker than the rest of the house. Positioned on the wall way above where any wisps of moonlight that might be there could reach from the kitchen window at the other end of the room.

What now? A torch? No, she didn't have a torch. A candle – a match? She wasn't aware there was either in the house. Gingerly, she traversed the kitchen to the window and peered out towards the sky – leaning across the sink so she could see further.

Off in the distance she could see a faint orange glow from the window in the caravan on the airfield. Maybe? She could wait here till morning, in darkness. She could go to bed early – sort it out tomorrow. Or she could put on her coat and go see if he had a torch – and a stepladder.

As she approached the caravan, she suddenly felt a little apprehensive. She hardly knew this strange guy who lived there. Would it not have been more sensible to go the house across the road – the one with the family of four who seemed *normal*? She drew a breath and told herself not to judge on appearances and consoled herself with the thought that just maybe he would be more shaken by someone banging on his caravan door in the pitch dark than she was actually doing it. She raised a flat hand and slapped the door, twice. The noise was louder than she expected. She gasped tinily to herself at that and cursed silently under her breath, nonetheless half amused.

There were noises from within, the caravan rocked slightly as he had obviously began to move. Then all noise and movement stopped. It was silent, and still. She sighed to herself and began to wonder why she had taken this course and not gone to the house over the road.

"Hey!" She called towards the door, "Hey, its me from the house over there ..." Stupidly she pointed behind herself and then realised that she could neither see the house, nor him her.

She heard him move, heard a few clicks then the door opened. He looked out. He had a woolly hat on and in the darkness he looked gaunt. "Whats wrong?" he asked.

She smiled. "I, er, the electricity has gone out. Its come on but not in our house. I know where the fuse box is but I don't have a torch – or anything ..." her voice trailed off as he stared at her. Not in a way that felt threatening but in a way that made her feel she was an inconvenience and she had intruded into his personal space.

He sighed and rubbed his nose with a finger. "Are you on your own?"

She went to answer but held her tongue. Was that a leading question and at the end of the day who the hell was he to ask?

"Did you just walk over here in the dark, without a torch? He asked before she answered.

She nodded.

"You should be careful, there are holes and shafts all around here. Its dangerous to be wandering about, especially in the dark you know ..."

"Ok, I will be careful." She said, in a small voice.

He grinned. "So, do you want to borrow a torch? Or do you want me to come back with you?

"The torch would be fine." She smiled.

He stared down at her in consideration.

"I'll come over, not right you should be wandering around in the dark anyway, not here. Where's your husband?

She answered too quickly, she thought. "Oh, he's not my husband." Then laughed, stupidly. "He's my brother." She added.

"Hang on." He ducked inside, grabbing a coat then sliding into it as he came down the steps and closed the door. He had a torch in his hand already and illuminated a beam in front of him.

He walked quickly, almost as if he had done this a thousand times, flicking the beam in front of him as he stepped.

"Keep behind me." He advised. "There are open shafts ..."

She almost jogged to keep up with him, tip toeing in his footsteps behind him. "You keep saying that." She commented. "What do you mean by "shafts"?"

"Holes" he replied. "Trapdoors, concrete shafts that drop straight down about twenty or thirty feet, connecting with storage bunkers below. A bit like manholes in the road only a lot of them no longer have covers over the holes, in the dark you could easily fall down them ..." his voice trailed off a little as he took a breath and strode on. "Probably kill yourself ..."

She made a face to herself in the dark behind him, a kind of a wry smile as she felt he was speaking to her like a stupid townie – which he probably thought she was – after all it was her that had banged on his caravan door because the lights had gone out.

He stepped over what was left of the boundary fence and stopped, turned slightly to her waiting for her to take a lead now he was on "their property" she ducked past him and he illuminated the path in front of her. She went straight to the back down, pushed it open and stood on the step waiting for him and his gift of light.

"Its pretty dark in here and we still haven't unpacked a lot of stuff so it's a bit of an assault course in here too!" She smiled, making light of his earlier comment but he did not react to it as he stepped inside. For a second or two he shone the beam of the torch around the house as if inspecting it but then caught himself and shone it on the floor in front of them.

"This way ..." she gestured, standing aside to let him lead. He stepped through into the kitchen and without a moment's hesitation shone the torch straight on the fuse box above the door going into the hallway.

"There." He said, walking towards it, "trip still out."

"I thought as much but couldn't see it!" She replied.

He stood below the box, reached up and flicked the switch back up. The lights came on. They both stood there squinting, plunged from darkness into bright white light.

He flicked the torch off, bounced it in his hand and turned back to her.

"Thank you." She smiled. "Must get a torch!"

"No problem" He looked around himself – looked slightly uncomfortable – clothes erring on worn, all slightly too big. His eyes were wandering around the interior of the room, but he was trying to look casual about it, like he wanted to stare but didn't want her to see him doing it. He caught her eyes with his but darted them away immediately.

"Hey, do you want a cup of tea or coffee – least I can do?

"Erm, no ..." He shuffled, "Its ok."

"No, its fine. The kettle was warm so it shouldn't take long to boil. What is it it? Tea or coffee?"

He paused, "Ok, tea please." And slowly sat back against the worktop. He stared at the fuse box again as she flicked the switch on the kettle and reached up for tea bags. Then he said. "Fuse box is in the same place."

She looked at him, "you know this house"
"You could say that."
"Did you live here once?
He shook his head. "No, a friend did. When I was a kid. Been a while since I was in here – its changed."
"Have you always lived here then?
"Born here." He replied, "My father worked on the farm here – lived in the house over there when it was still a tied cottage."
She stopped suddenly, one cup in hand and turned to him with a grin.
"Hey, I am so sorry – whats your name?
He raised his eyes to her, chin still down and there, just for the most fleeting moment of time, gave an impression that he did not want to tell her. "Jacob." He finally said.
She watched the word come from his lips almost as if it was a word he had not spoken for years.
"Hello Jacob" She stated with a smile. "I'm Marelle!"
He gave a little smile and nodded in acknowledgement. He was not comfortable here, almost looked like he wanted to run.
"So, how long have you lived over there?" She asked brightly.
"Years." He said, shifting his position and crossing his legs so that he rested against the worktop. In here, in her environment his voice seemed softer than she had remembered it outside.
"Have you always lived in a caravan?"
"No." He exhaled the word as if it was an absurd question. "I used to live in a house, here in the village."
She wanted to say '*what happened*' but she didn't. At this moment it was best to let it lie.
"So that's why you know your way around so well …?"
He smiled properly, finally – an unusually warm, boyish smile despite him being a good deal older than she was.
"Well, I hadn't even heard of this place a few months ago and now I'm living here!" Marelle continued, completing the mug of tea and handing it to him. "Maybe I have found the right person to show me around?"
"Oh, I don't think so." He said. "I kind of keep myself to myself. I don't get involved much with whatever's going on."
"Well I'll be here for a while, hopefully, if it all works out …I work from home, for my brother but I have also got to get this place straight."
He gave a non-commital smile in return.
Somehow the fact that she wanted him to ask her what she was doing here, and what she did for a living but by his demeanour he really didn't look as if he wanted to know.

"I guess I may have to trouble you from time to time." She gave a cheeky smile.

He laughed quietly. "I'll let you" which was probably the most positive answer she had had out of him.

Conversation with him wasn't easy but neither did she feel she wanted to get rid of him. There was a mindfulness about him she liked – a kind of being in the moment attitude she admired. Eventually however he left, out into the dark night again, along the path he had come and onto the airfield.

"Night." Marelle said as he walked away. Then, not resisting the urge, she said "Mind the holes!"

He replied as he walked, not turning to look at her to speak, but said "I know where they all are with my eyes closed.

And he disappeared into the complete darkness of the Suffolk countryside.

Marelle found herself staring out of the kitchen window the next morning – warm coffee mug in her hand clutched to her chest as the sun rose. There was something about this place – something that she knew would touch her life and make an impact.

She had been distracted by a box of old newspapers and magazines that she had found among her own boxes that had been left in the house when Seb turned up. He'd opened the door and walked in and Marelle must have physically jumped three feet in the air!

He just laughed. "What are you doing?"

"Oh, I just found this box with old newspapers in – looked interesting ... must be stuff from Uncle Dick."

She sat away as if she shouldn't have been rummaging amongst the papers in the box. "Wasn't expecting you ..."

"No, I wasn't planning to but, well I thought you'd been here a couple of weeks now – on your own." He gave her a lopsided grin "not straight yet?!"

"No, I'll get there ... are you staying?"

"Is there anywhere for me to sleep?"

"Oh yes, yes – its livable!"

It was, just – but the obvious truth was that she had spent the last two weeks moving boxes but never unpacking them, drinking coffee, reading bits of paper she found or staring out of the window and marvelling at the wide Suffolk landscape – and maybe, just maybe, thinking about Jacob. The house *was* livable, but only just.

Seb had other ideas. He unpacked boxes, tidied the kitchen, moved furniture, Marelle watched him, picked things up, put them down again.
"This is old rubbish, probably not worth keeping." He remarked picking up a newspaper out of the box she had been so engrossed in when had arrived.
"It is, but I want to look at them – they are old local newspapers from years ago. Dick must have kept them for a reason … its kind of interesting."
This is an old copy of the daily Express from …" he checked it loosely, "1963 for fuck's sake! Dick probably kept it because it had a coupon for cornflakes or something!" He turned it over in his hands to look at the back page.
"Yeah, well, I'll have a look and then chuck it out."
"You wont, you'll keep it. You'll fill this place with clutter …you cant live without it!"
"Yesh, yeah, yeah and I was always the untidy one and you were always so neat and organized." She wrinkled her nose at him "Creep."
Seb grinned, looking at the paper.
"Anyways, I thought you might be interested too" She added. "1963, closest we came to wipeout, wasn't it?"
"Yeah, it was – but theres not going to be anything in a daily we don't already know now."
"Well I'll keep it for the time being – you never know."
Later Seb suggested going to the local pub. They could walk there – it was only five minutes away. Be a good idea to meet some of the locals. Marelle wasn't sure – a village this size would take a long time to accept newcomers but if he wanted to endure that then she would go along with him and say 'I told you so' as many times as she possibly could!
The Black Lion was a tatty looking country pub with a low roof and mullioned windows. It had a large car park but the haphazardly parked vehicles, that looked like they had been driven in at speed and abandoned, rendered it quite full. The door was yellow, half glazed and there was a separate toilet block in a dirty pebble dash to the right.
Marelle tagged behind Seb, hiding in his shadow, feeling conspicuous. It wasn't packed but there was a group of young blokes at the bar. They were polite enough not to make a remark, but she could feel their eyes burning into them. Seb ordered drinks at the bar an then they sat, facing each other at a small square table. After an hour or so she felt that they had ceased to be a topic of whispered conversation. Seb had introduced himself to the landlord and she had said hello although no-one had really cared. Then they had sat to chat about what Seb needed her to do

in the next week. The group of guys at the bar got steadily louder which culminated in one of then suddenly proclaiming
"He's a total fucking weirdo!"
"Sam! Language!" The landlord said sternly.
"But he is. You don't fucking do that! Then he just glares at you and fucking walks away!"
"Sam!"
"Never spoken to him." One of the others commented. "Never."
"You cant fucking speak to him ..."
"Sam!" The landlord interjected again.
"He's a total fucking weirdo!"
Marelle had cocked an ear to them, half listening to Seb but getting dragged back to their conversation.
"They'll plough it all into the ground soon anyway and him and his fucking caravan with it." 'Sam' continued.
Marelle actually whipped her head round to look at them at that comment but on realising what she had done in reaction she quickly snapped it back to Seb and pretended to be listening intently to him.
The four lads moved out shortly after and Seb returned his and Marelle's glasses to the bar.
"Don't mind them" The Landlord said. "Heard they had an argument with the guy on the airfield today."
"Oh, I don't mind them?" Seb smiled. "We've met him too and they are probably right!"
Seb had two pints of cider in him and he talked constantly the whole walk back without realising Marelle didn't say a word. They were back in the house and making coffee when she said.
"He's alright, you know."
Seb stopped talking and looked at her "Who?"
"The guy on the airfield – Jacob."
"Jacob!!"
"Yeah, he's helped me a couple of times. The electric went off one night and he came in to sort the trip thingy out."
Seb stared at her. "Really?"
"Yeah." She said. "Keeps himself to himself but I think he's just quiet."
"Funny that's what they always say about serial killers!"
"Oh yeah, sure – and he's going to start a new career with me as his first victim!"
"Well when I find you dead I'll know" Seb quipped.
"Yeah, and I'll send you a postcard!"

The following morning she was sitting with a mug of tea looking through the newspapers again when Seb came down too.

"I was thinking ..." He began "Dick didn't move here until the late sixties – they must be the previous owner's rubbish!"

"Maybe." She mused, deep in thought. "Do you know about this?" She slid an open newspaper towards him.

He stood over her looking down at the newspaper spread on the table.

"Yeah. I've heard of the story." He said.

"What happened to him?"

He shrugged. "Don't know."

"Did they ever find him?"

"I don't know – doesnt it say?"

"Frankie Lee (11) went missing from his bed on 24th September. Mr and Mrs Lee said he had gone to his bedroom to complete his homework but when they checked in on him later he wasn't there. Local residents reported an explosion on the night of Frankie's disappearance together with some increased and suspicious activity around the nearby air base in the preceding days. Reports of unidentified flying objects in the area also led to speculation by some locals of alien activity centred around the USAF air base." Marelle laughed. "Really! They are deadly serious!"

"It was a Thor missile site in the 60s – it would have been top secret so stories would have abounded."

"What's a Thor missile site?

"It was a site on UK soil run by the USA which housed two or three Thor nuclear missiles pointed straight at Russia. I think there were about 20ish sites, all in the east – it was the height of the cold war."

"Wow!" she said. "Missiles, right here?"

He nodded. "Fun times! The missiles were huge and were mounted on skids – running tracks which they wound up into the air for deployment. The mountings for the skids are probably still over there and visible – somewhere on the airfield."

"We'll have to go for a walk and have a look sometime?" she suggested.

"Could do but whats-his-face will probably ask us what we're doing!"

She laughed, turning the page. "He's a pussycat!"

"Best friend, yeah, I know. Is there any update on where this kid went?"

" – No." Theres bits for 3 weeks or so then it stops."

"Probably turned up." After that coverage if he'd been found dead it would be in there."

"Mmm – but maybe they never found him?" She said.

"Well maybe he *was* abducted by aliens!" Seb stated, sarcastically.

Seb left that evening, leaving her with instructions on what her mission for the week was – what he needed researching and why so she could get on with his mundane stuff. Marelle had wanted to go and find the missile site but Seb had insisted that they at least put some effort into getting this place at least a little straighter instead. Now it was too late to go wandering over there but she could go tomorrow – maybe Jacob would be able to show her.

The following morning was another bright and crisp one. The air had a sharpness to it but the whole world lay still and cold without a breath of wind for now. When she stepped across the perimeter fence and onto the apron of the airfield she could see him in the distance. Half hunched over, he was making movements that suggested he was stabbing or prodding at something. As she neared him, along the path she had walked previously – just to make sure there were no shafts she could fall down – it looked like he had a long stick, prodding furiously down a hole. A few steps closer and she could see he was doing exactly that.

"Morning." She smiled.

He looked up at her briefly, then turned his head back down and thrust the stick into the hole a few more times.

"Morning." He finally said.

"I was careful. I walked along the same path!" she grinned.

"So I see." He said, not looking at her as he sighed and retracted the stick from the hole. It was long, twice his height and looked like a metal rod.

"What are you doing?"

He hefted the pole like a spear and stood upright. "Just checking. Not sure some of the local lads aren't stashing drugs and stuff down the holes. Caught them poking about up here the other day."

Marelle laughed, folding her arms. "Well, this place is certainly a hotbed of mystery and intrigue isn't it?"

He stood up to his full height, straightened his spine and lifted his head slightly. At that moment there was an intensity in his eyes that flared contempt for the moment they looked at her; just as quickly he moved them away. "What do you mean by that?"

Marelle laughed again, yes nervously, "Well ... this ... and, well we found some old newspapers in the house and we were reading about the strange disappearance of a little boy in the sixties. There was speculation he was abducted by aliens ..!"

He shook his head. "And people like you still believe that shit."

"Well, no ... but ..." She spluttered, almost feeling the nerve she had touched herself. "It was just what it said – we were laughing at it too."

"Its not something to really laugh about ... that's the problem, those stories re-surface again and again and everyone comes and starts poking around."

"It was in the newspapers. We were only reading them."

He turned and poked vigorously down the hole again,

"Did they ever find him?" She asked,

"No."

"What happened to him?" She pushed again, standing watching him with her arms folded.

"I don't know. Nobody does."

"Did you know him?" She looked up to his face when she asked but he remained expressionless as he rammed the pole down the hole. Then he paused almost as if he didn't want to answer that question, but he could not stop the words from forming.

"Yes, I knew him."

He then focused on the hole again, went to jab down it again as if just in good measure, then stopped.

"Where were the newspapers?" He asked.

"In the house. I thought they were Uncle Dick's but Seb says they cant be as he didn't move in until the late sixties."

"Hmm" He said.

"Do you want to see them?" Marelle moved a step closer and looked to his face a little more.

"No." He replied. "Its ok – I don't need to read about it."

There was a pause in conversation, a moment's silence which Marelle began to feel a little uncomfortable with. "I'm sorry." She finally said, very quietly, almost to herself.

Jacob stood there for a moment longer, staring down the hole. "No. no, its ok." He straightened up. "I'm going to go for a walk around the airfield in a bit if you want to come along?"

It was cold and a sharp wind was now starting to bite. Marelle ran back to the house to get her coat and then walked back to him. He was coming down the steps to the caravan, closing the door behind him. She raised her eyes to him, into his dark eyes and his clenched square jaw. There was a layer that he was hiding behind and she so wanted to peel it away, but she had also seen that vulnerability today and that had piqued her interest in him even more.

Jacob walked with a purpose, as if every stride was another accomplishment to his task in hand. He did not say much and if she wanted conversation then she had to prompt it.

"Is this your job then?" She asked, trotting along beside him as he walked the "perimeter", occasionally kicking or poking at things. "Are you the 'caretaker?'"

"I suppose its one of my jobs." He replied succinctly but weighed up the situation and added "I'm not a caretaker, more a watchman. I get paid a sundry amount each month to keep an eye on things – its not a lot but it feeds me."

"By who?"

"The developer."

She nodded "but Seb says it's been like this for years?"

"Yeah, things fell through, things got left. I've been on borrowed time here for the last ten years."

"What will happen?"

"I suppose they'll start by breaking the concrete, levelling the land …"

She smiled. "I meant to you!"

"Who knows? I'll end up somewhere. Maybe persuade a local to let me pitch in their garden."

She shot a glance at him. Was that tongue in cheek – was that humour from him – moreover, was that aimed at her? He gave no clues and just carried on. "Or maybe I'll just move on." He finally added.

Marelle looked up at him. He was unaware of her staring, studying him. How old was he? If he had known that kid in the sixties then it must have made him at least forty five now but he certainly didn't look it.

"They converted some of the old buildings into a business park – over that end – left pretty much everything here though."

"How big is the airfield?"

"It was massive, a lot of it has already gone – either back to the farms or converted for other uses. This is just the northern end of it left."

"Seb said there were missiles here?"

"There were."

"Where" She stopped and gestured around herself.

"Right there." He stood and pointed to a group of trees to their right.

"Nuclear missiles?" She asked.

"So we are told."

"Can we go and look? Seb says there are parts of the structures left there."

"There is." He said, tight lipped. "But not today – maybe another day …"

She didn't argue. There would be no point. "Did you see them?"

He walked on, head down while she stood and looked towards the trees. She ran to catch him up and thought he wasn't going to answer her last question. "Yes, I saw them," he said finally.

"Wow!" She laughed. "Were you scared?"

"Scared? When?" He asked quickly, in a manner that suggested he was perplexed she had even asked that.

"Well, with them – just being here?"

"I was just a kid. We liked watching them, but we weren't scared of them being here, no."

"We?" She asked, an eye cocked to him.

"Us kids … all of us." He said, shaking his head in a tiny involuntary way. "They were just here."

"Is it safe to go over there then?" She nodded back to the trees.

"As far as there not being any missiles there, yes."

She smiled. The more he tried to tell her less the more she wanted to keep drawing it out of him. As they continued in the almost frosty air, they came to a large set of metal padlocked gates close to the road coming into the village. A red pick-up truck was parked up against them and someone was standing beside it. Jacob's pace quickened and as they approached. Marelle could see the guy standing next to the pick up was taking a piss right through the wire of the gate. She laughed. Jacob didn't.

The guy zipped his fly, stood upright legs slightly astride eye to eye with Jacob who equally stood straight and eye to eye with him on this side of the fence. Eventually the other guy grinned and Marelle suddenly recognized him as the one from the pub the other night who had been swearing.

"It's a public road mate." He said, cigarette in his mouth. "I can be here as long as I want."

Jacob stood and stared at him.

"Not that you can stop me anyway – not you or your posh little friend."

Marelle looked around herself. Was he referring to her – is that how they perceived her? She looked between Jacob and the younger guy and back again wondering how long this may go on for. Then 'Sam" if she remembered correctly, turned with a sneer and climbed into the pick-up. With a roar of the engine as it started, he floored the pedal and spun the wheels, showering the gate with gravel. Jacob remained like a statue and watched until he had gone away.

"He was in the pub the other night." She said quietly, standing alongside Jacob.

"Sam Paske" He stated. "Works at the farm   bit of a clot – thinks he's the village hard man – just like his father did. Just lately him and his group of cronies seem to have a compulsion to trespass on the airfield. Like I said, I'm suspicious that they are trying to stash something or the other up here."

17

"I think they're more interested in winding you up! Just as an observation as an outsider – and no offence meant." Marelle offered.
"They don't wind me up." He swallowed and held that jaw so tight again.
"Well you stood there facing off like a couple of tom cats – I think him being there wound you up." She laughed, making light of her remark, surmising he would take exception.
He was silent for a moment then he walked off, quicker than before. After a couple of strides he stopped again and turned round to her as she followed.
"If you walk right down the run way – the concrete bit in the middle – it takes you to the pan handle where my caravan is. You know your way from there ..."
He pointed.
"You want me to go?"
He nodded. "Because you ask too many questions and that does really wind me up when people just come in here from their busy little lives somewhere else and start picking and poking around. You're not going to find anything now – you're not going to find a crock of gold at the end of a rainbow. Just leave it – just leave everything as it is." He raised his hand in exasperation, went to say something else but didn't then turned and carried on his black jacket flapping behind him as he tramped through the long grass.
Marelle stood there for a moment. She hadn't done anything! Sam had wound Jacob up and he had taken it out on her. For spite she felt like she wanted to walk a meandering path, all over the airfield until he yelled at her again, but she really wanted to take the quickest route back. So, she did as he suggested and walked right back down the centre of the runway. She didn't look back at him even though he occupied her thoughts every step of the way.

Trying not to think about him wasn't easy. She threw herself into the research for Seb for the next few days, but Jacob was never far from her mind – despite the way he had spoken to her. Half of her wondered if he was just that strange and volatile character as described in the pub that night but the other half still wanted to peel away his layers of defence and see what was really inside. She had never thought that someone that bit older than her would ever launch her into the feelings she felt right now but, she told herself, he was probably beyond domestication. Her head told her to leave well alone – just as Seb had in a roundabout way – but her heart – her heart wanted to discover him! Her mind, in its meanderings however, pulled her back to the newspapers time and time again. She re-read the stories about the disappearance of Frankie Lee in 1963. His parents had been pretty well off – his father was a Bank Manager and his mother had been a midwife. Frankie had a sister who was just two when he disappeared. He had been one of the brightest students in the class. By all accounts a quiet boy with only a couple of very close friends. There was one old photo of Frankie – obviously a school one – of a dark haired, smiling boy, smart in his school uniform and neat haircut. Just disappeared. In his room, doing his homework, then gone. Bed unslept in, doors and windows still closed, homework half done. Then there were the stories – alien abduction, "strange activity" at the air base. No trace of him anywhere; no clothes, footprints – body. Just gone – in this sleepy little village where everyone knew everything.

She imagined Jacob at the same age – they had probably gone to school together. Marelle tried to imagine the same cheeky, *happy* smile on Jacob's face as a child but she could only see the emptiness in his eyes and a skinny, sad little kid in her mind's eye – just like the person he was now. Just like he had never ever been a child.

She awoke the next morning with a new bright idea. He said she asked too many questions! Well to hell with it. It was how she was, she wanted to know but it didnt have to be Jacob who told her.

Marelle started where all life in this village ended up at some point – the village shop! It also served as a post office so it stood a good chance of pulling all kinds in. She had been in there once but admittedly preferred to drive to the supermarket in the nearest town. Nonetheless she walked in with a smile, bought a loaf of bread then asked casually:

"I've just moved into the village and wanted to do a little historical research – is there a good place to start?"

The shopkeeper passed her change over, "probably the library in town I don't think theres much in the village where you could look. The church I suppose? I've not been here long myself so not sure which direction to point you in."

Marelle smiled. It wasn't the answer she wanted. Then a voice piped up from behind the shelves.

"You know who would know all about the village?"A chubby blonde woman appeared from filling the shelves." She wore a blue tabard with the words 'happy to help' embroidered on it. "Mrs Avison – she lives in the little pink cottage on the edge of the village. I think she is one of the few people left who can go back a few years – she must be in her nineties – used to come in here and tell us tales about all of the locals and the village but I don't think she gets out much now."

"I don't know if she still lives there Jill?" the shopkeeper questioned.

19

"Oh, she does. My friend is a carer who goes in to her every day – still got all of her marbles by all accounts!"
Marelle smiled, "Ok – can I just go up there?"
"I am sure she would love it!" Jill said.
There was a distinctive feeling of déjà vu about knocking on stranger's doors in this village but the pink door with yellow roses around it was a little less daunting than Jacob's had been that night on the airfield in the dark. She knocked and waited.
It took a while but a stooped little old lady opened the door. She was smiling and holding on to a walking stick.
"Oh hello dear." She greeted.
"Hello Mrs Avison. I hope you don't mind me knocking on your door? You don't know me, but I have just moved here and I was trying to do some research about the village – the lady in the shop said you would be a good person to talk to?"
"Well dear, I've lived here all my life – I've seen some comings and goings alright." She chuckled – "I can probably tell you a few stories!"
Marelle smiled. "That would be great!"
"Do you want to come in dear?"
"Can I? Do you mind?" She felt a little guilty at obviously taking advantage of Mrs Avison a bit.
"Yes dear. It would be lovely to have a chat. The carer comes in about an hour but I haven't got anything else on until then." She stood aside. "Come on in."
The cottage was lovely. Typically the home of an elderly lady but cosy and extremely clean and tidy, perfused by the faint smell of furniture polish. Mrs Avison suggested tea but Marelle declined, she wanted to focus on the questions she had and tea would have been a time eating distraction.
Mrs Avison seemed happy in herself and delighted to talk. Her father had owned the butcher's shop and she had worked there too as she had got older. That had all gone now, converted into a house according to her. There was a period of general chit chat before Marelle could aim her in. She was trying to keep it jovial, keeping smiling but eventually she asked the number one question.
"I found some old newspapers in the house we've just moved in to – it mentions a little boy who went missing back in the 60s – I just wondered if you remembered anything about that?"
"Oh yes dear! What a to-do that was and that poor couple. He was a lovely little boy, very polite – and always happy – very intelligent too. He knew everything about those rockets they had on the airfield – knew every detail about everything."

"What do you think happened to him?"
"I don't know." She said and remained in thought. "He would come into the shop with his Mum – my dad knew he liked to talk about the rockets and he would tease him about them and then off Frankie would go telling us all about those rockets! Whats was in them and how fast they could go … he was *fascinated* by them."
Marelle smiled. "Did anything unusual happen before he disappeared? It said in the newspapers that there had been "strange activity" in the days before?"
"Well there was a lot of traffic. Mostly at night, big lorries and trucks. We had to hold tight on to the dog when we went for a walk! And that night – all hell broke loose! The place was lit up like it was daylight, sirens going off, people everywhere! They closed the road by the gates for a few days – we had to go on a detour to get to the shop."
"And that was the night Frankie disappeared?"
"Well yes. But they searched and searched for him and not a trace!"
" – and what about the guy that lives on the airfield now?" Marelle didn't segway it very well but she refrained from cringing and doubted Mrs Avison would really notice the awkward change in subject.
"He was Frankie's best friend! They were inseparable and to be honest with you dear, I doubt that child would have ever had a decent meal inside him if it hadn't been for Frankie's mother. Left to his own devices he was, wandering around at all hours! If anyone should have disappeared, then I would have bet on it being him. I know it was terrible what happened to his mother, but his father had a duty to that child!"
Wow! Marelle was taken aback. She hadn't expected that. "Sorry – what happened?"
"That young boy. Left to get on with it while his father drank himself stupid. I dare say he beat him as well."
"What happened to his mother?"
"Jeannie? Jeannie moved into the village just after the war. Ezekiel was besotted with her – took to her straight away. He was a looker … "She laughed "the one all of the girls wanted but Jeannie moved in to the village and within a year they were marrled."
"What happened to her?"
"She had Nat then fell pregnant again I don't really know what happened but she died giving birth to the second baby – Jacob I think they called him. Poor little mite, he didn't live longer than a couple of days either then he went to his Mum in heaven."
"How do you remember all of this and all the names so well?" Marelle asked, now slightly confused herself.

"Oh my dear I like to remember all of the people who used to live here ... it keeps my mind alive! I go along all of the houses in my mind and remember who lived there and all about them."

Marelle smiled again "So the guy who lives on the airfield is Nat?"

"Nathaniel." She nodded. "They all had names out of the bible Ezekiel, Nathaniel and Jacob. I'm pretty sure Nathaniel was the oldest and it was Jacob who died."

" ... and Ezekiel that's a strange name?" Marelle asked, not adding 'almost as strange as mine'.

"It was quite a common name around here then – I believe his father was also called Ezekiel too – everyone used to call him Ed for short. Very good looking young man in the early days."

Marelle laughed with her.

"Oh yes ... "She began and was then distracted by a noise outside. "Oh that'll be my carer ..." and she went to get up to open the door, in a hurry, panicked that she would not get there to have it open and ready.

"We'd better leave that for today dear." She said, "but its been lovely talking about this to someone who actually wants to listen! Come again – we'll save all that for next time!"

Marelle stood up and followed her to the door.

"Thank you Mrs Avison, I really enjoyed that – and I will come back again. If its alright with you?"

"Oh yes dear, please do" And she opened the door – expecting someone to be there. When there wasn't she looked out further. Marelle stepped out beside her and was immediately alerted to the beaten up old red pick-up truck parked in front of the house. Sam was in the driver's seat, window rolled down.

"You ok Mrs Avison?" He asked.

She looked up, not aware of him before that moment then smiled. As she answered a small dark blue car pulled up behind him. "Oh, hello Sam, yes I'm fine thank you. Just looking for my carer – and here she is. She pointed to the woman walking along the side of the car.

"Well you be careful Mrs Avison. You don't want to be letting strangers into your house."

"Oh go on with you Samuel Paske – she's not a stranger – and anyway, I didn't get to ninety five without knowing what I'm doing. You be on your way and stop worrying about me!"

Marelle stood upright and tried to perfect her thousand yard stare. He sat there for a moment then nodded to the approaching carer then drove slowly away.

Marelle drew a long slow breath after she had said her goodbyes and walked on. So, village life was still alive and kicking here – just hidden.

However, somewhere through it all there seemed to be a thread, albeit old, worn and about to break. She tried to get it straight in her head as she walked. Mrs Avison had obviously mixed up the boy's names in her tired old mind. So, Jacob was the son of a drunkard who had gone off the rails when his lovely young wife died giving birth to their second child. Jacob had been vagrant and uncared for but had been best friends with Frankie Lee and his family who had obviously taken him under their wing. That was until the strange disappearance of Frankie one night in the middle of some secret activity at the airfield.

Well maybe the second visit to Mrs Avison would definitely be in order.

With those thoughts in mind, she returned to the newspapers and pawed through them again. There was no reference or mention of a Jacob – or Nathaniel – or any other "friend" of Frankie Lee but Marelle made a mental note to ask Mrs Avison next time what Jacob's surname was – at least then she could research him a little more if she wanted.

It had been three days now since he had said she asked too many questions and had told her to walk back down the runway but she felt a surge of defiance in that she now knew a little more about him and the village. But in those three days she had not seen a sign of him – not poking down holes on the airfield nor walking the perimeter of it. She wanted to go and knock on his door again, but she wasn't going to. There was an intrigue about him that was constantly pulling her in his direction but she didn't want to appear as if she was chasing him. What she had thought of as attraction was probably tolerance on his part. Marelle decided to wait and see what happened.

This house had turned up at the right time for her. Marelle had been in a long term relationship – they had bought a house together but four years on they had just grown apart. They had both known it and realised it and the result had been an amicable and civilized break up. They'd sold the house and she'd been planning to bunk with Seb until she decided what to do. So when this house was handed to them it was the perfect opportunity for her to move in. It must have been fate.

Marelle stood in the kitchen staring out of the window, trying to find motivation to tidy the house. She had promised her best friend from back home that she could come down for the coming weekend which meant she had to try and get another bedroom ready. Seb had happily slept in among the boxes but Bella would probably be a little less happy with that arrangement. Bella was a bit of a rough diamond but her home was like an upmarket show house (mostly because she as rarely there Marelle had once commented) however, she knew Marelle and what to expect. She had never complained up to now in their twenty odd year relationship but sleeping amongst cardboard boxes may be taking it a bit too far.

So, Marelle was in the back bedroom, looking at the white and cream striped wallpaper and wondering exactly how old that was. It was clean and it was ok – but it was old and however much she studied it, it would still be old! She decided tidy was about the best she could do!

Then there was a sudden bang, bang, bang from downstairs, a definite knock on a window or door. She was expecting a delivery so brushed her dirty hand on her jeans and made her way downstairs. The banging came again but she realised it wasn't coming from the front door so she walked through to the back of the house.

There he stood, at her back door, hand raised and about to bang again. He raised his eyes to her with that hollow expression that defined him. Marelle walked through the kitchen staring at him all the way but he had already looked down. She reached out a hand and pushed the door handle down. She didn't take her eyes off him – he was wearing a black fleece with the neck zipped right up and looked pale, she thought. She opened the door and he straightened up.

"Hello." He said.

"Hello." Marelle tried to act cool and nonchalant but feared her eyes were dancing enough to give her true feelings away.

"I'm sorry about the other day." He stated. "I didn't mean to upset you."

"You didn't upset me." She said

" ... or make you angry with me."

That was more like it.

"Its just that ..." he began and Marelle stopped him, raised a hand. "Come in, I was making tea ..."

She stepped inside and he walked in behind her, shoulders stooped, eyes on the floor.

"I wondered could I see the newspapers?" He asked.

"Yeah, sure." She pulled a chair out from the table and gestured to it. He reluctantly sat down as Marelle filled the kettle then leant against the worktop as she waited for it to boil. Jacob had perched on the edge of the chair, one elbow on the table, his chin resting on his hand – eyes not on her as she studied him. He was attractive in a rough kind of way, his features quite chiselled with a well defined jawline. For someone who spent so much time outside his skin looked quite delicate and not ruddy as she may have expected. There was a gauntness to him and he looked pale due to his hair being dark. It just touched is collar at the back and the top was too long but he brushed it back from his forehead. He was tall but hid it with his stance; he was skinny but probably only because he didn't look after himself properly.

"Its just that the other day was a bit overwhelming, and I just needed to find space". He suddenly said.

"Well there was plenty of space over there!" Marelle said – it probably wasn't the right thing to say but he gave a brief little smirk at it.

"I'm just not a social person," Jacob stated.

"And I'm used to being with someone all of the time, with socialising and working with other people around me. Now I'm here and I want to make new friends! I can't help myself. I'm sorry." She replied with a smile, then turned to pour boiling water into the mugs. "I suppose it was bound to happen. Two opposites coming together, you know …" She brought her fists together in front of herself and made a gesture of an explosion, complete with sound effects then laughed.

Jacob stared at her as if she had just drawn a knife and was holding it at his throat – there was horror in his eyes for a fleeting second until he drew himself back again.

"So, lets start again!" She smiled, putting the mug down next to him followed by a biscuit tin. "I'll get the newspapers."

She brought the whole cardboard box through and placed it on the end of the table. He was sipping tea and staring into space when she came back but his eyes soon moved to the box. Marelle reached in and was about to lift the papers out when he said.

"So what are you doing here?"

She was surprised at him showing an interest in her and so she stopped to take it on.

"I mean …" he continued. "How come you have ended up living in this house?"

Marelle sat down, pushed the box to the side for a moment. "Well – Dick Saint was our uncle – our father's brother. Seb – my older brother – and me, are his only living relatives and, rather surprisingly, he actually left all of this to us in his will. I hardly knew him, but Seb visited a few times and knew him well as a kid. Seb has a family and works in the city. I, on the other hand, have recently split up with my partner – amicably I may add – and we sold the house we had. I was going to stay with Seb but thought I may a well move in here. We could have just sold it but well, that seemed ungrateful and unfair."

He now seemed filled with a new interest in her – she didn't know what had changed.

"So, I am here." She gestured. "I can work here as well – for Seb – so its perfect!"

"What exactly do you do?

"I research stuff for Seb – he's an editor of a colour supplement but he also writes a lot of stuff for other publications – I'm his researcher!"

"So, you are a professional at poking around?" He suddenly gave a small smile, fleeting – slightly odd but he did actually smile at his own quip.

Marelle laughed – God he had nice teeth too – "I wouldn't use the term professional but yes, I'm told I'm quite good at it! I trained as a hairdresser originally."

"Why did you stop being a hairdresser?"

"Had dreams of working in a top salon – doing celebrities' hair – but ended up in a pokey little place where you did the same styles on the same people week after week. It was so boring!" she sighed, "I do still keep my hand in though – I cut Seb's hair and a couple of friends too."

"You can do mine if you want." He involuntarily ran his hands through it, leaving it half sticking up, which was endearing.

She cheekily reached forward and ran her fingers through it with the touch of a hairdresser. Surprisingly he didn't flinch away from her.

"You'll have to wash it first! What have you got in it?

"Probably oil or grease from a tractor, been under one all day. I'll wash it. Maybe you can cut it next time?"

Marelle smiled. He was thinking ahead. "Ok, next time then."

She shifted her attention back to the box again, pulling it towards her and lifting out the pile of newspapers, placing it on the table and his eyes dropped to them.

"Here you go." She said. "There's something in most of them. The local ones have the best coverage."

"Show me." He asked. "You've been through them, so you know where to look."

Marelle stood up and began opening the various papers out on the relevant pages and spreading them before him.

"Here." She pointed. "This is the first one – it just kind of mentions it and then it turns into a bigger story. See – is that the little boy?"

Jacob stared at the small grainy black and white photograph for a good few seconds.

"Yes, that's Frankie."

"It says he was 11." She continued.

Jacob nodded then read through all in front of him. There was a prolonged period of silence as he did so, moving from one of them to the next then back again. He sat with his hand resting on his mouth and his elbow on the table.

"Haven't you seen these before?" Marelle asked.

"No." he replied, softly, deep in his own thoughts.

"He was a good friend of yours, wasn't he." Marelle questioned, sensing there was more going through his head than the words on the paper.

"He was my best friend, my only friend really – his parents were lovely too. I spent a lot of time with him. Now he will always be that child."

"Were you the same age?"

"No, I was younger than him by about a couple of years. He was super intelligent."

"And he just disappeared?"

Jacob nodded.

"And you were born in this village?" Marelle asked, making an attempt to snap him out of the dive he was in.

"Yeah." He finally said.

"Where?"

"The house over the road. Its yellow now – never used to be then. I was born there."

"Oh, the one over there." She gestured. "There's a family that lives there now."

"Yeah, it was sold off but it once belonged to the farm. They sold it when my father died."

"What happened to you then?"

"I wasn't living there then. I had been and I had worked on the farm but I'd gone away for a bit. I came back and then my father died. The farm wouldn't let me live in the house so I bought the caravan and pitched it on the airfield. Got away with it for a few years and then the developers started looking at the site. I talked my way into being allowed to stay there as a "custodian" while some issues were being sorted out. It went on for years getting passed around, changed, falling through, starting up again. I've hung in there but it will come to and end one day."

"What about your mother?"

"Oh she died when I was very young. I don't really remember her."

"I'm sorry." Marelle said.

"Its ok." He shrugged.

"And what about Frankie. Where did he live?" She asked brightly.

Jacob raised his eyes to her as hunched over the table.

"Frankie." He said. "He lived here."

Marelle physically felt the blood drain from her face. She had not been expecting that.

"Here." She said. "In this house?"

"Yeah.' He confirmed. "Your uncle Dick must have bought it right after Frankie's parents moved away."

"I'm sorry, I didnt realise …"

"Why should you?"

"So this was the house you used to come to? And which was his bedroom then?"

"The one at the back overlooking the airfield. We used to stand at his bedroom window and watch what was going on over the fence."

Luckily it wasn't the room she had chosen to sleep in, but it was the one she was making up for Bella and it was the one Seb had slept in – the very room Frankie had disappeared from. Suddenly Marelle felt alone in this house with a ghost; she shivered.

"That makes me feel a bit strange!" She laughed nervously. 'I didn't realise."

"He's not here." Jacob said.

"I know that, but well, he disappeared from here. We don't know why and we don't know what happened here."

"I should have said something before, but I didn't think it would bother you."

"It doesn't bother me – its just a bit of a shock. I've been reading about it all week and suddenly I'm sleeping right in the place where it all happened. What do you think happened?"

He shrugged. "I don't know." And shook his head.

Marelle was glad he had come back to her but aghast at his revelation. When he left, she wanted to ask him to stay but knew that would be totally preposterous and if she did he would probably never return.

"Pop around tomorrow, I'll cut your hair if you still want me to." She said instead.

"I'll see" was his reply as he stepped out of the back door. Then he stopped and turned back to her. "And I'm glad you didn't just sell the house."

Marelle smiled. And so am I, she thought to herself.

When darkness fell, she was constantly haunted by the thoughts of *that* child disappearing from *this* house and never being found. Every time her mind wandered to that she felt a chill overcome her. She wandered into the bedroom at the back and up to the window. It was a bright moonlit night and she looked out over what remained of the airfield just in the way that Frankie had all of those years ago. What had happened here? She still felt that Jacob wasn't telling her everything he knew.

TWO

Seb called her the next morning.
"Hows it going?" He asked.
"Fine," Marelle replied. "But did you know that this house is the actual house which that kid disappeared from?"
There was a pause. "No." He finally replied as her launching immediately into that fact had perplexed him for a moment.
"Well it is. The back bedroom is the very last place he was ever seen. Do you think Dick knew?"
"He never said anything – not that there was any reason for him to ..."
"He must have bought the house from Frankie's parents. The box of newspapers must have been what they left. It doesn't say in any of them that this was the house so he may not have known."
"And who told you this?" Seb asked.
"Jacob."
There was another pause – a little too pregnant to be benign.
"I also went and talked to an old lady in the village." Marelle continued. "Mrs Avison. She was lovely – she remembers all of the people who used to live here. She knew Frankie and his parents *and* she knew Jacob's parents too!"
"Why?" Seb asked.
"Why?"
"Why are you digging into this?"
"I'm *interested*!" She defended.
"Just be careful." Seb warned. "You don't know these people- and he's a weirdo who lives in a caravan on the airfield."

Marelle felt irked at that remark. "He's not. He's perfectly normal." She almost wriggled to herself in abhorrence as she actually said that but she added "I like him."

"Just be careful."

Marelle laughed. "Seb I don't think we have to worry about Jacob. If anything, he's the one that needs looking after."

"Marelle!" Seb exclaimed.

"He's kind of sad, I don't know what it is – he needs someone to look after him."

"He's a lot older than you."

"A bit, not a lot." She said. "Look he's fine. Leave it."

"What are you doing the weekend?"

"Bella is coming to stay. Why?"

"I was going to ask if you wanted to come to ours for the weekend. Give you a bit of a break?"

She laughed. "From what? I like it here."

"Well God help the village with you and Bella."

She laughed again. They had made mischief together over the years. Bella brought out the worst in her! "There's nothing to get up to around here so I think we will be fine!"

"Oh and Marelle" Seb asked. "Can you find time during your intensive researching into your potential new boyfriend and other waifs and strays to get my stuff back to me?"

"Yes Seb, its done – I just need to send it." She replied sarcastically. "And for your information, as you well know, knowledge is power"

"Yeah, well be careful."

So she spent the rest of that day doing Seb's work. Despite what she'd said it was not done. Seb knew that too and it was late afternoon before she emailed it to him. And it was late afternoon when Jacob wandered up to her back door. She was in the kitchen and saw him coming.

"Well hello." She said with a smile.

"Hi" He said with a small sigh. "Is now a good time?"

"For what?" She questioned.

"You were going to cut my hair."

"Oh that! Yes, its good – sorry I've just finished work – but its good – come in."

She offered him tea which he declined so she sat him down on a kitchen chair and ran her fingers through his hair again.

"Have you washed it?"

He nodded.

"It still feels really greasy – and its really thick. I think we are going to have to wash it properly! I can do it or you can jump in my shower?"

He shrugged. "You can do it if you want."

It had been years since she had washed anyone else's hair but she got him to lean head first over the kitchen sink and she made do without the aid of a shower attachment or mixer tap! Jacob had a lot of hair! She could feel it between her fingers and she probably spent a lot longer than she normally would have done gently lathering and then rinsing his hair with her body pressed against him and her arms across his back.

Jacob felt bonier than she had expected him to be. He looked far more "solid" than he felt bent over before her, quiet in his own usual manner. She gestured for him to stand up and threw a towel over his head as he did so.

"Right, wait here. I'll get my bag of tricks."

She came back with her bag and he was sitting on the kitchen chair again rubbing at his head with the towel. Marelle took a comb and combed through his hair. It looked even longer wet.

"So, what do you want me to do?"

He shrugged, "Just tidy it. Its too long – I normally hack it off piece by piece myself as it annoys me. I had it really short last summer – "

"Wont suit you." She commented. He had a strong jaw, almost square face and well defined cheekbones. "Well, I can tidy it up or you can let me loose and I can give you a great haircut."

"As long as you don't make me look stupid!"

She stopped and stared hard at him. "Trust me." She stated, walking around him. "But you're too tall ... here, try sitting on this." She pushed an old, shorter piano type stool towards him. It was covered in a tapestry depicting men on horses with bows and arrows. He swapped.

"Perfect!" She remarked, pushing the kitchen chair out of the way with her foot. She knew what she wanted to do – he probably wouldn't like it but it would look fantastic on him. He didn't seem bothered so she started cutting.

Jacob fidgeted, constantly. Marelle was tilting his head forward or asking him to keep still all of the time. This should have taken her fifteen minutes at the most but at this rate it would hours! Then he lifted a hand and started feeling what she'd done so far.

"Please!" She exclaimed. "Just keep still and keep your fingers out of it! Honestly, its like cutting a six year old's hair and believe me, I never liked doing that!"

"Well I cant see what you're doing."

"You don't need to see what I'm doing. If you carry on you'll have half a haircut and then you will be a laughing stock! Here, read a magazine." She thrust a copy of Cosmo into his hand.

He stared at her for a second with a look on his face that questioned why she had given him a women's magazine. She turned him forwards again. "Yeah, I know but just look at the pictures of the half naked women like all the other guys do!"

He did not take her up on that but managed to keep still for a prolonged period and she made progress – until she switched the clippers on.

"What are you doing?" He flew round, one hand on the back of his head.

"Its ok, I know what I'm doing" She stated with clippers poised. "Turn around."

Reluctantly he did but she could feel him tense as she used them.

"Do you put anything in your hair – apart from tractor grease?"

"No."

"It probably doesn't need it as its so thick but lets just do this." She rubbed something between her hands and then pulled it through the top of his hair. At the front of him she stood up straight – slowly, her eyes were only inches from his but she was finding it difficult not to smile at her handiwork. He raised his eyes and caught her gaze full on. Marelle smiled and stepped back.

Wow! She had created a work of art that leant itself to every inch of him. It was almost like this was the very epitome of his evolution and he had finally turned into the butterfly.

"You look amazing!" She said, smiling so broadly to herself and reaching out a hand for the mirror she had behind her. She hadn't wanted to give him the benefit of looking in it throughout as she had known he would probably have stopped her. He looked at himself, looked closer, sat back then ran his hands ove the back and sides of his head. Marelle had clippered the sides and back very short but left the top long which she had spiked so that it had height. It was almost a flat top with a shattered profile.

He was still examining his reflection. "It looks good but I think I will get a few comments."

"From who?"

"The lads on the farm for a start."

"Do you care about that?"

No, I'm not bothered." He confirmed. "Might frighten myself when I get up in the morning though!"

"You look fantastic!" she repeated.

'Thank you." Jacob replied with the tiniest of smiles playing at the corners of his mouth.

"Do you want to stay for tea?"

"Er, no, its ok. I'll get back over there." He picked up his coat and nodded towards the caravan.

"I know its ok but I've got to cook myself something anyway, to make something for two is not an issue. Not that I use the word "cook" in the true sense of the word – is mostly tin opening and microwaves – I'm no chef! Or we could get fish and chips?"

"It will be closed now." He stated. "I don't like fish."

"You don't like fish?" she repeated as a comment. "Well I can do beans on toast – if you're staying."

"Ok." He finally said without much more of fight.

"Good!" Marelle smiled. "Sit down again then."

"I can help."

"I'm not a good cook but I don't need help to make beans on toast!" She laughed.

Jacob ate in the same way that he approached most other things – with an empty detachment; everything happening around him and him just going through the motions. He was polite to a "t", chivalrous even but so detached. He shied away from eye contact but in those snatched seconds when he did allow his eyes to meet hers she felt a tiny moment of success like the sun showing through a cloud and these thrilled her more than she wanted to admit.

Then, half way through eating he suddenly reacted as if someone had told him to stop what he was doing. He put down the cutlery and went to put his head in his hands, he hesitated then instead pressed his palms into the sides of his head with his fingers around his eyes, which he closed. She stared at him, not sure whether to say anything. He must have stayed like that for a good few seconds.

"You ok?" she finally asked.

He exhaled quietly. Sat back and opened his eyes again. "Yeah – ok."

Marelle rolled her eyes to herself. What was that about? Was he in pain or had he been possessed by some demon for a few seconds. It was nothing in the grand scheme of things but it was strange!

"I was going to ask you if you wanted to come to dinner tomorrow night. My friend Bella is coming for the weekend."

"Er, no. I"ll leave a girl's night in to the girls!" He said.

"Bella's lovely – you'd like her!" Marelle smiled – but in reality she would probably eat him alive! Bella *was* lovely her mother was Italian and she had inherited her looks but she was very forward leaning and wouldn't hesitate to call a spade a spade! She also liked a drink, or two. She would probably be way too much for Jacob. But Marelle had thought about asking him.

"No, I'll decline. Thank you."

"We were going to pop down the pub on Saturday night – why don't you drop in and say hello?"

"I'll see." He said.

Marelle made tea without asking him or he would have said no and left. She didn't want him to go, not yet. She wanted to gaze at him for a little longer!

"Have you any hobbies?" She asked.

He thought for a second. "Not really."

"What do you do in your spare time then?"

"I don't really have any spare time." He replied.

"Well there must be something?"

"Do you?"

"Well put me on the spot! I used to love getting dressed up and going out to a party or something but haven't really done that for a while. I like reading – and researching things – I love clothes and fashion – not that its really obvious at the moment either! I guess since we had the house together and now – well -I've just not done anything much."

"I like being outside, walking around in the countryside." Jacob finally offered.

She nodded and smiled, aware that this conversation was not really going very far.

"I often used to have tea in here with Frankie." He suddenly said. "We used to have beans on toast too – his mother used to make it." He raised his eyes to her. Deep brown eyes. "Its strange to be doing it again."

"Well you can come here whenever you want – you know that."

He nodded, looking down again and picking at the edge of the table. At that point if Marelle had known Jacob better she would have wrapped her arms around him and hugged him. It looked like what he needed right at that moment, but she feared that doing that would send him running out of the house. Instead, she stood up to go to the sink but gave his shoulder a gentle squeeze in passing.

She couldn't hold him there much longer and shortly after he left. Standing at her back door for a second, thanking her for tea before he turned and walked off into the night with the haircut that had knocked ten years off him and tiny piece of her heart in his pocket.

Bella came running and screaming up her front path to throw herself at Marelle. Embracing each other they giggled childishly.

"What in hell are you doing in a place like this?"

Marelle laughed. "Oh it has all of the attractions!"

"Really! Well, you'll have to show me the sights as to me it sure looks like the arse end of nowhere. My God there's not even a motorway in the county!"

Marelle showed Bella around the house. She agreed it had potential even though it appeared to be very carefully hidden, somewhere! They were upstairs and in the back bedroom where Bella would be sleeping. Marelle hadn't told her about the house's history and wasn't sure whether to just yet. Bella wasn't the type to be bothered by it the problem was it would probably have the opposite effect. She walked up to the window and looked out. Bella had beautiful long, straight black hair which Marelle was jealous of every time she looked at her. Today it shone like silk as she stood staring out of the window.

"But good on you girl. Timing was perfect – even if the house isn't. Are you planning on staying here?"

"I'd like to. I've not been here long but this village has its claws into me already!"

"Have you got your green wellies yet then, or your four wheel drive?" Marelle smiled. "Not yet. Give me a chance."

"Whats that?" Bella asked, nodding towards the wasteland that was once the airfield.

"It was an airfield. It was a nuclear missile site in the 1960s apparently. Now its earmarked for development."

"What right behind you?"

Marelle walked up beside her. "Yeah, someday but word has it that its been standing like this for years – theres obviously some issue so its just been left."

"Is that a caravan over there?"

Marelle smiled. "Yes."

"Someone in it"

"Yes."

"Some local hermit." She laughed.

Marelle stared at it. "Let me tell you about Jacob." She said with a wink and walked away.

"Jacob! Who's Jacob?" Bella exclaimed. "What are you up to you little hussy? You've not been split from Chris for two minutes!"

Bella wanted to open wine but Marelle dissuaded her. "We'll have coffee."

"Ok, we'll have coffee then, but I was expecting to get into girly mode!"

"We can, later."

"So whos this Jacob? Does he live in the caravan?"

Marelle smiled. "Well..." she began.

Marelle told her all about Jacob but soon realised she couldn't tell her about him with mentioning Frankie. Bella was, of course, interested but Marelle left out the part about the bedroom. One coffee later Bella had opened a bottle of rosé and was appreciating its effect.

"So, what does he *do* then?"
"Oh, he's kind of a caretaker for the airfield – for the developers – and he works on the farm sometimes too."
Bella nodded grabbing a handful of nuts from an open packet on the table. "So he's got great prospects too! Bit weird, lives in a caravan, agricultural labourer – sounds like you're domesticating another waif and stray!"
"You sound like my brother."
"Why, doesn't he approve either?" Bella grinned.
"He doesn't need to – and neither do you!" Marelle pointed, smiling.
"Well I am sure when I meet him I will be as charmed and convinced as you are." She poured more wine. "How far have you got so far?"
"Well, not that far. I don't want to scare him off."
"You must have the patience of a saint."
"I gave him a haircut."
Bella laughed as she was taking a sip of wine and choked a little. "You gave him a haircut! Is that. A new part of the flirting process?"
"He looks amazing!" Marelle enthused. "Its probably was a bit young for him – but it looked *so* good!" She giggled. "He did look a bit like an 80s pop star but it suited him."
"An 80s pop star! What did he say?"
"I think he liked it."
Bella laughed. "Sounds like you just may have made him into a laughing stock."
"He liked it."
"Well that makes it even worse." Bella exclaimed. "I've got to meet this guy!"
They talked and laughed and drank into the early hours. Marelle was hoping that Jacob turned up "just by accident" the next day but it looked like he had gone to ground. He had still not shown himself by early evening, but Bella had kept her busy. Now they were getting ready to go to the pub. Bella had dolled herself up more than was really necessary despite Marelle warning her. With that Marelle had to also make an effort but just conceded to her best jeans and favourite cowboy boots.
"I'll drive." She said. "Its literally five minutes walk but its not a good walk in the dark – and especially when you've got those heels on!"
Bella was expecting a more lively place with a buzzing atmosphere and a queue at the bar to be served. It was quiet. There was a couple in one corner, the normal "pick-up crew" – including Sam at the bar, and them. There were mutterings when they walked in and probably comments

passed which she – and thankfully Bella – could not hear. They ordered drinks and sat down.
"When does it get busy?" Bella asked.
"Oh, in about half an hour." A man with his dog may also come in!"
He didn't, and by a quarter to ten Marelle wanted to join in with the drinking but she still had to drive home.
"We'll finish these and then head home, shall we?" She asked.
"Good idea. You've got a bit of catching up to do."
"Oh, I'll catch up – I've got a stash of Asti in the fridge." Marelle smiled.
At the point there was a loud and high pitched wolf whistle from the bar. It made Marelle jump and Bella turned around. With a smirk she turned back to Marelle.
"I say, is that your 80s popstar just walked in?"
Marelle looked around Bella and there he was, not a hair out of place but the brunt of a piss take.
"Fucking Hell! Who's a pretty boy!" Sam guffawed amongst the general childish chuckling of his little gang. "Fucking dick head."
"Jacob." Marelle called, ignoring them – as he was, "Over here ..." She gestured. That caused even more mirth, but he continued to ignore it and sauntered over to her and Bella, expressionless as normal.
"Come and join us.' Marelle stood up. 'This is Bella."
He nodded and gave a small smile in acknowledgement. He looked smart tonight – wearing clothes she was even surprised at. The black jacket he had on over a white t-shirt was the nicest cut and fitted him perfectly – sitting on his square shoulders with a sharpness. Teamed with dark, smart jeans and grey and white trainers he looked like he had also made an effort tonight.
"No, its ok. "Just popped in to get a couple of cans to take back."
"Ok, but you are welcome to join us."
"No, its ok, thank you." He backed away with a polite smile, a little nervous at being confronted by both of them at once.
"Do you want a ride back?" Marelle suddenly piped up, somewhat desperately, half getting up again.
"No, its ok. I'll, er, see you tomorrow." He offered in order to quieten her. Then he turned and walked out. Marelle watched him, liked what she saw, felt herself physically deflate. She turned her head to Bella with a sigh.
Bella kept her cool. "Bit old for you."
"I don't care – anyway he's a *bit* older, that's all." Marelle said. "Oh my God – he looks so good tonight."
Bella laughed. "He was getting the piss taken out of him, big time – due to that haircut!"

"He said it didn't bother him."

"Wow!' Bella smiled. "You actually told him you were going to give him a haircut that would make him a laughing stock!"

"No! ... No ... well oh just shut up Bella! If you weren't here I'd be running out after him."

"Be my guest." Bella gestured. "You've really got it bad with this one, haven't you? Does it actually *hurt* yet?"

"Its killing me." She sighed. "Come on lets go – we might catch him walking home – see if I can persuade him to get in the car."

"Marelle, this is stalking!" Bella joked, standing up and finishing her drink. They said goodnight to the landlord as they departed. Sam was coming back in the door as they left, he stood aside to let them through, examining his fingernails as they passed.

"Thank you?" Bella smiled while Marelle said nothing.

"It's a pleasure." He remarked.

There was hide nor hair of Jacob on the way home, but Marelle knew he had probably skipped off into the night.

"He's probably taken a short cut – he knows all the tracks and cut-throughs around here." Marelle remarked, driving slowly and straining to look into the darkness.

"He'll ruin those trainers.' Bella said, dryly but it was wasted on Marelle who was focussed elsewhere.

Eventually she pulled the car into her drive next to Bella's after driving home at walking pace.

"I believe theres a bottle in your fridge with my name on it.!" Bella grinned.

"I believe there's three!" Marelle added.

"Even better! Let's go girl!"

An hour later the first bottle was finished and they were onto the second. Bella was being loud as usual – telling Marelle about a recent trip to Spain which ended in chaos as one of their party got arrested in the airport for going to the toilet in the middle of the check-in area. Of course it was hilarious – mostly to Bella. They were both pretty drunk but Bella had the edge. She took a breath, still laughing, to top up their glasses.

"Bella!" Marelle suddenly said. "Bella, I really want him!"

"He's older than you. You need younger blood!"

"No, I don't. I don't!" I want him. He's good looking and he's gentle and he's kind – he's vulnerable and I can make him happy. I can make him smile again."

"Bella, he's weird."

"He's not. He's lovely – but he's fragile."

Bella laughed. "Fragile. Fucks sake Marelle! You know Chris has a new girlfriend? I saw him in Tescos the other day. Pretty little blonde thing – they seemed really happy. They were buying strawberries." She raised an eyebrow, made a serious face on purpose then laughed.
"I don't care."
"You do."
"I don't!" she argued.
"You do. "Bella laughed. "Your face went all tight when I told you."
"I really don't care."
"Do."
"Bella all I care about at the moment is getting Jacob to notice me – to *respond* to me."
"Well lets put money where all this is coming from, shall we? Get your shoes on, we'll walk right up to that caravan and ask him!"
"It's a quarter to twelve."
"Doesn't matter, does it? If he wants you he will be pleased. Come on, shoes on!"
Marelle sighed, pulled on her cowboy boots where she sat while Bella slammed her feet into her four inch heels.
"You're not going to walk up there in those?" Marelle laughed pointing to them.
"Watch me! – Bring this with us … we might need refreshments!" She grabbed the remaining, as yet unopened, bottle by the neck and swung it to her.
"I need a coat." Marelle scampered off, banging the door jamb with her shoulder and laughing. She came back with a padded anorak on, complete with fur trimmed hood.
"Will it be cold?" Bella questioned, standing there in a velvet mini dress, bare legs and four inch heels.
"I think so. Its always cold here." Marelle nodded. "Its quite near the coast I think."
To that Bella slung her long black, elegant coat. She put down the wine, wrapped the belt tight around herself in an untidy knot then picked the bottle up again. "Right!' She said. "Come on."
She got to the back door then stopped. "Do we need a torch?"
"Yes, but he will see us coming," Marelle said.
"Oh right, good point. Come on then." She yanked the back door wide open and they were out into the night.
'There are holes!" Marelle suddenly said. "Jacob always warns me there are holes. We mustn't fall down the holes. He knows where all of the holes are."
"I'm concentrating on not breaking a heel babe."

Halfway along Marelle stopped again. "Look I'm not sure this will work."
"Sure it will. Why keep fucking around – get it out in the open. Life is not a fucking rehearsal!"
"Yes, but he may be scared off. Its softly, softly." she whispered the last two words.
"Nonsense!"
"He'll flit away." Marelle made a gesture with her hand to illustrate.
"You gotta grab him girl. You've given him that sexy haircut he's gonna be a fanny magnet round here for sure."
Marelle laughed which started Bella off and they continued as a giggling, stumbling mess towards his caravan in the darkness.
They arrived at it standing there the night, still and silent. Bella gestured to Marelle to go ahead. The moon above them was full and clear, enabling them to see enough. Marelle hesitated.
"There are no lights on. "She whispered. "He's probably asleep."
"All the better." Bella whispered back, grinning "Put him on the spot!"
Marelle exhaled loudly and took a step forwards. She leant and went to bang a hand on the door but stopped. "If this goes wrong Bella I am going to kill you."
"Oh for God's sake. Get on with it!" She jumped forward and lumped her hand three times on the door. It made more noise than she was expecting, she made a face then giggled.
"Jacob!" Marelle shouted, her head close to the door. "Jacob, Its ok, its me."
"Its me!" Bella mocked. "Hi honey, its me!" she whooped then collapsed into giggles.
Marelle banged her hand flat on the door. "Jacob."
There was no reply. There was no noise or movement from inside the caravan. Marelle banged again "Jacob!"
"Oh Jacob, where art thou!" Bella sung at the top of her voice. "Juliet is here."
"Sssh!" Marelle shushed. "Jacob!"
Then she turned to Bella. "I don't think he is here."
"Perhaps he's out with his other girlfriend?"
"No. no. no." Marelle shook her head. "He does *not* have another girlfriend."
"Oh Jacob," Bella echoed.
"Hey maybe he's scared because we're drunk? His father was an alcoholic and used to beat him up!"
"Strewth!" Bella sighed. "And how do you know that?"
"I asked some people in the village."

"That's bloody stalking Marelle!" She warned. "Sorry I need a wee – hold this." She thrust the bottle towards Marelle before she staggered into the grass and began hitching her dress up.
"Bella – you cant!"
"Needs must and I'm not pissing on myself!" She squatted in the grass right next to Jacob's caravan. Rocking on her hanches in the heels she then went to stand up but stumbled as he reached to pull her pants up, took a side step where her heel plunged into the ground then crashed into the grass. Marelle began to laugh.
"Oh shit. Fucking shoes!" Bella exclaimed, kicking the shoes from her feet and flinging them into the air, one hit the side of the caravan with a sharp thud.
"`Get up! You're laying in your own piss!' Marelle laughed.
"No, its fine." Bella got to her hands and knees. Brushing herself down. "Give me that." She held out a hand to Marelle for the bottle and she handed it over.
"Shall we leave him a note?" Marelle suddenly asked.
"Good idea! Can he read?"
"Of course he can read! He's not stupid just 'cos he lives in a caravan – just sad." And she made a sad face to emphasise that word. "I don't have any paper though, or a pen."
"I might have a tissue ... " Bella began to search her pockets. Then her face lit up. "Here!" She exclaimed. "I've got a lipstick – write him a message on the caravan!"
"Oh no, he *will* be angry if I do that." Marelle shook her head.
"It'll wipe off if he doesn't like it. Here." She pushed the bullet of the lipstick up. "Go on."
"What shall I write?"
"Oh Marelle." She scoffed. "For fucks sake!" She lunged forward and drew a big love heart on the door. Marelle grabbed at her, trying to get hold of her hand and the lipstick, laughing and saying "no, no, no."
Bella laughed as she wrote *I love you Jacob xxx*.
"Bella!" Marelle exclaimed as Bella pushed her away.
"Its good. Its sweet. He'll love it."
Marelle stood there, unsure, swaying a bit, biting her lip. "Bella!"
"Look, look!' She laughed shaking the bottle of sparkling wine' Lets celebrate this!" She popped the cork with a loud bag and whooped loudly at the same time as the wine sprayed everywhere covering both herself and Marelle.
"I don't think he's here Bella." She said. "Or he doesn't want to answer the door. We had better go home now."

She drank from the bottle then handed it to Marelle who shook her head. Bella shrugged and took another mouthful. She turned to take another look at the caravan and then began to walk back. Marelle linked arms with her and they walked along together.
"Remember that time you got so drunk I persuaded you to climb up that tree in the middle of town?"
Marelle laughed. "Yeah! God, a policeman had to help me down …"
"You were so pathetic!" Bella remarked. "You just kept saying you were sorry!"
Marelle suddenly stopped, pulling back at Bella. She stood and looked up into the night sky – at the moon and a thousand visible stars on such a clear night.
"What?" Bella asked.
"Its beautiful here, isn't it?"
"Its bloody cold!" Bella offered in reply and pulled her on again. Suddenly she must have put her foot on a loose rock or stone as without warning she lost her balance. With a little scream she fell down again, dragging Marelle on top of her on the runway.
"Bloody hell" She cried. "I think I'm bleeding!"
"Where?"
"My knee – look!"
Marelle got to her knees and looked. "Its only a graze."
"Its fucking dangerous out here. I don't know about beautiful!" she moaned.
Marelle suddenly laughed. "Bella, where are your shoes?"
"Over there I suppose – I forgot to pick them up. I'll get them tomorrow."
"It is tomorrow." Marelle laughed, sitting on the concrete.
They finally picked themselves up and made it back to the house. They had left the back door wide open and all the lights on. They stepped out of the dark into the light, squinting.
"I'm done chasing weird guys for you! Look at my knees …"
They were both grazed and bleeding a little.
"Ooh they'll sting a bit tomorrow!" Marelle grinned.

THREE

Sleep was elusive for her in the degree she really needed it. Marelle was wide awake by seven and had got up by twenty-past. Surprisingly her head was not as thick as she had been expecting and she filled the kettle then stood staring out of the kitchen window. Maybe her sleep had been disturbed by the thought of the message they had left for Jacob and how she would explain it. Right now, she was more concerned about where he had been. They had made enough noise to wake the dead and she knew, if he had been there, he would have opened the door even if it was to give them a bollicking! She only hoped whatever Bella has persuaded her to do that it hadn't messed up what she was carefully culturing with him. She looked at her hands as their stinging suddenly reminded her that she had managed to skin them too when she had fallen with Bella. Marelle loved Bella to bits and had known her since school, but she felt that she had let her go too far last night.

With a sigh and a small smile to herself Marelle stared out at the wide flat land in front of her. It was getting later in the year and seemed to be turning a corner. Tilting her head to the side to stretch her neck she suddenly noticed a figure over near the fence. She stared. It looked like Jacob – he was leaning against one of the concrete posts – one arm outstretched against it, head hung down. Then he stood away, staggered for a stride or two, grabbed out at the concrete post again but missed and lumped down on his backside in the grass. What the hell was he doing? She watched. Was he drunk? He dropped his head into his hand against his knees and looked like he was preparing to settle down right there. This did not look right.

Marelle shoved her feet into her trainers and wrapped her dressing gown around her, tying the belt – she opened the door and started across the back garden. Marelle never took her eyes off him, quickening her pace as she realised he had the same clothes on he had been in last night.

"Jacob.' She called.

He was now sitting with his back against the concrete post, his head buried in his knees.

She stumbled up to him, placing a hand on his back as she squatted down beside him.

"Jacob are you ok?"

He lifted his head, there was blood across his face and his right eye was swollen almost shut. He was trying to focus on her with the other eye.

"Oh my God! What happened?" Marelle exclaimed, kneeling beside him.

"I fell over." He said, "I don't feel well."

"You *fell over*? Have you been out all night?"

He shook his head a little, squinted with his good eye and pressed his hand into his forehead. "I cant remember."

"Lets get you in to the house, we can ask questions later." She stood up and held onto his arm. "Can you stand up?"

With her hauling at him he managed to stand but was pretty unstable. He walked a step as she ducked under his arm to support him.

"Where did you fall over?"

"Sam hit me." He said.

"What!" Marelle gasped.

"He punched me straight in the face when I left the pub. He was coming out of the toilet. I walked off and was ok for a bit but then got really dizzy. I think I fell over and hit my head. I cant really remember where."

Marelle sighed. "He's a bully Jacob – you should have hit him back."

"That's what he wanted ... I'm not getting into that with him ..."

It was steady progress getting back to the house. They had to keep stopping as he would totally lose balance or just was not able to put one foot in front of the other. Marelle seemed to be supporting most of his weight but he was getting heavier on her. They eventually got to the back door and he managed to haul himself up the steps.

"Bella!" Marelle shouted. "Bella, I need your help down here ..."

She pushed him gently towards a chair and he collapsed onto it, closing his eyes and letting his head fall to one side.

"Jacob, wake up." She shook him gently. "Keep awake ..." She'd seen this in programmes on the television. She held his head with her hand. The blood across his face had come from his nose which had now stopped bleeding and was congealed. His eye had taken a direct hit – it was swollen and turning a dusky shade of blue.

"Bella!" She shouted again, this time turning towards the hallway. Jacob stirred slightly.

"Did you pass out?" She asked him.

"I think I must have done."

"You really need to go to the hospital." She said.

"I'm not going to the hospital."

"What?" Bella said from behind them, she had appeared in the doorway, in bra and pants. "Oh my God – whats happened to him?"

"Sam beat him up – Bella you need to be dressed!"

Marelle looked at the back of his head as it felt damp. She found a mess of drying blood. "Jesus!" She commented to herself. There was a deep, sharp cut that had bled and congealed but was still oozing blood through it. His jacket and t-shirt were soaked with blood. She didn't know what to do – truly she just wanted to call an ambulance. His level of consciousness was waivering – at times he was aware, but this was interspersed with times when he would 'drop off' and become unresponsive. She knew that was not good. And had he been out all night, laying in the pub car park or God forbid, beside the road. She was pretty sure he wasn't drunk or had even touched alcohol last night which made his demeanour even more worrying.

Bella arrived back in a t-shirt and leggings, her hair now up in a pony tail.

"What happened?" she asked, stooping down and staring at him.

"He says that Sam hit him when he left the pub, he became dizzy then fell over. He's cut the back of his head really badly. I think he passed out and spent the night in a ditch or somewhere …"

"Shit." Bella said. She reached out and touched his arm "Hey, hey sweetie, wake up!"

He didn't respond.

Marelle bent down beside him, placed her hand on his should. "Jacob!" she said, shaking his shoulder. "Jacob!"

He groaned a little, shook his head from side to said then opened his eyes.

"That's better." She smiled.

"I need to go home and get some sleep." He muttered.

"No you don't, you need to stay awake so we can work out what to do." Marelle warned.

"He needs to go to a hospital." Bella said.

Marelle sighed. "Jacob I really think we need to take you to a hospital …"

"No." He stated. "Im not going to a hospital. I'm ok, I'll be ok. I just need to sleep for a while."

Marelle stared at him then looked to Bella, she shrugged at her as if to say she didn't know what to do. The Bella walked towards him.

"Jacob you have quite a serious head injury and you are in and out of consciousness – this could be an emergency." Bella said to him. "You could be concussed or even have a bleed into your brain – we cant tell that and it will need medical treatment."

He shook his head then rested it on his hand on the table. Closing both eyes.

"Jacob, you really need to go to the hospital. I'm going to call an ambulance." Marelle exclaimed.

"If you call and ambulance or try to take me to a hospital I will never speak to you again!" He suddenly proclaimed. He opened his good eye and tried to open the injured one as he said the words with all the force he could muster.

Marelle sighed and paused for a moment. "Ok. You can stay here but I am going to keep a very close eye on you and if you lose consciousness we *are* going to a hospital."

Bella raised her eyebrows and shook her head but said nothing else.

"Well lets get this all cleaned up a bit – it may not be as bad as it looks." She headed to the sink and Bella followed her.

"Are you mad?" She hissed. "He's probably one step away from falling into a coma! There have been people die from head injuries like that you know!"

"I know but if he's adamant he's not going then I'm not going to fall out with him over it." She began running the tap. "There's some cotton wool in the bathroom, can you go and fetch it?"

When she came back Marelle had a bowl of water and was trying to look at the back of his head' There's a lot of blood but it probably looks worse than it is."

"Has he been fighting?"

"I don't think so. I think Sam just took an opportune swipe at him when he left the pub. Probably right before we left." She made a face as she looked at the wound. "Why don't you make some coffee".

"I don't think he should have coffee – doesn't caffeine make you bleed more?" Bella asked.

"I don't know, does it? Anyway, I meant for us!"

Marelle was not good at this. She hadn't really handled children, animals or sick people and was feeling her way now. Bella would have probably been better – she came from a big family – but Marelle didn't want to hand Jacob over to her. She had got most of the blood off his face and started on the mess at the back of his head.

"Heads always bleed a lot." Bella remarked. "You don't want to knock that scab off or it will start all over again."

"His jacket is soaked right through. Its as stiff as a board!"

"That'll need cleaning. Try explaining that when you take it in!" Bella grinned.

"Jacob, lets take this off." Marelle started to take the jacket off him, he woke up a bit and assisted. His t-shirt beneath was worse – his whole back was just a blood stain where it had spread out across the material in varying shades of rust. "Shit." Marelle gasped. "How much blood has he lost?"

"I don't think the initial slap in the face is the issue here, is it?" Bella added.

"I should take that off too but I haven't got anything else for him to put on and I don't want him sitting here half naked."

"You must have a big jumper or something?"

"I don't think anything of mine will fit him and I don't want to squeeze him into something too small. I've done it before – you think they are the same size as you but when they get it on its ten sizes too small!"

Bella stared at her a little oddly at that comment.

"Seb left anything here?"

"That's a point. He does sometimes leave a spare shirt or something. Go and have a look in the wardrobe in the middle room."

Five minutes later she waltzed back into the room. "Look what I found." She was holding a white, perfectly ironed shirt.

Getting his t-shirt off was more difficult – especially getting it over his head without disturbing the cut at the back. Eventually they peeled if off between them and Marelle folded it neatly. She noticed the label and held it out to Bella.

"Its Armani!" she mouthed a little surprised.

"Probably fake." Bella mouthed back. "But its fucked whatever it is!"

Marelle wiped some of the blood off his back and then guided him into the shirt. He was skinnier than she had expected and Seb's shirt drowned him – the sleeves were too long but he didn't seem to notice or bother. With a quick glance at him Marelle ushered Bella into the hallway.

"Why don't you go up and try to wipe that lipstick off his caravan?" She asked.

For a second it was obvious that Bella had forgotten what they had done last night at best she seemed to have partial recollection.

"Take some make up remover or it will smudge everywhere."
"Don't you want me to leave it?" Bella smiled, cheekily.
"No, I don't!" Marelle snapped. "Go!"
She returned to Jacob. Slouched on the chair, one arm on the table, the other limp by his side, his head dropped forward. The shirt was way too big. It had turn back cuffs but they were completely covering his hands. She gave his shoulder a gentle squeeze and he lifted his head up.
"How are you feeling?" she asked, quietly.
"Not great." He replied.
She gave a sympathetic smile. "Do you want to lay on the settee? It might be more comfortable?"
She managed to get him there, arranged pillows and he laid down. By the time she had run upstairs and grabbed a duvet he was asleep with his knees drawn up onto the settee. Marelle stood there staring at him. She just wanted to hold him, to lay down right there and cuddle him. Marelle wondered what he would do if she did that – and if he had ever been in a relationship before? Maybe all this time he had just been here waiting for her to come along!
It was a while later Bella stomped back in. Marelle was back in the kitchen, the kettle was boiling and there was toast in the toaster.
"Its come off but its left a bit of a pink stain." Bella confirmed.
"How much of a pink stain?"
"Quite a big pink patch" Bella said. "You cant see what it says but it's a pink patch."
"I'll have to play ignorant." Marelle sighed.
Bella pointed to the chair. "Where is he?"
"On the settee. He looked too uncomfortable here."
They left him there and Jacob slept most of the day. She woke him a couple of times to make sure he was still alive but apart from that he was pretty dormant. Bella made a move to go in the afternoon. She had already packed all of her stuff into the car and was just hovering now.
"Sorry it was so *eventful*!" Marelle smiled.
"Oh, it was fine. In years to come we will look back at this and laugh about it all! We painted the village red last night anyway!"
"Pink!" Marelle corrected.
"Yeah – pink. "She agreed. "Well, you take care – especially with him."
Marelle gave a smile and folded her arms around herself.
"He's not my type but, well I can see why you are so besotted with him. I only hope he feels the same way about you. Don't let him break your heart!" She warned, sternly.
Marelle laughed, "I will certainly try!"

"Come to mine next time – bring Jacob!" Bella smiled then gave her a quick hug. "See you soon, I'll call."

That left Marelle alone with Jacob. He was still curled up on the settee with the duvet clutched around himself. He'd been in this state all day and she was worried about him but was hoping that sleep would prove to be a healer.

As the evening drew on, she sat in the armchair opposite him. He still hadn't stirred but she didn't want to wake him as he looked so peaceful, for once relaxed. As night fell she decided to sleep in the armchair too. With moonlight washing in through the French doors looking out on to the airfield she drew her legs up into the armchair and settled her head back into the cushions.

Suddenly she was awake and was unaware of anything except consciousness for a split second. Her heart thrashing in her chest and her breath caught in her throat. The noise from the almighty crash that had woken her subsided and new noises clattered in. Then she came to, leapt up and lunged across the room to grab at Jacob as he had also risen to his feet. There was clutter all over the floor around him, the coffee table knocked over in front of him and a chair upside down to the right.

"Hey, hey, its ok." She clutched his side, trying not to step on any of the stuff that had come off the coffee table.

"You're at mine. Its Marelle, Its ok!"

He was completely solid, as tense as steel, rigid and almost shaking under her hand. The white shirt hung off him, covering his hands and he looked like a ghost in the moonwashed room.

"Hey come on. Sit down" She patted his arm.

He exhaled slowly and she felt some of the tension leave him.

"Shit." He said and sat down.

Marelle sat down beside him. He still looked confused and worried – totally bemused as to why he was here in the dark with her. He reached up and ran both hands through his hair.

"Where am I?" He asked.

"You're in my house. Sam hit you and you fell over yesterday?"

He let out another slow breath.

"You wouldn't let us call an ambulance so we agreed you would stay here so I could keep an eye on you. You've got a large hole in the back of your head!"

He felt it and winced.

"Don't you remember any of that?"

"I thought I was drowning." He said.

"Is that why you kicked the coffee table over!" She laughed.

"Sorry."

"Its ok." She laughed gently. "You've been asleep for the best part of 14 hours!" She explained. "I was worried about you."

He was searching for a memory, still not sure of where he was or why he was here.

"I think I can remember Sam hitting me now." He said. "I saw you with your friend in the pub then I left. Sam was coming in as I was going out. Didn't say a word just punched me straight in the face – then I've woken up here ..."

"There's been a day in between!"

He took a long breath, gradually finding his place in the world.

"How do you feel?"

"Sore.' He whispered. "Whats the time?"

"Erm ... a quarter past two – in the morning."

"I'd better go home."

"You had better stay right there!" she ordered. "I'll make some tea."

"But I've got to go to work in the morning and I can't go dressed like this."

Marelle stopped on the edge of the seat as she went to get up and stared at him. "Jacob you've got one eye swollen shut and a two inch hole in the back of your head. You cant remember yesterday and to be honest you're not making a whole lot of sense right now! You should have gone to the hospital by all accounts but I promised you I would not make you go. I don't think you should be going to work tomorrow."

"But they won't give me any more work if I don't turn up. I have been warned already."

"Is that on the farm?"

He nodded.

"Well, I'll call them."

"Please, don't." He pleaded. "I'll just go. It will be fine."

Marelle exhaled noisily and got up. "I'll make tea ..." She said with a sigh.

By daybreak she had failed to persuade him not to go to work. At least he was now lucid and able to stand and walk unaided. In the end he had conceded to let her go up to his caravan to get his work clothes while he had a shower at hers. He'd been reluctant to let her do so but eventually she had won the battle of wits.

So, she set off, jogging up the airfield with instructions in her head of where the key was and the combination to get it. As she approached, the large pale pink cloud of a stain on the caravan door reminded her there was still that to deal with. It may come off with some kind of cleaner, but she knew how difficult lipstick stains could be.

The key was in a key safe behind the wheel and the combination was 1008. She dialled it in and clicked the metal box open, then she had the key in her hand. For some reason she was expecting a mess inside the caravan, such a small space would be difficult to keep tidy and to live in, but she was surprised when she entered. It was pristine! Clean, neat tidy, everything in its place – there was no clutter – and no soul to the place. The clothes he wanted were exactly where he said they were, all neatly folded and ready for him to put on today.

"Fucking hell Jacob!" She said to herself as he went to pick them up but then her curiosity took over. She had been intending to play it cool. Get the clothes then go – not pry. But now she was here the urge was too hard to resist. She stood in his bedroom and opened the wardrobe door. That was not what she had expected either – he had some really nice clothes in there – smart suits and jackets, shirts that looked to be hand finished, new jeans still with the labels on. Everything was clean and pressed and ready – but never worn. She thought of the blood-soaked jacket and t-shirt she had stuffed into a carrier bag back at hers and thought she would get them cleaned for him. Then her eyes wandered to a pocket on the door of the wardrobe and she pulled out a red, leather bound folder. Carefully she opened it. It was photograph frame which folded in on itself. In the right hand side was a black and white photograph of a bride and groom. She looked closer – a petite, very slim blonde woman with high cheekbones and her fair hair scooped up into a bun. A beautiful, elegant young woman. Next to her in the picture was a much taller, dark haired man who was obviously the block from which Jacob had been honed. Except the man in the picture had a genuine, broad smile across his face. Jacob's parents she guessed – Ezekiel and Jeannie. But on the right she had to take a second look. For a moment she thought it was his father but by the clothing and the fact that the picture was in colour made her realise it was Jacob. He must have been in his late twenties, hair not dissimilar to how she had cut it now, slightly chubbier around his jawline and a smile on his face. It didn't look like a snapshot that somebody had taken, it looked like a professional shot. Marelle stared at it for a few moments longer wondering which one of the two pictures in front of he was the most tragic.

She put everything back as she had found it, locked the caravan again and made her way back to her house.

Marelle walked through the kitchen and the living room to the stairs and then she tiptoed up the stairs and crept silently along the landing, unannounced. The bathroom door was open but he wasn't in there. She tiptoed on to the open door of the back bedroom that had been closed. She leant forwards, slowly, looking inside, his clothes clutched to her chest. There he was, in the room, staring out of the window – naked except for the towel he held in his hands. Marelle stared, held her breath. There he was stripped bare in front of her, not an ounce of extra fat on him, his dark hair wet but still hanging on to the style she had cut it into, a bottom that looked as good out of jeans as it did in them and trickle of watery blood running down his neck. Marelle backed away, retraced her steps back down the landing and the stairs, right to the bottom. Once there she closed the living room door loudly and called. Jacob, I'm back. Do you want me to bring these up to you?" There was a smile on her face. He took a moment to answer and she heard him move back into the bathroom.

"Yeah, leave them on the landing. I'll be down in a minute."

When he came down he insisted that he didn't want breakfast but she eventually persuaded him with a bacon sandwich and a mug of tea. He looked better today – if you ignored the eye which was a deep shade of burgundy beneath it. He seemed to have stopped the head wound bleeding for now as well, but Marelle knew it should have been stitched.

"Are you sure you're ok?" She asked in his final bid to get out of the house as quickly as possible.

"Yeah, I'm fine." He said.

"Keep away from Sam." She added.

"I plan to."

"Jacob!" she called him back as he made a move. "Do you have a phone?"

"No."

"Well if I give you my old one which I keep as a spare will you give me a ring a couple of times during the day – just for today – just to make sure you are still ok?"

He looked at the phone she was holding out to him like someone had just told him to cut his own hand off.

"Please?" she pleaded. "I'm still worried about that head wound. Its got my number in the menu."

He had told her he was 'only clearing out ditches' behind the church today – which he said wasn't taxing. He looked up at her, looked down at the phone.

"Please!" She said. "Just ring me and say your ok – I wont expect an hour's conversation!"

He sighed reluctantly. "Ok."

Marelle smiled. "And if you don't call me, I'll call you!"

"I'll call." He said.

And with that he left – gone out of her house like a caged bird set free. She watched him walk away and felt an overwhelming sense that she may never get him in her hands like that again.

It got to eleven and he hadn't called. Marelle hadn't shown him how to use the phone – maybe she shouldn't have assumed he would know how to. She could call him but didn't want to do that, not just yet. Maybe if he didn't call, she could drive down to the lane behind the church and see if she could see him? Give it another half an hour she thought and go up to go to the kitchen. It was when she got there that her phone rang. Immediately she grabbed at it and was pleased to see her own face come up on the screen, almost breathless she answered.

"Hello?"

"I'm fine." He said. "Sorry, I was not keeping an eye on the time". His voice on the phone sounded richer, smoother and not having him in front of you avoiding eye contact focused it more.

"Hi." She smiled. "And you feel ok?"

"Yeah, fine." For the first time she realised he had no trace of the local accent. She hadn't even noticed before but his speech was quite precise.

"Well give me a call after lunch. Just to make sure."

She was sure she heard him smirk. "Yeah, ok, bye."

Marelle laughed to herself as she slid the phone back into her pocket. Was that a breakthrough? Had she actually asked him to do something for her and he had obliged? She flicked the kettle on and her eyes fell to the half empty bottle of make up remover still on the worktop and she remembered the pink stain. He wouldn't have had to chance to see it yet and she didn't really want to have to confess what they had done! So she had lunch then armed herself with cleaning materials and headed that way while she knew he was still out.

This time it mostly yielded to the bathroom cleaner – at least to a point where you couldn't really see it unless you were looking for it. She stood up and looked at it. She knew it was there but hopefully he would not notice. As satisfied as she could be she picked everything up and was about to head home when the phone in her pocket rang. Her picture appeard again and she knew it was Jacob.

"Hi!" She answered.

"Hi."

"Everything ok?"

"Yeah, just a bit tired."

"That's probably expected" She replied, still marvelling at how different his voice sounded when he wasn't in front of you! "Do you want to come back to mine again tonight?" She suddenly blurted out even before she herself realised how it sounded – probably distracted by Bella's shoes,

still in the grass! "Sorry, I meant, well … if you want to …" She spluttered and sounded stupid.
"Its ok. I'll go home. I'll be fine."
"Ok." She said and felt a little remorseful at her haste. She may have persuaded him to come back if she had been a little more reserved about it. "Well keep hold of the phone – you know where I am if you need me. The charge should last a few days."
"Ok, I will." He said. "See you soon. Bye."
And he was gone again.
With a sigh she tucked Bella's shoes under her arm and went home.
Bella called that evening with the opening words
"Well, did he survive the night?"
Marelle laughed and confirmed that he had but she'd had to let him out again! Bella was aghast that she had actually let him go when she had had him right there – naked as well! Marelle agreed, she had felt the same too but know she had to keep treading carefully on this journey.
The following morning, she so desperately wanted to call him. Several times her finger hovered over the phone the decided not to. She could see his caravan from the window but there was no sign of him – he had probably left already anyway.
Marelle left it for a bit, got dressed and made herself breakfast and was about to start some work for Seb that she had not been inspired to start as yet when she decided to go for a drive around the village – see if she could see him. She reversed her car out and headed towards the church. He had said he was "behind the church" yesterday so she turned down the little lane beside it and over a tiny hump backed bridge. The lane wound through a wooded bit and then out to open fields. She drove slowly, scanning from right to left. Then, in the distance she could see a digger, just sat at the edge of a field. It wasn't moving. She stopped the car on a verge and got out, standing up and shielding her eyes to see if she could see anyone in it. From here she couldn't. A minor panic overtook her. What if he was in the digger but had passed out – or worse? Marelle stared at it. Maybe she should call him anyway – maybe now was the right time. She ducked back into the car. Her phone had been in the centre console but had now fallen into the passenger footwell. She leant and reached for it but it slid further under the seat. She tutted and leant right into the car, feeling under the passenger seat until she grasped it in her hand. She almost didn't look at the screen and was about to dial the number when she noticed a text message from herself. Her heart slammed in her chest as she opened it. He had texted her! For God's sake that was the last thing she had expected him to do!
'Just been to yours but not in. RU around later? J'

"Shit!" She said out loud. "Shit!" If she had stayed at home, she would have been there.

'Back in 5 mins.' She replied. 'But yeah, be around later.'

She had put the phone down and got back into the car when his reply came through.

'Ok, See you later then.'

Marelle exhaled the breath she had inadvertently been holding, pulled on her seatbelt and started the car. Driving back past the church she noticed a small car park to the side, bounded by trees whose leaves were rustling gently in the breeze. Maybe she should take a look?

It was a beautiful church. Small, but neat with a copper topped steeple at one end. The graveyard was on all four sides with the older graves obviously towards the back left hand corner. It was quiet and peaceful with birdsong in the air and the spring sunshine just starting to warm. There were many old headstones in there, some so worn you could hardly read the names, some leaning over, some untended for years. She walked among them, reading the names and ages.

Mrs Avison had said that Ezekiel had been a popular name in the village. The first one Marelle came across was Ezekiel Ransome born in 1838 and died in 1887 – he did not appear to be buried with a wife and the headstone was large and grand. There were two others as far as she could see – both with the surname Frost. One was born in 1891 and died in 1946; his wife Juliet had died in 1951. The other was Ezekiel Nathaniel Frost. Unusually his wife's name was inscribed in the headstone first – Jeannie Alexanda. Marelle stared at the grave. She was looking at Jacob's parents. Jeannie had been 29 when she had died and his father had embarked on years of drinking to assuage the pain. Marelle remembered the happy couple in the photograph in Jacob's wardrobe; they were reunited here. She lingered for a moment before moving on and looking for a child's grave along with what Mrs Avison had said. She found nothing and concluded that Mrs Avison had probably got it wrong – she knew that Jeannie had died young but had in all likelihood mixed her up with someone else. However there had also been a practice of burying new born infants along with other people in graves that were available at the time. Maybe that was the case here? She didn't know and would have to dig further to find out.

She left the graveyard with a cold and melancholy feeling that one day Jacob's body would probably be buried here too.

FOUR

Jacob knocked on the back door at half past five. He was standing looking through the glass as she approached an opened the door – and didn't look like he'd just climbed out of a digger! The dark wash jeans he had one looked like one of the new pairs she had seen in his wardrobe and the navy blue shirt he had one was pristine and neatly pressed. Suddenly she felt scruffy in her leggings and sweatshirt and she as sure she hadn't even run a brush through her hair today!
"I wanted to say thank you for looking after me the other day." He held up what looked like wrapped fish and chips.
Marelle smiled, no, she laughed. "Oh that's so sweet! Come in ..."
"I also brought a couple of beers." He had a carrier bag with him and had obviously just been to the shop. Jacob stepped inside. His eye was a lot less swollen but a lot more black today.
"Thank you Jacob." She said. "Lets go through to the living room."
He followed her though and sat himself down on the settee where he had slept a few nights ago.
"Give me five minutes." Marelle said. "I just want to change out of these clothes."
She ran upstairs, stripped off and grabbed clothes which she pulled on quickly then looked at herself in the mirror. Her hair was a mess – but to be honest it normally was – and her skin looked dull and pasty. Marelle brushed her hair quickly, threw her head upside down and sprayed hairspray on the roots then did a thirty second make up she was proud of, considering. When she bounded down the stairs and skipped into the living room she instantly saw the back of his head

where the wound was still prominent and swollen. There was still quite a hole there and she could see fresh and dried bood.

"Right." She announced' That's better! I'd had a scruffy day today!" he gave a tight lipped little acknowledgement. "So how are you today?"

"Im fine. Was so tired yesterday! Had a bit of bother with the cut this morning but its ok now?

"Has it been bleeding?"

He nodded. "Scraped it on the floor this morning getting under a truck in the workshop!"

Marelle made a face of pain. "Did it bleed much?"

"A bit." He said.

They unwrapped the fish and chips. Jacob notably had sausage and no fish and they sat in her living room eating them and drinking beer.

"Did you see Sam?" She asked.

"Yes."

"Did he say anything?"

"No. And I'm not about to dignify it by saying anything either."

"Has he hit you before?"

"Accidentally."

"*Accidentally*?" She made a face.

"He was picking a fight with one of the other kids who works on the farm. I stepped between them and got a glancing blow. But this time I think it was meant for me."

"Its not right."

Jacob didn't respond for a while but then he said "Its ok. I'm not scared of him. He's just a bully."

"So, you weren't digging out ditches today then?"

He shook his head, eating.

"Why do you have to keep digging out the ditches? It sounds like something for bad behaviour! Shouldn't Sam be digging out ditches?"

He gave a little smile. "Its just clearing them out. They get full of silt and vegetation – and rubbish – each year. If they weren't cleared out then the roads and fields end up getting flooded. And you won't get Sam digging out a ditch! Its beneath him."

"But you're older than them – you've probably worked there longer than them. Shouldn't they be doing the mundane stuff?

"I'm casual labour – as and when – they're employees. They've all been to farming college."

"How long have you worked there?"

"Off and on since I was fourteen. A long time. My father worked there all his life."

"And you're not an employee."

"No."

"Why?"

He shrugged. "They don't like me, they all think I'm an idiot – but that's fine."

Marelle laughed. "What?"

"Its fine. I like it that way."

Marelle wasn't sure she understood what he meant by that comment, but she didn't push it any further.

"So you work on the farm when they need you and you 'look after' the airfield. Are there any more hidden talents?" She eventually asked, lightly.

"No" he said as he ate, not making eye contact.

Conversation was slightly easier with him tonight although it was far from flowing and she was still waiting for him to actually smile – to break that same smile on the photograph in the caravan. She couldnt help thinking that in a strange way Sam may have done her a favour and provoked some thawing of the ice and thankfully steered him away from Bella's attempts that night.

Marelle couldn't help herself from staring at him and twice he looked up and caught her doing so. He had brought two bottles of beer and she'd had one – she didn't normally drink beer but what the heck! He was more relaxed than she's seen him while conscious and she felt a warmth inside her of that achievement. She had finally made two mugs of tea and when she took them in her presented her with her phone.

"You can keep it if you want."

"No, its ok. Emergency over." He said which poured a little cold water on her earlier thoughts until he added. "I know where you are."

Shortly after he wanted to leave. Marelle didn't try to detain him, convinced that her slow approach was beginning to reap rewards. But, he was in her kitchen about to go out of her back door and she could no longer help herself.

"Jacob!" She called him back and he half turned to her. 'Thank you for this evening." She said and reached out to him, giving him a "friend to friend" hug as she may have done to Bella. For a second she felt him freeze, then relax then gently pat his hands on her back. Smiling but not wishing to push it she let go and backed away.

"See you later." He said and this time there was a hint of a tiny smile on his lips.

Marelle felt that she had made progress with him at last. It was slow but she had got him communicating with her, responding to her and that in itself was a victory she was proud of.

Over the next couple of months she maintained that. His trust in her was building. He would turn up more often, happily (although his face rarely expressed that) sit in her kitchen and have a chat. Sometimes she would see him walking round the airfield and would join him. She kept the questions to a minimum and he was relaxed with that.

On one weekend Seb and his family had turned up to stay for a couple of nights which had been inconvenient and unannounced. Marelle had obliged but when Jacob paid a visit and he had been completely overwhelmed by this. He had left after four or five awkward words and Marelle had been forced to wait until they were all still in bed the following morning before she had a chance to pay him a visit. His initial words to her were:

"You've got a houseful!"

But her reply had clarified it for him "Yeah, I wish they would go but its half his house so I cant chuck them out!"

Marelle had a relationship with Seb's wife Caroline which could be described as 'mutual tolerance'. She obviously thought Marelle as a little scatty, disorganized and needy. When they all finally left Marelle knew that the conversation in the car on the way home would have continued to express these views – now probably reinforced by Jacob's behaviour too!

On another day Marelle had found Jacob halfway round the airfield, kicking at one of the concrete posts with a look on his face which suggested he didn't want a conversation. She'd told him she would see him later and left him to it. Later she discovered that Sam had destroyed a moorhen's nest which Jacob had been watching and nurturing.

A second incident came to light when she saw Jacob was limping quite badly only to find out that Sam had pinned him up against the workshop wall with a forklift following him breaking up another brawl between Sam and one of the other lads.

"Just let them get on with it." Marelle had advised.

"If I do that then I end up getting dragged in anyway – or they break something."

A further evening with Bella had also transpired after she walked into Marelle's and asked if she could stay one night on her way to a music festival up on the North Norfolk coast. Marelle valued Bella's opinion on her progress, so she offered to cook dinner and invited Jacob. He of course took some persuading but she eventually got his promise that he would turn up. Bella was a slight worry too, but Marelle was confident she could control her! When she arrived, Marelle sat her down in the kitchen.

"You must be on your best behaviour, Bella – please!"

"I'm always on my best behaviour!" she laughed.
"Bella." Marelle said, sternly.
"Ok." She held her hands up.
"Don't mess it up for me. We came close last time!" Marelle smiled. 'That reminds me, I've got your shoes."
Bella laughed. "Oh God, I'd forgotten about the shoes."
"I found them in the grass – and I managed to get the pink stain off his caravan!"
"That was your idea!" Bella pointed a finger then laughed. "So, have you ..." She mouthed the words instead of saying them "*got him between the sheets*?" Then she grinned.
"God, no!" Marelle exclaimed.
"Well what *progress* have you actually made then?"
"I've got him starting to trust me ..."
"He's not a stray dog Marelle! And when does *trust* come into anything!"
Marelle sighed and stared at her.
"Ok, I get it. I'll be good." Bella replied.
Jacob stepped into the kitchen when they were both in there. The progress that Marelle wanted to demonstrate was written all over his face – he didn't want to be there but had turned up because she had asked him to.
"Well you look a bit better than last time we met." Bella said. "Last time you were white as a sheet, covered in blood, semi conscious and talking rubbish! You should have gone to hospital – I thought you were going to die!"
Jacob avoided eye contact by looking around the kitchen as he spoke. "I don't actually remember it but I'm still here."
Bella chuckled. "Guess you had a good nursemaid?"
"Yeah." He said.
By the time Marelle had the meal ready Bella had started on the wine and as they sat down proclaimed
"So it's the meal then the threesome then?"
Marelle physically kicked her so hard under the table that everything on it moved and the glasses tinkled together.
"Oh, sorry, that's tomorrow when I'm with Freya!" She checked herself but still with the sly grin.
Marelle managed to pull Jacob into some of their conversations, but he spoke as little as possible, mainly focusing on eating.
"Hey, why don't you come up to the festival with me? You can do a day ticket?" Bella suddenly asked.
"I'm not really into music like you are Bella." Marelle answered.

"Oh I'm not really into this stuff. Its usually some old farts playing shit from years ago but it's a big piss up and a chance to let your hair down." She explained. "Hey Jacob, you into music?"
"Er no, not much. I can take it or leave it."
And that was one of the longest sentences he managed all night.
As soon as he could escape he did, saying goodbye to Bella and thanking Marelle.
"Are you around tomorrow?" She asked as he left.
"Yeah, probably."
And Bella left in the morning. On the face of it she had been on her best behaviour and in a way, although she loved Bella to bits, Marelle was glad she would not be at the festival with her this weekend.
"And Jacob." She said as a final word to Marelle as she left. "He's lovely – I can see why you are attracted to him but Marelle – he *is* a bit weird!"

Marelle apologised for Bella when she caught up with Jacob on the airfield.
"I love her to bits, we've known each other for years bit she is a bit "forward leaning" sometimes!"
"I've met worse." He said in return.
It was Sunday evening, early Summer. The grass was green and dotted with wild flowers, the birds were singing and the sun was still shining.
"Are you walking up to the missile site?" She asked. 'We still haven't been up there."
"It wasn't what I had planned but I can do …"
"Its ok if you don't want to."
"No, no. Its fine. Come on then."
She walked across towards the belt of trees with him. Swallows and house martins were swooping around them as they walked, indulging in the bounty of small insects in the evening warmth. There wasn't quite so much silence between Marelle and Jacob now – conversation was still hard work, but less so. They rounded the trees and continued along a small track to what looked like a graduated concrete wall. The ground dropped away on one side the concrete so it was a foot high at one end and four at the other.
"Here we are." Jacob said. "One," He pointed. To two other walls set apart and staggered at about 45 degrees. "Two and three."
Marelle looked.
"This one is the best condition." Jacob commented nodding to the one close to them.
Marelle had expected more than this.

"This is all that's left now." Jacob said. "The missile would be raised on these "skids", three of them."
Marelle nodded and looked from one to the other.
"The trees never used to be there." He pointed again as he climbed up onto the concrete wall.
"And you can remember them?"
"Yeah." Jacob nodded. "You could see them best from that corner there." He pointed to the perimeter. "Where it dog-legs in."
She looked across before climbing up on the wall beside him." 'It would be a good view of the sunset from here." She commented.
"Due West." He said.
Marelle pivoted round in a small circle on the wall, taking it all in. Dark clouds had gathered above them now.
"Looks like ..." and there was suddenly a white flash of light followed by an ear splitting crack of thunder. Completely out of nowhere – so much so that she jumped and gasped, her hand on her chest. Jacob had jumped too and was now down from the wall.
"We'd better get off the airfield." He said. "Its not a good place to be in a thunder storm."
They began to walk and it began to rain. The odd large drop at first but with each stride it became harder and more frequent. The lightning flashed again and an almighty rumble of thunder shook the ground.
"Whoh!" Marelle exclaimed and looked to Jacob.
"Come on." He nodded. 'We had better make a run for it."
"We could shelter in the trees?" Marelle suggested, pointing to them.
He shook his head and waved for her to go in his direction just as the heaven's opened.
With the thunder and lightning crashing round them and the rain falling vertically like stair rods the noise was deafening. Jacob could shift, she granted him that and she was a way behind him. A crack of lightning seemed to hit the ground right next to them and it in all Marelle did let out a little scream at which he turned to see where she was, pausing and letting her catch him up. He sprinted to the caravan, ripped the door open and then pushed her inside as she came up the steps.
Inside, the noise was only slightly less as the rain hammered on the roof of the caravan. Marelle half gasped, half laughed as she turned to him with water dripping from her hair.
"Shit," she said.
He closed the door then took a deep breath – although he seemed less out of breath than she was. For a moment he was a little pensive but then he turned to her – reached past then passed her a neatly folded fluffy towel. Marelle took it and rubbed her hair, then her face and

finally wrapped it around her shoulders as she started shivering. Jacob had removed his t-shirt and had a towel around his shoulders too.

"I'm soaked right through!" She laughed, aware that beneath the towel the pale blue t-shirt she had one had probably been rendered pretty transparent. "And I'm dripping all over your floor."

"Don't worry." He said but threw her another towel onto the floor. She pulled her trainers off one at a time with the opposite foot and stood on it.

Outside the storm continued.

She stamped her feet on the towel to dry them but she was soaked right through to her bra and pants and was freezing.

"Go in there and get your wet clothes off." He nodded to the bedroom. "I'll find you something dry to put on." He passed her another towel.

Marelle ducked into the room and pulled the door closed. She stripped off her clothes – which wasn't easy in the cramped space with everything so wet. She folded it all into a pile then wrapped the second towel around herself, She felt like she'd had a cold shower and her skin was tingling with it. She turned and looked at herself in the small mirror, running her fingers through her shoulder length hair and pulling it back from her face. This must be where he slept – like the rest of the place it was impeccably neat and tidy. It was the same room she had come into the other week to pick the clothes up for him. Another peal of thunder split the air outside.

"Will this be ok?" He suddenly shouted through the closed door and made her jump.

She opened the door. He still had a towel around his shoulders, he'd taken his shoes off but still had the wet jeans on. He held up a grey jumper.

"Erm …" Marelle said. "It's a bit short. I've taken my jeans off!"

"Sorry, I was looking for something small for you! Hang on, let me come in here and see what there is." He pushed past her into the bedroom and she stepped aside as he moved to the wardrobe and opened the doors. Marelle moved alongside him to look in as well. He didn't seem to want her looking in the wardrobe as he pulled one door closed in front of her as he sorted through the clothes on the rail. Her eyes wandered to the red photo frame in the door, then back to him as she looked through the clothes..

"I've got a longish fleece in here. It will be too big but it will cover your modesty."

She smiled, leaning in slightly to look again. As he flicked through she could no longer control herself when she noticed a rather slim fitting pair of leather trousers. Her hand shot forwards and grabbed at them.

"Jacob!" he said with a grin. "Are these yours!?"

His expression didn't falter. He took them from her quickly. "Lets just put those back in here shall we." He said.

Marelle laughed to herself as he finally found the fleece he as looking for and pulled it out.

"Here." He said. "It will be warm and will be quite long on you."

"Ok, thank you, I'll pop it on."

He reached up and took out a top and jeans for himself and the red photo frame banged in the door pocket.

"Whats that?" She asked.

"Whats what?"

"The red thing." She pointed towards it.

"Its just a photo frame. Its of my parents." He said quietly and went to close the door.

"Can I see?" she asked.

"Its just and old picture."

"I'd like to see your parents." She smiled sweetly.

He sighed, a little resignedly and picked it out. Opening the frame out on itself he showed her the black and white wedding picture.

"Oh that's lovely." She said. "Your Mum is so pretty and petite!" She smiled up at him but as usual his face showed no emotion or expression. "And you look exactly like your Dad!"

"I never really knew my mother. She died when I was very young." He said,

"Oh, I'm so sorry." Marelle exclaimed softly. Moving the picture towards herself slightly as if to get a better look. In doing so she managed to get a finger in the frame and opened out the other side enough to see there was another photo. "Hey, is that you?"

He raised his eyes to her for a split second then looked away again. "No, its my brother."

At that precise second there was a simultaneous crack of thunder and lightning. They both jumped and cowered. It gave Jacob the change to wrestle the frame from her and replace it in the door pocket.

His brother?

"Are you twins?" She asked.

"No, three years difference. He was older than me."

'Was?" She questioned, tilting her head, wondering if she was on the verge of getting chucked out into the storm for asking too many questions and told to walk home.

Jacob nodded. "Took his own life."

She gasped, genuinely surprised. "Oh that's terrible. I'm so sorry." She felt bad for asking now. "I'm sorry I asked."

"Its ok." He replied. "It was a while ago now. His life and mine took two separate paths."

"Oh God. I'm so sorry Jacob." She said again.

He nodded his head in acknowledgement. "I'm going to put some dry clothes on."

Marelle left the bedroom and slipped into the large navy blue fleece he had handed her. It was long and quite large and came to mid thigh. If she put her hands in the pockets she could gather it around herself – and it was so soft and warm! While he changed she picked up wet towels and left her own clothes in a pile by the door. Moments later he emerged in dry jeans and the black fleece he seemed to favour.

Outside the rain was still hammering down.

"I'll boil the kettle." He said, "looks like this is in for a while."

Marelle sat on one of the benches and rested her head on her hand. At least the theory of a brother seemed to be true although Mrs Avison's recollection was obviously a bit patchy and not entirely correct. She had not seen a headstone in the churchyard but then, maybe there wasnt one. Jacob had said he had taken his own life, but not how. Maybe that was why there was no grave. While they both sat in his caravan waiting for the rain to pass Marelle felt that she had managed to peel away another layer at least and he had opened up to her and it was the result of her prodding. The rain lashed against the caravan and here she was, sitting in it in his fleece with no knickers on!

It was two weeks from mid summer but the storm took its time to move off and it was starting to get dark.

He walked back with her and she clutched the fleece around her as she tried to avoid the puddles with her bare feet in wet trainers.

"Well, we must do that again!" she grinned, finally standing inside her back door. "I'll get your fleece back to you."

"No worries." He said. "See you later."

"Night Jacob!" she smiled.

The weather the next day was a marked improvement. After all it was nearly mid summer and she would have hoped for something much better than what it threw at them last night. Her birthday was on the day before mid summer's day and nine times out of ten the weather was awful. Bella would no doubt be on the phone soon trying to organise a wild night out. Marelle sat back. She had been working all morning, her eyes were tired and it was lunchtime. There wasn't actually much in the house to eat and she hadn't bothered to make it to the supermarket yet, so she grabbed her purse and wandered over to the shop.

They stocked nice bread from a local bakery – she had discovered that when she had bought a loaf and asked about Mrs Avison. She picked a loaf and some "local grown" tomatoes and went to the till. The plump blonde woman she had seen before seemed to be on her own today – Jill, she thought her name was? She smiled at Marelle as she checked out the items.

"How are you getting on with your research?" Jill asked.

"Research?" Marelle questioned, for a moment wondering how she knew what Marelle did then recalling their previous conversation. "Oh, sorry – yes – I've been busy and haven't been able to get on to that for a bit. But Mrs Avison was brilliant – she knew so much about the village!"

"I bet she enjoyed talking to you?"

"Yes, she did. It was very pleasant."

"I see you've struck up a bit of a friendship with our friend in the caravan?" Jill continued.

Marelle stared at her. Gobsmacked that she had just said that – or even knew anything about her life at all.

"Er, yes – our paths do cross a lot as he practically lives at the bottom of my garden."

Jill smiled. "Well you've had an influence on him for sure. It hasn't gone unnoticed."

Marelle laughed. "What do you mean?"

"Well he's got a trendy new haircut and he's been waltzing about the village all dressed up. Linda says she's washing and ironing clothes she didn't even know he had!"

"Who's Linda?" Marelle asked.

"Linda Sharp – she does a laundry service for a few elderly and disabled people in the village ..."

"Well he's neither!" Marelle shrugged.

"Well she probably agreed to do his as well. All sorts of different stuff she said – twice as much as normal."

Marelle was a little shocked. Notwithstanding the fact that he got someone else to do his washing and ironing – and they hadn't even seen the leather trousers – but the fact the she, and him, were the discussion subjects of people she didn't even know.

"He'll be turning a few heads now that one! He was even in the chip shop the other day buying for two. Actually had a few words when he was in here the other day too – normally just skulks around with his head down ..."

Marelle clutched her bread and tomatoes and stood there smiling as benignly as she could.

"And we all thought he was just some recluse living in that caravan!"

"He's a really nice guy." Marelle offered. "that's the problem, everyone treats him like an idiot."
Before Jill started again, Marelle continued. "Well I'd better be going."
Marelle had wandered down there but strode purposefully back. Was everyone in the village talking about her and him? What other tales were they setting free?
The very idea of it plagued her all afternoon – then a new thought struck her. If they had noticed and commented, then so had other people. Maybe she had a new plan for her birthday.
She fended off Seb and Bella. However, Bella did remark 'Oh so you have *plans*! You go girl!'.
Marelle just prayed for good weather – so far it looked good but she hoped it would last. Jacob seemed oblivious to the village gossip and Marelle had not broached the subject. She had wanted to comment that getting someone else to do his washing was a little decadent but did not want to rattle his cage – not right now at least.
The weather had held and the day before her birthday she walked up to Jacob's caravan. The sun was out as the swallows were swooping around her but the caravan was locked and he was not there. She checked her watch. It was a quarter to six and he was normally here by now. Marelle waited for a bit, sat on the steps, walked around the caravan but there was no sign of him. It was odd but maybe he was still at the farm? It wasn't that late. So, she walked home again.
An hour later she returned. Nothing had changed, there was no sign of him. She banged on the caravan door a few times just in case he was there but there was nothing and he had to resign herself that he was not.
Marelle walked back again. Now her mind was racing. The last time he hadn't been here was when Sam had hit him. What if that had happened again? How would she know? Maybe she should drive around the village, look for him or look for Sam? But the last time she had done that he had turned up at her house and she had been out looking for him! She was plagued by the gossip in the shop as well – what if he had been taken in by someone else's charms?
She took herself home and sat herself up in the back bedroom where she could see his caravan. Dusk fell and it got as dark as it does in mid summer but she could still clearly see the caravan. It was ten forty-five and he still didn't seem to be home. Should she drive round the village? She wanted to but did not really see where that would get her? She rested her head on her hand. He'd asked her to cut his hair again the other day and she'd taken it as him liking the haircut she'd given him –

and he'd looked even better this time – but was it for someone else's benefit?

She suddenly awoke with a start, aware that she should not be asleep but a little confused at where she was. She shook her head and lifted it up, squinting she focused on the caravan. There was a light on!

Moving too quickly through the dark house, Marelle banged her knees and toes several times eventually bursting out of the back door and starting up the runway. She skipped up the steps and banged on the door.

"Jacob!" she shouted.

He had locked the door as she heard him unlock it before he swung it open.

"Whats wrong?" He asked.

"You weren't here. I've been back three times! I wondered where you were."

He smiled slightly. "I've been driving for the past five hours – sorry. I'm really tired."

He did look tired. He looked shattered.

"Where have you been?"

"Boss took me with him to pick up and old vintage lorry that he's just bought. Asked me to drive it home. It took hours and it broke down twice. Finally managed to bodge it and limp it back."

"Oh, I see. I was worried." Marelle confessed.

"So now I'm just going to try and go to sleep."

"Ok." She smiled. "But I just wanted to ask you if you would come on a picnic with me tomorrow evening? We could go up to the missile site and have a picnic as the sun goes down."

"Oh …" he said. "Ok, yeah."

Marelle grinned. "Great! Ok, I'll come to you, see you about six."

"Ok." He said.

"Well night night then, sleep tight." She smiled.

"I'll try." He answered as she turned to go. "Maybe bring an umbrella this time?"

Marelle laughed, "See you tomorrow."

Seb called her in the morning and wished her a happy birthday and she received a few cards in the post including one from Bella that made her smile. Bella's card was usually the rudest one she could find but this one had a picture of a fairy on the front and said "You can have one wish on your birthday … what will it be?" Then inside Bella had drawn little cartoons of her and Jacob (she knew it was Jacob by the hairstyle!) with lots of little hearts and kisses around them!

Shortly after she set off to the supermarket to buy everything for the picnic but ended up wandering around there aimlessly wondering what Jacob would like. She knew he didn't like fish and that was about all she knew. By the time she'd finished she had probably bought enough to feed ten people but had hedged all of her bets.

The day had been going too well and she began to worry, as she walked up to meet Jacob early that evening with the full coolbag, that someone would scupper her plans at this late stage. Marelle had put on a new pair of jeans, her favourite cowboy boots and a pale pink gingham check shirt; she'd washed and straightened her hair and was wearing make up. It was a relief to see his door was open as she approached, she walked up the steps and tapped lightly on the door. Jacob was standing just inside but looked up at her when she appeared.

"Hi." She said, smiling. "It's a nice evening."

"Lets hope it better than last time." He replied, slipping on a denim jacket over his black t-shirt and coming out to meet her. She backed down the steps and admired his bottom in the slim white jeans as he turned to lock the door.

They'd walked a few strides when he held a hand out for the coolbox and she passed it to him.

"What have you got in here? How many have you invited?"

"Just you and me." She smiled. "I've always wanted to do this."

"What?"

"A sunset picnic on a warm evening in the middle of the summer."

"You look nice." He said, looking straight ahead.

Marelle looked to him and smiled. "Thank you." And she felt that this had already got off to a good start.

They walked up behind the trees and out along the low concrete wall of the central missile skid. It faced directly towards the sun and had a clear view of it over the countryside. They sat on the wall at the end.

"Its still quite warm." Marelle commented, pulling the coolbox towards her. "Now do you want wine or a beer?"

"I'd rather have a beer." He replied.

She handed him one and opened the wine for herself. There were paper cups but that added to it.

"So – help yourself." She gestured. Taking items out of the coolbox and arranging them along the wall, hoping she had made some good choices.

Jacob was turned facing into the sun, his legs hanging over the side of the wall. Marelle sat perpendicular to him, watching him.

She liked watching him; you could stare at him and he was so wrapped up in his own thoughts that he didn't notice. Marelle looked at him in profile, staring into the sun and mindlessly popping food into his mouth. His features were quite strong in profile but the more she stared the more she could see the manifestation of the child he had long left behind. He picked the beer bottle up and drank before carefully placing it back down again. Marelle smiled to herself. There was a finesse about him, no doubt about it. He was far from *'the idiot in the caravan'* that everyone thought he was.

Then he turned to her gazing at him. She smiled.

"What?" He asked.

"Nothing." She said, "have I made some good choices?"

He nodded. "Mostly."

She would take that! "What have you been doing today?"

"Trying to sort that lorry out. Theres other stuff to do but that's his new toy so that takes precedence." He half turned and picked up some cocktail sausage rolls. "I sometimes think its the only reason he keeps giving me work – because I can usually double up as a mechanic."

"Have you been a mechanic before?"

"No, I'm just the one who always gets lumbered with that job, so it ends up being *my* job when anything goes wrong."

The sun was getting lower, it was deepening in colour now. The light that washed them was a warm, flattering pink. Marelle uncrossed her legs and lowered herself to the gound. She picked something out of the coolbox and walked up alongside Jacob as she still sat on the wall with his legs hanging down.

"I've got strawberries." She grinned, holding them aloft. Then handed them to him. He took one, took a bite then suddenly grabbed at her shoulder.

"Look!" He exclaimed in a whisper and nodded in front of them, A roe deer had ventured across the area, a small fawn at foot, stepping warily behind its mother as she stepped through the grass while making her way across.

"Sssh" he said.

Marelle stood alongside him, her hip pressed into his thigh, his hand still on her shoulder and the strawberries in her hand. A distance off to their right a barn owl flew its ghostly flight over the long grass of the airfield.

The deer walked on for a bit, stopped, sniffed the air then continued with its offspring meandering. Eventually they passed out of view and into the trees.

Marelle turned to him. "Did you arrange that?" She joked. 'This is such a beautiful spot."

"Its virtually the only one remaining. "He said, "Most of the others have already been broken up."
"Its special' She said, quietly, pausing for a second aligning her sight and checking her plan. "And today is a special day."
"Is it?"
"Yeah. Its my birthday." She said.
"Is that what this is for?" He asked, "why didn't you tell me? I could have got you something."
She turned to him. "You don't have to get me anything." She shifted her weight to her other foot. "But there is something you can do for me ..." Again, coyly, she turned to him.
"What?"
"This." She said and before the bird had time to fly she moved into him, placed her hands on his thighs, turned and kissed him. Not just a quick peck but full on his lips, searching his mouth with hers until she felt his hands around her. She moved between his legs and placed her hands up and around his neck. This was good, this was better than she had even hoped for and she felt that thrill within her. She broke away, stared right into his eyes, her hands still behind his neck, his around her waist. She rocked gently to and fro as she exhaled quietly. Jacob smiled. A lovely, sweet, quiet smile that wasn't just a token reaction. He smiled as he moved in to her lips again. The next time they parted she laid her head into his chest and he wrapped his arms around her. She could feel the heat of his body against hers and hear his gentle breathing as they remained there. This moment seemed to hold a reality to it that she had never felt before. It was like she had found her spot in heaven on this warm evening, enveloped in the golden sunlight with his arms around her and she wanted to stay here forever.
Eventually she sat away and looked up at him. The light was fading but she was sure there was a tear running down his cheek. He looked away. She turned his head back to her and gave him one straight kiss on the lips then wiped away the tear with her finger. She turned away, picked up a strawberry and placed it between his lips. Then with a grin she walked over and began tidying everything away. He sat there, eating the strawberry and looking out across the airfield as the light faded around them.
Marelle joined him on the wall, huddled up against him as they watched the final golden beams of light get pushed away by the darkening sky until they were bleached by the moonlight. He had placed his jacket around her shoulders and had his arm around her.
"Come back to mine." She said. "I'll make some coffee."
"Ok." He said, quietly. "But, Marelle ... lets not rush this."

She turned her head to him, half lit by the moonlight. "Why should we?" And she leaned up and kissed his cheek gently.

The following morning was a beautiful one. But when she opened the curtains, it was an even more beautiful one than normal. What she wouldn't have given to have Jacob stay the night – but that day would come. Today she was walking on air with every step and she couldn't wait to see him again but she didn't want to rush; she was not going to push too soon. She had opened the door and would leave it to him to come inside.

Jacob arrived at her back door late afternoon. It looked like he had come straight from work. He stood leaning against the wall with a coy little smile on his face. A smile at last! She was seeing a genuine smile, and she was proud that it was her creation. Marelle opened the door. He didn't move but lifted his arm to present her with a bunch of the most delicious cerise pink roses.

"Oh Jacob, they're lovely."

"I picked them." He said. "They grow up by the old mess room."

She smiled. "Thank you." As she leaned forward and placed a gentle kiss on his lips. Let me put them in some water. Are you coming in?"

No. I've just finished, I'm pretty grubby – I wanted to bring them here before they started fading."

"Ok. See you later?"

"Do you want to come for a walk?" He asked. "I need to clean up, but ..."

"Yes, that would be good." Marelle grinned. "Shall I come up to you, in about an hour?"

He nodded. "see you then." And let his eyes linger on her as he turned.

FIVE

Marelle was upstairs wanting to put "nice" clothes on but if they were only walking around the airfield she decided on clean jeans and a t-shirt instead. She applied make up and straightened the ends of her hair with the straighteners; thought about putting it up in a pony tail but then decided against that. Then her phone rang. It was Bella.
"Well?" she asked.
Marelle laughed. "What?"
"Well did you get your birthday cake and eat it?"
"That would be telling."
"You did – you crafty little bitch!"
"Steady on! It wasn't like *that!*"
"What do you mean? What was it like then?"
Marelle drew a breath, filled her lungs and felt herself swell with pride and happiness. "Oh Bella he is the sweetest, most gentle, beautiful person to walk this earth. And you know, when we were sitting out there and his arms around me ..." for some inexplicable reason Marelle found herself welling up. She continued and tried to hold on to it "it was like the point of my whole existence was to be there, in that moment, with him ..." she finally couldn't hold back the tears any longer. "I just wanted to stay there forever!"
Bella was unusually silent. There was a pause – something unheard of in conversations with her.
"Oh Marelle," she finally said "you've really fallen for this one haven't you? I've never heard you like this before."
Marelle sniffed, laughed, sobbed all at once. "They're happy tears Bella! I've never felt like this before!"

"So, what happened after that."
"Nothing, we just held each other. He says he doesn't want to rush things."
"Oh, I don't like the sound of that!"
"With anyone else I wouldn't either but with Jacob I take it as a positive in that he is thinking about it continuing."
Bella laughed. "that's a strange way of looking at it!"
"Well he's not straightforward is he? But I'm not letting him out of my grasp. He's a true angel – and he's mine!"
"Now you're going all spiritual on me ..."
"It was a very spiritual experience!"
"He's not part of some cult, is he? He's not brainwashing you, is he?"
"No, he's not!" She smiled. "And I'm going for a walk with him in a minute so I'd better go."
"OK." Bella said. "But be careful Marelle."
"Of course!" She said playfully mocking Bella.
"No, I mean it. You're so high I don't want to see the result of you come crashing back down again. Don't fall in too deep."
They said their goodbyes and Marelle checked her appearance in the mirror. Damn Bella, you could see she'd been crying now.
When she arrived at the caravan he was sitting on the steps eating a sandwich. He wasn't hurrying so she sat herself down on the two breeze block that for some reason had always been stacked by the door.
"Good day?" He asked.
"Not bad." Marelle smiled. "And you?"
"Yeah, ok."
Marelle reached across and rearranged his hair. "That's better." She said.
Eventually he finished and they walked off around the airfield but tonight he held her hand. By the time they returned he had his arm around her shoulders.
The wheat was high in the fields around here now, and golden. The evening sunshine played over the crop in an ethereal light. Jacob stopped and stared out over the crop and the wide Suffolk sky. Marelle stood alongside him and he moved behind her, her back pressed into his stomach; he wrapped his arms around her and rested his head on hers. Breathing together, still and just looking out over the scene in that early evening light. A soft breeze rose off the crop and ruffled her hair around her face. And in that moment Marelle suddenly *understood*.
With her back to him she felt a tear in her eye again. This was his universe and he had let her in.
"I want to stay here forever." She said with a lump in her throat.

He squeezed her gently and she felt him sigh. "I know ... come on I'll make you tea this time."
She stood in the caravan while he made tea. It was a small space and she had to keep stepping out of the way but she quite liked it when he brushed past her or reached across her.
"How do you have it?" He asked.
"Black, one sugar." she replied.
"That's good as I don't have any milk!"
She smiled.
He picked up both mugs and nodded for her to sit at the small table. Jacob put the mugs on the table but before he sat down, he took his wallet out of his back pocket and tossed it on the table. As he did a small metal object skidded across the surface and he grabbed for it.
"Whats that?"
He opened his fist. In it was a small metal badge in the shape of two stylized wings.
"It's a badge."
She took it from his hand and looked closely at it.
"It was given to me by one of the guys on the airfield when I was a kid. If we hung around the fence some of the guys would come over and give us things, sweets, chocolate – and this. A lot of them would tell us we weren't meant to be there but there were a couple that we got to know quite well. He gave one to me and one to Frankie. He smiled with a remorseful laugh. "Frankie often used to wear his."
She put it back into his hand and he closed his fingers around it. She clasped her hand over his.
"And you've kept it with you all that time?"
He nodded. "We said we would – as best mates – we said that we would always keep the badges with us."
Marelle smiled. "That's sweet."

Seb dropped a whole lot of very boring work on her the next day. For a change she decided to get on to it straight away and get it done. It took up most of her day and she was beginning to realise she would not be able to complete it and with that in mind she got distracted when on a geneaology website. She had Seb's log ins so had full access. Her fingers typed Jacob's name and she chose a birth date range and hit "enter". Sure enough she found him – he'd been born at the end of April and would be forty two now. Marelle was thirty four so that was not such a huge age gap as everyone was leading her to believe. She found his father, then his mother and began the search for the elusive brother. She found a Nathaniel Ezekiel Frost born three years before Jacob and died thirty two years later. So, he was right – and Mrs Avison had been very wrong with all of her ramblings. Jacob did have a brother, he had been called Nathaniel and he had died at the age of thirty four – the same age as she was now. 'Taken his own life' Jacob had said. Tentatively, she brought up the death certificate. During the course of her research for Seb she looked at death certificates all the time but as her eyes scanned this one she felt a chill in her heart. His brother had died of 'asphyxiation due to drowning'. Nathaniel Ezekiel Frost had taken his own life by drowning himself.

"Shit." She said under her breath. As far as she could recall there had not been a grave in the churchyard for him. Maybe she would check later. The person in the photograph Jacob had in his wardrobe could have been his twin. She hadn't looked at the small details but she had thought it was Jacob, albeit having a warm genuine smile on his face. And also, what Jacob had said 'our lives took very different paths'. Nathaniel had obviously moved away – his place of death was nowhere near here.

She had that in mind when she walked up to the caravan early that evening. The sun was still warm and high in the sky. The caravan door was open but she could not see him. However, as she approached she could hear tapping sounds and movement from the other side of the caravan. She walked forward a couple more steps and realized he was singing! Jacob singing! Marelle stopped in her tracks and listened as she held her breath.

'She broke my heart, when the corn was high, She broke my heart when she said goodbye, she broke my heart when she took my hand. And left me here such a hollow man." He then started tapping at something again. Marelle continued and peered around the end of the caravan.

He had a motorbike there, leant up against an old oil drum. He was crouched down behind it, tinkering with something.

"Where did that come from?" Marelle asked as she rounded the caravan. Jacob looked up at her. "Someone dumped it with a load of other stuff on one of the tracks. I had to get rid of it all but this didn't look too terminal."

"Can you ride a motorbike?"

"Yeah, I used to have a bike."

"Will it work?"

"I don't know if it will ever be roadworthy but I can mess about here with it."

She smiled. He actually looked excited about it.

"I don't know anything about motorbikes." She said, watching him. "Are you going to use it then?"

"Might do. I can go on the tracks so I could go to work on it."
"What was that you were singing?" She looked up at him as he stood up, squinting her eyes on the sun.
"Singing? Was I?"
She nodded. "Something about breaking hearts and corn."
"Oh that's an old song. I heard it on the radio earlier …:
"I don't know it."
"You're probably too young." He commented, walking around the bike. "Do you think she'll start?"
Marelle shrugged.
He kept his eyes fixed on Marelle, turned the key, kicked it into life and twisted the throttle. It started but was extremely loud and it emitted a huge cloud of blue smoke. He played with it for a minute or two and made it sound smoother. Then he stood it upright and slid a leg astride it, playing with the throttle. Once happy he kicked off and went forwards slowly, eventually moving in a circle around her. He did a couple of circuits as she pivoted around, watching him. On his third go around he opened it up and took off in a straight line up the runway. Marelle watched him; he did look extremely confident on it. He turned it around and came back towards her at speed then came to a halt alongside.
"Get on." He said.
Marelle laughed. "I don't think so."
"Come on. I'll look after you."
"I haven't got a crash helmet – and neither do you."
"Its ok, you're on private land. "He nodded behind him. "Come on, get on the back."
Marelle had never been on a bike.
"I'll take it easy." He said.
She stepped forward. "How?" she asked, laughing.
"Just cock your leg over and hold on tight to me."
She did as he asked, wrapping her arms around his waist.
"Just go with me – ok?"
"No, but go on." She said, apprehensively.
Marelle held him tight and buried her head into his back. He accelerated and made off steadily up the runway.
"Ok?" He turned to her.
"Yeah." She replied shouting over the noise and the breeze in her face.
"Want to go faster?"
"Go on then." She said.
Jacob opened it up, leaned into it and she held on to him for dear life. It was noise, and speed and the wind in her face – and Jacob in her arms.

He turned it round and went again. Straight up the runway, he pushed it faster still – Marelle screamed. Jacob laughed.
Despite everything Marelle was struck by him laughing – actually laughing! He drove back and came to a halt at the caravan. Her legs felt like jelly and she was still holding on very tightly to him.
"Been a while since I've had that!" He remarked, half turning to her.
"What?"
"A girl screaming on the back of my bike!"
"Sorry." She said, still clinging to him.
"I'm getting off now He said. "– you'll have to let go!"
She sat back, put a leg down then climbed off. Jacob did likewise.
"Not bad." He said, "For something chucked in a ditch."
Marelle turned to him. He was smiling and he was more than animated. Marelle grinned, happy to see him like this, to see a smile on his face like his brother's in the photo. He walked around the bike and held out his arms to her. They met in the middle and he hugged her to him. She laid her face into his chest with his arms around her then she turned her face up to him and kissed him gently on the lips; he responded by squeezing her softly as she did. Marelle opened her eyes and looked straight into his – she thought about his brother and the words on the death certificate.
"Want to come back to the house?" She asked.
They walked back down the runway. He had secured the bike behind the caravan and locked his door. He pointed out the barn owl to her again, swooping over the long grass to the other side. They watched it for a few minutes like a silent ghost, patrolling its domain.
"Its so beautiful." Marelle said.
"It is, but remember, she's beautiful but it will still end in a kill – for something."
That evening for some reason, Jacob seemed taller as he walked along with his arm around her shoulders, his head held high for a change. She wanted to believe it was her doing.
Then he turned to her with glint in his eye.
"Lets walk over to the river." He said, "We'll need to grab a couple of towels."
"Towels?!" She asked. "I'm not going *in* the river!"
"We can just get our feet wet. It's a chalk stream – its brilliant!"
Marelle did as he asked and took the towels but did not anticipate even getting her feet wet. He had an enthusiasm for this which she didn't want to dampen so she went along with it anyway.
"How far is it?" She asked.
"About a mile if we go on the tracks."

"A mile? We could drive?"

"No, no," he shook his head with a smile. "We'll walk." And he held out his hand to her.

It seemed a lot further than a mile, sometimes along defined tracks, other times through undergrowth but eventually he led her to a shallow bank which opened into a slightly wider bend in the river. It was surrounded by high grass and trees and the water was flowing quite strongly in the centre of the river. The water was clear, the bottom was gravelly, dotted with plants – almost like the bottom of a well kept aquarium. In the background there was a louder sound of rushing water but here it was relatively quiet and calm.

"We used to call this the 'calm pool'." Jacob said.

"You and Frankie?"

He nodded. "Further up at the weir it was 'the rapids'. We used to spend hours up here in the summer."

"Did you used to swim in here?"

"Yeah. "He nodded. "Still do, sometimes."

She glared at him. "You swim, in there?"

"Sometimes."

"How deep is it?"

"About six or seven feet in the middle."

He was staring at it.

"Are you going in now?" She looked to him and raised her eyebrows.

"I will if you will."

Marelle stared at him. Was he serious? He wanted her to get into the river? Right now, late evening with the sun already going down. She didn't want to, she hated swimming and it would no doubt be cold – but the look in his eyes was too much to turn down.

"I'm not a very good swimmer." She said. "It looks cold as well."

"If you sit there thinking about it you'll never do it. Just get in and get under the water!" He was already pushing his shoes off, pulling his t-shirt over his head.

She sighed and kicked off her boots.

He undid his belt, slid his jeans down and stepped out of them. He had red and white underpants on and Marelle began to laugh

"Where did you get those pants from?" They were like something you'd make a six year old wear.

Jacob ignored her and began to walk into the water, bending down and feeling it with his hand. Then he continued until it was above his knees.

"It goes a bit deeper suddenly here." He advised.

Marelle hesitated. "I think I'll keep my t-shirt on."

"Then you'll have nothing dry to put on afterwards."

True! She signed and pulled her t-shirt over her head, when she freed herself Jacob had swum into the middle of the river. She hurriedly stripped down to her navy blue satin bra and pants and stepped into the water.

It was freezing. Even just on her feet it took her breath away!

Jacob had turned and was treading water. "Get into the deeper water. It feels warmer."

She looked across at him, at the water, at the evening closing in around them and wondered to herself just what the hell she was doing. Then she took a breath and plunged in.

It completely wiped the breath out of her leaving her gasping and spluttering. Not swimming as such but just trying to maintain consciousness. Jacob moved through the water to her.

"Bloody hell Jacob!" She gasped, feeling for the bottom but only flailing at water.

"It drops down sharply." He said, coming to where he could reach the bottom and keep his head and shoulders above water and guided her up the bank to where she could do the same.

Marelle laughed, not through being cold, but through the moment she found herself in. She was shivering – Jacob hugged her to him. "You'd better get out if you're too cold."

She smiled. "I may need you to help me warm up again!"

She wrapped herself in a towel and sat on the grass beside the river. Jacob wandered out, picked up the other towel and at down beside her. She laughed and shook her head. "That was not one of the best ideas!"

"Why? I've been swimming in here since I was a kid!"

"You're used to it!"

"Ah, come here." He put his arm around her, squeezing her to him. She turned and kissed him gently. He stared at her, his dark hair just falling slightly over one eye, a somewhat cheeky look on his face. Marelle grinned back and placed her arms around his neck, she laid back and pulled him on top of her.

"That's better." She smiled and pulled him to her.

They ended up laying on the river bank, towels half covering them, Jacob's head against her breast, legs intertwined. It was getting dark.

"This spot hasn't changed since I started coming here." He said. "You cant get right to the weir now as its been fenced off but this bit is exactly the same."

"And you used to swim in here with Frankie?"

"Yeah. His mother would probably have grounded him forever if she'd have known and especially if she had found out we used to play at the weir as well."
"What's the weir?" She asked.
He nodded behind them. "It's a 'step' in the river where it drops from one level to another. The water there is deep and fast, you get an undertow. You could easily drown ..."
Marelle cringed slightly. Was he thinking about his brother? For a second he was far away. She felt a slight pang of remorse for steering the conversation that way.
"Come back to mine for coffee – or better, hot chocolate?" she offered.

A few days later, on her way back from a visit to town she swung by the small church again. It was a lovely sunny morning and there was a small yellow car also in the car park. Marelle wandered through and saw an elderly woman and a younger one over the far right. They were talking. She walked straight to Jacob's parent's graves and looked for Nathanial Ezekiel Frost. She walked slowly, staring at the stones, reading each name and not finding his. He obviously hadn't been buried here.
The other couple were moving closer to her and she looked up to smile at them.
"Morning." She greeted.
"Morning." The younger one replied politely. The older woman was lingering behind, poking through the grass with her walking stick.
"Hello." She said. "This is a lovely spot, isn't it?"
Marelle nodded. "It is, it's a very peaceful place."
"I haven't been here for over thirty years you know." She began a conversation. "I used to teach at the local school ...:
"Did you?" Marelle asked. "I've only lived here a short while but I have been researching the village."
"You'll know about the little lad who disappeared then? Terrible affair – I was his teacher."
"Really?" Marelle shuffled slightly. "I've been reading all about that, nobody seems to have any idea what really happened to him – do they?"
"Just disappeared. Right out of his bedroom into thin air! It was a terrible blow to all of us and to the children."
"Did you know Jacob Frost? I believe he was the little boy's best friend?"
"The Frost boy?" She asked. "Yes, how could I forget him? Went from a mischievous little scamp to a withdrawn silent little shadow overnight. I worried about that child but there as no safety net in those days ... still I heard he went on to win a scholarship to grammar school so it must have knocked some sense into him."

"What about his brother?"
She looked up at Marelle. "Brother? I don't think he had a brother."
"Mum!" The other woman called. "We'll be late!"
She turned to Marelle. "Oh well, been nice chatting to you. Good luck with your research."
Marelle watched them go then she turned back to the headstones. She stared at them for a while before she left.

Driving along the road by the main gate to the airfield she was initially alerted to two white vans parked in the gateway. They both had orange lights on their rooves and as she went past she could see two or three guys in hard hats and hi-vis vests. In the middle of them was Jacob, talking to them and pointing back at the airfield. Marelle slowed but he did not notice her. She drove home, parked the car then ran round the back of the house, over the fence and up the runway.
Jacob, was already walking down. He had a stick in his hand and was thrashing at the long grass as he walked. She could see the tension in his body even from this distance.
Marelle quickened her pace and walked towards him. His jaw was clenched and tight, his shoulders hunched and his face gaunt and expressionless again.
"Six weeks." He said across the distance.
Marelle reached him, reached out a hand and tucked it around his arm.
"Six weeks." He repeated. "And they move on to the airfield and start levelling ground. Eight maybe, if we're lucky."
"Have you got to get off?"
He nodded.
"Was that who was at the gate? I just drove past and saw them."
He walked on, quickly. Marelle held on to his arm and she could feel the tension in his muscles.
"You can put your caravan in my garden – or you can move in with me." She offered, trying to help.
"I need to speak to someone, can I borrow your phone?"
"Yeah, sure." She pulled it from her back pocket and handed it to him.
He took it and went into the caravan; she followed him inside. He took a notebook out of a drawer, flicked through then dialled a number. His eyes fixed into space as it dialled and rang.
"Hi, Mike? Its Jacob Frost – Project Emily, Thor site …"
Marelle stared at him. He sounded like he was disclosing secret information.
"Yeah, that's it." He continued after a pause. "The developers just pitched up – they are starting on the site in six weeks."

The other person spoke for a while. "Yeah, yeah." Jacob said "Ok."
There was another pause.
"I don't know." Jacob said. "Its still Devorah – yeah."
They spoke for a bit longer and it ended by Jacob asking to be kept posted and confirming he could pass on Marelle's number as contact. He handed her the phone back.
"Mike Nicholls – he's trying to get the Thor site to be made into a heritage centre – been trying for years. It's the only one left. I've spoken to him a few times and said I would let him know if anything was about to happen."
"Can he stop it?"
"I doubt it, at best we'll probably only get a delay. If he does manage it, then its only a very small part that will be saved."
Marelle sighed. She turned to him and hugged him but he didn't respond to her this time; just stood there and let her embrace him.
"It'll be ok." She said softly, resting her head against his chest, "Jacob?" She called him and tried to get his attention back. "Lets just calm down a bit and think about this."
He exhaled and relaxed a bit in her arms.
"I need to go off for a bit." He said, pushing her away softly. "I'm sorry but I've taken my eye off things and been distracted by you and ..." he stepped slowly away. "And now this has happened." He was rambling." And now there is only six weeks."
"I can help." She said, staring at him. "I'm here with you and I will help ..."
He looked at her with a sigh, utter pain on his face.
"All's not lost Jacob."
"I need some space. Sorry but I need to go."
"Go, where?" She asked, a certain panic creeping into her voice.
"Just off."
"Can I come?"
"I just need to be on my own for a bit." He flattened his hands as she went to follow him. "I'll be back later."
Seconds later the motorbike screamed into life and Marelle raised her hands to her head in pure disbelief as he disappeared up the runway. She swore to herself, watched him go then turned.
"Fuck." She said to herself. What was all that about? A couple of days ago she'd had him right there where she wanted him. He'd been happy and normal – responding to her. She had almost had him that night, but she had conceded to him 'not wanting to rush things'. Somehow, regret was a painful burden.

She returned home but was too panicked to do anything except pace about the house listening for the sound of that bloody motorbike. He had no crash helmet, no insurance and he told her that the damn thing wasn't roadworthy. And where had he gone? *'Finding space'* again? Was that a recurring thing with him? Marelle sighed and caught her breath – she was getting angry with him. She wanted to help him and be the one he returned to once he had found his space.

How quickly he had changed from smiling and laughing like the photograph of his brother to the stooped, gaunt, expressionless Jacob that she had first encountered. He had known all along that this would happen; he'd even joked with her about being on borrowed time here. But now, she understood that this would mean an end to his perfect little universe where he'd managed to hide for the past ten or so years.

The evening sunlight was coming to its usual golden hue over the airfield when she heard the distinctive sound of the bike. Marelle leapt up and went straight out of the back door, strode across the garden then shielding her eyes to the setting sun she looked towards the caravan and the place where the sound had come from. She watched and worried but eventually he appeared from around the caravan and began walking in her direction. A smile broke on her face in the realisation that he had come back and was coming straight to her. He was walking quickly towards her, determined in his stride, tall and lean, his jeans slightly crumpled around his ankles where they were not over his boots which were half done up, half unlaced. She looked up to him, he was wearing sunglasses – mirrored wrap round ones that he'd not been wearing earlier and his hair was slightly swept back from riding in the wind. In the evening sun her heart was doing backflips in her chest.

Jacob walked up to her. She looked up to him, not sure to be able to read his mood with the glasses on but they fell into a mutual embrace with him taking her in his arms and squeezing her tightly to him as though he had actually missed her.

"Are you coming over to mine?" She asked.

He nodded and walked on behind her.

In the kitchen she switched on the kettle and loaded the toaster. He rung his hands around a bit and hovered before he finally pulled out a chair and sat at the kitchen table.

"Where have you been?"

"I just rode about a bit then parked up and thought about things ..."

"I'm scared you're going to hurt yourself on that bike." She said, quietly.

"I'm fine."

Marelle smiled resignedly. "I wasn't expecting you to go off on that, I was worried."

"Sorry." He replied quietly. He was sitting there, tense and tight lipped, going through words in his head. Then he spoke.

"Ever since Frankie disappeared I've been looking for him. I have never given up hope that one day I will find him and I will know what happened to him." He took a breath. "He was the nearest thing I had to family and the only person I have ever trusted completely – even at that age I had learned that people were only out to hurt you. Frankie was different – he had nice clothes, he didn't speak like the rest of us and he was very bright – genius almost. He was rejected by everyone else because he was different and wasn't from round here. I was rejected by everyone because I was the son of the local alcoholic, because I was usually dirty and scruffy and hungry – pinching stuff, hanging around where I wasn't wanted ... we came together peering through the fence on the airfield and became a pair. He would bring me back here, give me food – his mother was lovely and treated me like one of the family. We were best friends and said we would always look out for each other – we would study hard at school, we would go to college, we would study nuclear physics and we would change the world. Then he disappeared."

Marelle put tea in front of him and a pile of buttered toast. If she had asked him he would have said he didn't want anything, if she put it in front of him he would eat. Then she sat down opposite and looked to him.

"Now, having said all of that I've spent thirty odd years looking for him – on my own. Nobody really bothers me – I'm just the weirdo in the caravan, recluse, village idiot, pikey – whatever they want to call me – it doesn't matter – but I've been here, looking, searching, *knowing* he is here somewhere. And I've known you a few months – weeks even but you came to me – you treated me like a normal human being, you trusted me, and you really made an effort to be part of my life ... its been along time since ..." he stopped and sighed. "I've never really been in a meaningful relationship, I've not really had anyone that mattered to me since Frankie – but I want to trust you – and I *have* to trust you."

"You *can* trust me Jacob. I am here for you, I promise."

He nodded. "What I am about to tell you I have never, ever told anyone but I've got six weeks to find him and I need your help."

"Find him?" Marelle asked. "You think he's dead and he's here somewhere?"

"He has to be." Jacob pushed the sunglasses up on his head and locked his eyes up into hers. "You see what it says in those newspapers isn't what really happened."

He stood away from the wall and looked up at the window. It was slightly open. It had to be nearly seven o clock, he'd been here for hours. It was cold and he hadn't eaten since dinner time. Frankie had said that it would make it difficult to sneak out if he had come in for tea tonight and Frankie had been sure that something big was afoot. He looked out as far as he could without moving out of the shadows where he couldn't be seen.

He stooped and scrabbled around on the ground, finding a small lightweight pebble which he took in his hand threw, very accurately, with a quick flick of his wrist. It clattered against the window and seconds later it had the desired effect. The window opened and Frankie looked out. He acknowledged with a wave then ducked back in again. Next time he appeared he pushed the window open wider and climbed out to sit on the window ledge in a way which suggested he had done it many times before he reached across to the thick, black metal downpipe on the wall, wrapped his hand around it and then climbed out with one foot against the wall, his other on one of the brackets holding the pipe to the wall. Before descending he reached over and pushed the window almost closed, but not quite. Deftly he shuffled and climbed down the pipe then jumped down onto the grass.

Without a word between them they moved off, little shadowy figures hopping over the fence at the end of the garden and running along the gap between the fences and the perimeter of the airfield. Once in the bushes at the far right of Frankie's back garden he finally spoke.

"Now remember, only use our code names. Don't say your real name!" he whispered. "My code name is Atom and yours is Storm."

He nodded in reply to Frankie.

Frankie continued. "I was watching earlier. They were moving things onto the launch pads. Two of the missiles are up but there are no floodlights on yet."

"Is the car with the flags still there?"

"Yes, its parked behind the bomb shed." Frankie referred to the building to the left of the kids which they called the 'bomb shed' because they thought it could have been where bombs were stored.

"Lets go up to the corner."

The corner had the best view. You could sit hidden in the bushes there and see everything. It was further away from the launch site however so at a slight disadvantage in the dark. They ran up to the corner and crawled into the bushes. They sat there a lot and the ground under the cover of the bushes was smooth and flat. Side by side they settled into place.

"Hey Storm!" Frankie said suddenly to see if he responded. He did. "Are you hungry?"

He nodded.

"Here." Frankie handed him a banana that he had in his jacket pocket. "Thought you might be."

He took the banana, peeled and ate it in chunks as they both earnestly kept their eyes on the launch pad, still in darkness.

"How long do you reckon Atom?"

"Not long Storm. Two are ready. I reckon the third one will go up and then they'll put the lights on."

Storm chewed on the last chunk of banana. "Thanks for the 'nana." He said.

"Didn't you have any tea?"

"No, there was nothing to eat and dad was out."

"Is he at the pub?"

"Yeah ..."

Frankie sat up and rested his elbows on his knees. "I think tonight is going to be very important. I think they might be testing the launch mechanisms." He sat there for a moment. "It is quite possible that they could start a chain reaction that could burn up the whole atmosphere you know?"

"We'd be dead then!"

"Very dead then!"

"Do you think you would hear a big bang and run away or do you think you would just be dead straight away?"

"I think it would be very quick, like a split second and you would be dead."

"What do you think its like being dead?"

"I asked my Mum that once. She said that being dead is like being how you were before you were born."

"Well I don't remember before I was born."

"That's what being dead is like then."

"Have you seen a dead person?"

"My grandpa died but I was shut out and wasn't allowed to see him dead. Have you?"

He shook his head.

A car drove past just inside the airfield. They were both silent as it passed. "That was a Jeep."

It passed right by and eventually parked over at the launch site. It was still not lit up yet – there were some lights on at the edge which allowed

you to see the two upright missiles reaching into the darkness and the activity around them but the big, white floodlights were not lit up.
"Sandra Kershaw had a bra on today."
"How do you know?"
I sat behind her. I could see it. She's got really big bosoms!"
They both laughed and giggled for a moment.
"You'd better come to mine after school tomorrow."
"Ta."
"Arthur Bond is saying he is going to beat you up on the way home."
"Did he?"
"Yeah, cos you beat Jonesey up the other day. I heard him say that you are 'going to get it' for knocking out Jonesy's tooth."
"I didn't knock it out, it was falling out anyway! He called you a monkey bastard."
"Whats a monkey bastard?"
"Said your mum gave birth to you after she had been in bed with a monkey. I hit him, hard."
"Is that how you cut your lip?"
"No. I had a fight with one of the older boys."
"What about?"
There was a long pause. "Nothing."
"Don't tell my Mum you've had two fights in a week – she doesn't like fighting."
There was whining noise from the darkness over the airfield for a few seconds then it stopped. They both stopped talking and looked in that direction.
"We could crawl right under the fence there."
Frankie looked across to where he was looking. It looked like a rabbit or a badger, or something, had dug a slight hollow under the fence. Enough for two small boys to squeeze under.
"They might shoot us."
"They won't shoot us. We're just kids! Come on …"
"Storm! Wait!" *Frankie called.*
He looked back, his thin face a white shape with two black holes for eyes in the darkness.
"Have you got your badge?" *he held his out, pinned to his chest.*
"Yes, here." *He fumbled in his trousers pocket and fished it out.*
"Lets do the oath."
"Good idea."
They took the badges and held them up to each other, then said together:

'I pledge allegiance to protect my brother at all odds and to do my duty to God.' Then they replaced their badges and held their palms flat together. 'As blood brothers.'

Then he was off, crawling along the ground to the gap under the fence. He pulled the wire up a little then ducked his head and shoulders under. With a lunge and flick of his legs he got through. Then he turned and lifted the wire a little more to let Frankie do likewise. Then they were both on the other side of the fence.

They ran, towards the far side of the launch pad, keeping in the shadows, along close to the fence. Then both of them crouched behind two enormous concrete blocks, twenty yards from the nearest missile.

The whirring noise started again, closer to them this time and with a crack and a creak the third missile began to slowly erect.

"They cost a million pounds each."

"Three million pounds, right there then?"

The third missile reached its fully upright position and with a loud click, locked into place.

"They'll pump in the liquid oxygen now."

"How can you have liquid oxygen? Is it like water?"

"No, silly! Its oxygen that has been frozen – it turns from a gas into a liquid."

Then suddenly the floodlights snapped on. It went from darkness to bright, white, blinding day light. They had both jumped initially but crouching behind the concrete blocks they laughed quietly to themselves. Once illuminated there was a visible mist cloud around the missiles, moving with a soft hiss and clinging around the missiles.

"Wow!"

Ten minutes later, after them watching a few men with clipboards walk around, there was a loud dual tone siren. They covered their ears and looked to each other with a grin. They were both excited, with a front row seat at the show, right there – in the airfield at the launch pad.

The siren continued, its now single tone wailing into the night.

Unexpectedly there was suddenly a loud crack like something snapping – audible even over the siren. A split second later all hell broke loose.

There was a loud hiss and suddenly one of the missiles was enveloped in an opaque white, swirling cloud. The noise became louder, a roar over the siren and shower of white hot sparks burst from the foot of the missile into the white swirling cloud. There was commotion and shouting from the launch pad, people running around. The Jeep drove off but the sound of thunder grew, the ground shook around them. They held their ears and gritted their teeth. Then incredulously, the missile lurched, there was a sound of twisted metal creaking and screaming, the ear splitting roar of

thunder that seemed to be shaking the whole earth right down to the core, flames, sparks, white hot gases as the missile began to rise.
They couldn't hold it there any longer and fear took over as they both held their ears and ran headlong for the gap under the fence, squeezing under, scrabbling legs, knees and hands, snagging clothes and grazing skin.

SIX

Jacob had his elbows on her kitchen table, his hand pressed to his temples, fixed stare into space – speaking constantly. It was like the floodgates had been opened and it was all pouring out.
"I was running flat out – faster than I thought I could ever run – there was noise and sirens and people running about shouting – cars. Jeeps, smoke, fire – and I ran. I thought Frankie was right behind me, I thought he was keeping up behind me when I got to his back garden and stopped by the fence. I turned to catch my breath and ask him what the hell had just happened – and he wasn't there. There was just me and the backdrop of chaos on the launch pad. I called him. Called his name and his code name in case he would not respond to his name. I expected him to come running up – he was never as fast as me anyway – but he didn't. I walked back along the fence, right to where the spot was where we crawled underneath, but I couldn't see him anywhere. There were men and vehicles near that spot so I didn't go right back. I waited near his garden for a while – hoping he would come running along from the other way, but he didn't. I remember I stood there waiting for ages – I was cold and hungry and with all that going on over the other side of the fence I was confused and scared. I began to worry that I would get into trouble ..."
"What had happened on the airfield?" Marelle asked.
"Years later – and I still can't be sure as it was classified information – it looks like something went wrong with the fuelling and the missile accidentally 'launched' but it came straight back down on itself and didn't explode. I don't know if they were fully armed." He sat for a moment then continued. "The thing is I *promised* him I would always

look out for him, protect him the same as he swore he would for me – but I didn't – I ran and left him."

"But you thought he was with you."

"But he wasn't and I didn't check. I just ran."

"You were just a kid Jacob. You were scared – anybody would have acted the same."

"But Frankie had saved *my* life!" He exclaimed then dissolved into a tirade of tears that almost rendered his words unintelligible. "He saved *my* life – not three days before that at the weir. We were running across from one side to the other but there had been a lot of rain and the water was high and strong. He'd told me already that it was dangerous and that we shouldn't be doing it, but I ran across, slipped on the slimy stones and fell in. I'm a strong swimmer, was even back then but Frankie wasn't. I must have knocked myself senseless and been caught in the current under the weir but he jumped in and dragged me out. I swear I was one breath away from drowning. I still remember opening my eyes and seeing Frankie – a silhouette in the sunshine, looking down at me – slapping my face and shouting at me. There were blackbirds singing …" he shook his head. "And it still haunts me – I still wake up and think I'm drowning and I see Frankie but this time he cant save me." Jacob sobbed, covered his face with both hands and ran his fingers up into his hair with his eyes covered while he cried. "And I left him – I ran away and left him behind – I didn't keep my promise to him. He uncovered his eyes but kept his hands in his hair pulling it back and enhancing the tortured look on his face. "And then he wasn't at school and no-one would speak about him – only in a whisper and not in front of me or the other children. Police came and poked around with sticks but they never found him. His mother wouldn't look at me after that – she stopped coming out of the house. He'd just *gone*." He sighed shakily. "I daren't say anything to anybody or ask anything, we shouldn't have been there and I was scared of the repercussions. Then his family moved away and everyone forgot about him."

"And you never told anyone that the stories in the newspapers were wrong?"

"I didn't know. I never read them until the other day! Everyone just used to say he had disappeared – which he had but the circumstances were not as everyone had obviously believed."

"And you think he is here?"

"I know he is here. I know his body is here and every single day it is calling to me but I don't know where he is."

"What do you think happened to him?"

"I think –" he started, stopped, took a breath. "The most likely explanation is that he fell down one of the shafts in the panic and probably broke his neck or worse, was injured and died down there. I've looked everywhere. I've had plans and schematic diagrams – I've looked ten, twenty, a hundred times and I've found nothing but ... he was just a small boy."

Marelle sat in his silence. He'd spent his life looking for that boy and in six weeks time he was going to lose the chance to ever find him.

"If I'd have waited ..."

"You can't say that Jacob."

"If I'd have kept my promise."

"Jacob, its not your fault."

"If I'd have told someone, if I hadn't have crawled under the fence – he would have had a life – he would have grown up ..." Tears were running down his face. "I cannot see this place dug up and built on and know that his body is still somewhere beneath it all while I am walking around on top of it ... and its all due to me that he never had a life – never had a chance."

Marelle stood up, she walked over to him and wrapped her arms around him as he sat there.

"Its ok Jacob. I will help you – I will push everything else aside to help you but I don't see what I can do that you haven't already done to find him."

"A fresh pair of eyes may see things differently and you are good at this. He turned and looked at her with a hope in his eyes that chilled her to the bone.

"We can try but Jacob, you can't blame yourself for this – you cannot spend the rest of your life blaming yourself for this – even if we never find him."

He turned slowly again, screwed his eyes tight shut and sobbed to himself.

As she held him it all made sense now – his constant patrolling of the airfield, his intimate knowledge of every inch of it; his compulsion to work on the farm so he had the chance to check all of the ditches that ran around the airfield. He had dedicated his whole life to searching for Frankie – and now he had a deadline.

When he stopped sobbing she sat beside him at the table. It was quite dark in the kitchen by now but he still had the sunglasses on his head. She reached out and clasped her hand over his.

"I'm glad you told me this and I am so pleased that you finally trust me enough to do so. I'm here for you Jacob, I promise."

He looked at her with those sad dark eyes and gave a tiny smile that he managed to hold on to or a couple of seconds before it faltered.

"Lets sleep on it tonight and in the morning we'll come up with a plan."

He swallowed and nodded.

"Why don't you stay here tonight. It's been a difficult day – I'd feel happier if you stayed here with me." Marelle asked.

"I'll be ok. I'm working at the farm tomorrow anyway."

"No ." She stated. "If we are doing this together then I want you to stay here tonight."

"Ok." He smiled. "But I need to be in a room on my own – I'm a bit of a restless sleeper."

"Oh, ok. If that's whats best?" At least he had agreed to stay.

She made a bed in the middle room for him and then made them both a hot drink. They sat in the kitchen drinking it without him saying much now, he was back to staring into space but seemed more relaxed than usual.

It seemed strange to her that he wanted to sleep in a separate room, but she respected that and met him on the landing between the bedrooms. He stopped and smiled softly down at her as she looked up at him. She placed her hands flat against him and tiptoed up to meet him.

"If you re lonely you can always come into my room." She said.

"I know." He replied.

He didn't come into her room – but as he had warned, he was restless. Marelle heard him all night long, up and down, walking around the room. At one point he went downstairs and she lay there in blind panic that she would hear the door go and he would leave. She breathed a sign of relief when he came back up the stairs. It must have been the early hours before she eventually fell asleep as she woke in daylight and heard him downstairs again. When she went down he was there in her kitchen making tea. He turned and gave her a smile when she walked in.

"So," she said when they were both sat at then table again. "I thought I could start by researching everything I can about Frankie's disappearance and this site and what happened on that night. When you come back, we can go through what happened again. We'll write it all down and go through it step by step …"

"Ok."

"As you said, a fresh pair of eyes … come back here after work." She said, "we need to be together."

Him stepping out of her back door that morning and going off on his own filled her with dread, especially after how he had been yesterday.

"Jacob." She called him back, "Come here."

She hugged him. "Be careful." She said as he hugged her back.
Marelle hit Google. She googled the village, airfield, Thor missiles, Frankie's name and many random phrases she thought may be useful. All she got were the same stories – the same paragraphs. As she had said, Frankie had disappeared and then he had been forgotten in the press – but not for Frankie's parents and Jacob – and it had consumed his life.
She had just found evidence that Frankie's father still appeared to be alive when her phone rang. She panicked that it was Jacob, so she answered it with a crushing anxiety.
"Hello?"
"Seb." He said. "Whats wrong?"
"Nothing." She laughed.
"I'm just calling to check that you are coming to Abbi's party on Saturday – if you are staying, and if you are bringing anyone with you."
"Sh…" Marelle began as this had completely slipped her mind but she managed to change it to "Sure!"
"Oh good. Are you coming the night before?"
"Er, probably not. What time is the party on Saturday?"
"Well. She's thirteen and she's been promised a proper 'grown-up' party with a disco – we've said seven in the invitations."
"I'll probably come straight there – where is it?"
Seb sighed. "Marelle, you were sent an invite!"
"I know, but well, I lost it."
"Its at the Social Club – where we had the christening?"
"Oh, ok."
"And you're staying Saturday night?"
"Erm, I can do, saves me driving home late."
"And are you bringing anyone with you?"
Marelle paused. A million thoughts were in her head at that moment. "I might bring Jacob actually."
"Jacob!"
"Yes, why?"
"I thought maybe Bella – all the kids love her – Abbi even asked if she was coming."
"I don't think she's free – I think she was going to Spain with a group of friends this weekend." Marelle lied. "If you don't want me to bring Jacob then I wont but you never minded me bringing Chris to yours …"
"No, but we *knew* Chris. So, are you and this *Jacob* an 'item' now?"
She felt slightly reprimanded by her brother. "Yes, we are." She said. "And I'll bring him with me on Saturday, we'll stay the night and drive back on Sunday."

"Ok." Seb said. Marelle knew he was wondering how to break the news to Caroline that they would have a complete stranger who was in all likelihood an axe murderer in her perfect house – *and all night*. While Marelle herself was wondering just how she was going to persuade Jacob to go with her.

She started the best way she knew when she walked up to his caravan and stuck a note on the door which said:

"Don't eat, I've cooked. Come straight over when you get home.'

Jacob turned up at six which, from previous experience, was about the time she'd expected him. He'd obviously smartened up after work and walked into her house with a sigh.

"Ok?" She asked.

He nodded. "What is this in aid of?"

She laughed. "Nothing – I thought we could talk about my efforts today."

"Well?"

"Its early days Jacob. I've been through everything I can find about the village and the airfield – and Frankie. There is nothing new …"

He looked despondent.

"Its going to take a little while. You've got to gather everything together first."

"I know – but – six weeks."

"We'll do our best."

She had made an enormous shepherd's pie. It was a tried and tested recipe and she had served him a huge portion.

"You trying to fatten me up?" he asked.

"No, no! I like you just the way you are!"

Halfway through she broached Saturday. His first answer was an unconditional 'no' – which she had expected.

"You've just got to sit there and have a beer, smile at the kids …" Marelle explained. "We can stay that night and come straight back the next day."

"I cant." He stated. "I'm sorry but I cant."

She smiled. "I don't think it would be a bad thing for you to come with me. It would give you a bit of a break – a bit of space."

"That's not the kind of space I need!"

"I want to show you off!"

"What?"

"I want everyone to see you are with me … I'm proud of you!"

He obviously didn't know what to say to that, so he said nothing. He carried on eating for a bit, then he spoke again.

"I'll come with you but don't expect me to be the life and soul of the party."

Marelle smiled broadly. "Of course not! I just want you to be there with me."

"And I'll be expecting you to hold my hand at all times ... !"

She laughed. "Well you can guarantee I will do that."

After dinner she went through everything she had researched that day. He listened.

"There's nothing different." The belief is that he disappeared from his room. So all searches were based on that fact. As you said, they probably searched in the wrong place ."

He nodded.

"Do you have a plan of the airfield?"

"Yeah, back at the caravan."

"Well if you can bring it down I may get a few copies done at the shop so we can write on it. I think our next step is to go through what actually happened again and see if anything stands out to us."

"Ok, I'll drop it off in the morning." He wouldn't stay that night. But he held her tightly and kissed her with an urgency she hadn't experienced from him before. He looked her in the eye and with a new depth and gave her a meaningful smile as he left.

And as promised he brought the plan in the morning. Overnight Marelle had a few thoughts which although she probably knew the answers, she raised them anyway.

" – why don't we tell the police all about this?"

He stared at her in disbelief that she had even entertained that idea.

"What do you think would happen if we told the police we thought Frankie's body is around here somewhere. For a start it would be out of my hands then, secondly there would be too many questions asked. If they actually listened to us they would pile in and the whole area would be cordoned off ... I want us to find him first. We can cross the bridge of letting authorities know when we come to it."

"I did think that would be what you said." She replied.

Then she offered him her old phone again. He didn't want it, but she said if she needed to contact him urgently or ask any questions it would save time. He agreed on that basis and took it.

By Friday they had written all over several plans of the airfield, discussed several possible scenarios of what may have happened and pulled from it one unnerving conclusion.

"So, when you ran you went straight under the fence?" Marelle asked.

He nodded. "I ran from the concrete blocks to the wire – I didn't stay in the shadows but took the most direct route."

"Are you sure that Frankie came under the wire too?"

"No." Jacob said. "I thought he did but I can't be sure."

"Could he have got under it ok?"
"I think so, he got under it the first time – although I did open it up a bit, but it would have been the same when we went back. He was a bit chubbier than me, but I would have thought he could have squeezed under ok."
"If he didn't, then what do you think he did?" What would you have done?"
Jacob thought. "Probably tried to hide."
"Where?"
He looked at the plan. "Where we were hiding I suppose, but that would have meant running back towards the explosion."
"Where else could he have hidden?"
"Without going right out onto the launch site, not anywhere really. He could have stayed in the shadows but with all of the lighting on there were very few dark spots."
"Did you get seen?"
"I don't know. It was chaos."
Marelle paused for a second.
"So – say he didn't get under the fence and there was nowhere he could have hidden. He would have been right in the middle of it all, lit up by the floodlights."
Jacob kept looking at the plan.
"What would have happened then?"
"Some one would have seen him and stopped him I suppose, I don't know. We shouldn't have been there – I don't know what would have happened to him if he had been caught but either way surely his parents would have been contacted. He was an eleven year old child essentially playing ..."
"But it was a top secret site!"
"What are you saying?"
"Maybe he "disappeared" because of that. Maybe he never left the airfield, or fell down a hole."
"So are you saying someone could have grabbed him and 'got rid of him'?"
"It's a possibility. It would make sense."
Jacob looked totally unconvinced that this could ever happen.
"It was at the height of the cold war ... the world was on the edge of nuclear annihilation."
"But we were just kids!"
"Did that matter? What had you seen and what had you done?"
"No – !" He shook his head.

"I must admit it does seem unlikely – as you have said, you did make friends with some of the guys on site and that they were always giving you things bit, its always something to consider – if we don't manage to find him."

She looked at him and somehow, this consideration seemed to have made things worse. The look on his face haunted her and she began to wish she had not come up with this inconceivable idea.

"Its just another possibility to add to the list ... "She said, quietly but knew what he was thinking. "But even that does not mean its your fault!"

When Saturday arrived Marelle was glad that she had persuaded him to come to Abbi's party with her. He was still pinched over what she'd said last night, obviously hadn't slept and looked like death warmed up on Saturday morning. She needed to get him away for a day and get his head somewhere else. Noted he was reluctant to go – even more so staying away for the night but by four thirty she had him in her car ready to leave. He'd not been in her car with her before but was now sat in the passenger seat looking much better than he had earlier. She pulled out of the drive and he lowered his sunglasses. Marelle smiled. He didn't know how good he looked and she could hardly wait to parade him in front of Seb and Caroline.

It was the best part of a two hour drive and he probably wouldn't say a lot during the whole journey so she told him to find a CD and put it in. She was half interested to see what he picked from the dozen or so that were scattered around the car, some in cases, some not. He found one which was not a proper pre-recorded CD but instead a home burned one with flowers and hearts drawn all over the disc.

"Whats this?"

She laughed. "You don't want to play that! It's a CD of a band Seb used to be in when he was at Uni – its awful!"

He looked at her and pushed the CD into the slot. Marelle shook her head.

Jacob did physically wince when it crashed into life. He listened for a bit then to Marelle's surprise began to sing along with the lyrics.

She looked at him. "You know that!?"

He finished the second line. "Yeah." He said. "Is this a punk version?"

Marelle grinned. "I don't know what it is. I only know it as they used to play it."

"So you've never heard the original?"

"No, never! I'm too young" She smiled.

"Well theres a one." He said.

Marelle nodded to the CD. "Take it off for God's sake. I haven't heard it for years and I don't really want to now! Pick something sensible."
He looked through the CDs again. "You're a bit of a rock chick, aren't you?"
"What!" She laughed. "Most of those are Seb's." She smiled to herself as she drove, then added. "I'm just amazed you knew that song!"
"Oh, I was young once. I went to "Uni" as well …"
Marelle turned her head and stared at him then looked back to the road. "You went to University?"
He nodded.
"And what did you study?"
"Nuclear physics."
She whipped her head round and glared at him again, probably longer than she should have from behind the wheel. "Really!"
He nodded.
"Wow!" She said and laughed gently to herself. "So you're not just a pretty face then?"
"Well, I might have been that once."
She laughed at him and raised her eyebrows.
Apart from that revelation he didn't say much more during the journey. Marelle eventually put the radio on in the end and sang along to a random assortment of music. Jacob didn't but he did question her theory on someone having "taken" Frankie on the airfield that night, it was obviously still concerning him deeply.

The parking at the venue was limited but then they arrived at half six Marelle managed to squeeze the car into quite a tight space right by the main door.
"Right." She said sitting back in her seat, studying and smiling at Jacob. "I need a drink. Hopefully the bar is open."
"Haven't you got to drive to your brother's afterwards?" Jacob asked, one eyebrow raised.
"We'll leave the car here. Someone will be able to give us a, lift… I can guarantee Seb or Caroline wont be drinking!" She opened the car door as wide as she could in the small gap and slid herself out.
Inside the disco was already set up, playing quiet music in the background but the main lights were still on. The bar was in a separate room at the back of the hall and there were a few people around that area. Jacob walked in beside her and she crooked a hand into his arm. He looked up and around himself, staring up at the lights, balloons and various decorations around the hall.

"Marelle's here!" Somebody suddenly shouted and a young girl in jeans and trainers with a sparkly t-shirt came running up to them. She threw herself at Marelle and hugged her, making her have to let go of Jacob in doing so.

"Hi Abbi" She laughed. "Happy Birthday! I sent your present to Daddy."

"Yes, thank you. "She smiled, then looked to Jacob. "Who are you?"

Marelle laughed. "Abbi – this is Jacob."

She stared at him quite coldly, Jacob managed a smile but that was about it.

"We are going to get a drink, is Daddy in there?"

"I think so." She replied, still staring at Jacob before she turned and ran off to her friends again.

Seb was in the bar, standing with Caroline. He was talking to someone Marelle didn't know, Caroline was talking down sternly to Bobby, their son who was reincarnation of Seb.

Her brother spotted Marelle approaching and beckoned her closer with a smile.

"Hi." She smiled at them all. "This is Jacob."

Seb reached out to shake his hand – Jacob obliged but it was awkward.

"I believe we have met before!" Seb said.

"I think so, yes." Jacob confirmed, withdrawing his hand to his pocket.

Caroline eyed him and managed a tight smile when he noticed her staring at him.

"This is my little sister and her ... partner." Seb said to the other guy who he had been chatting to. "John is our neighbour." He explained to Marelle.

There was a great deal of very small talk. Seb tried to involve Jacob but quickly stopped when he was confronted by single word answers and a lack of attention on him. The place was filling up with forty or so twelve year old girls and a few token boys to keep Bobby company together with various parents who braved to stay. The disco cranked it up and the lights dimmed in the main hall. Marelle looked to Jacob and he looked a little stressed by it all.

"Erm, shall we go and find somewhere to sit?" She asked him but loud enough to let everyone know where they were going. They took their drinks – Marelle was already on her second – and found a seat toward the back. Jacob still had his sunglasses on but Marelle didnt comment. He was happier to sit down in a dark corner and drink a beer beside her and from what she could see had even began to relax a little. She sat close to him, her hand on his thigh, singing along to the music and tapping her hand in rhythm.

"You ok?" She asked.

He nodded. "This isnt really my 'thing'".
"Its not mine either but it keeps everyone happy! This is pretty good – its normally round to Seb's for crisps, cake and jelly."
"Oh, nice." He commented.
She laughed and laid her head against his shoulder for a second. There girls were all dancing on the dance floor and Marelle was struck at how mature their mannerisms looked. She didn't think she'd been like that at twelve!
"Smile!" Somebody suddenly said. It was Caroline with a camera. Marelle turned to her and smiled but Jacob ducked behind her and put his hand up to his face.
"What are you doing?" She asked as Caroline walked away making a face.
"I'm sorry but I don't like my photo taken." He apologised.
She smiled and ruffled his hair. "It wont steal your soul you know!"
"I'm not sure I have one to steal anyway." He remarked.
With a sigh Marelle turned to cuddle him in consolation. "In an hour and a bit this will all be over!"
She tried her hardest to chat with him, laughing at the kids dancing, taking the piss out of Seb and making faces behind Caroline's back.
"You'll get us in trouble." He warned her.
"Give over, they're used to me. Take me as I am – they know how I am!"
"Are you a bit drunk?" He asked.
"No - !" She exclaimed although she had drunk four, or five, glasses of wine – she couldn't really remember. But, she was a little touched by him saying that and decided there would be no more for her tonight if he was worried about it.
"Its ok, don't worry. I'll look after you." She said.
At that point Abbi and three of her friends came up to them. Marelle lent forwards, Jacob sat back. As she raised her eyes to Abbi she couldn't help but notice Seb and Caroline standing over near the bar door, glaring at them. Caroline had her arms folded.
"Marelle, will you come and show us how to do that dance again? The one we did at Christmas …"
"Oh, I am sure you can remember it – go and ask the DJ to put it on."
"I cant – and it was so much fun! Please Marelle!"
"You go and I'll shout to tell you what to do."
"Its not the same. Please!" She pleaded, pulling at Marelle's arm.
"Oh Abbi … "She stalled but caught Seb and Caroline still staring at them. She laughed. "Ok, ok then but only for two minutes." Abbi pulled at her and she stood up, looking back down at Jacob.
"You be ok? I'll be back in a tick – unless you want to come and join in."

He gave his normal tiny smile. "No, its ok."

Abbi pulled her away from him with a small cheer from her and the friends. One of the other girls ran over to the DJ and a few seconds later La Macarena started up and Marelle took to the helm to go through the actions with them.

She glanced across to Jacob a couple of times and he seemed content sitting there drinking beer from the bottle – not really watching her, or anyone else.

La Macarena, 5,6,7,8, Cotton Eyed Joe and Saturday Night later she looked again and he had disappeared. Marelle stopped immediately, stock still on the dance floor and looked about for him. Abbi pulled at her arm to continue but she took her hand.

"I need to go and sit down for a minute Abbi – give me a few minutes and I'll be back ..." She moved off, leaving Abbi standing and shrugging. Marelle scanned the room, she couldn't see him anywhere. She bit her lip and started towards the bar.

Then she saw him, coming out of the toilets with Seb. Marelle sighed in relief to herself – there he was and it looked as if those two were actually having a conversation. But as she stepped towards them, she realised Seb was shoving Jacob. He pushed him forwards as Jacob turned slightly to him. The second shove was more violent and Jacob was somewhat unbalanced by it.

"You cant hang around in there mate."

She heard Seb say over the music.

"Whats going on?" She asked,

"Take him home." Seb said.

Marelle stared at him, then at Jacob. Jacob was looking at the floor, he raised a sideways look to her but he still had the sunglasses on.

"What?" she asked.

"He knows what. Get him out of here. Take him home. We can talk about it later but I don't want him here."

She stood staring at Seb, reached out and took Jacob's arm.

"Seb!"

"Go!" he shouted, pointing to the door.

Marelle had never seen Seb this angry before. He could be grumpy sometimes, frustrated with her and her inadequacies but never angry like this. She stared right at him, angry herself now but took Jacob's arm, squeezed him to her and walked away.

She took him through the main doors, out to the car park and turned to him.

"What happened?"

Jacob inhaled. "He just called me a paedophile."

"What? Seb?"
Jacob nodded. "I went into the toilet for a minute. Next thing he comes in and tells me I cant hang around in the toilets at a kids party."
Marelle could not believe what he she was hearing. They had just been kicked out of a twelve year old's birthday party.
"I was only standing in there – it was a bit overwhelming, so I went in there for a minute or two, waiting for you to come back."
She sighed. Standing in the car park, holding on to him, the music from the disco pounding in the background.
"Fucking paranoid!" she exclaimed. "Get in the car. I'll be back in a minute."
"Marelle." He said. "I wasn't doing *anything*."
"I know you weren't." She said. "He's a fucking moron and she's behind it ... get in the car and wait for me."
Marelle stormed back in, slammed through the doors and headed for Seb who was standing chatting to Caroline.
"What the fuck do you think you're doing?" She exclaimed.
Seb placed a hand on her shoulder and pushed her out of the room and into a corridor behind the bar. Caroline followed.
"You called him a fucking paedophile. What fucking reasons do you have for that!"
"Marelle calm down."
She shrugged him off.
"He was only standing in the toilet!"
"One of the kids came up to me and said there was a strange man in the toilets banging his head against the wall. I went to look and there he was, doing just that."
"Well that doesn't make him a fucking paedophile does it?"
"I don't know. I don't know what he was actually doing in there but a grown man hanging around in the toilets at a kid's disco has some serious implications to it."
"We could call the police you know." Caroline added.
Marelle flew at her. "Call the fucking police then – because someone went into the toilet! Are you as totally fucking stupid as you look?"
"I'm not the stupid one Marelle ... I'm not the one parading around some mentally ill idiot who cant be trusted to be left on his own with children."
"Don't you dare try that tack!" She made a lunge towards Caroline and Seb stepped between them. "Caroline, go and make sure Abbi is ok. I'll deal with this."
"You really are a vindictive bitch you know – always have been." Marelle took one last verbal stab at Seb's wife.

"Marelle!" Seb called her attention. "He's not right, is he? For God's sake he's sitting in a dark room with sunglasses on, he wont speak, doesn't make eye contact, doesn't want his photo taken ... Jesus he's a head case and there is no way on this earth that I am going to let him hang around in the toilets here with the kids – what do you think would happen if the kids got wind of this and told their parents? It just takes one mention of that word and we're all finished."

"You're a fucking wanker Seb. You're so far up her arse you cant think for yourself or see things how they truly are! He's not mentally ill, he's not retarded – he's got a degree in nuclear physics! Everyone treats him like shit but if you take the time to get to know him you would realise he is the sweetest, kindest person on the face of this planet."

Seb laughed. "I'm not discussing this now. I'm not arguing with you now, not at Abbi's birthday."

"Oh no, that's right. Make the accusations then wipe your hands of it. Saying something like that can ruin someone's life. He's not in the best place at the moment anyway. You're such a fucking bastard Seb."

"Marelle – cant you see it? Can't you really see it? If he's not a paedophile then he's an alcoholic or a druggie. I've seen it before, I know. He's not right and you're going to get dragged down with him if you carry on. I've seen it before, many times."

"Fuck off Seb. You don't know. You haven't got a fucking clue. He didn't want to come and I made him. Blame me if you have to blame someone but don't start slinging mud at him."

"Just take him away from here. I don't want him here and I don't want him near the kids. We'll talk tomorrow."

"No you wont. You wont fucking speak to me ever again. You or your fucking wife."

She went to walk away.

"Go to the house, we'll talk about it sensibly tomorrow."

"Fuck off." She snapped. "I'll take him home – to my house."

"Its our house – and you're too drunk to drive."

"I'll drive if I want to."

"Marelle!"

"Fuck off. You want this, you've got it!"

SEVEN

Marelle stormed outside, slid into the car and turned to look at Jacob. He'd removed the sunglasses. How could anyone in their right minds accuse him of any of these things?
She sighed. "I'm sorry." And she leaned forwards to kiss him across the car.
"Did you hit him?" He asked.
"No, but I wanted to."
"So do I." Jacob stated.
"You should have."
"No – that would have made everything a million times worse. Sometimes you just have to walk away from things."
Marelle turned her head and kissed him again, almost angrily but he responded and kissed her back.
"I know I've done nothing wrong." Jacob explained, breaking away. "And thats the only thing that matters."
Marelle gave him one last kiss, then settled into the driving seat with a sigh.
"He's a fucking wanker." She hissed and turned the key in the ignition.
She was so angry that she could feel it bristling inside her, tingling and her fingertips as she drove. A couple of times she was a bit jerky with the car and she found herself concentrating a lot more than usual. They were just leaving the town and heading for the dual carriageway when Jacob said –
"Pull over, I'll drive."
"Its ok."
"I think you would be over the limit if we were stopped."

"I've only had two. We just got chucked out of a fucking twelve year old's party!"

"You've had a lot more than two – I'm happy to drive."

"I don't think you would be insured to drive my car." She replied.

"I'll take a chance."

She shook her head. I dont want you losing your licence over this … that would be a disaster!"

"You'll lose yours if we get stopped." He warned.

"I don't care. I'm not going anywhere and anyway it will be on Seb's conscience for making me drive."

All the way home she protested about Seb and Caroline.

"I cannot believe they said that all about you! I simply can't believe it" she said for the umpteenth time "They are so fucking paranoid – both of them – about their fucking kids! Just putting two and two together all the time …" She quietened for a bit and then. "How fucking dare he? Oh, it would have been fine if you had danced with them on the dancefloor – touching and messing around with them but go and stand in the toilets and you're a fucking paedophile."

Jacob didn't really respond to any of her outbursts but sat quietly in the passenger seat.

"What did he say to you in the toilet?"

"He said *what are you doing* when he walked in and then pulled me away from the wall – he said *you cant hang around in here mate* and then he pushed me out of the toilet."

"Did he hurt you?"

"Not physically, no …"

"I looked across and saw him shoving you out of the toilets. What a fucking prat."

She finally pulled the car into the drive just over two hours later. It was ten past midnight on a clear moonlit night.

"I'm never fucking speaking to him or his bitch of a wife …" She was still proclaiming as she got out of the car " .. and his fucking kids. What precocious little brats they'll turn out to be …"

"Doesn't he own half the house?" Jacob asked.

"Doesn't matter, I still don't have to physically speak to him. Anyway, I could always buy him out." She locked the car door and staggered a little as she walked around it. "I'm making some very strong coffee – come on."

Marelle was still fuming. She had never felt this angry about anything ever before and this was firing her up beyond recognition. *Why* and *how* could anyone ever accuse Jacob of that? And *how* could Seb make allegations on him being an alcoholic or a junkie? He didn't know him!

Jacob had been standing in the toilet just to find himself space and Seb – egged on by Caroline – had deduced at that point that he *had* to be a paedophile. How? Just *how*? She angrily flicked the kettle on.

"No coffee." Jacob said. "I'm not likely to sleep well as it is and coffee wont help."

"I'll make you hot chocolate."

"No, I'd better go." He shuffled and did that apologetic little smile.

"No – I don't want you to be on your own tonight. Stay here – I don't really want to be on my own either …"

He looked slightly put out, yet torn at wanting to stay.

"Its not going to be a good night … and …" he began to plead a case but Marelle suddenly launched herself at him.

"Sssh." She said and kissed him, roughly. Anger channelling in a new direction. He responded with equal attention. Then she was all over him, pushing herself against him, her hands behind his neck pulling him into her further. Then she placed one hand on his bottom forcing him into her hips as her other hand slid fingers down the front of his jeans, gripping at the waistband and pulling at him.

"In here." She whispered, her lips close to his neck.

At no point did he stop her or resist her, but instead went along with her as she pulled him into the living room. He staggered forward under the guidance of her strategically placed hand with her lips constantly against him. Marelle could hear own breath in her head as she pushed him backwards into the living room and then trapped him against the wall. She felt his hands in the small of her back as her own undid his belt, then his jeans so she could slip her hand fully inside. At that point he tensed in a way that wasn't what she was expecting so instead she undid her own jeans and pushed them down.

"Jacob." She said, dragging him forwards until she could recline over the arm of the settee and pull him in top of her.

"Hey – "He said.

"No, no, no …"Marelle smiled and silenced him with her tongue inside his mouth and her hands firmly on his bottom forcing him towards her and between her knees.

There was nothing gentle about her approach, just an angry and unrelenting urgency. Forcing him against and into her. Holding onto him so tightly it was a wonder he could take a breath; running her fingers up and into his hair and twisting a handful into her fist, grabbing every last inch of him in any way she could and roughly consuming him into her. This was rough, messy, hostile, urgent and unco-ordinated but amidst all of that there was a harmony that fulfilled the need that had taken over her.

It was probably over much quicker than either of them felt and as Marelle clutched him to her in that conjugated embrace she closed her eyes tight shut and felt the tears well up inside her. He exhaled gently in her ear. She cried.

"You are too beautiful for this world Jacob – you are too perfect for this world." She sobbed. "I cant let them keep hurting you like they do."

He relaxed against her and buried his head in her shoulder.

"I don't want to ever let you out of my sight." She cried softly.

When the sun breached the horizon and shone straight into the open window of the bedroom Marelle stirred and squinted open her eyes. She should have pulled the curtains – it was probably five o clock in the morning. She lifted her head to see the clock and suddenly saw Jacob beside her in the bed.

From the confusion of returning consciousness Marelle was suddenly very awake as last night came crashing back into her head. She sat herself up gently and looked down on him. He was asleep; his head against her pillow with his dark hair spiky and unkempt, the sheet pulled up to his chest, one arm out and folded against himself, the other bent so he rested his head on his hand. Marelle smiled and was touched by an immediate thought that his skin was very pale for someone who worked outside so much. His arms were skinny but muscular with the tone apparent in their bent state. With her own nakedness becoming apparent to her she pulled the sheet around herself as well as she sat gazing at him – she wasn't sure why as she certainly hadn't shown any modesty last night. In fact, as she remembered it, she had shown very little except anger fuelled animal instinct – but, he was still here, right in front of her. The act was still fresh in her mind but how much persuasion it had taken to get him to stay the night she could not recall. Marelle stared at him, at his face, his high cheekbones and strong jaw and smiled to herself as the thought of it all came back to her.

Jacob opened one eye and stared at her, squinting the other one.

"Hi, "she said, sweetly.

"I felt you staring at me."

"You don't normally notice."

"I always feel you staring at me!" He revealed.

He opened the other eye and stared right into her. He avoided eye contact a lot but when he didn't he stared right into your soul.

"Was I a bit forceful last night?" She asked, biting her lip.

"A bit." He said.

She gave a small smile and a shrug. "I'm sorry."

"Its ok. I've had worse."

She scoffed and slapped him on the shoulder playfully. He grinned, closed his eyes and nestled his head into the pillow. This was a Jacob she had not seen before!
"Did you sleep ok?" She asked, not recalling him repeating the actions of previous overnight stays.
"Mmmm" He said.
"Good. "She smiled. "Wait there. I'll go and make some tea." And she stopped to gently kiss his forehead.
Marelle slid out of bed and grabbed her cerise pink, silk dressing gown off the chair, slipped into it and tied the belt around her waist. She walked over to the window and looked out.
"Oh my God!" She laughed. "Did I park the car like that?"
"I did offer to drive." He muttered from the bed.
"It is about one inch away from the house, and the window is open!"
"You were a bit drunk."
"I didn't think I was *that* drunk!" She laughed as she left him in her bed and went downstairs.
She may have not remembered getting to bed but the trail of clothes – both hers and his – between the living room and the bedroom was a telltale sign of how it may have gone. She also suspected that she had been behind most of it. She picked it up as she went, finally walking through the living room to the kitchen. She put the clothes in a pile on the table and switched the kettle on. The back door was also still unlocked and she tutted to herself as she went out to close the window on the car. While she did she saw her mobile phone still on the dashboard. There were three missed calls from Seb – the last one at one forty five in the morning. Marelle gripped the phone to herself and went back in. As she made tea and a pile of toast she realized it was still only six o clock in the morning. Probably Jacob's normal time for getting up but a good two hours off hers – and it was a Sunday.
From the kitchen she heard him move into the bathroom and then back again. She placed his mug of tea on the bedside table then slipped back under the sheets with the plate of toast in between them. He sat up, ran his fingers through his hair then reached for the mug with a yawn.
"I'm really sorry for what Seb said last night." Marelle said.
"You don't have to apologise. You didn't say it, he did."
"I know, but he jumped to a conclusion – which is so wrong." She replied. "He's tried calling three times last night." She added. "I'm not answering or ringing him. Let him stew. I'm not speaking to him – pretending he cares now – if he cared he wouldn't have said what he did."

Jacob didn't comment but stared blankly at the foot of the bed while he ate the toast.

Seb tried calling at nine o clock then again at ten. He didn't leave a message – Marelle just let it ring out each time.

Jacob put the clothes back on he'd been wearing last night and said he was going back to the caravan.

"Oh. Ok." Marelle said.

"I've got to sort stuff out for tomorrow and I wanted to mess around with the bike." He explained. "Shall we have a look over there later?" He nodded to the airfield. "Look at the plans and have a think about the theory you came up with?"

"Er, yes, no problem. Shall I come up to you?"

He nodded.

Marelle walked over to him and took both of his hands in hers, holding herself close to him.

"I don't want you to go."

He laughed a little. "I'm only over there."

"I know but I want to be with you."

"Come over on a bit then. I'll be there." He replied, looking down at her.

"Ok." She smiled, still holding his hands and looking up at him.

Then he smiled. A proper smile, a smile that gave him a little dimple in one cheek. Marelle smiled and went up on tip toes to kiss him.

"See you in a bit."

Jacob's plan for later was to go out onto the airfield and walk out all the possibilities they had discussed. He had plans of the original site and they went through all of the what ifs they could come up with. He retraced the steps between where the fence had been and where the missiles were; where they were when the explosion happened; where he ran to and the ways Frankie could have run.

"So did he definitely follow you off the airfield?"

"I don't know."

"Well, if he had then he would have been behind you surely?" Marelle asked.

"I would have thought so – but he wasn't."

"So say he couldn't get back under the fence – where would he have run to?"

They looked at the plans. There had only been one building; the one they had called 'the bomb shed' then nothing until the buildings over the very far side of the airfield. Most of which were long gone. It was doubtful he would have run back towards the explosion and why would he have run right to the other end of the airfield, through all of the people and vehicles and so far away.

"Surely he would have run home?" Marelle questioned. "If he was scared he would have run home."

"That's always what I thought but he didn't – or he would have been there."

"So …" She mused. "He disappeared *on* the airfield and never got off?"

Jacob sighed. It was a theory he didn't like.

"No." He said.

"It would explain why he has never been found." Marelle offered.

"But I cannot believe that someone actually took him on the airfield and killed him?"

"It might have been an accident?"

"But if that was the case then why didn't they give his body back?"

"Depends on what they did to it." Marelle said but then instantly regretted it.

Jacob looked at her with an intense gaze. "That doesn't bear thinking about."

"I know, but its a theory. Where else would he be? What else could have happened to him?"

"I don't know, but I've spent the last thirty odd years trying to work it out …"

"Maybe it's a theory we have to consider. It won't be closure for you though."

He stood there, staring at the ground for a moment, trying to take in that she could be right.

Then two shots rang out. He lifted his head.

"They were gun shots." He said. "No-one should be shooting on here – "He walked away quickly, away from the missile sites, around the trees with her following.

Once they rounded the trees and stood on the airfield proper, they could see where the shots had come from. There, at the main gates were two or three vehicles – one of them a white panel van with someone standing on the roof of it, a gun raised and aimed onto the airfield. Right beside it was a familiar red pick-up truck.

Jacob flew, right across the airfield, Marelle in tow shouting

"Jacob, they have guns!"

She was gasping for breath when she got to the gates. There was Sam on top of the van, casually swinging a shotgun around. On the ground were two of his henchmen that Marelle had seen with him in the pub.

"What are you doing." Jacob asked.

"Oh, just shooting a few rabbits."

"Well you can't shoot on the airfield."

"Well, I'm not on the airfield." Sam laughed. "Touché dickhead!"

The other two laughed and Marelle realised they were all drinking.

"You don't have permission to shoot on here."

"So, what are you going to do about it, pretty boy?" Sam mocked.

Jacob stared at him. Marelle moved closer and clutched at his arm. "He's got a gun." She whispered. Jacob ignored her.

Sam laughed. "Aaah, look at his little girlfriend – she's worried dickhead, back down."

They all laughed again.

"Nice to see you've got a girlfriend really I suppose, always thought you were a fucking shirtlifter! Bit of a little shrew this one though – surprised you can handle her. Nice tits and arse but a right little shrew! Bet you've been knocking one out over her every night in that fucking caravan though, haven't you?" He made a wanking gesture. "Seen the old caravan a-rocking, haven't we?"

Jacob never said a word.

"Her friend is alright though – wouldn't mind giving that one over a five bar gate!"

They all laughed.

Marelle tugged at Jacob's sleeve.

Then Sam raised the gun and fired a shot. Marelle jumped but Jacob didn't move.

"Get off the roof and go." He said.

"Make me." Sam laughed. "I'm not on the airfield. And anyway – it'll all be gone soon. All dug up and covered in concrete. I'm doing them a favour, putting them out of their misery – they won't have a home soon – just like you. You and your little bunny friends!"

"And until then this is private land and you do not have permission to shoot here."

"What are you gonna do about it then, dickhead?"

"I've given you a warning. If you don't go I will call the police."

Sam laughed loudly. "Call the police! You won't call the police – you never do – you *avoid* the police. You're shit scared of them! Got some deep, dark secret I reckon. Hey!" He called to Marelle "Did he tell you about his deep, dark secret?" He asked. "He won't call the police. Fuck off and go give her one. She looks like she's gasping for it – not that you'll keep it up for long will you, pretty boy!"

Then Jacob launched himself at the fence, climbing up it very deftly and cocking one leg over the top.

"You step over here and I'll beat you to a pulp that she wont recognize."

113

"If I call the police you'll lose your gun licence and probably your driving licence too."

"Well fucking call them then."

Jacob sat astride the top of the gate. He turned to Marelle.

"Call them." He said. "Call them then hand me the phone."

Marelle fumbled for her phone.

Jacob turned back to Sam. "Now get down off the van and piss off."

Sam looked at Marelle with the phone.

"Police please." She said, the reached up to hand the phone to Jacob.

Sam suddenly decided to get down. Once on the floor he pointed the gun up at Jacob.

"Yes please." Jacob said. "I've got someone threatening me with a shotgun."

Sam shook his head at Jacob as he conceded and got into his pick up truck, throwing the gun in with him. The other two got into the transit van and as suddenly as that, they went. Jacob watched them go then he climbed down from the gate and handed the phone back to Marelle.

"We should have really called the police." She said.

"Be too much trouble. "Jacob said.

"You really need to do something about him." Marelle commented.

"He's just a coward and a bully. He wont do anything because he knows it will have as much impact on him as it will on me. He stands to lose as much as I do."

"But he *has* done things. He hit you, he's driven at you with the forklift, he's just waved a gun around in your face and shot over our heads. I don't call that 'doing nothing'."

"Its nothing." Jacob said. "He's a coward."

"I think he needs bringing down." Marelle stated. "Sooner or later he's going to follow those threats through."

"Nah. He's not. He's a coward – he likes showing off and getting a reaction from his friends – and I'm the target. He wants me to retaliate but if I do that will be his opportunity to turn it all on me."

"But he could have killed you the time he hit you – you seem to brush that off as nothing, but you were lucky …"

"I did the damage when I fell over."

"But you wouldn't have fallen over if he hadn't hit you!"

"He's an opportunist. He has a go when he gets the chance. He was drinking tonight – he doesn't have a gun licence and he'd got the work van up here. If he thinks he is going to get reprimanded, he will back down."

Marelle sighed angrily and asked herself why everyone treated him like shit and why he let them!

They walked back to the house, made tea and discussed Frankie. Jacob was undoubtedly uncomfortable with Marelle's theory. He could not believe that such a thing could have taken place. If she pushed it, he got more uncomfortable with it. But with his thirty odd years of fruitless searching, it was beginning to look like a possible answer. He also refused to stay at hers that night which upset her a little. She felt bad letting him go off into the night – thinking about Frankie like that and looked disturbed about it.

"I'll be ok." He said to her as she hugged him in the doorway. "Sometimes I just need to be on my own you know."

She lay her head on his chest. "I know, but I like having you here."

He squeezed her. " ... and I like being here ... I'll see you tomorrow, ok?"

She smiled and nodded. "Ok."

Then he kissed her and went off across the airfield.

Marelle sighed and took herself to bed alone.

She was sure she heard the motorbike fire up and go off in the morning at about half six. She didn't like him riding the bike – not so much worrying that he would hurt himself on it but more that he might just keep going and not come back to her.

There was still some work for her to complete for Seb – which she would do. Whether he sent her any more would remain to be seen but, Seb being Seb, probably would. However, she didn't need to speak to him and didn't want to. Her focus was on helping Jacob in his search for Frankie. She didn't want to believe that Frankie had been taken on the airfield either and she didn't like the reaction that it had provoked in Jacob, but it was looking like the most likely answer. Unless she could find something else to open up a new line. Over breakfast she looked at the plans again, read all of the notes she had made – looking any anything that might afford her that opening.

There was nothing she hadn't looked at a hundred times but then she wondered if there was anything Mrs. Avison may be able to shed light on! She had said she would visit again, and it had been a couple of months. A little excited at her flash of inspiration, Marelle dressed and headed out.

The sun was warm and she decided to walk. Maybe pop into the shop and buy her some flowers and chocolates on the way. When she walked in Jill was behind the till again.

"Good morning." She smiled, watching Marelle intently.

"Hi." Marelle smiled. She had a bunch of flowers she had picked from the display outside and was looking for chocolates, she turned to the counter.

"How are you" Jill asked.
"I'm good. Thank you."
"I see you and Jacob are getting along now?"
Marelle smiled. "Yeah, he's a good guy."
"You've managed to turn his head. Been living on his own all the time I've been in the village ..."
"Oh I don't think anyone has ever given him the time of day before." She stated, bluntly.
"He's not been the most friendly face around here but, he has been much better lately." Jill replied.
"How long have you lived here?" Marelle asked.
"Oh, about nine or ten years now." Jill answered. "Is that all?" She nodded to the flowers.
"Oh. No – I was going to see Mrs. Avison again – do you know what kind of chocolates she would like?"
Jill stared at her. "Mrs. Avison died about a month ago."
Marelle went cold. She felt like she'd well and truly put her foot in her mouth.
"Oh God! I didn't know." She gasped.
"She's buried in the churchyard, her funeral was a couple of weeks back."
"Oh, ok – that's really sad." She said, feeling awkward. "I'll take the flowers and put them on her grave." She offered as a kind of compensation.
Marelle felt terrible – although she had no reason to – but she took the flowers back and then got into her car to drive to the church. So, that was one good source of information gone forever and she would never hear the the tales of Jacob's family that she had promised.
Mrs. Avison's grave in the churchyard was over to the left. It was still obviously a new grave although Marelle guessed it was in with her husband as it was between existing graves. The headstone had been removed to add her name but there were still flowers and wreaths on there – her full name – Edna Louise Avison – told Marelle that it was her grave. She knelt down and took the flowers out of the packaging. A thought crossed her mind that maybe she should put half on Jacob's parent's grave – it would be a nice gesture. But, on second thoughts, she decided not to. If he saw them it would open a can of worms. So, she placed the flowers on Mrs. Avison's grave.
"Thank you for telling me your stories." She said quietly then paused at the grave for a couple of seconds before she stood up.
Slowly she walked over to Jacob's parents grave and looked at it. The churchyard was pretty today with sunlight dappling through the leaves

and birds singing in the background. The sun played across the names of Jeannie and Ezekiel as she looked upon them. Marelle smiled as she stood there.

"Your son is a good man." She said to them for some reason. "And I wont let anyone hurt him. I promise."

It brought a lump to her throat for some reason she had to walk away. Then her phone buzzed in her pocket. Quickly, she fished it out and looked at it.

It was Bella. Marelle smiled to herself and answered.

"What the hell has he done?" Bella exclaimed immediately before Marelle had the chance to speak.

For a moment Marelle was stumped by her question, then she realized. "You've seen Seb?" She sighed, moving towards the bench over near the stone wall.

"Yes, I was going in to the petrol station and he was coming out. I just said 'Hi' but when I came out he was waiting and grabbed me! I though he was going to mug me!"

"What did he say?"

"He was angry!"

Marelle sighed.

"What the hell did Jacob do? Seb said to me that he didn't want him anywhere near him, Caroline or his kids – and he said he wasn't too happy with him being with you either!"

Marelle exhaled loudly.

"What the fuck did he do?"

"I don't even really want to talk about this ..." Marelle began " ... but we went to Abbi's birthday party on Saturday, she had a disco – I ended up dancing with her for about 15 minutes. Jacob decided to go into the toilet because he 'wanted some space' – Seb found him standing in there and accused him of being a paedophile. Frog marched him out. I naturally had an argument with him and then followed Jacob. I drove home drunk."

"Oh wow!" Bella laughed.

"Bella, its not funny."

"I'm sorry. It is – what was he doing in the toilet?"

" – nothing! Its stupid! Its fucking stupid – and his fucking bitch of a wife is behind it."

"What did Jacob say?"

"What do you think he said?"

"Nothing?" Bella asked.

"I could have killed Seb. I'm not speaking to him. Full stop."

"I am a bit lost for words." Bella said.

"How the fuck could he come to that conclusion – for Jacob for God's sake! He also said Jacob looked like an alcoholic or a druggie – said he was mentally ill!". "Oh God!" Bella said. "He's a bit quiet, a bit weird but he's not any of the other things!"
"Exactly," Marelle said. "It was a cruel and horrible thing to say – and I'm not speaking to him – ever again."
"Oh dear." Bella sighed. "Is Jacob ok?"
"Yeah, he's ok. Its either not gone in or he's had a lifetime of being treated like a piece of shit and it means nothing to him. If someone called me a paedophile I'd be livid. I am livid!"
"As long as Caroline doesn't go blabbing to her stuck-up friends about it." Bella remarked.
"I don't think she will – its too much of a dirty word for her to mention."
"Shit." Bella exclaimed, then added. "Seb did ask me to try and talk you out of being with him ... I told him I was not going to interfere in your life!"
"Thank you." Marelle answered. "You don't believe him do you?"
"Of course not!" Bella stated. "Jacob's quiet, he's a bit off – wont make eye contact with you – but well, he's quite sweet and he's kind – and he's got a sexy haircut!" She added, just trying to make Marelle laugh.
"I'll tell you what though ..." Marelle began. "I drove home pretty drunk – he offered but I wouldn't let him drive – I was so angry – but we had the best angry sex you could ever imagine!"
"What!"
"I was wound up and forced myself onto him." She laughed. "It was wrong, I know but I somehow wanted to take my anger out and prove to Seb that I am serious about Jacob – and that he is *mine*!"
"Oh wow!" Bella grinned, audibly.
Marelle was still sat on the bench and staring across at Jacob's parent's grave as she spoke.
"Was it good?"
"It was excellent!"
"And he stayed the night?"
"Yep! Woke up the next day with him beside me and our clothes strewn up the stairs."
"Wow he's a dark horse isn't he?"
"Well to be honest I didn't give him much choice!"
They both laughed. There was a moment before they stopped and Bella said:
"You know you need to have this out with Seb. You don't want that hanging over you ruining everything."
Marelle didn't agree but knew her friend was right.

"Well, maybe." She said.

"If I see him again, I'll try to have a word …"

They finished their conversation and Marelle sat back on the bench. She was looking at her emails on the phone to see if Seb had sent anything or tried to communicate when she heard another vehicle pull into the car park. She decided to wait until whoever was in it had come into the churchyard before she made a move. She looked up when she saw movement out of the corner of her eye and was astonished to see the tall lanky figure of Jacob walking towards her, his head on one side looking at her in a questioning manner.

"I saw your car in the car park." He said. "What are you doing here?"

"I just came down here. I didn't know Mrs Avison had died." She nodded to the grave and he looked.

"Did you know her?"

"Not really but I spoke to her when I first came here – I was doing a bit of research on the village – she was very welcoming and knew so much about the place – I went into the shop and happened to mention her and found out she was dead – I just brought some flowers."

He was looking at the grave. Marelle shielded her eyes looking at him.

"Why were you researching the village?"

"Just curious – not being from around here. I wanted to know what I was getting into." She made light of it. "Where have you been?" She turned to see the same white van that Sam had been on top of standing next to her car in the car park.

"Pick some parts up that had been delivered wrong." He finally sat down next to her.

"She probably told you a whole lot of rubbish anyway." He said. "Her memory was going but she wouldn't have it – if she couldn't remember she'd make it up – so totally convincing though."

Marelle laughed. "I guessed that! Tried to convince me your name was Nathaniel!"

He shifted his feet, his boots weren't done up and he had his jeans tucked into them. "See what I mean." He said.

"I know." Marelle chuckled and leant her head on his shoulder. "Its so pretty here."

"Its full of dead people!"

"It's a very pretty spot though."

"Have you been here before?"

"Couple of times.'

"Why?"

She didn't move as she answered. "Same reason – churchyards are always a good place to start."

He sat there for a moment, staring into the direction of his parent's headstone.

"That's my parent's grave over there." He nodded.

Marelle lifted her head. "I kind of worked that out." She replied.

"And my grandparents."

She hadn't realised that but could see it now. For a while she paused as he just sat there, knees apart, elbows on his knees.

"Is your brother buried here?" She finally asked.

"No." He said quickly. "He was cremated and his ashes scattered. I am not sure where. I wasn't involved – he had a circle of close friends who organized it all."

She stared at the graves. That was odd but, as he'd said, their lives had taken different directions.

"How's work?" She asked.

"Ok."

"Coming to dinner tonight?"

"Mmm." He said. "We're not making any headway about Frankie, are we?"

"We're trying Jacob. I know you don't like my theory but its looking more and more possible. But we can still look at the other conclusions – tonight – after dinner?"

"Ok." He said.

"I'll be looking for any clues or ideas this afternoon that may point me in a different direction."

Jacob sat for a minute. Then he pressed his hands on his knees to stand himself up. "I'd better go or I'll be accused of going awol again! I'll see you at about six then?"

"See you at six." She smiled broadly in reply.

He walked away without looking back.

Jacob seemed a little despondent that evening. He ate quietly avoiding eye contact as much as possible and had slipped back a few steps. He also looked tired.

"Whats wrong?" she had asked.

He sighed heavily, sat back and looked at her with his mouth tense.

"I just don't think we are going to find him."

"We'll try Jacob." Marelle replied. I'm looking into things all of the time – it just needs one little clue that is the final piece in the jigsaw."

"But I've been looking for most of my life and I haven't found him. Whats different now?"

"A fresh pair of eyes?"

He shook his head. "They're going to raise this to the ground and we will never find out what happened to him ..."

"We've got time Jacob."

She stared at him as he stared off to her left, his jaw clenched and tight. "I was planning on speaking to Mrs. Avison today – just to see if she had any little gems of information that may have helped – that was why I ended up in the graveyard."

"She wasn't a reliable source – "

"Well, not now anyway."

They talked for hours, discussing possibilities, going over the same ground again and again. If he'd run off the airfield then why hadn't he been behind Jacob or gone home – it was literally yards away from the airfield. He had suffered some kind of incident in getting off the airfield or someone had taken him on the airfield. If he'd fallen down a hole then Jacob had searched every hole on the airfield a hundred times. It only left one possibility.

"I just don't believe that happened to him." Jacob said. "I just feel it wasn't what happened to him."

And they were back off at the beginning again. Marelle hugged him as he sat at her table, rubbing her face into his hair and touching her hand onto his.

"Stay tonight." She said.

He slept in her arms, curled against her like a frightened child in her bed. Some way into the night he awoke with a start, waking Marelle and making her jump too. Amidst it, she comforted him, held him and he slept again with her arms around him and his heart beating against her. Marelle closed her eyes and wondered again on the fragile thing she held in her arms.

The following morning he appeared happier. She made him breakfast and saw him off with a kiss and a cuddle at her back door. She had also suggested that he leave a few things here so he didn't end up having to rush off to the caravan in the mornings. Whether he would or not was in the lap of the Gods. She watched him walk up the runway in that lanky unhurried pace he normally adopted.

There had been nothing more from Seb, but she hadn't lost any sleep over it. Marelle spent her time trawling the internet, looking for something that might give a clue to Frankie's disappearance and subsequent whereabouts but she found herself constantly going down rabbit holes which led her to dark and mysterious stories of Suffolk folklore – which were of no help even if they involved green children or phantom houses!

It was coming to the point where all she could suggest was for them to physically examine every inch of what remained of the airfield, but it had been thirty odd years since the child had disappeared. She truly wanted to help Jacob and she feared how he would take it if the bulldozers moved in and they had not found Frankie but as the days passed she was realizing it was probably something she was going to have to find out.

Just after lunch she heard his bike start up. Every time she heard it she felt a little stab of anxiety inside her. Maybe it wasn't him – but she knew it was. Marelle walked through to the kitchen and out of the back door. Yes, she could hear it. Walking towards the edge of the airfield she heard him rev it up and start off. Seconds later she saw him zipping across the far side of the airfield. Where was he off to? A couple of minutes later he came back, then round again. Marelle stood and watched for five minutes or so as he flew around in circles at the far side. She wondered if he had seen her but pretty soon he headed down the runway at full pelt, put a boot down, swung it round and flew back again. She smiled to herself as he repeated the same circuit. Then he disappeared from view but she could still hear him and it sounded as if he was going round in circles over the far side near the farm. Ten minutes later he came flying down the run way again but this time kept coming and stopped at the foot of her garden – sunglasses on, hair swept back and a broad grin on his face.

"What are you doing, apart from shaking the whole village out of its sleepy little skin?"

"I knocked off early. They've got an electrician in doing stuff so I couldn't do a lot in the workshop – and Sam's trying to annoy me…"

"What he done this time?" Marelle asked as he tentatively looked over Jacob for wounds.

"Its nothing much – just got a new trick of taking plugs off things and taking things apart then leaving them in bits. He's doing it to annoy me – he'll start getting annoyed trying to annoy me and then off he'll go …"

"Sensible." She said.

"So I've knocked off – doing the right thing - if theres nothing I can be doing then I wont make them pay me for it."

The bike was ticking over noisily between his legs.

"Want to come on the back?" he asked.

"What, like this?"

"Yeah, get on, you'll be fine."

"Hang on … "she gestured. "I'll just grab a jacket, it was cold last time."

He sat and waited for her to come back, playing with the throttle and revving the engine. Marelle came back with a denim jacket on and trotted up to the bike.

"Hop on and hold on tight." He said.

She did, wrapping her arms tightly around him and burying her head into his back as he kicked it into gear and started up the runway.
Jacob restrained himself with her on the back. She knew he did.
"Go faster!" She shouted in his ear.
The second time up the runway he did open it up a bit more. Marelle laughed and enjoyed the feeling of him in her arms as they flew along. He carried on around the top of the runway, along the side by the main gate then down to behind the missile pads. Pulling around in what was left of a panhandle he out his feet down and stopped.
"What?" She asked.
He was looking down the airfield. A view she was not used to and it slightly disorientated her as landmarks she knew seemed to be in different places to where she would have expected them to be.
"Nothing." He said quietly. "I just got a strange feeling ..."
"What sort of feeling?"
"Anxiety. Foreboding."
"Are you ok?" she asked.
"Yeah, I'm fine. You ever get that? For a second or two you just get an overwhelming sense of doom?"
She let go of him, climbed off the bike and walked round to face him.
"No." she shook her head.
He shrugged, then smiled. Maybe its just me then!"
She stared at him "but you're ok?"
"Yeah, I'm fine." He said, then grinned.
Marelle stared at him, saw herself reflected in his sunglasses. Eventually she smiled.
"Can I have a go?"
"On this?" He asked, doubtfully.
"Yeah."
"Have you ever ridden one before?"
"No."
"And I've seen you drive a car so, no."
"You can teach me." She smiled cheekily. "And anyway, I was a bit drunk that night."
"Nah ..." he shook his head. "No, you'll hurt yourself."
"Because I'm a girl?" she asked.
"Of course not!"
"Please Jacob!"
He sighed and got off the bike, cutting the engine.
"One very little go then!" He stood to the side. "Come on then – and make sure you do exactly what I say – nothing more and nothing less."
"Ok." She said.

He nodded his head. "Get on then."
He held the bike while she climbed astride it.
"You have to hold the bike up when you're not moving – its heavy and if you let it go past the point of no return then it will drag you over with it."
Marelle nodded.
"Ok." He pointed to the right handlebar. "That's the throttle – its your accelerator – you turn it *towards* you. But be careful with it – be gentle – its not like driving a car."
"Ok."
He pointed to the left. "This is the clutch – it works in the same way as one on a car but you control it with your hand. You change gear with your left foot."
She looked confused.
"Right." He turned the key in the ignition. With his hand over hers he twisted the throttle and revved the engine. "I'll put it in gear." He flicked the pedal with his foot while pulling in and holding the clutch.
'Take hold of the clutch." He nodded, pulling her hand and wrapping her fingers around it. "Now its just like a car. Bring up the revs and let out the clutch – very slowly – until you get the biting point and you can feel the bike is ready to go."
He did it with her, his hands over hers a couple of times so she could see and feel it.
"Now, the important part. Your rear brake is under your right foot ... only use the rear brake!"
"Whats that for then?" she asked, nodding to the right handlebar.
"Don't worry about that. Forget about that – you wont need it." Jacob replied. "Now have a couple of practices with the throttle and the clutch on your own ..."
Marelle concentrated, revved the engine, let the clutch out; revved the engine and let the clutch out. After a few more goes he let her move off.
"Lift your feet up." He called.
The bike moved off, under her control, slowly and she laughed. He was jogging with her.
"No faster." He said.
Marelle laughed and went a bit faster anyway.
"Hey, stop – brake!" He exclaimed. "Right foot!"
She obliged him and slowed with a grin as he caught up to her again.
"That's enough." He said. "I'm worried you are going to hurt yourself."
She came to a stop, was a bit late putting her feet down, did it quickly and unbalanced herself. If Jacob hadn't steadied it and took the weight she would have ended up beneath it.

She laughed.

"Come on, get off before theres an injury."

Marelle cocked her leg over and stood beside him and the bike. She felt like her father had just been teaching her to ride a push bike for the very first time.

"Its complicated, isn't it?" She exclaimed.

"Its no more complicated than driving a car." He stated. "Its practice!"

"How long have you ridden bikes then?"

"Probably since I was about fifteen. Come off a few times as well!"

'Take me right round the airfield!" she said with a glint in her eye.

"I'm not sure how much petrol we have left but hop on then. If we run out we'll have to walk back!"

He rode along the back of the airfield, down the side, along the bottom by the house then started up the far side with the intention to finish with a quick blast right down the runway to her back door. The far side that they started along adjoined the farmland – most of the fence was missing here but there was a definite demarcation between airfield and farmland. This was the way he often went to work in the mornings. Here, Jacob opened the bike up alongside the hedgerow on their left between the edge of the airfield and the grass track that ran along the field on the other side of it. Marelle clung on and leaned into him. They passed the end of the hedge and were heading for the large oak tree which stood right on the boundary corner of the airfield when there was suddenly a flash of red to the left that caught her eye. Her brain processed it as a vehicle, very close to them.

Marelle heard Jacob say "Fuck" which stuck in her mind because she had never heard him swear like that before. Suddenly he accelerated, crossed onto the farmland and headed for a bank on the other side of the track. The tyres of the bike bit onto the looser ground, ran up the bank and into the hedge as behind them the other vehicle glanced into the trunk of the oak tree.

Everything happened too quickly to register what was actually going on. One moment she'd been holding on to Jacob, flying along with the wind in their faces and his t-shirt rippling around her hands and the next she felt twigs and branches flicking into her face and she was laying on her back, staring up at the powder blue sky dotted with tiny white clouds. Immediately, her brain was searching for injury and pain but she stretched her legs out and suddenly began to scramble to her feet as everything began to dawn on her. All body parts seemed to be working and she turned to look for Jacob. His arm was suddenly around her shoulders as he had appeared from the opposite direction. Marelle turned towards him and looked into his face. His lip was bleeding.

"Oh my God! Are you ok?" He asked in a panicked voice.
She nodded.
"Are you sure – nothing injured?
"You've cut your lip." She said.
He took her face in his hands. "Just sit there for a minute – get your bearings – " He said right into her face. "I'll be back in two seconds." He stood up. "Don't move."
She watched him start up the bank at the edge of the field that they had just crossed. He was holding his left side and limping but it did not impede him. Not taking any notice of what he had said she got up and followed after him.
Jacob topped the bank and almost ran down the other side, the loose surface tripping him a little. The red pick-up truck was crumpled against the tree. As Jacob approached it the driver's door opened. Marelle started down the slope after him.
"You stupid fucking little twat!" Jacob exclaimed to Sam. "What are you doing up here!"
Marelle heard Sam say something in return but it wasn't clear however she did hear the word 'cunt'. He was obviously a bit dazed by the impact; she walked up behind Jacob she saw Sam half floundering in the cab with the door open. His nose was bleeding and it looked like he had smashed it into the steering wheel. The engine had stopped but there was a loud hissing noise.
"Waiting there for me, weren't you! Weren't you!" Jacob shouted at him. "You could have killed her!" He walked into the gap of the open door. "You'd better get one of your little friends to come and tow this thing away – you cant leave it here "Fuck of." Sam bawled. "I will fucking kill you ..."
Without warning he suddenly punched Sam right in the face. Marelle even winced at the unexpected and explosive reaction from Jacob.
"What for? Because you've crashed your truck into a tree – what's that go to do with me!"
Jacob turned away and walked up to Marelle. He put his arm around her and guided her back up the bank.
"Jacob, you're hurt ..." She began, turning to him and trying to look at him.
"Lets get away from here before he comes to and decides to retaliate ... "He walked her up the bank. "You sure you're ok?" He asked.
She nodded. "I think I may have a few cuts and bruises but I'm ok."
The bike was a way away, lying on its side in the grass. He picked it up.
"Is it ok?" She asked.

"It'll be fine. Nothing I can't fix – its you I'm worried about." He pushed the bike. "Come on, you ok to walk?"
"Yeah, of course. "She ran a little to catch him up – he seemed to have an urgency to get away.
"You've got a little cut on your cheek." He said.
She felt it and discovered blood. It didn't feel too big or too deep. "What about you?" She asked.
"I'm alright."
She walked up beside him and slipped an arm around his waist as he strode on with the bike. He winced slightly.
"I'm sorry I had to do that." He said. "If I hadn't have accelerated and gone up there he would have hit us and we wouldn't be walking away. He was waiting behind that hedge, probably been watching me. I saw him at the last moment and knew there was a rut in the track right there that he was about to hit – that would have sent him straight into us. So I had to accelerate out and risk ditching it."
He was definitely limping now.
"You could have been killed. I'm not taking you on it again, not with him around."
"I'm not blaming you Jacob!" She said, "I asked you to go round there."
They were back on the airfield and heading towards her house. Sam didn't seem to be coming after them.
"Will we get in trouble?" She asked.
"For what?"
"For making him crash into that tree." She asked.
"I didn't make him hit the tree. He was being an idiot and did it himself. I wasn't even there …"
"But you hit him."
"Nah, he did that on the steering wheel, didn't he?" Jacob grinned. "Lets keep it that way."
Marelle smiled and turned to hug him. He gave her a quick one armed hug as he held on to the bike. When she stood away, she lifted his t-shirt where he had been holding his left side. She gasped. There was a bloody and still bleeding hole and a huge graze. The skin around it was already purple.
"Its just a graze. I did it on an old stump of a tree that was sticking up it looks worse than it is, honestly."
"You're hurt." She said.
"I'm fine." He gave her a smile to prove it. Let's get back to yours, I could do with a mug of tea!"
He was wincing a bit more with the motion of walking as they approached her house. Marelle was walking along with her hand on his

arm when she raised her head and saw someone in her back garden, walking slowly towards them up her garden path.

EIGHT

There, in the garden was Seb, standing there now and looking at them. "I made a special journey down here to come and have a sensible conversation with you but I can already see I've wasted my time." He said, coldly.

"No-one asked you to come Seb." She said and they stopped a few feet away from him.

"What the fuck are you doing?" He exclaimed. "And have you been on *that*?" He pointed towards the bike that still had soil and grass stuck on it.

"Yes." She said defiantly.

"It doesn't look roadworthy and you don't even have a crash helmet – you've fallen off it, haven't you?"

"It wasn't our fault." She began then remembered Jacob's words.

"You could have been killed!" Seb pointed at Jacob. "Are you totally fucking stupid? Jesus, I don't even know why I'm asking you that! I know you are."

"Seb either apologise for what you said about Jacob the other day or fuck off!" Marelle raised her voice.

Seb laughed. "*Me*? Apologise to *him*?"

He walked towards them. "I came here to have a sensible conversation, not to apologise. Maybe take the time to see it from your point of view – but not to *apologise*."

"Look – I'm sorry." Jacob suddenly said. "I want to say I'm sorry for my misjudgement at Abbi's party – but all it was ..."

Seb glared at him.

"Jacob!" Marelle exclaimed. He shot her a glance and she said "Sssh!"

"I respect you for saying sorry but describing it as a '*misjudgement*' kind of misses the mark a little. While I appreciate your apology it does not change my opinion. I don't want you near my family. *Any* of them."
Jacob made a little face of resignation but said nothing more and just stood there.
"If you're not accepting his apology then piss off – back to your bitch of a wife and her precious little world."
"Marelle. Five minutes – in the house!" Seb said.
"You do not speak to me like that!" she hissed.
Jacob nudged her. "Go with your brother – hear him out. I'll stay here and have a look over the bike – go on." He said quietly.
"Jacob – who's side are you on?"
"Just go and hear him out. I'll be here – "He nodded.
She sighed angrily and glared at him with her mouth tight.
"Five minutes." She said and walked towards the back door.
"I wont credit you with sense. But thank you." Seb said to Jacob.
"I don't like conflict." He replied. "And I don't like you hurting her with this stupidity. That's all I'm saying ..." And he turned away moving the bike to the side and kicking the stand down, leaving Seb to follow Marelle into the house.
She flew at him as soon as he walked through the back door.
"You can thank Jacob for this otherwise I would not be giving you five minutes."
"Yes. He seems charming." Seb said sarcastically. The he sighed and appealed to her in a pleading tone. "Marelle ..."
"Sebastian!" She said in retort.
"Look at it from my viewpoint. You had a stable relationship with Chris – you had a house together, you were the perfect couple. Then it was 'oh I'm finishing with Chris, I'll come and live with you for a bit ...' then we get this house and its "I'll move in there' which was fine and you could 'live there while we decide what to do with it'. Then you have suddenly taken up with this weirdo who lives in a caravan – you are besotted with him – despite the fact that he's probably a nutcase, or an alcoholic, or a junkie or God forbid, a paedophile!"
"He's not a fucking paedophile!" she gasped.
"Well he seems happy to stand around in the toilets at a kid's party, watching them come and go – what the fuck are you doing Marelle?"
"For the record Chris decided to finish it and for the record he was boring ... he was becoming fat and middle aged!"
"So whats this one then?" Seb asked with a cruel smile on his face.
"Well. Yes, he'd probably older than Chris but he doesn't have that middle aged attitude ..."

"Exactly! He seems to have the mental capacity of a fifteen year old! Whats wrong with him hey? Is he mentally retarded?"

"I am not talking to you Seb. Fuck off!"

He sighed. "Look I cant tell you what to do. You're an adult – you can make your own decisions but you are my little sister and I care for you. I don't want to be picking up the pieces, I don't want to be bailing you out of jail, I don't want to be – God forbid – identifying your body …"

"For God's sake. He's not going to kill me!"

"Looks like he had a good try today."

"You said it Seb. I can make my own decisions – and I have."

Seb nodded. "Its your decision. "He nodded. "But I don't want him anywhere near me, Caroline or the kids – ever." He held up a finger.

"Well I don't want you near him either – not if you are going to treat him like shit and accuse him of things he would never do and which you have not evidence for."

"Fine." He shrugged. "I suppose that the nearest I am going to get to resolving this."

"It is."

He stared at her. "Just be careful."

Marelle stared blankly back at him.

"Finished?" She asked.

"No – are you still working for me?"

She swallowed, "yes, if you want me to."

He nodded.

"Well off you go then. "She said. "I've got to go and make sure he's alright."

Marelle watched him go – right out of her front door, into his BMW and away. As she walked back through the house she could feel her cheek stinging and her back beginning to stiffen up a little. She walked out to Jacob. He was sitting on what remained of one of the concrete fence posts, beside the bike.

"Ok?" he nodded.

"Not really but, as they say – you cant pick your relations!"

He gave a little laugh.

"Are you ok?" she asked.

"Yeah "

"Let me see."

You've got a cut on your cheek."

"I know … its nothing … come inside." She nodded.

"You're going to be black and blue tomorrow!" She commented, lifting up his t-shirt again. "Look at it!"

The tree stump had taken a lump out and then left a long, wide graze. All around it was a shade of navy blue.

"It probably needs cleaning up" She said. "And your lip …"

"I think I bit it."

"It's a bit swollen." Marelle put a finger on his chin as she looked to check it.

"And what about this?" He asked, pointing to the cut on her cheek – it wasn't deep but it was stinging. He examined it. "I don't think it will scar."

"I don't mind if it does – I'll always have it to remember you – "

He gave a little smile, looked touched – almost as if he was about to cry. He hugged her tightly.

"I'm sorry" he said with a breaking voice.

"Hey, its ok. I'm fine." She stroked his hair. "Why don't you go and have a shower – or a bath if you want – it might help."

"Mmm, ok." He said. "I did say I was going to leave some stuff here, didn't I?"

"You were!" She said, "But …" She held a finger in the air and went to one of the cupboards in the kitchen and handed him a carrier bag. "I did take the liberty last time I was at the supermarket. You'll have to supply the clothes but everything else you need should be in there!"

She had bought them a while ago but hadn't wanted to be preposterous as to put them in the bathroom.

He smiled. "Thanks – maybe we'll take the bike back later and I can pick up some clothes."

Marelle grinned to herself as he went upstairs. That meant he was planning to stay.

And that night she lay in bed with him, this time curled in his arms. He's said he was sorry so many times and was far more worried about the very few grazes she had than he was about his own injuries. He had said more than once '*I could have killed you.*' And now he just wanted to hold her. To Marelle that meant he cared for her.

They fell asleep in each other's arms but she was woken when he got out of bed at some point during the night. She heard him go to the bathroom but when he didn't come back when she had expected, Marelle got up and went along the landing.

He was standing in the back bedroom, looking out of the window,. She walked into the room and joined him. They were both naked as she slipped a hand around his arm and stared out of the window with him.

"You ok?" She asked.

"You know I think he's still out there. I just *feel* that he is there. I try to focus on his spirit and summon it to call to me. Sometimes I feel it – sometimes I *know* he is still there."
She squeezed his arm.
"Right now Frankie, right now I need you to let me know." He said.
Marelle stared out. The moonlight stripped the colours to monochrome blue yet made the view flat and calm. All this space; all of Jacob's universe. Over on the airfield was his caravan, she could just see it from here. Looking at it from her window she wondered if he felt like the first men on the moon staring back at earth from the satellite's surface. Soon it would be ripped away from him and with it the hope that he would ever find Frankie or truly know what had happened to him.
"Come and find some dreams." She said. "They might give you the answer."

He didn't get the dreams and he didn't get the answers. Jacob didn't sleep much after that. He was tense – she could feel his body against her throughout the rest of the night. Now he was sitting in front of her eating toast and looking anxious. This morning, as predicted he was black and blue – they'd compared bruises earlier; his were much worse and by the way he was moving, were hurting him. The cut on her cheek was a little tender and she had a large bruise on her right hip – it was a bit stiff but not too painful. It could have all been so much worse.
At least that morning he didn't have to rush back to the caravan, but he would have to walk to work. She'd made him breakfast and was sitting opposite him.
"I can drop you off if you want?"
He shook his head. "I can walk, it doesn't take long."
"But you're limping."
"I'm not."
She smiled. "But if you want me to I can. I don't actually know where the farm *is*."
"I can cut across the back, quicker than you can drive me down the road. I'll get the bike going again in a few days ..."
"Do you reckon Sam will be at work?"
"He may be."
"Are you worried about him?"
"No."
"He did say he would kill you ..."
"He says that every time!"
"Well keep out of trouble with him."
"I'll try." He said. "I'd better go."

"And you're coming back tonight – for dinner?" She asked with a glint in her eye.

He gave a smile. "Ok."

That evening it just felt so right. Jacob came home to her after work; she'd cooked dinner and they sat down and ate. She was so happy to have finally reached that level of 'normality' with him. Was she finally 'domesticating' him – as Bella liked to put it – after so long at large in his own wilderness?

There was, of course, still the issue of Frankie and that chasm still studded her time with Jacob with little shards of fear and desperation. He'd been looking for over thirty years and had not found him – Marelle was here to help all she could, but in all honesty, she was running out of ideas. She did fear what would happen they day they started breaking ground but hoped her being there for him would comfort him.

"So, was Sam there?" She asked as they sat in the kitchen.

"Jacob was eating in his usual manner – full attention on what he was putting in his mouth. He nodded. "Yes. He was. Got two stitches on his nose and apparently crashed his truck when a deer ran out in front of him.!"

"Really!"

"Yeah. Good idea!"

"See. If you stand up to bullies they back down. You should have thumped him ages ago."

"Mmm." Jacob mused. "I'm not proud of it. I don't like violence, but on that occasion, he deserved it. I don't really care what he tries to do to me, but he could have killed you – and I wasn't just turning a cheek on *that*."

Marelle smiled. She was touched by that comment; the day was getting better by the minute.

After dinner he wanted to go back to the caravan to 'check everything was ok'. Marelle duly went with him, walking along side by side in the strong evening light that bounced back at them from the concrete of the runway.

Even Marelle was quieter tonight; she too felt a longing for this place now and an ache that it would soon be gone. She kicked stones around outside while Jacob went into the caravan. She wasn't sure what he was actually checking but five minutes later he came out again – in different clothes. Marelle looked up at him – he had the sunglasses pushed up onto his head.

"Has anything changed much around here since Frankie disappeared?" She asked.

"Well, yes. But the landscape is pretty much the same."

"Were there any special places you and he had where he may have gone to?" She asked.

"Why?"

"Just wondered if Frankie may have made his way to one of those? When I was a kid there used to be a tree we always used to sit in. It had white bark that peeled and one long wide bough that ran horizontal. We used to sit astride it …"

He shook his head. "I searched all of those years ago. If he had been in any of them, he would have been found."

"Everyone thinks he disappeared straight out of his bedroom – but he didn't."

"What are you saying?"

She shrugged. "I don't know. I'm just thinking out loud." She paused. "Jacob, what if we *don't* find him?"

"Then I'll go to my grave without ever knowing what happened to him. I live in hope that we may meet up on the other side and he can tell me." Marelle smiled a little, but it brought a lump to her throat.

" .. and what if we do find him?"

He drew a breath., looked away from her, pulled down the sunglasses and stared out over the airfield. Marelle wanted to take a picture of him like that, she wanted to remember him like that forever.

"Well." He finally said. "I will know what happened to him. I will know that despite it I had looked after him all this time; I had guarded him from other harm."

Marelle walked up to him and slid her arms inside his, clasping them behind his back.

"I just wish I could wave a magic wand and find him for you." She said, hugging him to her.

He smiled sweetly down at her and returned a gentle hug before he walked on with his arm around her shoulders.

They ended up at the Thor site, walking up hand in hand and looking into the sunset. Jacob sat on one of the walls and pulled her between his knees, her back to him, his arms around her. Everything now seemed golden and still and silent.

"Your guy hasn't called back" Marelle said, "about saving the site?"

"Nah – It'll take a few weeks, but I doubt it will get him anywhere. I'm not expecting a miracle."

Marelle turned and faced him, looking onto his eyes. He leaned forward and kissed the cut on her cheekbone.

"I'm sorry." He whispered.

"Its ok."

"I'm so very sorry." He said, again, reaching up and brushing her hair off her face as he kissed her.

Then in the dying evening sunlight, there on that site Jacob made the first move, leaning into her and gently laying her down on the wall, his mouth against hers as she felt him undoing his belt. This couldn't have been more different to her anger fuelled onslaught as he fell upon her with an extreme gentleness that she was devoured by. For someone who said he had never had a meaningful relationship he certainly knew how to play a good tune. He was gentle and *so* kind, *so* considerate. He genuinely was the most beautiful person she had ever come across and right now he was both in her arms and inside her; out here; on the spot where the missiles had once been. How could such a beautiful human being not have been snapped up years ago and now be living a as a married man with three kids? Jacob was one of those people you would spend your whole life asking 'why' about but hoping your trust and love would win him and intertwine your lives together forever.

Jacob stayed at the house again that night which pleased her even more. He seemed to be moving in bit by bit, day by day. But that was just what she wanted – him living day to day with her. She'd bought the winning ticket and now she wanted the prize.

Marelle had made him breakfast and he'd gone off to the farm. He said he would see her later and she planned to have a good trawl through whatever she could research in the hope of finding Frankie. By eleven she was stalled with a mug of tea, the internet and her notes. Seb had sent stuff through which she was chipping away at but prioritizing Jacob's research. Then her phone rang.

She sighed and picked it up – expecting it to probably be Seb – or at a push Bella – but she would be at work now and wouldn't normally call at this time. She was surprised to see it came up as herself but then remembered Jacob still had her old phone. That was odd – but she was delighted – what did he want?

"Hiya!" She answered brightly.

There wasn't an instant answer, but she could hear muffled noises.

"Jacob?" She asked, thinking he had probably pocket called her.

Then, " ... let me have the phone sir ..." a voice said.

"Jacob?" She called again, worried now.

"Hello?" An unfamiliar voice greeted.

"Hello! Who is this?" Marelle asked, completely in the dark as to who this was or why they were calling her.

"Is this Marelle?" He asked.

"Yes – who is this please?"

"My name is Daniel, I'm a paramedic and I'm currently with Jacob."

A paramedic! She panicked.

"Is he ok?" She gasped, "Whats wrong?"

"Im afraid he has suffered an electric shock from some equipment here in the workshop ..."

"What!" Marelle exclaimed. "Is he ok? Where is he?"

There were muffled noises again. The next voice she heard was Jacob.

"Marelle, can you come down here?" He asked but his voice sounded funny, very lethargic.

"Yes, Jacob. I'm now coming – how do I get there?"

There was a pause.

"Jacob?"

"I cant remember." He said.

"Jacob, let me speak to the paramedic." She asked, calmly although her insides had gone into turmoil.

"Hello." He said.

"I don't know how to get there – I've never been ..."

"I turned into the second entrance after the village shop on the right. Wrights Farm. Where are you?"

"I'm literally two minutes away – I'll be right there." She said hurriedly, getting up to leave as he finished the call.

What! Her mind was screaming at her. *What*!? She drove down the street, past the shop and looked for the second turning. There it was, an entrance with two curved brick walls and two aluminium gates which were open. It led onto a concrete yard with various barns and buildings – over to the right she could see the paramedic's car so drove over to there and parked alongside it.

The sun was hot today and the whole place dusty. There were no shadows as the sun was directly overhead. Just in front of the car was a shutter door that was pulled up – it looked like what she would expect a workshop to look likes so she tentatively walked in.

There was an inspection pit with no cover, a workbench and various tools laying about the place. Over the back she could see the paramedic, his back to her so she headed that way.

"What happened?" she asked as she approached. "Jacob, are you ok?"

The paramedic looked round and moved to the side slightly. Jacob was sat on a chair, he had a blanket around him – he looked cold and appeared to be trembling slightly. He was as white as a sheet to the point of being grey and looked shattered and clammy.

"He wants me to go to hospital?" Jacob said – "Tell him I'm not going."

The paramedic smiled and turned to Marelle. "He's had quite a severe shock, he has burns on his hand – I've checked his heart and it's a bit fast – in these circumstances we normally want the patient to attend

A&E for further check-up and monitoring. He's been very lucky – shocks like this can cause a cardiac arrest."
"How did it happen Jacob?" she asked.
He shrugged.
"He just picked up the angle grinder and switched it on." A voice said from the far corner. Marelle spun around to see a very young, spotty faced guy in green overalls. He looked almost as white as Jacob and scared shitless.
"Were you in here?" She asked.
He nodded. "He switched it on, there was a loud bang and he flew across the workshop. I thought he was dead. I called the ambulance." He mumbled.
"Who are you?"
"Ryan." He said.
"Was Sam in here too?"
He shifted his eyes for a second. Then nodded.
"Fucks sake!" Marelle said to herself. "Where is he now?" She asked Ryan.
Ryan shrugged. "He went out, I think he thought he was dead too."
She turned back to Jacob. "This has got to stop." She said. "Right now Jacob."
"The ambulance will be here in about five minutes." The paramedic said.
"I'm not going." Jacob said.
"You wont get him to a hospital." Marelle warned.
The paramedic made a little gesture which suggested that would not be the best decision.
"I can keep an eye on him. Its fine." Marelle stated.
"I would strongly recommend he goes. After an electric shock like this there can be repercussions – even a long time afterwards ..."
"Like what?"
"Heart problems, cardiac arrest, organ failure, anxiety, depression – not to mention he has quite a bad burn on his hand that will need dressing ..."
"I'm fine." Jacob said and sounded slightly better now than he had on the phone.
"His heart rate is quite fast. I'd like to see it settle down a bit." The paramedic said.
Marelle sighed.
At that point the ambulance turned up and it all started over again. From the conversation it seemed that Jacob and Ryan were in the workshop with Sam hanging around. Jacob picked up the angle grinder

and bang! Next thing he'd been unconscious on the floor – Sam had fucked off and Ryan had been left to deal with it; which he had by dialling 999. They'd told him what to do and the paramedic had been close by – hence he'd turned up first. Now Jacob was being poked and prodded again and wasn't enjoying the experience.

Then to add to the melée, in walked an elderly gentleman in a khaki quilted waistcoat, jeans and wellies.

"Whats happened?" He asked.

Marelle listened as it was all explained again, and she got the impression that this was the farmer.

"What happened Jacob?" He asked.

"I cant quite remember."

"Who called the ambulance?" He asked.

"I did." Ryan said. "I thought he was dead."

"You should have called me straight away – I don't like coming back and seeing ambulances and paramedics in my yard ..."

"Erm ... excuse me ..." Marelle interrupted, gaining his attention. He smiled purely because she was a reasonably attractive female.

"Oh, hello. And you are ..."

"I'm Jacob's partner."

"I never knew he had a partner."

She smiled and continued. "I don't know if you are aware, but your other employee, Sam, has a habit of trying to antagonize or hurt Jacob – I think he may have had something to do with this ..."

"Marelle!" Jacob suddenly shouted.

"Oh, I don't worry too much about that lot, bantering and picking on each other – they do it all the time."

"But this happened using your equipment in your workshop."

"Marelle!" Jacob said loudly again.

"He could have been killed."

"Marelle leave it!" He exclaimed.

"No, Jacob. Its got to be said."

The farmer sighed. "Well, we'll have a look into it ..."

"He'll need to take the rest of this week off – he needs to rest ..." Marelle said.

"That will be fine, I understand that ..." The farmer answered.

"No, I can come in tomorrow. I will be fine!" Jacob piped up.

The paramedic shook his head.

"No Jacob, you're not!" Marelle told him firmly. "You're coming home with me and you're going to spend the next four days getting over this. In fact, I think you should reconsider working here ..."

"No, Marelle, No!" Jacob protested.

"Its ok Jacob. Take the rest of the week off – then come back on Monday – don't worry about it." His boss said.

Jacob shook his head.

"Don't worry about the money Jacob, you're more important!" Marelle said.

"I'm not worried about money …" he said in reply. "I've got money – just leave it – it was an accident."

Marelle sighed noisily.

"If you are refusing to go to the hospital then we will need to complete some paperwork." The paramedic explained.

"Is that safe now?" Mr Wright, the farmer asked, gesturing towards the piece of equipment on the floor.

"Its off and its unplugged, but I wouldn't say its safe." Ryan replied.

Then as Mr. Wright walked across the workshop to have a closer look at the strewn angle grinder he farted, quite loudly – more than once but not one person in the whole workshop said anything, or even smiled. Marelle, in all the confusion and chaos had to turn away and hide her face as she simply could not hold on to it.

"I'll speak with Sam." Mr Wright said. "And you Ryan … Jacob, you go home and take care of yourself."

With that he left.

When Marelle turned back to Jacob she had tears rolling down her cheeks and was still struggling not to laugh. While they were completing their paperwork she kept hearing it over and over again and each time it started her off. Jacob was reeling off information about himself that was not entirely accurate, but she was giggling too much to correct him, so she let it be.

Eventually everyone left but with a warming to Jacob to rest and to call 999 if he suffered any other symptoms or his condition worsened. He was able to walk to her car and get in but was still seemed shaky. She climbed into the driver's seat beside him and closed the door.

"Whats wrong with you?" He asked.

She grinned. "I'm sorry – but didn't you hear that? He farted when he walked across the workshop!" She was suddenly crying again as she burst into more giggles – probably fueled by any adrenalin in her from the whole incident.

"Yeah – he does that all of the time." Jacob said dryly, but obviously didn't find it as funny as she did. He closed his eyes for a second as she started the car. Then he added. "Its ok until you're stuck in a lorry with him for hours"

Marelle laughed. At least he was having a joke with her but she needed to get him home and get to the bottom of what had really taken place.

It was a two minute drive home and she reversed the car into the driveway so he would be closer to the front door. By the time she'd walked round the car he was out.

"How do you feel?" She asked.

"Bit weird." He said." Feel like been hit in the chest with a wrecking ball."

She threw him a glance.

"I know." He remarked. "But I'm not going."

"No, but you are going to stay here for the next couple of days and *rest* – just like they said. You're not going to work and you're not messing around with that bike."

"Can't, its still broken." He commented. "But if I'm forced to 'rest' over the next couple of days I can get it fixed."

He did seem fine, if a bit distant – but that was part and parcel of Jacob anyway, so she didn't let it play on her mind too much. She commented on his hands being shaky but he told her that the paramedic said that was due to the shock to his body and should subside. The burn on his hand had been dressed and didn't appear to be bothering him. He said he wasn't hungry and didn't want anything to eat when she asked him but again, that was normal for him. He said he wanted to go to the caravan to get some clothes and look at the bike. Marelle persuaded him it would be best to bring the bike back here – at least that way she could keep an eye on him – and for him to at least leave tinkering with it until tomorrow. He said 'he would see' but by the time they had walked up to the caravan and back he was beginning to fade a bit.

So they at on the wooden bench in the garden. The sun was still hot, but she sat up close to him and rested her head on his shoulder.

"Do you think Sam was behind it?"

"I think that may have been a step too far – even for him. I think it was an unfortunate accident."

"But you said Sam had been taking things apart – and the electrician had been in too."

"Its just a coincidence."

"There is not such thing as a coincidence." She remarked. "Things happen due to things happening."

"That's very cynical!"

"Yeah, well; that's the difference between you and me. I see the worst in everyone, and you look for the best."

"Hmm." He said.

"Anyway, I think it may be time to consider not working there anymore … you can do better Jacob – and lets face it Sam isn't going anywhere is he?"

Jacob sighed. "I like working at the farm – I've been there off and on since I was twelve or thirteen …"
"But he's going to end up killing you!"
"Of course he isn't."
"Jacob he's already nearly done it three times!"
"I don't think he means things to go as far as they do."
She shook her head. "He's dangerous."
"I'm not scared of Sam – and I don't want to leave the farm."
"But you've got a degree in nuclear physics – surely that means something?"
He paused before answering. "I haven't actually got a degree in nuclear physics."
"You said you had – the other day!"
"No, I didn't. I said I went to Uni and I studied nuclear physics – I didn't say I actually completed the course."
"You dropped out?"
"Yeah …"
"Why?"
"Lets just say I was distracted."
"By what? Was it a girl?" Marelle lifted her head and looked at him.
"No. It wasn't a girl. It was a number of things at the time and I – well, I didn't finish."
Marelle laid her head back down. She could hear him breathing; she could also hear Seb's voice in her head too.
She reached her arms around him on the bench and cuddled closer to him.
"Ow!" he complained softly.
"What?"
"The bruise on my side really hurts at the moment!"
"Let me see …"
"No, no, no, its fine. You just caught it wrong."
She lay her head against him again and closed her eyes. Happy that he was here with her like this.
That night Marelle didn't give him much choice about staying. There was not a snowflake in hell's chance that she was going to let him go off on his own and she didn't even let him entertain the idea of sleeping in another room. She wanted to keep an eye on him and for that reason she was sleeping right beside him.
Which was fine to begin with. She fell asleep snuggled against him in her bed. This was shattered when she was woken with a start by him suddenly scrambling to an upright sitting position and saying,
"Your ghost is within me."

Marelle sat up and stared at him. It was dark in the room but the light from the moon gave a blue-ish glow to everything. The room was not overly warm, but she touched his arm and it was wet and cold. The sheet on his side of the bed was damp too.
"Jacob." She said, "Are you ok?"
He didn't reply immediately and took a few seconds to come to his senses. He let out a held, steady breath.
"What was that about?" She asked, touching his cheek and finding it too covered with a sheen of sweat.
"Did I say something?"
"You said *'your ghost is within me'*!" Marelle explained, looking up at him. "What did you mean?"
"Nothing."
"Why did you say that?"
He sighed. "I don't know." He swung his legs round and stood up a little too quickly, throwing himself off balance so he had to grab onto the back of a chair.
"Where are you going now?"
"Toilet.' He said and she watched him bump into the doorpost as he walked through. He returned a couple of minutes after and curled up tightly on his side beside her.
It seemed like only minutes after when he got up again – went to the bathroom then went downstairs. Marelle lay there listening; he was in the kitchen – maybe he was making himself a drink? She listened as she lay there until she heard him unlock the back door and open it.
Marelle was up like a shot. Dizzy in the darkness and giddy she ran headlong down the stairs.
"Jacob!" she called after him, through the living room and into the kitchen. The back door was open and he was halfway up the garden path, naked.
"Jacob, what are you doing?"
"Lets go up to the weir." He said.
"Not at this time of the night I'm not." She said, clutching his arm. "... or naked. Come on, back indoors."
"No. I need to go now." He insisted. "*Now*."
"Jacob! Come back into the house."
"We can walk up there from here."
"No – come back to bed."
"I'll go on my own if you're not going to come with me."
Marelle held on to him but in sheer exasperation she sighed. "I'll drive us up there, but come and put some clothes on first."
"It will be better to walk. Someone will see the car."

"No-one's going to see the car at this time of the night!"
This was blowing her mind! She had no idea what was going on or why he was insisting on doing this but, she went along with him. He dressed – a bit haphazardly and she threw on clothes and grabbed her car keys – pushed him into the car and drove up the road to the spot where he had taken her before. She parked in a shallow run-in at the side of the road. He got out immediately and started off. She locked the car, panicked and ran after him.

"Jacob!" She called a little fruitlessly and ran behind him.

He walked past the 'calm pool' and headed in the direction of the noise of rushing water. Marelle wrapped her fingers around his arm and went with him. There wasn't really a defined path but he knew the track well. Soon they came to a four feet high chain link fence with signs on that said 'Danger! Keep Out! Deep Water'. For a moment he stopped and looked at the fence then headed for a wooden gate to the right. Seconds later he was over the gate and heading down the bank.

"Shit Jacob." She moaned to herself as she made a complete hash of getting over the gate and following him.

By the time she grabbed his arm again he was standing on the edge of a brick built wall, level with the bottom of the bank but descending beneath their feet vertically down into the thrashing water.

He was standing on the edge, staring down into the water. Marelle suddenly felt scared of him and what he may do. She had his arm and looked up at his face which was tilted downwards gazing into the water. In the moonlight his cheeks looked hollow and his eyes not visible – just black shadows.

"Jacob." She said but he seemed far off.

If he jumped he would take her with him; she clutched at a handful of his t-shirt in the small of his back as well. She wouldn't be able to save him – or herself either for that matter if he jumped and took her with him – her only option would be to let him go.

"Jacob." She said again but he remained staring down.

She tugged at his t-shirt, pulled at his arm to try and get him to step back. The sound was almost mesmerizing; the moonlight glinted on a line of flagstones across the top left edge of the weir, above the falling wall of water. Was this where he had fallen in as a kid? How on earth had Frankie – a weak swimmer – ever dragged him out of that?

"Jacob." She tugged him back. A step. "Come on – we shouldn't be here and its dangerous."

Marelle shivered and felt a chill pass over her soul. Why was she even letting him do this? She looked down to the noise of the water below. His feet were right on the edge, he had his head bowed still staring down into the dark, raging waters. And Marelle sensed him staring the devil in the eye right at that moment. Taking a chance she stepped alongside him, pushing hard at his shoulder, twisting him away until he staggered a step backwards. She shoved him again, almost shoulder in to him and he stumbled backwards, his feet hitting the rising ground behind them and he lost balance and sat down heavily.

"Jacob!" she shook his shoulder, crouching beside him. "Don't do this to me!" She put a finger under his chin and turned his face to her. "You scared me."

Then he held out his arms to her which she happily fell into.

"I don't like it here ... I don't want to be here right now!" She said, "Come on, lets go home."

It was more difficult getting him back up the bank than it had been coming down but she pushed him in front of her, not letting him out of her sight. Once over the fence and in the car again she turned to him.

"Jacob, sometimes you scare me!"

"Sometimes I scare myself." He said in a quiet solemn voice.

They got home, went back to bed and he slept like a log without another word. When she woke again with sunlight streaming through the windows, he was beneath the duvet, only his hair visible. She smiled to herself and went downstairs to make tea.

He still hadn't stirred when she came back up with two mugs and placed them on the bedside table. Climbing back into bed beside him, Marelle lifted the duvet off his face, rolling it back and looked down on him with a smile on her face. Then she leaned down and gently kissed his cheek. Jacob stirred a little, shifted position slightly and settled his head further into the pillow.

"Come on sleeping beauty, I've got a mug of tea for you."

He opened his eyes and looked back up at her – this morning they had a sparkle to them again. Pushing himself up into a sitting position, rubbed his hands through his hair and took the mug off her as she held it to him.

She grinned. He looked so adorable with his hair ruffled like that!

"Jesus I've got a headache." He said in a low voice.

"I'm not surprised after last night's antics!" She commented. "It's a wonder I haven't got a headache too!"

"Sorry, did I keep you awake?"

Marelle stopped midway to take a sip from the mug and glared at him. "You could say that." She said.

He didn't remember. He honestly had no recollection. She had stood with him on the edge of the weir looking into the water, petrified that he would jump but this morning he knew nothing of it.

"Jacob!" she stated. "You honestly do not remember what you did last night?"

"No."

"You made me go up to the weir with you at about two in the morning! I think you would have gone on your own but I found you in the garden – "

He looked at her. The glint in his eyes had turned to bewilderment. "The weir?"

She nodded. "Before that you woke up with a jolt, sat bolt upright in bed and said '*your ghost is within me*' as well ... scared the shit out of me!"

"I'm sorry. I don't recall any of that ..."

"Well you did. I thought you were going to jump into the weir. I was scared!"

"Why would I do that?" He asked.

"I don't know Jacob – if you don't know whats going on inside your own head how am I supposed to have any clue?"

Marelle snuggled close to him. "The paramedic did say you may get some weird symptoms ..."

He stared into space and sipped the tea.

"Lets hope it's a one off." He finally said.

"You scared me last night. I didn't know what you were going to do." She said. "You know I had hold of the back of your t-shirt trying to hang on to you."

"Oh my!" He said. "I didn't mean to scare you but I honestly don't remember any of that."

"Just don't do it again!" She joked, but meant it.

That morning he went outside and began tinkering with the bike. Funny how he hadn't mentioned Frankie for a day or two – Marelle had begun to worry that his memory had been affected by the shock – what with that and last night's behaviour – maybe she would test the water later. She had some work to do for Seb but also wanted to continue reading something she had started researching about Suffolk as well. Marelle set her laptop up in the kitchen so she could keep an eye on him out of the window. Every now and then she looked up and saw him happily working on the bike – engrossed in what he was doing – like a six year old playing with a favourite toy. She smiled to herself as she worked.

She'd just stood up to make a drink when her phone rang.

"Hi Bella." She said.

"Oh you sound happy! Whats occurring?" Bella asked.

"I'm just watching Jacob through the kitchen window." She replied, casually. "He's outside tinkering with an old motorbike he's picked up

– got some old ripped jeans on that are a very good fit and a tight black t-shirt ..." She mused.

Bella laughed "Ooh I like a guy on a motorbike!"

"Hands off, he's mine." Marelle warned.

"So, it sounds like you're having a good week?"

Marelle laughed, "Well no, not really."

"Oh, why?"

Marelle took a breath. "Well – we both fell off the bike the other day. Then Seb turned up unexpectedly as we were walking back with the broken bike, both covered in cuts and bruises! Then yesterday Jacob was electrocuted!"

"Electrocuted! Do you mean he got an electric shock?"

"Yeah – he was using some tool in the workshop at the farm and got a shock off it knocked him out and one of the lads there thought he was dead and called an ambulance!"

"Oh my God! But it sounds as if he's ok now?"

"Well, he is but he's been told to rest for a few days – he was a bit weird yesterday – went sleepwalking last night – but he seems to be ok today."

"Oh, so just a normal week then?"

"Yeah." Marelle said, her attention now on Jacob as he stood up and waved to her through the kitchen window.

"Did you sort it out with Seb then?"

"No – "She replied. "We argued. Jacob actually apologized but Seb wouldn't accept it. I think we've agreed to disagree – said he didn't want Jacob anywhere near him or his family and didn't approve of me being with him either, but he know he cant stop me and he's got it all wrong anyway."

"Oh dear!" Bella replied.

"Sod him." Marelle laughed.

"Well I'm free this weekend – you wanna come to mine for a change? You can bring lover boy?"

"Oh no, no I don't think that would be a good idea – I think its best to keep him out of social situations because people get the wrong end of the stick with him all the time ... and you're going to want to drag us to a club or something."

"Well I'll come there then." Bella stated.

"You're welcome but I'm not going anywhere – I don't want to leave him alone at the moment."

"Say, why don't we do the *boyfriend test*?"

"No Bella – not with Jacob. He doesn't really drink.

"Well that makes my life easier – and more interesting!"

"No Bella."

"Oh come on, he could do with loosening up a bit! I wont get him paralytic – just – nice and loose."
"He wont drink. You cant make him."
"Oh I have my ways. If he wont play we'll stick a few shots of vodka in his bottle of beer!"
"Bella no." Marelle sighed. "Not Jacob."
The *boyfriend test* was a game they'd played many times. Stay sober but get the guy in question drunk enough to show their true colours!
"I've got an idea …" Bella continued. "We can have a barbecue – what guy can resist playing with a barbecue?"
"I don't have a barbecue."
"Jacob has one. I saw it when I was cleaning lipstick off the caravan door."
"No Bella."
"Oh come on Marelle! Borrow his barbecue, let him play with it. Get him all nice and fuzzy and see what comes out!"
"No!"
"Well just the barbecue then?"
Marelle sighed. "Oh Bella!"
"Go on. It'll be fun,"
"Where have I heard that before?"
"I'll see you on Saturday then?"
"Bella!" Marelle exclaimed. "I don't know, and I don't want you getting him drunk either."
"Just a little bit. Loosen him up."
"I guarantee you wont get him drunk."
"Well that's fine then! I'll see you Saturday … get the barbecue. I'll bring the booze."
Marelle sighed and stared out of the window. He wasn't looking at her this time. He was trying to straighten a piece of metal that had got bent in the accident and was concentrating on that. She was about to put the kettle on when the doorbell rang.
She wasn't expecting anyone and had though it would probably be Seb having seen the error of his ways but when she opened the door it was Mr. Wright from the farm.
"Good morning." He greeted. "I was looking for Jacob – general consensus of opinion is that he is here."
She smiled "yes, he is … come through."
"How is he?"
"Seems ok – but the paramedic said to keep an eye on him as things can manifest themselves quite some time after." She walked through to the kitchen with him following. "He's outside."

She opened the back door.

"Jacob, someone for you."

He looked up, saw Mr Wright and stood up. Wiping his hands down his jeans.

"Morning Jacob." Mr Wright said. "I just wanted to let you know I had the electrician look at the angle grinder – he said it looks like it was an unfortunate accident with a pretty old piece of equipment. I've scrapped it and I'll buy a new one. Good to see you're ok though."

Marelle looked to him as she leaned on the doorpost, arms folded. This was going to be a standard compensation waiver conversation she suspected.

"Ok." Jacob said. "Do you want me to come in today?"

"Oh, no, no – its fine. Take a few days to make sure you are over it – come in on Monday. I'll make sure you get paid for these three days."

"Thank you." Jacob smiled in his best 'just being polite smile'.

Marelle smiled cynically. So that was all his life was worth – three days pay?

" … and I've been thinking …" Mr Wright continued.

Marelle listened harder. She didn't like '*I've been thinking*' conversations.

"I'm looking to step back a bit – let Adam take the reins a bit and I was planning to collect a few more vintage vehicles – maybe its time to offer you full employment – mainly as my mechanic but to help on the farm as well if needed. Separate the workshop and let Adam take control of the lads and the farming."

Jacob nodded. "Ok."

"Well lets get the harvest and summer out of the way – Adam leaves college soon and he'll be back for good. Carry on as you are for now, give me a few weeks to sort everything out and then we'll look into taking you on as a full time employee."

"Sounds good." Jacob replied.

"Good." He said. "Very well. I'll leave you to carry on with that …" he nodded to the bike.

"Ok, thank you." Jacob said and turned back to the bike.

"You'd better come back through the house?" Marelle gestured. "Be bad luck to go through the back way …"

He laughed. "Oh I'm not superstitious!"

She closed the back door as they went into the kitchen.

"I didn't know Jacob had got himself a young lady!" He chuckled. "I used to know Dick who live here."

"He was my uncle." Marelle said. "He left me the house."

"Oh, I see. And you're going to stay here?"

She nodded.

"My father would never take Jacob on as an employee you know – he let him down once when he disappeared for a few months. My father said he was unreliable and wouldn't take him on permanently when he came back. He's been working for me for ten years now and hasn't missed a beat so I think he's proven himself since then. It was just around when his father died so there was probably a good reason for his disappearance. Still, he's a good worker ... quiet, keeps his head down." He nodded and continued walking through the house. "Always been good with mechanical things. When I first saw him, I knew he was a bit of a petrol head – I was too I suppose! He always liked bikes but I remember for a time he had a silver Corvette Stingray – I often wondered how a young lad like him working part time on the farm could afford such a thing but – well – it was his money and his life. Don't know what happened to it ... "

"His father worked on the farm too didn't he?"

"Oh yes, had a bit of a drink problem after his wife died – we knew but cut him some slack. That's how Jacob ended up working on the farm – he used to help his father a lot – used to cover for him a lot of the time – yes he's been around for while!"

"And did you know the Lees who lived here before Dick?"

"Oh yes, the boy that went missing?" He mused. "Knew *of* them, didn't know them well."

"Do you remember when the boy disappeared?" Marelle pryed.

"Yes, I do. It was just after I married my wife – we'd just come back from a working holiday on my cousin's farm in Australia – we came back right at the time he'd gone missing. I helped the police when they searched the farmland around here ..."

She looked at him. He liked talking. "What do you think happened to him?"

"Who knows? But I always say they should have looked a little closer to home. You know what they say? Most murders are committed by family members! I always found it strange that they moved away pretty quickly ..."

"You think maybe his parent's killed him?" She gasped.

"Well, I didn't say that, did I. But, well strange things happen in small villages." He got to the front door. "Its good to see Jacob is ok."

He reached for the door and at the same time let rip a loud, involuntary fart, Marelle tightened her lips and let him go closing the door behind him. She was laughing as she walked back to the kitchen. Jacob walked in as she returned.

"What?" He asked.

"I wouldn't go in the hallway for a bit!" She grinned.
"Oh he didn't, did he?"
"Fraid so. Whats wrong with him?"
Jacob shrugged. 'Too much rich food?"
Marelle smiled.
"In wasnt expecting that. "Jacob said quietly. "He has always point blank refused to give me a permanent job before ... I don't think Adam being in charge will go down well." He grinned
"Who's Adam?"
"His son. Bit of a hooray-Henry – he wont be popular with Sam and his cronies."
Marelle smiled. "Good – and with a bit of luck you wont have to deal with Sam anymore either."
"We'll see. Its just a promise at the moment."
"Its just a bloody carrot!" Marelle remarked. "He's offering you that so you don't try and sue him for getting a shock off his equipment."
Jacob laughed. "You're so cynical."
"And you always look for the good!" She quipped. "Well heres one for you. Bella's coming the weekend and she's spied your barbecue at the caravan – wants me to ask you to bring it down here so we can have a barbecue on Saturday."
He gave a lopsided smile.
"Are you up for that?"
He shrugged. "Ok. I guess I can just about handle the both of you."
"Are you sure?"
"As long as you hold my hand!"
They sat down for lunch. Jacob said he wasn't hungry and didn't want anything, but she made him a sandwich anyway and sat herself down.
"Mr Wright has an interesting theory about Frankie." She began.
"Has he?" Jacob asked. "Did you ask him?"
"Conversation came up as he was leaving. Said he knew Dick and the Lees before." Marelle explained. "He seems to think that his parents may be behind Frankie's disappearance!"
"What?"
"He said they should have looked closer to home. He said most murders are committed by family members!"
Jacob stopped chewing the sandwich he had decided to eat after all. Sat back and ran his hands through his hair before shaking his head.
"But that doesn't exactly help us in finding him, does it?"
"Maybe we should look in this house?" Marelle asked.
"Well as a last resort I'll rip all of the floorboards up. "He said. "But I don't think for one second that his parents killed him!"

He didn't like that theory. Like when Marelle had said about Frankie being taken on the airfield – Jacob went all quiet and withdrawn compared to how he had been with her earlier. She knew he was going through every aspect of it in his head and not liking what he was thinking. She hoped he would sleep that night.

Marelle was tense when they went to bed which impacted on her getting to sleep. She must have eventually dropped off only to be woken suddenly by violent movement and the racket of stuff being knocked over. Just as she had shook sleep away and sat up, Jacob slumped back down to sit on the edge of the bed, his back to her. He'd clearly leapt up from the bed in a single movement and managed to knock everything off the bedside table in doing so.

"Sorry." He said when he realized she was awake too now.

Marelle slid across the bed and cuddled against his back

"Come on. Its ok." She whispered.

He gently lay back down beside her and she held on to his arm as they both fell asleep again.

"I'm going to the supermarket." She had announced the following morning. "Are you coming?"

"No." he said, staring out of the window.

"Ok – well I'll be about an hour, maybe an hour and a half – will you be ok?"

He nodded.

"Ok then." She felt uncomfortable leaving him here on his own and he seemed very distant this morning.

"Can you get me some petrol?" He suddenly asked.

"Petrol? What for?"

"The bike."

"Oh, ok – yeah. What shall I get it in?"

"Good question." He said. "The can I normally use is at the workshop." He reached into his back pocket and took his wallet out, handing her a twenty pound note. "You might have to buy a petrol container at the garage …"

"Its ok, I'll pay for it." She smiled, shaking her hand at the money.

"No." He shook his head and held out the money to her insistently.

She wasn't going to argue and took it. "Just ordinary petrol?"

"Just ordinary petrol will be fine."

She left him in the knowledge that at least he wouldn't be going anywhere on the bike.

Friday at the supermarket was a nightmare. Marelle's mind was never organized enough for shopping and she made the usual impulsive and haphazard purchases which included stuff for the barbecue that Bella had instigated. Marelle still wasnt sure she wanted to go through with this – not with the state his mind he seemed to be in at the moment but she went along with the idea so far.

Getting the petrol had added to the complexity of her trip. This was something she'd never done before and although a simple enough sounding task proved to be a complicated one. She hadnt realized you had to have a certain colour and size of container or how quickly it filled up with petrol and she probably spilled a few quid's worth. Eventually she secured the precious cargo in the back of her car, hoping it wouldn't spill on the way home.

NINE

Marelle reversed the car into the drive and opened the hatchback on her way to the front door. She was expecting Jacob to be outside in the back garden. He wasn't. The bike was still there and didn't look as if it had been moved since yesterday. Marelle turned to start looking else where when she heard a noise from upstairs that sounded like wood being thrown down followed by a loud rumble as if someone was pushing furniture across the floor. Curious, she turned and headed up the stairs. There were more noises which sounded like a large piece of furniture being moved; she followed the direction of the sound – it seemed to be coming from the back bedroom overlooking the airfield. The door was open, she walked in on tip toe, wondering what he was doing but stopped in her tracks and could not help herself but exclaim "Oh my God Jacob. What are you doing?"
She teetered on the edge of a hole in the middle of the room. Jacob had pushed all of the furniture to the sides of the room, with stuff piled up on the bed, pulled up the carpet and had taken up about sixty percent of the floorboards in the room. Right at the moment he had his back against the wardrobe, trying to push it along by about six feet so he could, presumably, remove more of the floorboards. It was solid and heavy and despite his strength, it wasn't moving far.
"Jacob, I was joking!" She gasped. "Bella will be staying in here tomorrow!"
"Its ok, I'll put them back." He said, standing up and away from the wardrobe.
Marelle looked into the hole. She could see all of the joists, the pipes, wiring and the back of the ceiling below.

"Jacob." She sighed.
"You put the idea in my head – I didnt want to leave any stone unturned."
"But you knew he wouldn't be in here. You knew he was on the airfield when he disappeared."
"No, I don't know." He stated. "I had to look."
"Why this room? What makes you think he would be in this room?"
"The floors downstairs are solid – I haven't looked in the other rooms." He stated. "But I found this."
He walked towards her, picked something up from the floor and held it out to her. It was a large, square biscuit tin with a picture of a red London double decker bus on the lid. It was dusty but the colours were still vibrant beneath the layer of dust. He walked over to the side of the room where there was still a platform of floorboards left and knelt down.
"Look."
She went over and crouched beside him. "What is it?"
"It was under the floorboards – it was Frankie's."
"How do you know?"
"He opened the tin, took out the contents item by item and laid them on the remaining floor. "Its his stuff. He had an obsession with burying a time capsule somewhere – this may have been the start of it ..."
"Did you know it was here?"
He shook his head.
On the floor in front of them was a folded piece of paper, a plastic elephant, a die cast model of a car, a foot long piece of black metal with some numbers painted on it in white – there was also a photograph but Jacob held on to that.
"Read that." He pushed the folded piece of paper towards her.
Marelle opened it out. It was A4 and covered in neat, black handwriting which. She read aloud.
'I, Frankham G. Lee have left this here so you have been able to find it. By this time I will be a nuclear physicist and you will know my name alongside Albert Einstein and J. Robert Oppenheimer. The items in here are important to me:
1.   A Jaguar e-type car. I will drive this car when I am grown up. It will be a V12 Roadster in British Racing Green.
2.   A mastodon. It is a private joke. You will not know the joke but you will ponder on it.
3.   The stolen number plate from a Willy's Jeep. My best friend gave this to me as a birthday present. To you it might look like rubbish but to me it is one of the best gifts I have ever been given.

4.   A photograph so you can see what I looked like and what my best friend looked like. You may laugh at us, but we were real once.'
Marelle had read it out loud but wished she hadn't. Her voice was broken at the end and her eyes were full of tears. Jacob knelt before her with his head bowed and the photograph clutched in his hand.
Marelle swallowed. "Oh God."
Jacob sniffed and looked up, he was crying. He held out the photo to her. It was small, black and white but very clear and perfect. There was a woman – presumably Frankie's mother – crouching beside two young boys, holding a birthday cake. It looked like summer – they were in the garden, behind this very house and the woman was wearing a sleeveless dress and had a broad, happy smile on her face. The two boys stood side by side. One was in a dark, smart blazer with a white shirt beneath; he wore shorts; his hair looked black and was cut onto a short, neat style. He had his chin down but his eyebrows raised with a grin on his face. Frankie. Beside him, slightly shorter, a lot skinnier was the other boy. Thin faced, hollow cheeked, sharp high cheekbones, pointed chin. There was a grin on his face as he pointed comically at Frankie. His clothes were scruffy and there was a hole in the jumper he wore, one side of the collar of his shirt was out, the other tucked in, he had shorts on too and his needs were knobbly on his slender legs; lighter in colour than Frankie's his hair was longer and scruffier but pushed away from his face so that it stuck up here and there on his head and looked spiky. Jacob.
Marelle stared at it.
"It was his birthday." Jacob said in a quiet and shattered voice. "I remember the day so well. Just after his Dad took the picture a Vulcan bomber flew over, really low. Frankie was convinced his father had arranged it!"
"Whats a Vulcan bomber?"
"Huge delta wing bomber, made to carry a nuclear weapon. British plane – beautiful thing – loudest plane you'll ever hear but so majestic …"
She watched him. He was back there.
"I gave him the number plate off the Jeep on that day. I didn't have anything for his birthday so when I saw the Jeep parked outside the shop, I managed to rip the rear plate off it. Cut my fingers nearly to the bone – had to wipe the blood off it before I gave it to him."
"Looks like he loved it!"
"Yeah … things were simple then …" He sat there, silent, holding the photo but then began to cry. Really cry, silently, his shoulders shaking as he hung his head and placed a hand up to his eyes.

Marelle slid sideways to him, wrapped an arm around him. Frankie's words came back to her and she felt the tears welling up again. They held each other amongst the scattered furniture and ripped up floorboards with Frankie's memories around them and his words in their heads which would remain with them forever.

After a while Jacob sighed and sat away from her.

"I'll put it back."

"Put it back!"

"Yeah, its where Frankie wanted it, he didn't mean *me* to find it."

"You can't put it back – you cant just leave there under the floorboards."

"Its safe there. He left it for someone else to find ..."

"And someone who it means nothing to – someone else who will think its junk and throw it away! *You* found it Jacob – Frankie would be glad that you found it – it means more to you than anyone else on the face of this planet! Keep it and keep it safe."

He sniffed. "Maybe."

She rubbed his back. "You'll have to put the floorboards back though."

She watched as he put the things back into the tin. He closed the lid and sighed.

"I just know he's here, somewhere. I can feel him – and I can imagine him saying the words he's written – I just don't know where he is." And he snapped the lid closed again.

It took him most of the afternoon to put the floorboards back, followed by the carpet and the furniture. Marelle unloaded the shopping and went up to help but proved to be more in the way than anything else.

Marelle watched him. He was good with his hands but sometimes she thought it wasn't what he was truly put on this earth to do. He stayed there that night for a third night in a row and all night long Marelle pondered on calling Bella off – this wasn't a game she wanted to play with Jacob but, then again, she *was* curious.

The barbecue gave them a hard time. Jacob suggested it wasn't a good idea to try and carry it all the way down to hers – she thought he was back pedalling but then he asked if they could put it in her car.

"Will it fit in there?" She asked.

"You could get probably get the whole caravan in there!" He commented.

It entailed driving up to the main gates, unlocking them, driving down to his caravan, shoving it in and then doing the reverse. It took them over an hour but eventually they placed it in her garden and he began getting it ready.

Bella arrived just after lunchtime. She bundled in with a bag full of bottles and a hug for Marelle.
"Bella." She said quietly, looking to make sure Jacob was still outside and out of earshot. "Bella, go easy on him. He's a bit fragile at the moment ..."
"Why? What have you done to him?" Bella laughed.
"Nothing – but he's just been electrocuted, remember? And he has a "few things' going on – what with Seb and everything."
Bella gave her a hard stare. "We're all going to have fun. Relax!"
They both walked out into the garden. Jacob was poking at the barbecue. He'd got changed a little while ago.
"Oooh, I like a man with confidence!" Bella remarked. "White jeans and a barbecue – that's confidence!"
Jacob turned and gave them a smile. Bella eyed him and grinned.
"Nice jeans! Bit snug!"
Marelle jabbed her in the ribs as he turned back to the hot coals.
The white jeans were a bit tight – Marelle doubted she could have got into them, but they did look good on him!
"Right." Bella smiled. "Lets get the party started!"
Bella followed Marelle into the kitchen and picked up two bottles of wine from the bag she'd brought with her.
"Whats it to be?" She asked.
"I don't mind."
"No, I mean for him." Bella nodded towards the garden.
"Oh I don't think he'll drink wine."
"Oh sure he will!" Bella smiled. "Well lets go for pink wine – he's got white jeans on he can have pink wine!"
Marelle laughed. "Stop going on about his jeans!"
"I can hardly!" Bella grinned. "They don't leave much to the imagination!" She wandered around the kitchen with the bottle. "You got a corkscrew? I broke the first rule of pissing it up! No screw top!"
Marelle opened a drawer and handed one to her. Then she turned to her friend and asked
"Bella. Bella, Seb hasn't put you up to this has he?" It had been playing on her mind for the last few days.
Bella stared back at her, slightly aghast that Marelle had even asked that let alone thought it. "What! No, of course not. I don't give a fuck what Seb thinks. I'm doing it for you ... but I can tell he's a keeper ... in those *very* tight white jeans!" She grinned, then added "... but he did say to try and persuade you to keep away from him. I just wish I'd been there to see you give him a piece of your mind!"
"He's lucky that's all he got." Marelle said, angrily.

"Still ..." Bella mused. "You did say you had some great angry sex on the back of it." She winked.

Marelle smiled coyly and followed her outside.

Bella handed Jacob a large glass of wine.

"Its that or nothing I'm afraid." She said. "I forgot beer."

Jacob didn't protest but took the glass and held on to it while he poked the barbecue.

Everything went well. Jacob was happy with his task in hand an acted like any normal guy – albeit quiet – and kept out of the way while Marelle and Bella continued in their normal giggly way.

After eating and picking at whatever was left for a good while – which was somewhat dominated by Jacob insisting everything was practically cremated because, in his own words 'he'd had the shits once from a barbecue and wasn't going to suffer that again'. He had come out with it as such a proclamation and in such a way that they had both fallen into a fit of giggles over it. Jacob couldn't see what was so funny and had remained at the barbecue with a straight face which made them laugh even more.

"He really, actually fucking means it!" Bella had giggled to Marelle.

Then the attention had turned to the motorbike. If she had thought about it beforehand Marelle would have suggested that they had put it out of the way – but she hadn't and now Bella was looking at it.

"Take me on it!" She asked.

"Nah! I'm not taking anyone on the back of it again." He had replied.

"Oh go on. *Please*?" Bella pleaded.

"Go on Jacob!" Marelle joined in. "Bella will love it. She won't be scared like I was."

"I'm not sure its working properly yet."

"You started it earlier ..." Marelle commented.

Jacob sighed.

"Go on ... *please*!" Bella said again.

"Quickly then." He said and walked towards the bike. The key was in it, and he kicked the stand away and moved it away from the wall.

"Have you been on a bike before?" He asked her.

"Of course I have!" She replied.

He pushed the bike to the airfield and sat astride it.

"Come on then."

Bella was enthusiastic, she ran over to the bike and climbed on behind Jacob.

"Hold on tight." He said and kicked the engine into life. Bella hugged him around the waist and they started off up the runway. When they went faster she could hear Bella screaming – not out of fear but

whooping with sheer delight. Marelle laughed to herself and stepped to the side to get a better view. They went right up to the second turn around and started back. Bella suddenly had both of her arms in the air, still screaming. Jacob stopped the bike, put his feet down and turned to say something to Bella. When he obviously didn't get the answer, he waited. Marelle watched him fold his arms and just sit there. Eventually he started of again, this time Bella kept her arms around his waist. He came back to Marelle, a broad smile on his face.
"What happened?"
"Oh he's feisty today, isn't he?" Bella exclaimed. "Told me to sit down, shut up and hold on to him or I would be walking back!"
"You're a bit heavier that Marelle and if you had kept that up, we would have both been off!"
"Oh my!" Bella laughed. "This one really has no social filters with a little bit of wine added, does he!" But she was laughing as she patted Jacob's shoulder. He was still smiling broadly so Marelle smiled too and gave him a little kiss.
Bella looked at them both and grinned.
They went back to the garden, drank wine, started the barbecue off again and had the same argument about the food being burned then spent the evening sitting in the warmth of the gently glowing coals. Despite the efforts, the alcohol inside Jacob only had the effect of making him appear more 'normal'; relaxed, joining in the conversation and joking along with them. Bella's plan seemed to be working and she keep topping his glass up when he wasn't looking and he was a good deal more relaxed than Marelle had ever seen him before. She and Jacob were sitting on the wooden bench, his arm around her shoulders, the wine glass in his other. Bella was on a garden chair separate from them.
"We had a hard time getting the barbecue here. Marelle had explained. "I had to put it in my car!"
"You got that in your car!" Bella exclaimed.
"After a fashion ..."
"It's a big car." Jacob said. "Why have you got such a big car?"
"Because Seb gave it to her!" Bella chirped in.
"He did not *give* it to me. I *bought* if off him." Marelle corrected. "He had a '*camping phase*' and bought it for that but Caroline didn't like camping, so he sold it to me."
"I did wonder why you've got a car like that." Jacob said.
"Whats wrong with it? It's a Mercedes!"
"It's a family car." Jacob remarked.
Bella laughed.
"Yes – and we got the barbecue in it!" Marelle had the last word.

"We should have just had the barbecue at your caravan Jacob. It would have been fun and we could have just crashed out in it at night." Bella piped up.

"Nah, nah, nah." Jacob shook his head. "Cant ... I don't have a toilet."

"Well what do you do?" Bella asked.

"Shit in a bag and chuck it out the window!" He exclaimed, pointing at Bella.

"He does have a toilet." Marelle said but Bella was laughing with Jacob.

"Wow! He does have a sense of humour!"

"I am not joking." He continued, taking a big mouthful of wine and cuddling Marelle closer to him. "This is just like the old days ..." He sighed.

"What *old days*, Jacob?" Marelle asked, quick enough to pick up on what he'd said.

He laughed and told her "Ssshh" as he turned to her and surprised her with a full on, tongues and all kiss.

Bella made a 'fingers down her throat' gesture and then grinned.

"Get a room you two."

So try as hard as Bella had they could not elicit anything adverse from Jacob whatsoever. The only tiny chink of light had been his comment about the 'old days' but it could have just been a one off remark that meant nothing. In fact, this evening had only gone to show his growing trust and interest in her.

Although Marelle had pre-warned Bella of Jacob's night time escapades he slept soundly right through until he did eventually wake Marelle in daylight when he got out of bed. Marelle questioned why she always forgot to pull the curtain as sunlight streamed in through the window. Maybe it was so dark outside here and there were no streetlights to light up the night that she never realized they were still open. She opened her eyes, squinting for a moment or two until they adjusted and she saw him sitting on the edge of the bed, his back towards her, bowed and his head dropped. She could see his backbone and ribcage as he hunched forwards. He yawned and groaned.

"Ok?" Marelle questioned.

"Mmm" he said. "I'm going to have a shower."

"What time is it?" Marelle asked, pushing herself up and looking at the clock. Half past six or thereabouts. He stood up and in all of his nakedness went to go out of the room.

"Remember Bella's here!" Marelle reminded with a grin.

"Oh, I don't mind."

"No, but I do!" She exclaimed. "Put my dressing gown on."

Without argument he slipped into her pink silk dressing gown and held it around himself – it fitted where it touched and that was about it. Marelle laughed and stretched out across the bed.

Fifteen minutes later he had gone downstairs and Marelle had followed shortly after when she heard him open the back door. When she got there, he had filled the kettle and switched it on and was now outside sitting on the bench, dressed now and with sunglasses on. Marelle joined him – he had a hangover, she could tell but he didn't want to admit it.

"Bit delicate?" She asked.

"A bit. I've not felt like this for years and years. This is what happens when I drink wine plus Bella just keeps filling your glass up!"

"I know. You have to keep hold of your glass with her around – she just wants everyone to have a good time – just like she is."

"I think her heart is in the right place." He commented.

"Oh definitely. Bella is one of the good guys – you can trust her and she will always be honest with you – too honest sometimes!" Marelle smiled.

"How long have you known her?"

"Since school. We have got up to a lot of mischief in our time – but never trouble. She can get wild if she's being egged on."

" – and no boyfriend yet?"

Marelle laughed. "Hundreds of boyfriends but no 'significant other'; she likes flirting too much!"

"What does she do?"

"Believe it or not she's a primary school teacher!"

Jacob gave a little laugh and winced at the same time.

"She cuts loose when she gets the opportunity but otherwise she is 'Miss well behaved.'!" Marelle smiled. "I can guarantee she'll get up and want a huge breakfast!"

"Count me out of that one." He said quietly. "How much did I drink?"

Marelle shrugged. "I don't know really. Theres one left in the fridge, I bought two, Bella bought four ... I think?"

"Jesus!" He said. "Have you got any paracetamol?"

Marelle laughed. "Yeah, hold on."

When she returned outside with tablets and a glass of water he pointed to the sky above the airfield at a large bird circling above on a thermal. It had bands of white on the underside of its wings and a forked tail. Marelle looked up, it looked like an eagle.

"Red kite." He said. "Not seen one of those around here for years."

As predicted Bella got up an hour or so later full of life and talking breakfast.
"Hey, why don't we barbecue breakfast?" She enthused.
"No. I don't think so – its probably only you eating anyway." Marelle replied.
"Only me?"
"Jacob is a bit 'delicate' and I don't really do big breakfasts. I'll just have toast in a bit ..."
"Wow! Whats wrong with you two? What are you made of!" She smiled. "Ok, I'll cook my own but theres no nicking the bacon when you smell it!"
She went inside and cooked her own breakfast. Jacob watched the red kite for a while until it disappeared with Marelle sitting beside him in the early sunshine. Bella eventually came back outside with her breakfast and a mug of builder's tea, sat down in the chair with it on her knees and tucked in.
Jacob had coffee. He looked at her when she sat in front of him.
"You're not having any! You said no!" She joked, waving the fork at him.
"Its ok." Jacob said, sipping coffee.
"You need fattening up!" Bella remarked. "Look at you. Its criminal that you could get into those white jeans last night!"
"I'm ok." He said.
"That wasn't a big sesh anyway. I'll get you well and truly plastered next time!" She winked at Marelle.
"Theres one bottle of pink sparkly left." Marelle said.
"Well we'll keep that for next time!" Bella laughed.

Jacob was still there when Bella left. He'd been tinkering with the bike and cleaning the barbecue and was now still in the garden when Bella was getting ready to go.
Standing in the kitchen with Marelle they both looked out at him in the garden.
"Look at him." Marelle smiled warmly. "He's just so irresistible!"
Bella laughed. "You've done well, turning him round!"
Marelle thumped her playfully on the arm then looked out at him again and smiled.
Bella stared at her. "I've never seen you like this!"
"I've never met anyone like him before!" Marelle sighed. "Its like he's just been waiting here all of the time for me to come along ..."
"I wouldn't doubt for a minute girl that's he's not been a player in the past. He knows what he's doing!"
"He told me he's never had a meaningful relationship."

"Probably had loads that he didn't give a shit about then!" Bella grinned.
Marelle shrugged. "Who cares? He may have belonged to somebody else once – but he's mine now!"
"When's the wedding? I'll make sure I'm free!" Bella smiled and raised her eyebrows.
" – he'd run a mile!" Marelle whispered.
Bella grinned. "Yeah, and a little while ago you said he'd run a mile if you tried to kiss him – now look where you are!"
"Well I wouldn't have to invite Seb, would !?"
They both laughed.
"I'd better go." Bella said, she walked to the door.
"I'm off Jacob – see you soon."
He looked up, didn't say anything but raised his hand and gave a small smile.
She grinned. "You make sure you look after her, wont you?" She called to him.
He looked to Marelle then back to Bella with a lopsided grin on his face. "I'll try." He replied.
For the rest of the day he seemed quite subdued, even by Jacob's standards. Marelle put it down to him being hungover – he didn't normally drink much, and they had put it away a few bottles between them although she had actually drunk very little. She'd caught him now and again standing staring into space for a good few minutes at a time but he may have just been watching something on the airfield. Marelle had let him be – just happy that he was at her house in her garden.
Later on, he said he would go back to the caravan tonight. Marelle made a sad face at him.
"I'm back at work tomorrow so I'll be off early." He explained.
"I don't mind ..." Marelle offered. "Please ... you could move all your stuff in here if you wanted?"
He gave a strange little laugh which came out to Marelle as a warning.
She stopped and stared at him, wide eyed in that her mouth had run away with her.
Jacob realised that his response had deflated her somewhat and he shook his head and smiled as he stood looking down at his hands on the back of the kitchen chair.
"I will stay tonight but I *will* need to go to the caravan for a couple of nights ..."
She smiled. "I didn't mean to ask you to 'move in' as such ... but ... well ...."
He smiled. She liked his smile and seeing it more often made it even more appealing.

"I know." He said. "I like being here. I like being with you but sometimes I need to be on my own."

"I don't like you being on your own when you are upset about Frankie."

"I've been on my own virtually since the day I was born. "He said, quietly. "And nothing has happened to me yet."

He moved away from the chair and stood behind her, his hands on her shoulders.

"Its just part of being me ... and being with me. Pretty soon I may be looking for somewhere to live anyway, I wont have much longer over there. Its been my home for the last ten or so years, so I want to go back now and then while I still can."

She sighed, lifting her shoulders up and down under his hands.

"I understand ..." she replied, softly. "I just worry you'll go and never come back!"

He came round to the front of her and stared right at her, right into her eyes.

"And why would I do that? Hey?"

She shrugged. "Sometimes I feel that's what you're going to do ..."

He shook his head. "I'm not going to do that!" And he pulled her in to him for a hug.

That night was awful. Apart from the night he had gone to the weir this had to be the worst one she had spent with him. He must have woken up with a jolt an either sat bolt upright or stood up at least ten times. Marelle lost count but was lucky if she had grabbed twenty minutes sleep between each episode. Sometimes he looked to still be asleep, sometimes he was definitely wide awake; sometimes he swore; sometimes he was silent; sometimes he said a random word. The most legible that she heard seemed to be 'just fucking lunatic' to which he stood up and stared out of the window at the night with a sigh before he walked back and got into bed again.

"Whats wrong?" She had asked, sensing he was awake.

"Nothing." He replied.

She snuggled herself into his back and lay her head against him. He felt tense; she could hear his heart beating. Marelle closed her eyes and listened. As much as she got close to him and as much as she tried to hold him to her heart, she felt she would never fully know what was within his. But as she listened, she was perfused by the dark thought that one day, inevitably, that his heart would stop beating and he would exist no more; just as she would and everyone else she knew. That made any time she had with him so precious and a world without Jacob seemed like her own nightmare stretching into the night. And with every beat she knew that was a passage of time that had gone forever – a moment together that was forever lost.

Marelle hugged him very tightly when he left in the morning. He looked kind of sad today – like the clock had been turned back a couple of months but she put it down to lack of sleep – maybe? Jacob kissed her goodbye tenderly and then got onto the bike.

"Jacob, maybe you should get yourself a crash helmet if you are going to keep riding the bike ..."

He gave a little smile. "I'll think about it."

" – Have you got the phone?"

He nodded, about to start the bike.

"Call me at lunchtime."

He dropped his arms to his sides as he sat astride the bike. "Why?"

"Because I cant go the whole day without hearing your voice!"

Jacob gave that half cheeky smile that she liked so much.

"Ok."

He called her just after one. She loved his voice on the phone – it sounded so different to when he was in front of you. It was much richer, and you got a sense of how well he pronounced his words.

"What are you doing?"

"Calling you ..."

"Very funny!" She laughed. "Where are you?"

"In the van. I just pulled over to call you. Been in the workshop this morning."

"And you're ok?"

"I'm fine."

"I know you said you wouldn't stay tonight but, are you coming to dinner?"

There was a pause. Then he laughed gently. "Yes, I'll come to dinner."

Marelle heard the bike coming and was surprised he hadn't walked down. She went straight through to the kitchen, but he was already coming through her back door. He had obviously been to the caravan first as he was smartened up and clean. He walked through the door and placed a brand new, black crash helmet on her table. He turned his eyes to her with that slight smile that actually looked a little bit self satisfied tonight.

"Better?" He asked.

"Thank you Jacob." Marelle beamed and could not help herself but to give him a hug. The thought that he had actually been into a shop and purchased this was a revelation in itself. Where she did not know but at least he had made the effort to do as she asked. He still seemed quiet and did not have his usual enthusiasm for food. Conversation was a bit hard, but he seemed relaxed and happy enough to be there.

Over the meal a strange hazy yellow light had filled the world outside. Marelle commented as she stood looking out of the window after washing up.

"Theres a really weird light out there ..."

"It's the harvest." He said. "They've started so there's a lot of dust in the air. If its an easterly breeze its probably dust coming over from the Sahara too. It happens a lot this time of year."

She pointed out of the window. "But this is really odd. The sky is pale yellow."

He got up and stood beside her, looking out of the window.

"I've seen it like this before." He looked for a bit longer. "Shall we go out for a walk?"

It was weird. There was a density to the air that she had never felt before; it was warm and muggy and everything was bathed in the eerie yellow light. Even the sun that was beginning its westward journey was a very, very pale yellow in the dust filled atmosphere.

"The sun is almost white." She said. "It should be a yellow sun!"

He gave a wry smile and walked her out to the airfield. She took his right hand and gripped it in hers.

"This is weird." She said again.

"Frankie used to say it was an 'end of the world sky'. Like the world was about to end but no one else had realised and you could feel it dying beneath your feet ..." Jacob said, almost with a smile. "Or the sky after a nuclear blast ..."

"You kids really had a whale of a time, didn't you!"

"Its what we talked about!" He shrugged. Then was silent for a while, wandering beside her – no purpose to his stride tonight.

"I keep thinking about his words on that note in the biscuit tin." He said quietly after a while. "He said 'you may laugh at us but we were *real* too once.'"

Marelle tightened her grip on his hand.

"He used the word *real* which gave it an existence – a personality, ambition – a life and a legacy. We were *real*."

Marelle didn't know what he was getting at so said nothing.

"Its that one word that makes me think we all underestimated Frankie. He had a much deeper understanding of everything that no one realized. There was something "untapped" about him that no one will ever know about – or what it may have led to."

Marelle walked beside him, still unsure of what he was talking about but remaining silent.

"And I can still feel that. I still feel like he is here …" Jacob stated, determinedly, "I think he is here, somewhere. "He paused and drew a breath. "I'd like to dig this whole place up."
"What? The whole airfield!"
"It's the only way we would know."
"But can you?"
He laughed. "No – its over a thousand acres – that's whats left now … and it doesn't end there. How deep do you go? Notwithstanding that it would take me longer that we have left plus I don't have my own excavator." He sighed. "Its too late."
"Do you think he's buried here then?"
"He's here – I don't know if he was intentionally buried but he's still here …"
"Would they not discover him when they start building?"
"Probably not. Even if they have archaeologists in then they'll just do a couple of trenches. What's the chance of one of them being hitting the correct spot?"
He looked at the ground in the clinging yellow air.
"If we don't find him before they move in then he's gone forever."
The hazy sun was catching all of the fluffy heads of the dandelions and illuminating them in the ethereal light. There were millions of them. The grass was knee high and dry, dotted by a thousand pastel hued wild flowers.
"Where did you put the biscuit tin?" Marelle asked. She had noticed it missing earlier.
"Its safe."
"Where is it?"
"Its ok, its safe." He repeated.
"You didn't put it back under the floorboards?"
"No. Its safe. Its ok."
"Where?" She asked again.
"I buried it."
She stopped and stared at him. "You *buried* it!"
He nodded.
"Why?"
"So its safe."
"Surely it would be safer in the house?"
He shook his head. "Its safe. Its ok."
"You haven't buried it on here?"
" – no! Of course not!" He exclaimed. "No one else will find it. But I know where it is."

Marelle sighed as she looked up to him. He smiled and she lay her head against him so he could wrap his arms around her.

"Look at this place." He said, his head resting on top of hers. "Just look at it. How can they take this away? How can they reduce all of this to concrete and tarmac? Hey?"

Marelle turned her head and looked at it. If it had been a painting, you would have questioned its integrity.

"Have you heard from that guy?"

"No – but he's got your number. He'll call as soon as he hears some anything but all he can hope to save is the actual missile site – not this."

Marelle turned herself around against him, her back into him, his arms around her from behind. She reached her hand up to grasp his against her chest.

The scene was an unearthly one. Bathed in a golden yellow light, still and warm. The air full of illuminated motes of dust and flying insects. The grass high and proud – burnished by the sun and bejewelled by flowers in pastel colours as bright as the day. Birds were singing, the solitary cry of a buzzard above – and all in this tiny little universe, all bounded by the perimeter fence. Maybe this was an end of the world sky – the portent of things to come here. Maybe this was its last day in the sun.

"I wish i could put all of this in a box and climb inside with it ... shut the lid. I could die a happy man then."

"Jacob!" she reprimanded quietly. "Don't say that."

"Three score and ten. I've had over half ..."

"Don't talk about things like that." She said.

"Why, its inevitable ... it's the only thing in life we can count on ..."

"Count on? Like its something you are *relying* on?" She asked. "You can count on me – death is inevitable, yes but don't talk like that!"

Behind her he sighed and gave her a little squeeze. She gripped his hands tighter in hers. She didn't like him talking like this – she always had it in her mind of his brother's fate and the way Jacob was sometimes made her uneasy with that history. Marelle didn't want any thoughts of this entering her mind as she couldn't imagine a world without him now. There was always a morbid curiosity to ask more about his brother, but she always felt a discomfort from Jacob. Digging any deeper might open a wound that would never heal.

Eventually they wandered back. He was intent on sleeping in the caravan tonight. He picked up the crash helmet from the table and put it on top of his head before he leaned forward and kissed her. Then he pulled the helmet down.

"I cant see your face with that on." She said.

Her gave her a look with his eyes that suggested he was smiling.
"Be careful!" she called after him – he'd not ridden the bike in the dark before – at least not to her knowledge. "See you tomorrow."

The whole room had a pale blue hue to it, with the cool colour adding to the feeling that this brought. She was expecting to see her own breath condensing in front of her as she exhaled heavily and closed her eyes for a few seconds in preparation. When she opened them again she could see Seb's solemn expression glaring back at her with 'I told you so' emblazoned in his blue eyes.

The grey door in front of her opened slowly, only a foot or so and a young woman came through it. Her blond hair was pulled back tightly into a bun, no make up, pale blue shirt and navy blue trousers. She had no colour in her face.

"Would you like to come in now?" She asked in a quiet voice which did not penetrate the cold air and walked a step forwards as she spoke. Marelle nodded and they went through the door, moving into a space between that and another door. The space was lit by a single strip light, glaring coldly.

"Do you want to be by yourself?" I can wait outside or I can come in with you if you would like me to? Its entirely up to you."

"I'll be ok by myself." Marelle replied dryly, her voice sounded tiny with the vacuous atmosphere of the small space.

"He's just in here." The woman opened the second door.

Marelle looked at her, no expression on either of their faces as she passed through the door and into the other room.

The walls were dark grey, the floor and ceiling white – it was lit by LED downlighters that robbed any warmth that may have existed from the area. Behind her the door closed with a gentle click. She took a breath and focused on the centre of the room.

Jacob lay on a bed there. He was covered from the neck down by a pale blue sheet, perfectly pressed and totally creaseless. Marelle could see the shape of him beneath it, his long legs and his feet beneath the sheet at the end. She walked forward. Running a hand gently along the side of the bed and up to his shoulder where she stopped and looked down at him.

He was perfect. His features so precise and chiselled, his broad forehead, so smooth and flat, his cheekbones so defined, his features all in such a perfect balance and harmony. But his eyes were closed and his skin so pale. His lips were in a tiny smile but unmoving.

Marelle wanted to look into those eyes again; to see his soul within connect to her again. She wanted to kiss those lips and feel his ribs expand under her hands as she held him.

"Jacob." She said and stared hard at him.

He did not stir; he did not move; he did not breath. Marelle reached up and ran her fingers through his hair. It had flattened so she stood it up again as she had always done, flicking her fingers through the ends to make them spiky.

She lifted the blue sheet. Just enough to look at his chest, his collarbones, his arms flatly by his sides. Those hands, practical and able to turn themselves to anything yet so gentle and caring – so subdued when they could have fought.

He'd drowned they said. Drowned! How could Jacob have drowned when he was such a strong swimmer? Just how? She looked at him, skin so perfect but so pale, so smooth. There was not an ounce of fat on him but he was not skinny; his muscles all defined but not bulky. The bruise from the time they'd fallen off the bike was still visible. It had faded but was still there as it would be forever now.

Her eyes wandered to his chest – still not moving – and she though about his lungs inside – about their last taste of air and the water that had taken his life still within them.

She shook her head in disbelief. Lowered the sheet and looked down into his face. With a featherlight touch she caressed his cheek, but she was shocked by the cold plasticity of it. She felt her lip begin to tremble as her touch gained no response. She touched his other cheek with her other hand and held his face in them, staring down at him. Then she tenderly placed a kiss on his forehead. Swallowing back a whole tidal wave of emoting she gently placed her lips onto his.

As cold as stone and with all of that soft gentleness gone from them. Marelle kissed his lips and looked into his face but there was not a single flicker of a heartbeat within him.

Then the tears came and the flood of emotion as she could contain it no more. Marelle bent double and sobbed so intensely it robbed her own lungs of air as she closed her eyes tight shut and screamed into the silent room.

Marelle awoke with a breath in her throat and tears streaming down her face. She sobbed as she sat up in her own bed and felt for Jacob. She panicked in that moment as her brain struggled to untangle nightmare from reality which took too long as she began to sob harder. Clasping her hand across her mouth and losing her breath in the screams and sobs she was unable to control. Grabbing her phone from the bedside table in sheer desperation she dialled with only one thought in her head.

The phone rang. Marelle looked at the clock. It was twenty past three. The phone rang and rang.

"Jacob." She said to herself. "Jacob!"

The he answered. Voice gruff and croaky, sleep audibly falling from him. But alive.

"Hi." He said.

Marelle cried and sobbed, unable to get any words out for a good few seconds.

"Hey, hey! Whats wrong?" He asked, calmly. "Whats the matter?"

She took a breath and rubbed her eyes with the heel of her hand. "I thought you were dead."

"What?" He laughed.

"I dreamed you were dead ... I was with you in the morgue." She dissolved into tears again, crying bitterly.

"I'm fine. I'm here!" He replied, soothingly.

"I thought I'd lost you!" She sobbed.

"I'm fine. It was just a bad dream – it was just a silly dream!"

She cried down the phone.

"Marelle, are you ok?"

"No – " She cried. "I need to see you!"

He sighed, almost mournfully. "Ok, I'll come over. I'll be there in two minutes, ok?"

"Ok." She cried.

"I'm fine Marelle. I'll see you in two minutes."

Marelle heard the bike start up across the airfield. Thirty seconds later she ran downstairs and through to the kitchen, fumbling with the key in the lock, she finally opened the back door, still sobbing to herself with hands shaking. Outside it was a pitch black and pretty moonless night. She pushed the door wide and stood out on the step as Jacob appeared out of the darkness. She burst into a flood of tears as soon as she saw him – running towards him and meeting him halfway along the path. In a tirade of tears and snot she flung herself at him and held him tightly to her.

"Its ok." He whispered, hugging her back. "I'm here, I'm ok."

She cried and looked into his face, held his hands in her hands, looking into his eyes. She gripped his arms, touching every inch of him, crying all of the time.

"I thought you were dead!" she cried.

"I'm not. You can see I'm here, you can touch me and see me!"

"Oh God!" she sobbed. "It was so real Jacob ..."

He hugged her to him. "Come on, lets go inside."

Jacob walked her in. She was still crying to herself and clung to him. He sat her down at the kitchen table and flicked the kettle on.

"Why on earth are you dreaming something silly like that?" He asked.

She shook her head. "It was so real. You were there in the morgue, right in front of me. I touched you but your body was so cold and lifeless ..." She looked up into his eyes as tears streamed down her cheeks.

"Its ok. Its not real." Jacob said, placing his hands over hers.

They drank the tea he made and Marelle calmed down a bit but kept dissolving into tears. He said he would stay for the night and eventually climbed into bed by her side and wrapped an arm around her.

"I can still see it all so clearly." Marelle said. "It will haunt me forever. Don't let that ever come true."

Jacob squeezed her. "That was just a dream, but I promise I wont ever let that come true."

Marelle was still shaken by it when he left in the morning. It was only now as he stood in her kitchen in daylight that she realized he must have thrown on random clothes and come straight down to her last night. He stood there now in old, ripped jeans with a creased navy blue shirt and his unlaced workboots. He also hadn't bothered to wear the crash helmet in his mercy dash to her last night. Marelle hugged him tightly until she could feel his bones beneath her hands.

"You going to be ok?" He asked.

"Yeah, as long as I know you are." She replied.

"I'm fine!" He said with a smile that was now looking familiar. "Flesh, blood and heart still beating!" He rapped his knuckles against his chest.

"Well lets just keep it that way." She remarked. "See you later."

He nodded. "I'll have the phone if you need to make sure I'm still alive!"

She shot him a glance and shook her head playfully back as he set off on the bike.

It had shaken her to the core. Never before in her entire life, had she experienced a dream that was so real and so tangible that she found it hard to believe it had not actually happened. The image of Jacob on that slab was still vivid in her mind and the cold sting of the utter, utter lifelessness of him when she had touched his skin. Sure, she'd had nightmares or stupid dreams which woke you up with a start, heartbeat racing and adrenaline pumping but nothing that had driven so icily into the very core of her in the way this had.

The overbearing fact that was still clawing at her heart was that she would find life without Jacob unbearable. She could not imagine a world without him or never setting eyes on him again. What had started as a meagre curiosity had grown legs and arms and now clutched tightly at her heart. Marelle had always been one to fall deeply – if anything mattered to her it mattered heart and soul to the point of obsession. Jacob was more than that. She'd always known she was in deep with him for what he was and how he looked but now she knew her life and his were woven together in such a way that she must ensure they were never parted or her own heart would not be able to continue beating.

Bella had always laughed at her; always getting into serious relationships while Bella cast anyone aside with abandon. Marelle had been with Chris for just over eight years and had not broken it off first. She supposed she would probably have still been jogging along with it now. However, she had never, ever felt like this about Chris – he had been the right person at the right time – this was different. Jacob was the point of her existence, and all of this had happened to bring them together. She knew now she was meant to be with *him* and nothing on this earth was going to take him away from her.

He came to her that night and stayed without argument. Marelle found herself staring at him even more than usual, mapping every last inch of him in her mind even more intensely than she had before. Little things she'd not noticed previously were suddenly obvious to her – like the way his left eyebrow was very slightly higher than the right one; the smooth, straight concave curve of his noise which she'd always thought of as straight and sharp, the absolute squareness of his shoulders ... and when he looked at her now, how he focused on her. Jacob was the master of looking at you without engaging with you ... he had that thousand yard stare that would look in your direction but see right through you. It was a learned skill no doubt that he had perfected but now, when he looked at her, she did not see that anymore – she saw his eyes perfectly focused on her and her alone.

He hadn't said anything more about wanting to dig up the airfield, but she knew he was desperately trying to think of something. She'd spent days on the internet now to no avail – just the same articles and the same stories. Marelle had tried every search combination she could; she had searched random words that might yield results and she had even read numerous other cases where kids had disappeared thinking that it may lead to something that would put her on the correct course. Most of them were found within twenty four hours, alive or found later dead. One that had remained unresolved for over thirty years was rare if not unknown in all she read – so nothing had really helped. This morning she returned to searching Suffolk archives and news stories.

At lunchtime she went out, stepped over the fence and began to walk up the runway. She knew Jacob wouldn't be there but she just wanted to walk up there on her own, just to see if she felt the spirit of an eleven year old boy guiding her to him.

All she felt was the heat of the sun on her back as she walked up the concrete strip. She stopped to look in to the distance, shielding her eyes against the sun and suddenly noticed a vehicle at the gates. She stopped, stood and stared. It was a large blue lorry with what looked like equipment on the back of it. Her heart lurched and she felt panic course through her as she felt in her pocket for the phone.

Jacob answered with worry in his voice.

"Hi – everything alright?"

"I'm fine but theres a lorry with construction stuff on it at the main gate."

There was silence for a moment or two.

"Are you there?"

"No. I'm halfway up the runway. I was going for a walk when I saw it."

He sighed. "I'd better come and see what they want. Shit!"

"They said six weeks, didn't they?"

"Yeah ... they have keys ... they can get on if they need to ..."

"Did you want me to go and see who they are?" She asked.

"No. no. Its ok. I'll come down. I'll take an early lunch."

Marelle carried on walking towards the gates, Jacob would no doubt be there before she was.

As she approached, she could see the lorry had two portacabins on it, there was a driver standing at the gate and a telephone, papers in hand. When he saw her coming, he looked hopeful and gestured to her but at the same moment Jacob turned up in the other side of the gate in the white transit van. The driver was about to call to Marelle when Jacob walked round behind the lorry. He had sunglasses on again.

"Can I help?" He asked.

The lorry driver looked between them. Marelle walked up to the gate and watched through the chain link fence.

"I've got to drop these off here." He said and held out the paperwork. "Told to ask for someone called Frost."

"That's me." Jacob said.

"They said you would open the gate so I can unload them."

"I can but I didn't think work was starting yet ..."

"I don't know anything about that – just picked them up from one site and told to bring them straight here rather than back to the depot ... I only know what I'm told ..."

Jacob sighed. "Do you know where you've got to put them?"

"In there." He said, pointing.

"Devorah have their own keys ... "

"Who?" He asked. "I don't know anything about that – I'm just the transport company. I get told to go from A to B. I don't know the whys and wherefores."

Marelle stared at him as Jacob read the paperwork. He looked quite business like in doing so and she gave a little smile to herself.

Jacob sighed again. "Ok." He handed the paperwork back. "I'll let you in – I don't know where they've got to go – just put them anywhere – but on the concrete, not on the grass."

Jacob walked up to the gate face to face with Marelle the through the wire. She smiled at him but he bowed his head and undid the padlock. Then he opened both gates, dragging them across the concerete until they were fully open. He stood by one as Marelle stood by him.

"This is unexpected." He said.

"Its sounds like he's just dropping stuff off."

"It's the thin end of the wedge. They've staked their claim now – it'll be this every couple of days."

The lorry moved onto the airfield then over to one side where there was a larger concrete area. Jacob left her side and walked over to there. She watched as he directed the lorry driver, told him where to put the portacabins, oversaw them being lowered down from the lorry, then guiding it backing up to depart. Finally, he pulled the gates to with the two bright blue portacabins now standing on the airfield and walked back to her. He looked defeated.

"You could have refused to let them in." She said.

"Whats the point?" He answered. "Just makes everyone's life difficult. If I start getting reticent it will get me chucked off sooner."

"What are they for?"

He shrugged. "Offices I suppose – for the hoards of people who will be crawling about all over here."

"Can't you call thy guy who's trying to save it?" She offered.

"He'll call if he has any news. Its not the whole airfield anyway – just the Thor Site – it probably wont stop most of the work – if, that is, he gets any joy." He looked contemptuously at the blue buildings then turned his back on them.

"I'd better get back."

"Don't you want to come home and have some lunch – now you're here?"

"No – I don't feel much like eating." He replied.

She gave him a smile and grabbed his hand.

"Jacob." She pulled him to her. He reciprocated, hugging her, kissing her once then kissing her again – the second time he meant it!

"Sorry." She said when they broke apart.

"What for?"

"For calling you. If I'd have not said anything then they may have gone away."

He gave a lopsided smile. "They wouldnt, don't worry – if they're there they'll come in …"

She looked to his eyes but only saw herself reflected; she wanted to reach up and take the sunglasses off; but she didn't.

"Well be careful then." She said, oddly. "I'll see you later."

He went out of the gate, pulled the chain through and locked it. She was standing right against the wire, her fingers through the holes, forehead pressed to it. Jacob jangled the keys in his hands then came back to her. He kissed her gently on the forehead through the wire then he walked off with a grin.

Jacob turned up on the bike at a quarter to six but was massively distracted. He picked at food, didn't want to make conversation or eye contact and was walking around with his shoulders hunched. She had tried consoling him with the odd hug or peck on the cheek, but everything just seemed a distraction from the cold hard truth that he had chosen to concentrate on.

He eventually stood up with a sigh and announced:

"I'm going off on the bike for a bit. I'll only be on the airfield …"

She wanted to go with him but didn't want to add to the burden he was so obviously carrying.

"But you'll come back here, wont you?" She asked.

"Yeah, I wont be long." He replied, taking the crash helmet with him.

Marelle heard the bike for a bit. Then it stopped. The sun was getting low in the sky. She knew where he was. By now she could tell by the sound of the bike where he was on the airfield. Smiling to herself she picked the bottle of pink fizz out of the fridge that Bella had left behind and set off at a brisk walk.

Marelle rounded the trees and walked up to the missile site. The bike was parked up beside the one facing into the sunset and Jacob was there, sitting on the low wall, his back to her, his face to the sun. he had one leg drawn up, his chin resting on his knee. She didn't want to make him jump so she walked a little closer before she said:

"I thought you'd be here. I'd say a penny for them but I know what they are."

Jacob turned his head slowly and looked to her as she walked up to him. She gave a smile and stood on the ground against his extended leg.

"It's a beautiful sunset again." She said.

"Suffolk knows how to do a sunset." He remarked.

"I brought this in case you wanted to make an evening of it?" She held up the bottle.

He shook his head but held out an arm to wrap around her.

"I don't want to drink at a time like this …"

Marelle cuddled in to him, standing the bottle down in the grass.

"If there was anything I could do, I would." She said with her head against him. "Can we buy it?"

"Its millions." He sighed. "Prime development land, out of town industrial site."

"Cant we contaminate the land?"

He gave a laugh that had no humour in it. "I don't think so." And he hugged her to him, tightly.

Marelle felt his pain; she felt that moment when he had unlocked that padlock and opened his universe wide; when he had been forced to allow them that foothold – that moment when he felt all was being lost.

TEN

They remained like that for a while, his arm around her, huddled to him, both staring into the sunset without saying a word.
Eventually he sighed. "So this is it then?"
She turned her face to him, not sure what he meant.
"This is how it ends ..." He said quietly. "A gradual onslaught of machinery and people onto here – next week it will be something else, then something else ... then people will come, and they will start tearing this apart. This is how it ends – thirty two years of searching. I always thought I would find him."
"Jacob. "She said, holding his hands as he stared into the sun. "Its not over! We've still got a bit of time."
He shook his head. "But theres nothing we can do."
Marelle sighed. "Well cant you borrow the digger and start digging it up – like you said?"
He shook his head.
"Its not over yet." She stated. "We've still got time."
The sun was getting lower, escaping for another day; the light was pinkish red. He was till staring into the sun; she looked to it as well. He waited until the glowing ball of fire sank below the horizon then he stretched both of his legs down and stood on the ground. Marelle turned to him and hugged him – he felt tense.
"I'll walk back." He said, turning to pick up the helmet. He gave a sigh as he did so.
Marelle thought about all she'd read in the past couple of days and sought in desperation for answers. He turned back to her with the helmet in his hand; a last bit of sunlight caught it and it reminded her

of what she'd read about the 'glowing eyes' of Black Shuck in Suffolk folklore.

"What was Black Shuck?" She asked him, pretty randomly and out of the blue as her mind wandered.

He gave a small and tight grin – "Black Shuck is a demon dog who roams the Suffolk countryside – my father once …"

If blood could drain instantly out of someone's face in a more visible way than it did from Jacob's right then, Marelle had never seen or experienced it. He froze and stared back at her. His eyes flickered for a second and the helmet fell from his hand into the grass. He had the weirdest expression on his face that fell between abject fear and wretched misery. He clapped a hand across his mouth as his eyes dissolved into an expression that was wild.

"No, no, no, no, no!" He whispered, coming forwards towards Marelle, then turning suddenly and clamping both hands on his head as he stared at where the sun had been.

The noise that came from him was unearthly; it was sob that rattled with a scream in it that he expelled until there was no more breath, then he turned back to her, his mouth half open, his hands still on his head.

"Jacob, what is it!" She asked, scared now.

It was like he couldn't breath, it was like fear and realization had completely paralysed him and he just stood there gasping.

Marelle grabbed him, shook him before he fell onto her, his head over her shoulder and he gasped a noisy breath in again.

"Jacob!" she said, holding him, his full weight against her. He staggered, she pushed him back to the low wall and sat him down.

"Jacob!" She said, right into his face, he stared at her, trying to form words, shaking his head.

She shook him. "Whats wrong? What did I say?"

His head seemed to wobble on his neck, he lifted his chin and looked her right in the eyes. His face seemed so thin, his eyes so dark and his chin so pointed as he drew himself into that position. His dark hair was longer than it had been, but it stood up on his head from his running his fingers through it moments ago. Right now, he looked possessed by some demon that had come out of her mention of Black Shuck. He gasped in a breath and she realised her was trembling beneath her hands.

"I know where Frankie is." He said.

The kitchen was dark and cold. He walked in furtively and warily, opening the latch on the door and sliding around into the small space where it was ajar. No-one was home; there was not a fire and there was no electricity as the meter had run out that morning. Moonlight illuminated half of the kitchen. He walked in, dragging his feet and slumped down on a chair. For a few moments he sat there in the darkness; his stomach rumbled, and he could hear his own breath in the sharp coldness. He shivered. Then with his dirty little grazed hands he pulled the candle in the holder forwards to himself, pulled a match out of the box on the table and struck it. The flame came to life with a hiss, grew and reached up into the cold, dark air. He lit the candle then shook the match until the flame died and a wisp of smoke curled away, marking its existence. The yellow light from the candle illuminated his face. Its light flickered on the walls in a macabre dance of light and shadow. There were tracks of tears on his face although he couldn't remember crying.

He sniffed and sat playing with his fingers in the light of the flame. He shivered again. If he went to bed it would be colder. At least here he had the candle and the light. His mind re-ran the events over and over again, his face in a tight uncomprehending expression and his eyes looking towards the cold, hard floor.

After a while he got up and filled the kettle from the tap, turned on a gas burner and lit it with a pop. The blue flames licked around the bottom of the old kettle when he placed it on the ring. Going along the cupboards he searched for tea, or coffee, or something. There was nothing. That was normal and if there had been anything he would have been better placed to leave it for his father for the morning. Behind the sink there was a milk bottle with an inch or so of milk in it, he eyed it but decided to leave it there. The kettle boiled and he switched the gas off. Lifting a mug down from a hook along the shelf he poured in hot water and then stirred in two teaspoons of sugar with the crusted up spoon out of the sugar bowl standing next to the milk bottle. While it was hot it could warm his hands, when it cooled her would drink it.

His father's car pulled up against the house. It sounded loud, as if he had parked right on the garden near the front door. The engine wound to a stop and he heard the driver's door slam. He expected his father to burst in through the side door straight away but there was a delay, followed by a second car door slamming. Footsteps approached the door, slower than usual, laboured with mutterings and swearwords. He stood up and had one hand reached up to the latch when the door unexpectedly flew open, knocking him and sending him backwards – he thrust out a hand to steady himself, but in the process knocked two empty pans from the side of the cooker onto the floor. There was an almighty crash in the dark of the otherwise silent kitchen as his father rolled in through the door.

"What are you doing in here?" He snarled, obviously surprised to find him there. In his arms he held something wrapped in a blanket. It didn't

appear overly heavy but was bulky and he was struggling to get it through the doorway.

"Get to bed!" he shouted as the miasma of alcohol and cigarettes filled the kitchen with his breath. There was a sheen of sweat on his father's face and his dark hair was flopping over his forehead. "Bed!" he shouted again, still struggling to get through the door.

"Whats that?"

"Never mind!" His father raised his voice again angrily. "Get out of here!" With some exasperation he finally backed out of the door. Laying the bundle down in the passageway by the back door and the shed.

"What is it?" His small voice asked again.

"Nothing. Go to bed."

"Whats in the blanket?" He asked with the curiosity of a child.

His father looked at him, his face red and angry . "I've just run over Black Shuck. I need to bury him …"

As his father turned away, he sidled up to the half open door and peered through the gap. In the darkness he could see the grey mound on the floor, the blanket haphazardly covering it.

"Get out of here!" His father suddenly snorted, turning back and finding him in the way, staring at the bundle on the ground. "Get out!" He shouted in a desperate and irate voice; he raised a hand and swiped it down forcefully against the side of the child's head. His hand swiped again immediately. Still recoiling from the first fist, he ducked away, ran out into the dark hallway and up the stairs to his cold, dark bedroom.

That night he slept in his clothes under the scratchy blanket and did not acknowledge the tears that ran down his cheeks.

Marelle raised her eyes to Jacob in the gathering darkness. He was in pieces and fragmenting before her very eyes. She felt that she had to gather him up both to keep him together and make some sense of what he had just told her.

Right now, he was walking round in small circles with his hands on his head, sobbing to himself.

"Jacob, sit down." She said, sitting herself on the wall. He continued pacing, breathing heavily, sobbing, saying 'no' and shaking his head, "Jacob."

He stopped and stared at her. "I know where he is." He said. "I know where he is!"

With that he lunged at the bike – Marelle leapt from the wall and in one stride grabbed him. He was in no fit state to start off on the bike.

"Jacob, no!" She said, "Wait, tell me where he is and why you think he's there …"

"He's over there. He's in the garden!" he exclaimed, wide eyed and no longer in control of any aspect of himself.

"Which garden?"

"*Our* garden."

She looked at him oddly then realized that he meant the garden of the house where had had lived as a child.

He made another unearthly screaming, breathing sound and just stood there as he cried. "No!" He had out his hands on his head again. "No!" he cried, bending over, then crouching with his head in his hands.

She went to him, placed an arm around his back.

"Jacob, come back with me and tell me all about this."

"No!" He suddenly exclaimed. "No. We need to go there now …"

"We cant Jacob, its dark."

He stood up and turned to her, crying bitterly and burying his face into her.

"Its ok." She said. "Lets go back and talk about this – nothing needs to happen right now."

It was like leading a zombie back to her house, Marelle wasn't sure how she managed to get him and the bike back but they both eventually stumbled into the kitchen and she turned on the light.

Jacob looked awful, almost unrecognizable; it was as if weight had dropped from his face instantly and darkened his eye sockets. He was shaking and could hardly make it to a chair.

Marelle put the kettle on, locked the back door and pocketed the key. No-one was going anywhere tonight.

'So," she said, eventually sitting opposite him with a mug of tea. He had one too but was staring at the floor with eyes that were as lucid and awake as glass. "What are you saying?"

"My father ran him over and told me it was Black Shuck."

She stared at him.

"He told me that. He was drunk and angry – he hit me pretty hard and I was scared. I didn't put two and two together – I'd forgotten about it until you mentioned Black Shuck."

"You can't be sure Jacob. Perhaps he did run a dog over?"

"It was the same night …" He stated, shaking his head. "Black Shuck is a myth."

"I know but, well, do you really think it was Frankie he ran over?"

Jacob nodded. "I know it was."

Marelle shivered.

"He was drunk." Jacob said. "He was *always* drunk. There's a cut through at the corner – Frankie must have gone under the fence and ran the other way, straight down the track through the allotments and onto the road ..."

"Surely your father would have said if he had run over a child?"

Jacob snorted. "You think so? What – when he was blind drunk, driving home – probably with no lights on – he would have lost his job, his home, ended up in prison probably – or lynched by the villagers. He was a coward – he killed Frankie and told me it was dog."

Anger was setting in now.

"Maybe it *was* a dog Jacob. You don't know."

"One way to find out." He said.

She stared at him.

"Dig up the garden where he buried him."

There was silence as the whole situation slowly sank into her.

"He buried *something* in the garden – I never gave any though to it after that night. He just got worse – he just hit me more and more if he saw me or if I even spoke – Frankie had gone and my life was hell – why would I think anything of what he did that night?" He stood up. "I'm going to dig the fucking garden up now."

"No Jacob – no you cant just go and dig up someone's garden at night. Think about yourself in this ... you don't want to make it worse for you." She grabbed him. "Lets think about it first – *please*."

He looked at her hand on him, sat down and began to cry again.

She let him cry; she sat across the table from him with her hand clasped over his, not saying a word. If he stopped sobbing it took only a few seconds to start again once the thought of it all entered his brain again.

"We've got to be sensible Jacob." If you go ploughing in – which I know you want to, and I can understand why – its going to be a mess and you're going to end up either hurt or in trouble." Marelle eventually offered.

He was staring at her hand, crying silently.

"If you really think that Frankie is buried over there then maybe we should tell the police."

That animated him. "No –!" He shouted. "No!"

"It may be the best thing to do."

"No, no, it's the worst thing. What questions do you think they'll ask? Hey? They'll want to know how I know."

"Then we can tell them ..."

" .. and they'll really believe me?"

"I believe you."

He shook his head. "No police. I want to find him – I don't want anybody else finding him." And he started to cry again.

Marelle watched him cry. Ok, so no police.

She could not console him, whatever she did. Any suggestion she made was instantly rejected – Jacob was so far out of reach at the moment it was like she had a different person sitting in her kitchen. Marelle decided to let him just cry and rant as much as he wanted. He sat at her table all night. The hours passed in that arduous but vicious circle until eventually he began to tire. Soon he had laid his head on the table; by four thirty in the morning he was asleep. She decided to leave him there and sat herself in a chair opposite with a duvet around her. He needed sleep and she needed to keep an eye on him. Tomorrow was a new day. Marelle kind of dozed now and then but never fell into a deep sleep. Jacob remained out for the count; totally and completely sound asleep on her kitchen table. He didn't look comfortable but she didn't want to disturb him, so she let him be. When sunlight began to come into the window, she expected him to stir, but he didn't. Marelle got up quietly and closed the blind in the kitchen. By eight he was still dead to the world as she slipped silently out to the hallway with her phone.

Marelle found the number for J.F Wright and Son – Farmers and dialled the number. A woman answered in a hurried voice.

"Hello."

"Oh, hello. Could I possibly speak to Mr. Wright please?"

"Who is it?"

"My name is Marelle, I'm Jacob Frost's partner. I spoke to Mr. Wright the other day."

"Hold on."

Seconds later Mr. Wright spoke. "Good morning."

"Hello Mr. Wright. It's Marelle, Jacob's partner ..."

"Hello my dear." He said. "How can I help?"

"I'm ringing for Jacob. I'm afraid he's been really unwell all night – he's got a bit of a tummy bug I think. He wants to come in to work but I think he should stay at home today – if only to stop everyone else getting it!" She bluffed in a voice that was as honest as the day was long.

"Ok, ok, yes I agree. Its no problem and thank you for letting me know."

"Ok, thank you. I'll tell him." She smiled.

"Let me know if he needs another day tomorrow – and I hope he feels better soon."

"That's very kind, thank you." Marelle replied and said goodbye. She was not sure that would be the case.

By ten o clock she began to worry. She almost wanted to check his pulse and hovered over him for a good few seconds. He *was* breathing; she could hear it. His head was resting on his arms folded beneath it, his eyes closed and no visible tension in his face. Marelle stared at him. He looked deathly pale in the dim light with the blind half closed. His hair needed sharpening up a bit – she could see to that later. He just didn't look a patch on his normal positive self but a night asleep on her kitchen table together with yesterday's events were probable contributors to that.

Marelle was hungry and she needed coffee but didn't want to wake him. Her head was banging through lack of sleep, but he slumbered on.

Just before half past ten he stirred, sat up and looked around himself with the face of a confused three year old, woken suddenly from a nap. He looked at her, looked about himself then sat himself up fully, slowly. "Morning." Marelle smiled, reaching up to open the blind. The light flooded in and he squinted as it blinded him.

He sighed, "what time is it?"

"Half ten – you've been well out of it!"

He suddenly stood up, giddy from sleep, wobbled and steadied himself on the worktop. "I've got to get to work."

"No you haven't, I called them. You're not going anywhere today. Sit down."

"What?"

"I called Mr. Wright – you've got a tummy bug – don't want to pass it on to everyone else, do you?"

He stared at her "Why?"

"Because after last night you are in no fit state to go to work or operate machinery."

He sighed again. "What did he say?"

"He was very nice about it."

"I wish you hadn't done that ..."

"Why?"

"It just makes me look stupid – getting you to call in for me – I need to be able to keep working there."

"But you can! Its just one day off sick! Its fine – no-one suspects anything or even questions it. And to be frank Jacob – you just need someone looking out for you sometimes ..."

He looked tired, standing there, gripping the back of a chair.

"I think there's some things we need to talk about." She said. "But why don't you go and have a shower and I'll make coffee.

He closed his eyes for a second or two, opened them and stared at her. He gave a long sigh then took himself upstairs.

Coffee and toast were on the table when he came back downstairs. Jacob had put clean jeans on but had come down with his t-shirt in his hand. Marelle didn't stare but she was not used to seeing him so undressed during the day. It reminded her of the dream of him in the morgue – the protrusion of his collar bones and the taughtness of the skin over his torso. The bruise from the bike stil poked out of the waistband of his jeans but was a more dirty yellow colour with a brown centre now. He put his head through the t-shirt then sat down with it just round his neck. He'd combed his hair back and into a side parting – it didn't suit him, she thought but as soon as his hair started to dry it would stand up again anyway. He sighed, placed his elbows on the table then rested his chin on his hand.

Marelle caressed his bare shoulder as she walked by to get her mug of coffee. She sat down opposite him with a smile.

"So, shall we go through what you told me last night? Now that we are both a little more used to the idea?"

He made a little grimace; bobbed his head.

"Yeah." He finally said. "I've been thinking about it."

Marelle smiled at him in encouragement.

"I think maybe I should go on the rest of this journey on my own ..." He avoided eye contact with her when he said it.

She was shocked to say the least; she felt the bottom drop out of her world at that moment with the gravity of what he'd said, pulling at her insides.

"Jacob, no!" She gasped. "I said I'd help you, I'm in this with you."

He shook his head. "I don't want to drag you into anything – I don't want you getting hurt."

She shook her head. "No Jacob. The only thing that is ever going to hurt me is not being with you."

"That's possibly one of the implications ..." He said.

"What do you mean?" Jacob if you're saying things like that then I'm not leaving your side."

"I don't know what's going to happen if he is there, but I don't know what's going to happen if he's not either ..."

Marelle swallowed noisily.

"Nothing Jacob, nothing is going to happen. I'm not walking away from this – how could I? How can you even say that?"

"You wanted to call the police."

"I said that because I thought it would be easier for you! I'm not going to do it ... I'm with you in this Jacob – I wouldn't do anything you didn't want me to. I promised you all of this and I keep my promises!"

She found she was almost crying.

"My whole fucking life is a lie!" He said.

"Of course its not!" She cried, wanting to hold him but scared of what reaction she would get. "Don't say things like that! We're so close now Jacob ..."

He looked at the floor, sniffed, didn't say anything.

"Jacob, I'm here with you all of the way no matter what – I promised you before and I promise you again. I dreamed you were dead the other night – I've never felt like that ever before – don't push me away again now!"

"Again?" He asked.

"Yes, again! That day on the airfield when you told me I asked too many questions and told me to go away. You made me so angry!"

He smiled. A warm genuine smile, which, when given lit up the room with his humility. "I'm not pushing you away. I just don't want to hurt you."

"You're hurting me now."

He sighed.

"Please Jacob! I've been thinking about this too – there is a way ..."

He raised his eyes to her.

"I think we've got to make an excuse to dig around there and then 'accidentally' come across whatever is down there."

"And how do we 'make an excuse' to dig up someone else's garden?"

"Well, can't you dig out a ditch nearby ..."

"And just accidentally dig a lump out of their garden?"

"Yes!"

He thought about it for a moment. "And wouldn't it be a bit strange if I happened to accidentally dig up a lump of their garden where there just happened to be a body?"

She shrugged. "These things happen ..."

He stared at her, the t-shirt still just round his neck. She pushed toast towards him.

"Eat." She said "I've put that lime marmalade on it that you like."

"How do you know I like lime marmalade?"

"Because you always eat the bits I put it on!"

He raised his eyebrows.

"Is there a ditch along the garden?"

He nodded.

"Cant you dig that out and accidentally take a bit too much away?"

"I don't think that ditch has been cleared for a while. When my father died, and they sold the house off they kept a strip of land at the back of it to dig a drainage ditch. That part of the field used to flood really bad. So, they kept that land and dug out a ditch. But right after that the council did a lot of drainage work along the road which sorted out the problem in the field. The ditch is always pretty dry and doesn't get cleared out as often as its not a priority."

"Well, maybe you could do it."

He was thinking about it.

"Couldn't you just say you had to dig out a bit of their garden to … find a pipe or something .. then go in there? We could go and ask the people who live there if it was ok if we did that?"

"I can't remember how close the ditch is to the part where I think Frankie might be buried …"

"Well can't we have a walk up there and have a look?"

"I could have a look …"

"If we had a look and it looks possible, we could go and knock on the door to let them know what we wanted to do. We could lay it on really thick … say it was very important for the farm – and that we would put it all right again afterwards." She explained. "Which we would."

"We?" Jacob asked.

"Yes, 'we' she stated. "I'm here to help Jacob; I'm here until we find him – no matter what!"

"Let me think about it.' He said.

"I'll go and knock on their door." She said. "I don't mind."

He ate one piece of toast then finally put the t-shirt on properly. His hair was still quite flat with that odd parting which she didn't like and was itching to run her fingers through it.

"It might work." He finally said. "Wright's going away for two or three weeks from Monday so I'm free to do what I want. its probably better if I tell him that ditch needs clearing though – at least then it won't be random."

"Perfect." She said.

"Ok, we'll go and have a look then we can finalise the plan." He added. Marelle tilted her head. "*We?*"

"We." He stated.

ELEVEN

Today he was remote to say the least. It was as if his mind was off somewhere else, but his body was functioning in 'limp mode.' What he had said that morning had chilled her to the bone but the idea she had fabricated on the hoof had pulled him back to her – but it had scared her.
They drove up the road to the field behind the house where he used to live and he told her to pull into the entrance to the field. It was possible to see the front of Jacob's old house across the road from her property but to get to the back was a short drive down the main street and along a lane through the fields at the back of the house. The crop in the adjoining field had been harvested and he assured her that the car would not be in the way. They got out and walked along the edge of the stubble field; first along the front by the road the took a left right-angle up the side of the field towards the back of the house Jacob had grown up in. The field had been harvested but the grass in and along the ditch was long and sunbleached. The ditch started halfway along. Slowly they walked towards the house, now painted yellow. There was an oak tree at the extreme right-hand side of the garden, right on the edge of the ditch. Jacob walked slowly to the other side of the tree, then stood looking at the house.
It had been extended to the left and had a relatively new looking conservatory on the back. It all looked very neat and tidy. The garden was almost a perfect square, quite flat and featureless except for a small greenhouse and a table and chairs on a concrete patio beside the conservatory. There was no door on the back of this house like hers, but

it had a small passageway leading from the front to the back on the right hand side with the 'back' door half way along there.

Jacob was standing staring at the house.

"Which was your bedroom?" Marelle asked.

"Top right." He stated. A small window, set high on the first floor. "It looks much grander than it used to. Looks like its loved and looked after."

"So this ditch is new?" Marelle asked, pointing to it.

"Well, relatively. The garden used to come to about here ..." He drew a line with his foot. "They kept this strip and dug the ditch. Before that you could walk right out onto the field. He stepped to his left a little. "Used to be an old apple tree about there – they must have chopped it down."

"So, where ..." Marelle asked, not really knowing how to express it.

"About here." Jacob extended his arm and looked down it with one eye closed. "The ditch has actually brought the spot well within the reach of the digger."

"How do you know exactly where ... "

"Just looking at the back of the house – it was next to a rhubarb patch, right in the middle. My father had a greenhouse beside it, but it was massively overgrown and wild by that time. I'd say its probably in line with me here, about two or three feet in."

"Can you get to it?"

He nodded. "But I'm going to have to dig into their garden by two or three feet – I've got to be accurate, if we go with your story of having to dig a culvert in. I'll only have one chance, I just cant keep on digging."

Marelle absent mindedly pulled dead heads off the dry grass and scattered them as she too stared at the house.

"Be nice to pace it out from the back of the house but I think I can work it out from here."

"So you say Mr. Wright is away from Monday – are you going to do it then?" Marelle questioned.

"I cant really do it before. I can say the people in the house asked me if we could clear the ditch – it is a bit of a mess."

They both stood staring at the back of the house. Jacob started walking up and down, pacing it out where he was.

"You reckon you know where?"

"Yeah." He confirmed, standing straight and pointing into the garden. "Here." He looked tense as he said it, defiant, staring into the garden as a woman appeared from the conservatory and began walking across the garden towards them.

"Oh dear." Marelle said under her breath.

The woman walked across. She had a towel in her hands and kept walking straight towards them. She probably in her forties, dark hair pulled back into a short pony tail. Marelle had seen her before, usually ferrying children in a dark grey four wheel drive. She strode up, smiling at least.

"Hello!" She greeted in an overly jolly way. "Can I help you? I've noticed you've been staring at my house for a while?"

"We're from the farm." Marelle replied, brightly and confidently. "We are planning on clearing this ditch next week – it hasn't been done for a few years ..."

"Oh, ok. It is a bit of a mess! My husband was going to ask at the farm if it could be tidied up a bit – so that would be good!" She smiled.

"Ok, no problem." Jacob said.

Marelle looked to him, he had pulled the sunglasses down.

"We might have to dig a culvert in here for a couple of feet – there should be a drainage pipe under there, somewhere!" He explained. "I'll try not to make too much of a mess, but I'll put right anything that needs doing afterwards."

"Ok, that won't be a problem." She smiled. "When will you do this?"

"Probably on Monday." Jacob replied.

"Oh, that's fine! We've got a family party on Saturday, but Monday will be absolutely fine. There probably wont be anyone here then – I will be at work and my husband is in Europe for a few days ..."

"Ok." Jacob nodded. "Many thanks for your co-operation, much appreciated."

"Perfect!" Marelle remarked to him as they began to walk away and head back to her car.

When they finally stood beside it, Marelle reached up to him and ran her fingers through his hair so that it stood up and got rid of the side parting.

"That's better!" She said, "It needs a trim ..."

"You can take it all off if you want." He replied.

"No –!" Marelle answered. "No Jacob, it wouldn't suit you, I like it like this."

He had that lost, despondent look about him – far from a smile and avoiding eye contact.

Marelle reached on her tiptoes and kissed him once.

"We'll do this together." She said, with a smile. "No matter what we find."

"Hey! Hey!" Somebody called unexpectedly, grabbing both of their attentions. It came from up the field in the direction they'd just walked down. Striding towards them was the woman from the garden, she was smiling and waving the towel in the air to get their attention. She hurried up to them, a little breathless. She must have crossed the ditch somehow.

"Just had a thought …" She explained with a smile. "My husband wants to start a vegetable patch at just about that spot in the garden – if you could, well – just break the surface in our garden for that it would be a huge help …"

Jacob stared at her from behind his sunglasses.

"If you can?" She asked, expectantly smiling – "I'd be happy to give you a drink for it …" She added as an incentive.

"That would be fine, wouldn't it?" Marelle interjected before his blank staring became suspicious. She turned to him for confirmation. "In the circumstances we'd be happy to do that for you!"

"Yeah, yeah." Jacob finally replied, "that won't be a problem. I can reach with the digger."

"Great!" She laughed, clapping her hands together with the towel between them. "Just a square would be fine – as a starting point for him!"

Jacob nodded. "Ok."

"Great! Glad we can all help each other!" Marelle smiled.

They got into the car.

"Now I'm digging a vegetable patch too." Jacob remarked.

"Well thats just handing it to you on a plate, isn't it – you can pretty much dig where you want…" Marelle smiled. "They actually *want* you to dig their garden up!" She tried not to sound too enthusiastic in the circumstances. "And they're not going to be here … we really couldn't have asked for more."

"It's a sign of fate." Jacob said. "Someone up there wants me to find him."

Marelle gave a sympathetic smile. "Maybe they do."

The trick now was keeping Jacob grounded until Monday when he could take the digger up behind his old house and dig into the spot where he was convinced Frankie lay. Everything had come together in such a way that even spiked Marelle's belief in something much higher being at work here. Despite everything and despite her resolve to go on this journey with Jacob she was, deep down inside, doubtful that this would have the outcome he yearned for. Jacob spoke about his father with little kindness but even so Marelle could not believe that a man who was a father himself could – albeit accidentally – run over a child then take the course of action that Jacob claimed he had. Their plan had come together but she suspected they may find the remains of a dog or other wild animal down there. But, as with her floorboards, Jacob needed to look for himself.

"How long will it take?" She had asked with him sitting on a chair in her kitchen while she trimmed his hair following another argument about how much he wanted her to take off.

"About a day. All being well I'll get up to there by mid afternoon. I'll have to start at the bottom and clear the whole ditch out otherwise it will look suspicious."

"Can I be there?" Marelle asked, "I want to be there."

"That'll look a bit strange wont it? You hanging around while I did out a ditch?"

"I could sit in the car." She suggested. "I can bring you lunch ..."

"I don't think I'll feel like stopping for lunch." He said quietly. "I suppose we could get away with you sitting in the car."

Marelle stood back. "There." She said. "I'm leaving it like that – it looks too good to ruin by taking more off."

He looked in the mirror. "Ok." He sighed.

She placed her hands on his shoulders as she stood behind him. He was tense, rigid beneath her hands. He'd had a momentary loss of control when he'd made the connection between her mention of Black Shuck and where Frankie might possibly be but now he'd gathered himself inwards, bottled it away inside and once again adopted that air of indifference. Marelle had to admit to herself she'd noticed he pulled the sunglasses down when talking to strangers – that was his final shield of defence behind that air of indifference that he hid himself behind. She'd often thought about wanting to peel away his layers – as yet she hadn't completely managed that but at least she had exposed them – if only to herself.

The crying distressed wreck he'd been the other night was probably the tiny, exposed, soft body of his true self – let loose for that period when his emotions had finally turned the key and let what was really beneath it all visible.

She squeezed his shoulders slightly. He was just sitting staring at the floor. Marelle wanted him to stay tonight – she wanted him to stay every night but especially now when she was so worried about what he may consider if he was on his own. She had locked the doors last night and kept the keys with her – she didn't know what he would say if he knew but right now her priority was to keep him safe.

He did go to work the next day, on the bike with the crash helmet on. Her only worry with that was Sam but hopefully he'd scared himself with the electric shock enough to wind his neck in. Jacob was keen to get there and begin making moves to execute their plan. In the end he had stayed the night, strangely without much persuading and he had slept soundly with his head on her breast while she had played with his hair. Marelle just had to keep it that way for the next three nights. After that they would likely be back where they had started and she could relax a little.

Saturday he had hung around. She had expected him to hook off on the bike but instead he tinkered with it. At one point he even had the bonnet up on her car – said he was checking it for oil and water because he didn't suspect she ever did! But if it kept him occupied then she was happy. A couple of times she looked out and he was just standing there, staring out across the airfield – stock still and deep in thought or otherwise. She'd spied on him tinkering with the bike or when he was looking at her car. He had a methodological approach to everything, thought about everything carefully – worked with confident hands and a surety with anything mechanical.

Mid afternoon she walked out to him with a mug of tea. He was standing with one hand on old concrete fence post, staring up the runway.

"What're you doing?" she asked.

"Nothing. Just wondering …"

"About what?"

"Life, existence and everything." He sighed.

"Oh, ok." She handed him the mug.

For a moment she stood there with him, staring out at the airfield too.

"Well how say tonight you get your glad rags on and I take you out for a meal – just you and me?"

"Where?" he asked.

"Quiet little restaurant, near Birdfield – I've driven past it many times – looks lovely …"

He made a face for a fleeting second. "I'm not sure."

"Just you and me…" She said. "No one else. It's a tiny place so even if its full it wont be crazy. Just the two of us, we've never actually been out together properly before …"

"I don't really do things like that Marelle." He excused himself.

"Well I'm taking you. Treats on me. All you've got to do is look nice!" She took his arm. "For me …" She added. "No one will know us there, no-one will recognize us, we wont have to speak to anyone else!"

"I know." He said with a certain reticence. "I'm just not comfortable doing things like this."

"Why?" she asked with a laugh. "Whats so intimidating about it?"

He shrugged. "I just don't like social situations."

"But why? Whats happened to make you so uncomfortable? I'm not asking you to stand up in front of a crowd and make a speech, or dance or sing in public! Its hardly going to be a social situation. I've picked the

smallest, quietest place I can find. I just thought it would be nice to go out – just you and me – as a *couple*!" There, she'd said it.
He didn't react, just stared at the airfield for a good number of seconds. "Ok." He finally said.

Marelle was thrilled, so thrilled that she didn't protest when he said he would go back to the caravan to get changed – leaving her there to do the same.
Tonight, she wanted to dress up for him; he'd never seen her at he best after all – probably, normally, at her worst. So, while he went off to the caravan, she pulled out clothes that had not seen the light of day for years. She spent ages doing her hair and make up to perfection then stood in front of the full length mirror in the spare room and had to admit she was pleased with what she saw. The tight, black off-the-shoulder slinky dress had not had an outing for ages, she liked how slim she looked and the way the four inch heels made her legs look long and slender. With her hair in a half up, half down style it also made her look taller – which she also liked. Just touching up her lipgloss in the mirror she heard the back door open and close.
Marelle didn't rush. Firstly, because she had four inch heels on and secondly because she wanted to make an entrance. So, she walked slowly down, took careful steps through the living room and into the kitchen doorway.
And there he stood. She'd wanted to make an entrance but there Jacob stood in all his well groomed glory in the middle of the kitchen floor wearing the black jacket she liked him in that had survived the blood from the cut on his head – now cleaned and perfect again. It fitted him so well, hanging so pristinely from his square, straight shoulders, sleeves of the jacket the perfect length. It was very slightly fitted and worked so well with a plan white t-shirt beneath. He had black jeans on that looked brand new teamed with a plain, but smart belt and a fantastic pair of black and white patterned, pointed boots, complete with silver tips.
He'd done his hair, actually made it spikier – maybe for her – and he had a glint in his eye with that lopsided grin on his face. A warm genuine smile, a perfect smile.
Marelle smiled; she thought about scrapping dinner and pushing him against the kitchen table right now!
"You look nice." He said.
"Nice?" She laughed.
"Different!" He replied. "I've not seen you dressed like that before."
She grinned. "I scrub up well …"

"I can see." He commented.

"And you're not so bad yourself! In fact you're pretty damn hot!" She grinned and could not help herself but plant a kiss on his lips.

With the heels on she was more his height, shoulder to shoulder with him which was nice, but she preferred him being taller than her.

Marelle smiled at him again. How could this be the same guy she'd knocked on the caravan door of in the dark when she had first moved here. But he was, and it had been all her own work bringing it out of him.

"Thank you." She said.

"What for?"

"For coming tonight. For being you!"

He raised one eyebrow, looked like an awkward six year old which made her smile again.

"Why not let me drive?" Jacob asked.

"No, its ok."

"You can have a drink then, I don't want to …" He suggested.

"You're not insured to drive my car."

He shrugged. "I'm probably covered third party on my own insurance …"

Marelle considered it for a moment.

"Doesn't seem right, you taking me, I should be taking you." He said.

"Ok, ok, then." She finally conceded.

It was strange being in the passenger seat in her own car. Stranger with Jacob driving. She had not been driven by him in a car before, but he drove in the same way he approached everything – with a workmanlike methodology! He drove smoothly and considerately, reversing the car perfectly into a parking space outside the restaurant with a precision and accuracy she could have only dreamed of! He opened the car door for her, and she took his arm as they walked across the small car park.

The restaurant, quaintly called 'the Mustard Pot' was a low ceilinged, thatched building, criss-crossed inside by exposed studwork. It was small but fairly busy. There was a bustle which meant they could get lost in it but not enough to intimidate Jacob. Marelle had booked this a few days ago and had specifically asked for a quite corner table and that was exactly what they were led to. They weren't too close to anyone else and Marelle let Jacob sit with his back to the wall. All in all he seemed happy. When he relaxed and smiled Marelle loved him all the more! He'd turned heads when they'd walked in – Marelle had noticed and she was proud. Now he sat across from her, right where she wanted him. For some reason Marelle had expected him to struggle with making a choice from the menu but he had no problems and ordered what he wanted without hesitation. Marelle had a glass of wine, but he ordered coke.

"So?" He asked, "what is this in aid of?"

"Nothing, I just thought it would be nice ..."

"It is, but I feel that you have a motive." He grinned.

"No, nothing. I just wanted to go out with you, like his, as a couple, on a date."

He smiled, raised his eyebrows. "Fair enough."

Marelle chuckled. "Are you not used to going out like this?" She was teasing him.

"Not for a long time, no." He replie. "And to be honest, not ever, really."

"How come?"

"How come?"

She nodded to him repeating her question. "How come someone like you has never been on a 'date' like this?"

He shrugged. "Just didn't – not with a girl anyway."

"So you went on a date with a boy then!" She knew what he meant but liked teasing him.

"No." He smiled. "If I've been in a restaurant, its been on my own or with a group of people ..."

"Don't believe you." She said. "You're too damn cool and sophisticated to have never done this!"

"Me, sophisticated?" He laughed.

"You look it." She mused, leaning towards him.

He smiled, a little embarrassed and looked down. Marelle looked briefly to her right. There was a larger party just along from them, eight people; a family she guessed as there were two older people, two younger couples and a couple of teenagers. They weren't noisy and were engaged in their own conversations – and just far away to not be a problem. However, as she glanced across, she caught one of the females staring at them; no, staring at Jacob. Marelle glared back and the woman looked away again. Marelle looked back to Jacob.

"You can have one drink." She said to him, "If you want?"

"No, I'm ok."

"You sleep better when you've had a drink." She remarked.

"I know. But I don't want to go there – or else where does it end?"

"What do you mean?"

"Well, you drink to give yourself confidence; because you're feeling down; because you're bored – or because you cant sleep – it's a slippery slope and I've seen it all first hand." He sighed. "I can take it or leave it but I'm not going to start using it like that."

Marelle smiled at him. Shit, he looked so good tonight! Then she caught a glimpse of the dark haired woman on the table beside them, staring at Jacob again.

This was no coincidence. Jacob hadnt noticed, Marelle had. She stared her down again, but she wasn't looking at Marelle – she was staring at Jacob.

Their first course came and they tucked in. Twice more Marelle caught her staring again. She staked her claim, leaning forward and kissing him full on the lips with a lingering note.

"Oh wow what was that for?" He asked.

Marelle gave a cheeky smile. "Just felt like it!"

She wanted to ask him if he knew the woman who obviously couldn't take her eyes off him and at the same time, she wanted to confront her. But if she did, either it would break the spell or probably send Jacob into tailspin.

Marelle kept quiet but made sure she had staked her claim as publicly as possible. Sometimes she touched his face, tousled his hair, held his hand across the table all the time shooting meaningful glances at the – not unattractive – woman on the other table with her languid dark eyes firmly fixed on Jacob.

In her snatched glances, which she was trying to accomplish without Jacob picking it up, Marelle surmised the woman was probably a bit older than her – pale skin, dark hair, dark eyes, too much make-up (but perfectly applied). She appeared to be with a partner in the group who seemed unaware of her fixation on Jacob.

"Just going to the toilet." Jacob stated and regained her attention on him. "Too much coke!"

Marelle smiled. "Ok, I'll just be here!"

Jacob got up, averted eyes to the floor and walked towards the toilet door. Marelle sat and watched. It seemed to be a one in and one out toilet so he couldn't get accused of hanging around in there but nonetheless she sat and watched the door with baited breath, waiting for him to reappear.

As she sat and stared at the door, to her utter disbelief the dark haired woman from the other table was walking towards the toilet. She wore a tight red dress and had a flirty wiggle to her walk. She flicked her hair over her shoulder as she approached the door.

"No you fucking don't!" Marelle said to herself and pushed her chair out from the table – as she stood up the door opened, and Jacob emerged just as the harlot in the red dress was about to enter. Marelle froze. For a second Jacob and the woman were face to face, barely a foot apart in the doorway. Jacob immediately looked uncomfortable, virtually

flattened himself against the open door and looked straight down at the floor. She smiled and Marelle heard her say
"Oh sorry!" In a flippant way.
Jacob said nothing, he waited until she had gone into the toilet then unflattened himself and walked quickly back to Marelle at the table where she had sat down again.
"Ok?" She asked.
He nodded.
Marelle didn't want to start the conversation here, so she bided her time. The woman came out of the toilet again, shot a glance at Jacob and returned to her own table. Marelle glared at her – who the fuck was she? Jacob seemed oblivious and remained focused on Marelle and as sweet as he ever was. She held onto his arm when they left, smiling broadly and laying her head against him as passed the other table who were still there. Marelle didn't look back but knew they were being stared at.
Out at the car she forgot she wasn't driving and went to go to the driver's door, fumbling for the keys until Jacob swung them in front of her.
"I'm driving, remember?"
She laughed and moved round to the other side of the car. Once in she pulled the seat belt around herself and turned to Jacob.
"Who was she?"
"Who?"
"The woman in the red dress who was trying to get into the toilet when you came out?"
Jacob gave a little laugh. "I don't know but they need to make the door a little bigger!"
"But she seemed to know you."
"Know me?"
"Yes, she's been staring at you all night. Every time I looked up, she had her eyes fixed on you like something possessed." Marelle explained. "I shot her daggers a few times but she wasn't looking at me ... then you go into the toilet and she follows!"
"I didn't really look at her. Can't say I knew her though ... maybe she's seen me around the village?"
"Seems like she's not from round here. I caught some of their conversation and it seems like some kind of family get together from far and wide."
He stared at her in amazement. "You don't miss much, do you?"
"Born nosey and I ask too many questions too – apparently." She smiled.

"I don't know her." He said with a finality, then added. "I'm sure if she'd have known me then she would have said something when we met in the toilet doorway."

Marelle doubted it. He'd looked like a scared child. "She obviously has a fixation on you."

He started the car.

"Sure she's not an old girlfriend or something?" Marelle questioned.

"Marelle there are no 'old girlfriends' around here – or anywhere really." He did sound a little abrupt when he said that which surprised Marelle and made it sound like a sore point which made her even more suspicious of the woman in the red dress.

He may have sensed he'd replied a little tersely because he added "If you make me look this good then you've got to be prepared to fight them off!" With humour to deflate the conversation.

"Oh I'll fight them off, tooth, nail and stiletto!" Marelle replied. "Its just odd. Its like she wanted to say something but didn't."

"Maybe you scared her off."

"I was going to confront her when she went to follow you into the toilet but then you came out… but I didn't really want to make a scene. I didnt say anything to you because I knew it would make you feel uncomfortable …"

"Well let's forget it shall we? She probably thought I was somebody else." He replied. "Obviously some rich tycoon who lives around here – and not some weirdo who lives in a caravan!"

Marelle smiled. "Well I like the weirdo who lives in the caravan." And she huddled to him as he drove her car home.

Jacob seemed to forget about it – maybe because he hadn't actually experienced it all night – but it still played on Marelle's mind. She would not have done that. If she fancied someone, she may throw a few cheeky glances or at least say something – but if the guy in question was obviously with another girl and not in the least bit interested then why would you keep staring with that intensity? Maybe it was a case of mistaken identity? Maybe Jacob was right.

He stayed again that night without question and slept with her clasped in his arms; her back against his stomach and not stirred until the dawn when the rising sun awoke him and he sat on the edge of the bed

Marelle opened her eyes and looked at his back. He looked thinner. His head was bent forward, staring at the floor, his elbows on his knees. The clock said ten past six. She stretched her legs out as she slid across the bed, placing one leg each side of him and sitting up with her face against his back, her arms around his waist. She kissed the back of his neck.

"Morning."

He sighed.

"Whats the matter?" She asked.

"I was laying here thinking about tomorrow."

"I was trying not to think about tomorrow." She answered, squeezing him gently.

"Are you coming down there?" He asked.

"Yeah, I'll wait in the car. I can see you from there."

"It'll be two or three hours before I get to the garden, you needn't come down all day."

"What are your feelings on this?" Marelle asked, quietly.

He paused for a while before replying. "I think he's there."

"Really?"

Jacob nodded. "Everything points to that now – everything comes together and delivers me there ..."

"You don't think it was just a dog?"

"Why would he make such a palava about burying a dog? At worst you would leave it in the road, at best you would try to find the owner – you wouldn't bring it home and bury it in your garden."

"You did say he was drunk. Maybe he panicked?"

"He was permanently drunk, had no capacity for remorse, or honesty ... just fear and anger."

"Do you remember him before he started drinking?"

"Hardly ..." he said, sighed with her cuddled up to him so that she felt his ribcase expand against her. "I remember him showing me an ear of wheat once. In a sunny cornfield at harvest time. I remember the heat of the sun and his gentle hands pulling apart the ear of wheat to show me the individual grains, golden and ripe. I remember that."

"At least it's a happy memory." Marelle commented, her face against his back.

"Then after that I was pretty much fending for myself."

"What about your brother?"

"He's dead."

"I know he's dead but where was he?"

"He lived with my father's parents." He said quickly.

"Why?"

He shrugged. "Guess it was when my mother died – he went to live with them and I stayed with him."

"Surely it would have been more sensible to send you to them and for him to look after your brother – who was older?"

"I don't know the whys and wherefores – I was just a kid." He replied "I don't know what went on – I was just getting by day to day. When I met Frankie life was much better."

Marelle hugged him. She closed her eyes and lay her head against him. If – and to her it was a big if – she expected nothing more than old dog bones down there – if indeed there was anything at all – if he did find Frankie's body buried in that spot then not only had the body of his best friend been laying buried in that garden for years but it had been his own father who had killed him. Even if it had been an accident what would that do to Jacob?

"No matter what Jacob – you know I'm here for you. No matter what, I'm not going anywhere – I promise." She whispered.

Sunday was solemn. He functioned but on a medial level; no highs or lows, no light or shade. He did what he had to but was otherwise preoccupied. There was a feeling of anxiety – of knowing what tomorrow may bring but walking headlong into it nonetheless. The sun shone, the sky was blue and the birds sang. The world was turning and revolving around him but in his world he was frozen in the anticipation of all his greatest fears being realised tomorrow. But he was so completely focused; he had to make this look plausible and Marelle could feel the tension as he struggled to hold on to it.

That night he wanted to be alone and told Marelle that. She didn't want him to be on his own, but she saw that nothing would change his mind tonight.

"I just need to be on my own tonight." He said. "I want everything clear in my mind – what I'm doing and how I'm doing it." He said, standing in her kitchen. "I'll be ok."

"Well call me if you need me." She asked, then hugged him. "Call me in the morning – before you leave. Then I'll come up and park in the lay-by."

He nodded.

She looked up into his eyes and he stared right into her. There was an emptiness there tonight – like looking into a deep, dark, bottomless hole. She closed hers and kissed him until he responded and pulled her to him.

"Be careful." She whispered, holding his shoulders in her hands, looking her eyes into his.

He nodded again and turned to leave. Her hands did not want to leave him, moving from his shoulder, to his arm, to his back as he left – went out of her door and along the path to step over the fence at the end. She stood and watched him walk away across the airfield in the last light of the evening; his tall, thin frame moving slowly on a fixed trajectory without a glance back.

Marelle couldn't sleep; didn't want to sleep, scared of what dreams would flood in if she did. It was three in the morning, and she was still standing in the back bedroom looking out of the window. All was quiet and all was dark. She reached for that thread in the dark between her and him but could not find it tonight. She panicked, cried to herself, wished for morning yet feared its arrival.

TWELVE

Jacob called her at half past six. She was ready and waiting and answered on the first ring.
"Jacob." She said.
"I'm leaving in a minute." He replied, his voice sounded rough and tired. "I've got to get the digger and drive it up there. I left it ready but someone has probably used or moved it. I dont want to be there too early. Aim to get there about half eight, start about nine. Should be getting that way by lunchtime …"
"I'll come up about ten." She said.
"You'll be there for hours!"
"I'll be ok." She replied. "Are you?"
He paused momentarily. "Yeah, I'm fine." Which said a whole lot. She suspected he hadn't slept either, nor eaten – then, neither had she.
"I'll see you later then."
"Yeah."
"Ring me if you need me to come sooner." Marelle told him.
"I will." He answered. "Bye."
The hours until she could get into her car and drive up to the lay-by crawled so slowly, she felt like the whole day had passed and she began to worry he would have already got to that spot by the time she got there. She had managed to make a flask of coffee to take with her but knew he would not eat anything, and she didn't feel inclined either. Marelle sat and watched the clock, counted every second as the hands moved towards ten and she deemed it was ok to go.
She was trembling when she reversed the car out, thinking it was Jacob who had driven it in last, and made her way up the road. Her breath was

arrested in her throat until she pulled into the lay-by and saw the yellow digger halfway along the ditch. Breathing again, she got out and began to walk up. Marelle walked along the edge of the line of stuff he had dragged out of the ditch. It was neat and tidy; the ditch deep and flat on each side. Where he had dug beyond the surface the ditch was damp and muddy; where the detritus had been turned out onto the field there was a layer of greyish, black mud on top. In the warmth of the morning, she could smell the damp mud and the decomposing vegetation. She approached the digger, not sure if he had seen her or not; for a moment she stopped, looked up to the cab, waved a bit but he didn't notice her. She had his head turned slightly away, staring into ditch ahead. Marelle walked forwards a bit more, closer, staring up at him, almost on tip toes to make herself visible. Then he pivoted the digger, turning the arm and bucket back towards her – and spotted her. Marelle smiled and waved but he, almost angrily, gestured with his hand for her to get out of the way. Reprimanded she hopped back a few strides and watched him as he stopped everything and climbed out, down the step then onto the caterpillar tracks before stepping down into the stubble field.

"Never walk behind a digger like that when its working!" He exclaimed. "It swings round 360 so could easily hit you. If the bucket hit you you'd be dead."

"I'm sorry. I thought you'd seen me."

"No, I hadnt." He said sternly. He was locked into the mission; focussed. "I should wait in the car. I'll let you know when to get out."

"Can't I stand and watch for a bit? The sun is nice ..."

"It stinks!" He remarked. "You can if you want but it would look a bit odd with you standing watching me ..."

She sighed. "I suppose so."

He wasn't making eye contact today, looking everywhere but at her. "Do you want some coffee – I brought a flask."

"No, I'm fine, thanks."

"Doing ok?"

"As well as can be expected."

She nodded.

"I'd better get on." He looked towards the digger, then added in a quiet voice. "I just want to get this over." As he walked away.

Marelle went back to the car and sat in it, in the driver's seat so as not to look suspicious and began her vigil.

She put the radio on in the car quietly, changed channels a couple of times until she settled on one. For a bit she watched him intensely – methodically dragging the crap out of the ditch, piling it neatly then turning and scraping the sides of the ditch, clean, smooth and straight. Then moving along a bit to start again.

Jacob had said he liked doing this – it was mindless and gave him time to think. Today, she surmised it was anything but and each bucketful drew him closer to the spot in the garden where he believed Frankie lay.

Marelle was sitting in her car, back to the driver's door, watching the digger go through the repetitive motion when her phone rang laying in the centre console of the car. She picked it up but did not recognize the number – curious she answered while keeping her eyes on Jacob.

"Hello."

"Good morning, could I speak to Marelle Buckleigh?"

"Speaking – who is this please?"

"I'm calling from The Mustard Pot restaurant – I believe you dined with us on Saturday?"

"Yes, that's right."

"I've been asked to pass on a message from another of our guests on Saturday – if, of course, you are content for me to do so?"

"What is it?"

"I've been asked if I can pass on a contact number. The other guest believes she may know you and would like to get in touch."

The woman in the red dress!

"Ok, who was it?" Marelle questioned.

"The lady's name is Anna Dawson ..." she reeled off a telephone number while Marelle fumbled for a pen in the car and found one – scribbling the number on an old petrol receipt.

"She asked us to pass her number on – with a message to call her if possible."

"Ok." Marelle replied. "Thank you. I'll think about it."

So, the woman in the red dress, Anna Dawson, thought she new them – or knew Jacob. Marelle would be interested to hear her story despite a voice in the back of her head telling her to leave well alone. She dialled the number, it rang three times then a woman's voice answered.

"Good morning?"

"Is that Anna?" Marelle asked.

"Yes, speaking."

"I've been passed your number by The Mustard pot restaurant near Dirdfield – you left your number and asked if I could get in touch?" Marelled explained.

"Oh wow! Yes – I didn't expect you to call back and definitely not so swiftly!"

"How can I help?"

"Well, firstly I must apologise for me asking you to call. Its terribly cheeky and a little presumptuous. I assume you must be the lady in the black dress who sat just along from us?" She went on.

" ... yes ..."

"Well, the guy you were with – he doesn't happen to be Ezza's brother, does he?" Anne asked, quite enthusiastically.

Marelle took a breath. So, she was staring at Jacob.

"No, he doesn't have a brother." Marelle stated not going into detail – his brother had been called Nathaniel anyway, so it wasn't worth pursuing.

"Oh, ok." She sounded deflated. "I'm sorry then, my mistake. My brother used to work with Ezza you see, and I know from him that he had a brother who lives around this area too ..."

"Well its not him I'm afraid." Marelle said.

"No, ok. Sorry to have bothered you – it is a case of mistaken identity I guess."

"You should have asked us on the night." Marelle began. "You were staring quite intently and it was a bit unnerving. He's been unwell lately and it was a night out and a break for us – it was made a little uncomfortable by your staring. Luckily, he didn't notice ..."

"Oh, I'm sorry. I didn't mean any harm, I'm sure you understand. He just looked *so* like Ezza – I was sure he had to be his brother ..."

"Well he isn't." Marelle reiterated and said nothing more.

"Well, ok, thank you for calling me anyway and clearing that up." She said tersely. "Goodbye."

"Goodbye." Marelle echoed.

She pushed the button on the phone to end the call. Cheeky bitch! But at least she now knew it *was* a case of mistaken identity for someone called Ezra! She'd tell Jacob later, right now he had something else on his mind.

Marelle looked across to the digger. He'd moved on a bit. Maybe next time he moved he would be in the region of that spot. They were close and soon he would know for sure. Marelle wanted to get out and go up there but knew he wouldn't want her right there. He'd said he would let her know and at that moment, in the focussed state he was in, she knew she was probably best placed to stay there.

Watching him go through the same motion, time after time with a patience that was beyond human – especially when with each movement he drew closer.

He moved the excavator along again. Marelle was certain he must now be at the spot where he was planning to reach into the garden. She stretched her back in the car; lifted her head to see better. The arm of the digger reached across instead of down. Marelle watched; she waited and she watched.

The repetitive movement had changed. The digger arm was not going up and down or pivoting in an arc to deposit the stuff from out of the ditch. It was extended slightly but not moving much. Marelle began to wonder what he was doing – had he found something? Maybe he was going to dig down from the top? She shifted in the car, finding it hard to remain there – straining to see either Jacob in the cab or what he was doing.

The vegetable patch! She suddenly remembered. Was that what he was doing? Scraping a square of earth away at the top first? He probably was; one last thing to do before he started digging further.

The excavator suddenly stopped, the arm, bent down in a neutral position. Marelle watched for the cab door to open. It didn't. She shifted her position in the car again and was about to get out when the digger started moving again. Scooping down into the ditch as before and raising a bucket of tangled undergrowth, dripping black mud. Then he was making smaller movements again, tidying the edges and smoothing the sides. She looked at her phone briefly, worried that she had turned it off and he may have tried to call her just now when he had stopped. It was on and there were no missed calls. She raised her eyes.

The cab door was swinging open and she could not see Jacob. Marelle gasped to herself and twisted to open the driver's door.

Almost falling out she found her feet and scrambled along side the pile of debris that had been deposited on the field. Her pace quickened; she ran.

The door of the cab was swung wide open, Jacob was in the ditch one leg on the bank, one on the other side, astride it – avoiding the worst of the mud. He had dug out a perfectly square patch on the surface of the garden – edges neat, soil flat and even. But now he was stopped looking at something, a couple of feet down from the level of the vegetable patch. There was a piece of material poking out of the side of the ditch. It looked greasy and wet – just a two inch by two inch triangular corner. Jacob flapped it with his hand, looked at it closely.

"What is it?" She asked, standing at the top edge of the ditch, in a clear space between debris and the edge of the ditch. She'd sidled up past the digger to get there. This time he didn't reprimand her but turned his head at her voice. Pushing away from the far side he scrambled back up the bank to where she was.

He raised his eyes to her. His hair had flopped over his forehead a bit and his face was solemn, his mouth tight and small. He held out a clenched hand towards her. Marelle looked to it as he slowly opened his fingers. There, in the palm of his hand was a metal badge – two wings – dirty and slightly corroded but exactly the same as the one he had and which he had shown her in the caravan that night.

Marelle looked up into his eyes as he closed his fingers around it again. There was a look of knowing in them as he turned away and climbed back into the digger.

She moved away and to the side. If she stood to the side of the digger where he hadn't yet cleared, she could see better. Suddenly she felt cold and shivered as she stood there. The digger started moving again and she looked up to Jacob's face in the cab. He didn't look at her – just kept his eyes fixed on the spot on the side of the ditch.

Marelle became aware of her own breathing as she stood and watched the digger bucket scrape gently across the topsoil. Taking away an inch at a time. Slowly, carefully he operated it to remove the layers of earth away with such a delicate touch. He worked away, opening a trench down from the top, perpendicular to where the triangle of material was visible on the side of the ditch. Then he pulled back the digger arm and stopped. He got out of the cab again and made his way into the ditch. Marelle moved forwards to the edge of the ditch as he positioned himself at the far side of it. One leg higher than the other, bracing himself against the slope of it by digging his feet into the surface in a wide stance.

The trench down from the top was one, maybe two feet deep. He had stopped as there was also the same material now poking out of the top layer of soil that remained. Jacob began slowly scraping the soil away from the top with his bare hands and shovelling it down into the ditch around his feet.

Marelle stood and watched, her arms wrapped around herself as a chill passed by her. He was working slightly quicker now, leaning into the side of the ditch as he dug away with his hands. Bit by bit he exposed the material which was buried there – something was bundled up under the material as he moved the earth away. It was still partially buried beneath the undisturbed soil further back in the garden. There was a shape to it which was becoming apparent and Marelle did not like it. Something was wrapped in that material.

Jacob had exposed one end of the object. It was not level with the ground and this end was at a slight upward angle. The part sticking out of the ground was about two feet in length, probably a foot proud but with a roundness to it that looked ominous. Jacob stopped. He stood there in the ditch, his legs and torso now leaning against the sloping wall of it that he had dug earlier. He'd long stopped trying to keep out of the mud and was plastered in it up to his knees. The top half of him was against the dryer ground but digging with his hands had spread damp earth all down the front of him too. He was looking at what he had uncovered; pondering now in those final seconds just what the decomposing blanket held from him. But that was it. He could peel away the thin veil of fabric and he would see just what, or who, his father had buried there all those years ago. He replaced his hands on the blanket, almost like a child feeling a Christmas present for shape, weight, form. He stood with both hands placed on it.

"Sweet fucking Jesus Christ!" She heard him whisper as she stared down at him.

Jacob pulled gently at one end of the cloth, looking for an opening. He found it and began to fold the material back, carefully with gentle, steady hands.

Marelle watched, staring down at the back of his head, hardly daring to breath or move herself. He'd paused. She could hear him breathing. Slowly he pulled back the material and looked upon what had been wrapped inside.

It was stained and muddy from time under the soil, weathered by years of rain, wet, cold, warm. By years of abrasion in the soil, rocks, worms, roots of plants and stones in the soil once cast upon it. She saw what looked like the smooth dome of a skull, a human head in the throes of thirty odd years of decomposition, she saw bone, teeth and hair. And she saw Jacob stand there in the ditch, laid against the mud staring at what he had finally revealed.

She was not sure if she let out a gasp, or a cry or indeed made any sound at all as she looked on but she raised a hand to her mouth and felt the need to turn away and leave Jacob in that moment alone.

Marelle walked two steps away and turned her head to look out across the stubble field. The sky was a pure azure blue, studded with tiny white, fluffy clouds here and there; the stubble was holding on it its golden hue in the warm sun and the birds were singing – a skylark– if she remembered correctly how Jacob had pointed the ascending song out to her. House martins swooped around her and the excavator; a soft breeze soughed across from the west and ruffled her hair slightly away from her face. Marelle felt numb but she raised a hand and wiped tears away from her eyes.

"I'm sorry." She heard Jacob say, quietly from the ditch. "I'm so sorry …" and his voice cracked. "I'm sorry." He cried. There was no wailing or beating but the emotion could be heard in his voice. She stepped forward and looked down on him. He had both of his hands around what remained of the body, one on each side, his head bowed and his shoulders shaking as he cried those silent, anguished dry tears that were wracked with pain and loss. Those mute, hacking sobs that were the worst kind of tears.

"Jacob." She called but her voice hardly made it out of her throat. "Jacob, I'm here."

He didn't acknowledge or respond to her, but she did not say anything else. Folding her arms around herself she stepped away again.

Standing in the sunshine, here in such a peaceful setting it was hard to accept what was going on in a hole in the ground a few feet away from her. After over thirty years of searching he had found the final resting place of Frankie Lee. The circumstances of how he came to be buried where he was were going to be harrowing to deal with but at the moment the only fact that mattered was that Jacob had found him; he had been right and Frankie had always been here.

Marelle looked into the distance. Surrounded by that flat Suffolk landscape she felt she belonged here now. In all of her wildest imagination she would never have thought that this small village would integrate itself so wholly with her DNA and that she would have met someone like Jacob here. Someone so unique and gentle; someone so different from anyone she had ever met before; someone she knew she wanted to spend the rest of her life with.

She turned suddenly at sounds of movement from the ditch; stepping forwards closer to the edge. She saw Jacob place a hand on Frankie whom he had covered with the fabric again. He paused for one more second before turning and making his way up the steep bank of the ditch. He climbed out slowly, tiredly, holding with hands and feet as he he made his way up. Then stumbling as he finally stepped out of the ditch.

The black mud from the bottom of the ditch had soaked his feet and legs up to his knees, it had dragged up the front of him in a messy swirl. His hands and arms were painted with a thin layer of dried mud. At some point he had obviously wiped a hand across his face too and the smear off mud was striated with the tracks of his tears. He was a wretched sight as he stumbled towards her, and she held out her arms to him.

Jacob fell into them, heavily and for a second Marelle felt she was holding him up. He cried again, burying his head into her shoulder. Marelle held him and stroked the back of his head with her hand.

"Its ok." She whispered.

Then suddenly he pushed away from her, ducking to the side, bending his head forwards and dropping to his knees as he choked and vomited. He spewed and coughed and sobbed on his hands and knees beside the scene. Marelle moved to him, stopped to place a hand on his back but he staggered to his feet and wrapped her in his arms again, hugging her tightly as if his life may actually depend on his contact with her right now.

"Its ok. "She said, turning into tears. "Its ok ... you've found him – he's safe now." Standing beside the excavator, on the edge of the ditch, behind the house where Jacob had grown up. "You were right. He was here. You haven't got to search for him anymore. He can go back to his family and he can be safe forever."

Jacob suddenly pushed her away while staring her in the face. Hollow, empty eyes from his grubby, mud-streaked face.

"No!" He said. "No! He stays here."

Marelle stared back at him.

"He stays here. I know where he is – we'll leave him here, undisturbed ... I'll fill it in again."

She shook her head. "You can't do that!"

"Why? I found him, he's here ... he must stay here."

"But his family will need to know he's been found. We need to tell the police so they can contact his family."

"No!" He pushed her right away from him. "They didn't care about him. They moved away and left him here. They didn't care! They didn't spend over thirty years of their lives looking for him. He's staying here. I'll fill it in again." He stepped towards the digger.

"Jacob, no! You can't. Its not right!"

He shrugged her off as she tried to take his arm.

"Jacob you cant just fill the hole in again!" She exclaimed, calling after him, pulling at his t-shirt. "Jacob!" She exclaimed.

"Fuck off!" He shouted at her and the intensity and volume of his voice halted her instantly.

"Whats going on?" Somebody suddenly called.

Marelle snapped her head towards the sound of the voice and was faced with an ernest looking man dressed in a maroon cardigan with a white shirt and, incredulously, a navy blue bow tie. His head was almost bald and he wore thin, round glasses. He stood in the garden.

"Whats going on? I've been watching you for the last few minutes ..."

Who was he? They'd been told no-one would be at home today. Now he was standing there and didn't look like he was going to abide with Jacob's last suggestion should he decide to utter it again.

"Nothing." Jacob said. "Go back inside. I'm filling the hole in – you shouldn't be near a digger when its working."

"You're on the other side of the ditch and I'm in my garden." He looked down into the ditch. "Whats going on? When my wife told me about this, I was suspicious ... my meeting was cancelled so I stayed at home to watch – we've lived here ten years and no-one has ever done this before

– why now? What are you trying to hide down there?" He peered down. "You've both been behaving strangely and now you look like a couple of guilty children – whats the game, hey?"

Reality had ripped a hole and rushed in like water breaking the banks of a dam. Marelle looked at him, into the hole then across at Jacob – who was climbing into the digger.

"Whats that down there?" The guy in the garden asked, pointing with some urgency. "Theres something buried down there, isn't there?!" He exclaimed.

Marelle stared at him and she began to cry. Tears streamed down her face as she nodded. Jacob was now in the cab of the digger, the door was swung open, but he started it. Marelle turned to him.

"Jacob! Stop!" She shouted but he ignored her.

The guy in the garden ran forward, shaking his hands in the air.

"No, stop! Stop!" He shouted.

But Jacob extended the digger arm right into the garden as far as it would reach, bit deep into a section of lawn and pulled the bucket back, rolling a pile of earth and turf in an ever growing pile towards the ditch. Marelle ignored what he'd told her earlier, ducking under the digger arm and running towards the cab but he didn't look at her.

"Jacob please! You cant just bury him again – please – Jacob! Stop!"

He pulled the digger arm right back for a second swathe. Marelle ducked out of the way but saw an opportunity as he retracted the bucket again.

She jumped into the ditch, through the mud and scrambled up the other side just as the bucket reached over her head. She stood above the body of Frankie in the shallow gulley, one leg each side on the earth above, facing Jacob as he arced the digger arm above her and started to pull another swathe of soil towards her.

"Stop!" she shouted, her hands in the air but aware the digger arm was above her and the bucket was travelling towards her from behind. If he pulled it into the hole to rebury Frankie he would pull her in with it.

"Stop!" She called again, staring at his face in the cab; fixed and frozen, not even sure if his eyes could see her. Marelle stared right into his face, stared so hard, willing him to look at her as she could feel the soil piling up behind her. She stared right into the very depths of him, right into a soul that was ripped into a million pieces right now but right into the beacon of light she knew was still shining in there.

He raised his eyes to her. There was no love in them, no hope or joy anymore. She stared into them; his mouth was tight and clenched. The next second would determine everything. Marelle raised her chin defiantly with her hand in the air.

He stopped.

The arm stopped; the moving soil stopped. Marelle started breathing again.

"Stop, Jacob." She said, almost in a whisper.

He stopped the machine and the engine died. The silence rang in her ears until the birdsong and buzzing of insects filled that void again.

Jacob collapsed into himself in the seat of the excavator. He began to cry again. Drew his knees up to his chest and wrapped his arms around his legs, burying his face in himself.

Marelle dropped her arms to her side, she hung her head for a second then slowly made her way back across the ditch. Her legs were shaky and she herself felt sick, but she could hear his defeated sobbing and it pushed her on.

"Whats wrong with him?!" The bow-tie guy asked in a stupid. Half-sarcastic voice behind her.

"He's found a fucking body in your garden – we think it's a child – *that's* whats wrong!" She turned to him, shouting then scrambling towards Jacob.

"I'm calling the police." He stated like a threat and went running back towards the house.

Marelle stood on the digger track and climbed onto the step into the cab. Jacob was in a ball, sobbing loudly, crying like the child he had been when he'd last seen Frankie alive. She held on to the side of the door and leant in. hugging one arm across his back.

"I'm sorry." He sobbed. "I'm so sorry!"

"Its not your fault Jacob. It'll be ok now – it's the right thing to do. Its ok."

She leant in to him, reached behind his hands clasped tightly around his legs.

"Hey, give me your hand ... come on." She weedled her fingers into his until she managed to grip his hand in hers.

"It'll be ok. Come on ..."

"He's still a child but look what I've become ..." He cried.

"You've become the kindest, greatest person Jacob! You became the best friend anyone could ever have had, and you've never forgotten Frankie." She whispered to him. "He will be ok now – he can have a proper funeral and a proper resting place."

"They cant take him away."

"They will have to Jacob – but he will be looked after now – we've got to hand it over to the police now ..."

"No!" He cried. "Don't involve the police!"

"We've got to Jacob. We have no choice ... he's gone to call them ..."

He began to sob again.
"Come on. Lets go and sit in the sunshine ..." She squeezed his hand. "Come on, I need a hug too!" She smiled, "come on Jacob ..."
It took a minute or two but he eventually unfolded himself and holding her hand stepped shakily down from the cab. Marelle steered him back away from the ditch and walked with him round to the far side of the digger where the sun was strong. She sat him down on the digger tracks and then sat herself down beside him.
"You're covered in mud!" She said with a smile. "Look at me too!" She reached up and turned his face to her. He looked a mess, a wretched wraith in front of her, his face tear and mud stained, his hair full of mud flopping onto his forehead.
"It'll be ok. Just tell the truth – you can tell them as much as you want ... you can always tell them more later ... ok?"
He averted his eyes down.
Marelle gave him a gentle kiss on the lips which he hardly responded to but nonetheless accepted.
The guy in the bow-tie came back. He had a cordless phone in his hand.
"The police are on their way." He announced, walking along the other side of the ditch in his garden so he could see them.
"I'm sorry I swore at you." Marelle said. "It was a bit fraught."
"That's ok. I understand. "He said, but didn't really sound as if he did. "The police said not to touch anything. We all need to keep out of the way and wait for them to arrive."
Marelle nodded.
Jacob now had his head in his hands. She had a hand across his back which she patted gently.
"Is he ok?" the man asked.
"He'll be alright." Marelle answered. "Its been a bit of a shock ... to all of us ..."
He hung around, almost as if he was keeping an eye on them. He wandered up and down, the phone in his hand. Eventually he stopped.
"I'm Derek." He said.
"I'm Marelle – this is Jacob." She replied, if only out of politeness.
"You've already met my wide – Patricia.?" He said.
Marelle nodded.
"Patricia the stripper!" Jacob suddenly said, quite quietly and began to laugh.
'What?" Marelle asked, smiling.
Jacob put one hand to his forehead but kept looking down. He was actually laughing quite uncontrollably at what he'd said.

"Sshh Jacob." Marelle whispered but couldn't help smiling as he fell into a fit of giggles.

"Whats he laughing at now?" Derek asked.

"I'm not sure." Marelle answered. "Don't worry he's in shock ..."

But she really didn't know whether to laugh or cry with him; it was extremely random behaviour and if he couldn't keep a straight face when the police arrived it may be difficult to explain. Derek looked at him as if he was a complete lunatic as he continued to laugh alongside Marelle. She smiled with him for a bit, talking to him quietly but he continued inanely giggling with without looking up from the ground. Eventually though it dissolved into tears again and he was sobbing.

Derek shook his head and began to wander away from them, further into his garden.

The police arrived. Two uniformed officers had obviously gone to the front of the house but were now walking warily around the side of the building. Derek went running towards them, waving his arms and pointing back towards the ditch.

Marelle raised her head but kept an arm around Jacob. She was fine with speaking to them but was worried of what may come out of Jacob's mouth.

Nonetheless the next two hours were an expanding flourish of activity. The uniformed officers spoke to both of them, asked basic questions, spoke to Derek. Then they began to cordon off the area around the ditch, securing the site. Jacob was now watching, silently with a blank look on his face. Surprisingly he had answered their questions – basically what, when and where – without losing too much composure but that had just been an initial round of questions – there would be many more to come.

More police arrived, some in uniform, some not. Forensics arrived in a van, put on white protective suits. More people asked more questions, all going over the same ground. All of the time Marelle sat glued to Jacob's side, still on the tracks of the digger.

Essentially, their story looked straight. He had been clearing out the ditch, seen something sticking out of the ground, gone down into the ditch to investigate. 'I thought it may have been someone's beloved pet buried there' he'd said. He hadn't wanted to disturb it too much so had unearthed it carefully with his hands then discovered it was human! The only question had been him trying to rebury the body.

"Why did you try to put the earth back in the hole?" The question had come from the plain clothes officer, Marelle had forgotten his name or rank.

"I don't know; I just thought it was the right thing to do. I wasn't thinking straight – I'd just found a body in a ditch ..." Jacob said in monotone.

"He didn't mean any harm." Marelle piped up in defence.

The inspector flattened his hand to her. "Let Mr Frost answer."

"I just wanted to bury it again quickly, I suppose I was scared ..."

Jacob looked up at the tent they were erecting over the hole.

"May I have a word?" The police officer asked, directed at Marelle.

"Yes ..." Marelle replied, standing up and walking towards him. "But I don't want to leave Jacob – he's in a bit of shock and he may wander off – this is all very traumatic for him ..."

He sighed, turned and called one of the uniformed officers. "Jones – can you sit with him for a minute?"

He obliged, came over and sat himself about six feet away from Jacob, who ignored him.

Walking away from the inspector spoke. "Forgive me if I'm overstepping the mark here but does Mr Frost normally have full mental capacity?"

"Yes!" Marelle exclaimed. "He just seems to have been really traumatized by this." She sighed. "He's had a pretty traumatic life and things have been piling up on him a bit lately too ..."

"What kind of things?"

"He's from a broken family, brought up by an alcoholic father – his mother died when he was a baby and his brother committed suicide. He's not let people get close to him – he's being bullied and victimized by other people and he's about to lose his home too – please be easy on him – this may have pushed him over the edge."

"Does he live with you?"

She was taken aback by that question. "Well ... yes ... but his home is in the caravan on the airfield."

"Oh, I see." He said. "The developers are moving in soon I believe?"

She nodded. "He also gets overwhelmed by certain situations, like this. He's not happy in a crowd – he likes his own space."

"Ok." He said. "Sorry for asking, I just wanted to check. We have people who can assist if there are mental health problems."

"What will happen now?" Marelle asked.

"Forensics will examine everything – the coroner will take charge of the body until a formal identification is made. Once this and a cause of death are established then the body can be handed over to his next of kin. However, bodies do not usually end up buried in gardens without any foul play ..." He stated.

"Can I go back to him now?" She gestured towards Jacob.

He nodded. She walked back and he followed her.
"Ok Jones. Stand down." He said.
Marelle sat close to Jacob, He sighed.
"I know who it is." He suddenly said.
The Inspector turned back to Jacob. "You *know who it is*?" He asked. "How do you know who it is?"
"Its obvious." Jacob said, his dark eyes fixed straight ahead of him, focusing on no-one. "The boy who went missing in the sixties. His body was never found – the police searched for weeks back then ..."
"How do you know?"
"I was born here ... I was in the village when he disappeared ... I thought you would be aware of the case ..."
"I'm not from round here." He justified himself.
"He disappeared. His body was never found. Its him." Jacob said.
"Do you remember the boy's name?" the inspector asked.
Jacob nodded. "Frankham Lee – but he was known as Frankie."
Taking the witness statement from Jacob started off fine. The inspector had decided to undertake it himself there, by the digger and Jacob had agreed he was comfortable with that. He was fine; he was concise and totally together – until he got to the part where he had climbed into the hole. He broke down in such a way he could not go on and stood up, walking off to stand near a tree a few yards away. Marelle got up and went to him. He was standing with his face only a couple of inches away from the trunk of the horse chestnut tree, staring blankly at it.
"Hey, are you ok?" She asked.
He stared at the tree for a few seconds more. There were tears streaming down his cheeks, he looked tense and ready to explode. The mud on his face had dried; tears had left rivers through what was there, and his hair was plastered down, half of it falling into muddy spikes.
He nodded, finally.
"Lets finish this and we can go home." Marelle said quietly to him, reaching out to his arm and folding her fingers around it.
"I don't want to leave him here ..."
"He's been here all that time Jacob."
"But he was safe; now he's not safe; now they are prodding and poking at him, taking pictures of his decomposed body under their lights. There's no dignity."
She sighed, unfortunately, she could not deny any of that.
"And what then?" He asked. "They'll take him away and I won't know where he is."
"He'll be in the morgue."

At that word he crumpled again, placed a hand on the tree trunk and leant his head on it,

"Its ok Jacob, he won't come to any harm now – he can have a proper funeral, a proper resting place so we will all know where he is ..."

"I wish I'd never found him. They said there would be no-one here ... I wanted to cover him up again ... leave him be ..."

She gripped his arm. "Jacob, you know we couldn't do that."

"I could have. If I had been here on my own, I could have done that. It would have all been ok and he would not be violated like this."

Marelle felt a little upset at that remark. "Maybe you could have but it wouldn't have been the *right* thing to do."

"In *who's* opinion?" He snarled. "In *their* opinion. In *your* opinion – but not *mine*."

Marelle sighed. "Well, it's happened like it did – we cant turn back time."

He stared at the tree intently then suddenly turned from it. Threw himself at her and sobbed bitterly. She hugged him and patted his back, staggered herself by his sudden action.

"Sorry." He cried. "Sorry."

"Sssh!" she whispered. "Its ok."

He held her and cried for a couple of minutes then wiped his face on the back of his hand. He took hers then began to walk back to the inspector who was waiting for them.

There began a further half an hour of Jacob avoiding eye contact, speaking in single word answers and going over it again and again in his head until there were words on paper that everyone was satisfied with for the time being. Finally, he signed it as indicated by the Inspector.

He passed Marelle his card. "If there is anything else then ring me, *anything*; however small." He said. "And if you feel that you need some counselling then let me know as I can probably arrange something."

Jacob didn't respond.

"Can you let us know of any updates?" Marelle asked. "I think it would help Jacob if he could know details as they are released?"

He nodded.

"Can we go?" Marelle asked.

"I've got to take the digger back." Jacob stated.

"You can go but nothing can be moved until forensics are happy. It will have to stay here for now."

"Ok." Marelle answered and took Jacob's hand.

"There are press about." The inspector warned. "Don't say anything to them beyond that police are investigating an incident."

"Press?" Marelle asked.

"Yeah. I think its only local at the moment."

"Why are the press here?" She added.

He sighed. "I'll walk down with you." He said. "Its probably best that he doesn't speak to them ..." He nodded to Jacob.

They eventually walked back into the house. It was a quarter to six in the evening. Jacob wandered into the kitchen, placed both of his hands on the table and stood there, head bowed. He sighed.

Marelle stood and stared at him, her arms wrapped around herself. Today he looked older; the dirt gathered in the lines on his face; the darkness apparent around his eyes. He looked shattered, broken into a thousand pieces now – scattered before her; the piece with his smile missing.

There was a complete and vacuous silence hanging in the air; the clock ticking, checking off seconds as time passed; her own breathing noisy in her head.

She stepped forward and laid herself against his back, wrapping her arms around him.

"You did it." She said. "You found him Jacob."

He didn't move or reply for a good few seconds.

"We found him." He eventually said. "I probably wouldn't have considered looking in my own back garden."

"After all these years though. You found him – just like you always promised."

"And now it hurts more because of that." He whispered quietly, staring down at the table top. "I found him and I lost him, all in the same day."

"You haven't lost him Jacob. You know where he is now, where he'll always be. He's safe now."

He sighed. "Can I have a bath?"

She smiled and stood away from him. "Of course you can – leave your clothes and I'll wash them for you."

With a quick little smile and minimal eye contact he walked through and went up the stairs.

THIRTEEN

Marelle sat herself down. Today had been so carefully planned but it had run away with them. She too felt shattered – but physically. She had held herself and Jacob together for as long as she was able to. Admittedly she had not thought about the press – the inspector had got them into her car and away. Hopefully it would not be a big story, or even in the news for long – if at all beyond local interest and people generally had short attention spans.
She took her phone out of her pocket and placed it on the table. For a moment she stared at it then picked it up and dialled.
"Hello? Marelle?" Bella answered.
"Hi Bel, you got a minute?"
"Yes, of course! Whats wrong? You only ever call me 'Bel' when something's wrong!" she answered. "He's not left you has he?"
"No, no! He's here – he's in the bath actually."
"And you're not up there in it with him!?"
She gave a small smile to herself. "No, we've had a pretty traumatic day."
"What happened?"
"Jacob found a body when he was digging out a ditch. He thinks its that little boy that went missing in the sixties."
"Oh my God!" Bella gasped. "Oh my God, I can't even begin to imagine that. Is he ok?"
"As ok as can be expected but he seemed pretty traumatized."
"And you ... are you ok?"
"Yeah. But I'm worried about him."
"Did he see the body?"

"Yeah." Marelle said. "It was wrapped in a blanket – he thought it was maybe someone's pet been buried there – he didn't want to disturb it, so he got in the hole and unwrapped it."
"Oh hell." Bella exclaimed. "Were you there?"
"Yeah, I'd just taken him lunch ..." She explained. "I don't know how to help him. We've been stuck there with the police all day – the press were there too."
"Just stay with him. Be there for him. Can the police arrange any counselling or something?"
"Yes, yeah – they did say that but, well, he knew that little boy, didn't he?"
"Did he?"
Marelle couldn't quite remember how much she had told Bella. "Yeah. They were best friends. He's told me all about him."
"And now he has discovered his body?"
"Well, he thinks its him ... there will need to be a formal indentification."
"Oh Jesus!" Bella said.
"I know, I'm sorry but I just wanted to talk to someone about it."
"No, no ... that's fine. I'm listening babe ..."
Marelle sighed. "He's in the bath now – he was covered in mud. *I'm* covered in mud.'" She laughed.
"Marelle." Bella suddenly said, quite sternly for her. "Marelle, what are you not telling me?"
In that very split second Marelle's eyes flickered, she pondered on the path to take; whether to open the floodgates and let everything she knew flow out to Bella – even stuff she'd promised not to mention to anyone. In that moment the years of trust and friendship she had with Bella were flaunting their strength and bond to her. They'd shared everything – love, loss, despair, happiness, drunken stupidity – even boyfriends on the odd occasion ... but ...
"Nothing." She exclaimed with a little laugh. "What do you mean!"
"Its like you've got an apple and you're cutting all the good bits off to give to me but theres a rotten part of it you are keeping to yourself."
"What?" Marelle exclaimed "Nothing's 'rotten'!"
"You know what I mean." Bella stated. "You remember the time when we were kids? Where we used to sit and thrash out every problem we thought we had?"
"Yes! I was telling Jacob about 'the tree' the other day!"
Bella gave a small sigh. "Well right now you'd be sitting in that tree."
"Its nothing." She said lightly. "Its just been a shit day and I wanted to talk about it."
"Well if you're sure." Bella replied in a resigned tone.

"Sure I'm sure!" Marelle laughed.

"You need a girly night out with me – up here – like we used to." Bella offered.

"That's the last thing I need at the moment! Maybe when we've got over this!"

Bella sighed. "You've never been this besotted over anyone like this before – not even Chris. Whenever you've hooked up with someone in the past, we've still always had the same relationship – but this time its like you've taken him into yourself so intrinsically. I've had other friends who suddenly meet *'the one'* and they just fade out of my life. I don't want you to fade out of my life …"

"Bella. I wont! I've called you now, haven't I? You were the first person I wanted to speak to!" She said in exasperation at having to have this conversation with Bella.

"Well just be careful."

"I can be careful!" she said. Thought for a moment then continued. "I'm just scared about losing him."

"Losing him?"

"I had a dream, well a nightmare that he was dead – that he had drowned himself and I was with him in the morgue. It was so *real* and it was so awful. I called him in the middle of the night to come over just so I could touch him and know that it wasn't real. It made me think of life without him and I don't think I could ever face that now."

"Oh Marelle, it was just a dream!"

"Well it got me thinking."

"Its just your brain firing off when you're going to sleep – it doesn't mean anything …"

"Maybe not. But it scared me."

They talked for a bit more. Bella lightened the mood, made Marelle laugh. Finally happy that Marelle was ok she said her goodbyes but added

"Just be careful. I don't want to see you hurt."

She had just put the phone down on the table when it rang again. Assuming it was Bella once more having thought of something else she wanted to say Marelle picked it up and answered without looking at the screen.

" – yes!" She mocked.

"Marelle?" it was Seb.

Marelle tightened her lips and considered cutting him off. "Yes, what? I thought it was Bella otherwise I wouldn't have answered."

"Are you ok?"

"Yes, fine thank you."

He tutted. Yes, he actually tutted. "Marelle stop it."
"Stop what?"
"Being like this with me!"
"Huh!" She gasped. "Stop being like that with you, but you wont stop being a cunt over Jacob!"
"I reckoned it would only be ten seconds before his name cropped up."
"Look, get to the point or I'm pressing the button and if you have just called to let me know what a loser he is then you then its bye bye."
"I called because I just saw you and him in your car being hustled by the press ..."
"Where?"
"On telly."
"On telly? Me and Jacob?"
"Well, it was your car and there were two people in it – it was a local story but it made it onto the end of the national news. They found a body?"
It had quietened her.
"Yes, Jacob was digging out a ditch and he uncovered a body ..."
"Where?"
"In a field on the other side of the road. He was digging out a drainage culvert and ..."
"Wait!" what? Why are you using words like 'culvert' you don't even know what a culvert is!"
"Its what Jacob said. No I don't know what one is but its what he was doing."
" – and?"
"And he uncovered something wrapped in an old blanket buried in the hole. He thought it was someone's pet that had been buried there so he got into the ditch to have a look and it was a body."
"So it was buried?"
"Yes, been there years by the looks of it. Jacob thinks it may be the body of Frankie Lee."
Silence for a bit.
"Why does he think that?"
"Well its obvious – he disappeared and his body was never found – it has to be him ..."
"It said someone was '*helping police with their enquiries*' is that Jacob?"
"No!"
"Did you give a statement?"
"No. Jacob did – that's all. He's not helping them with enquiries. They said we could go – they'll identify the body then it will be handed over to the family."

"How do you think it got there?"

"Well I don't know."

He sighed. "Exactly! It was buried – *hidden* by someone. There'll be an investigation it will be treated as a murder investigation in all likelihood …"

"Well that may be but that's got nothing to do with me – or Jacob."

"Are you really that stupid Marelle?" He asked. "There will be a thorough investigation into everyone. They'll start poking around and if anyone has the same thoughts that I do about Jacob well then what?"

"Are you really that stupid Seb?" She mocked. "He *found* the body. He didn't *kill* it or *bury* it!"

"Can we be sure of that?"

"Fuck off Seb. He was a kid when Frankie went missing. For fuck's sake, he's in pieces about finding it – he's in a complete fucking state – why are you trying to pin the blame on him?"

"I'm not but somebody might."

"Oh piss off! No one is going to blame him for this!"

"Well I suggest you keep your mouth shut or you'll get dragged into this as well. Its friendly advice Marelle – for your own good."

"I don't need your advice Seb. I've told you before – "

"I'm only trying to help Marelle – I saw it on the news and thought I would call just in case you were stumbling over the edge of a cliff."

"Well I'm not. Thank you. Goodnight." She pressed the button. "Fuck off Seb." She said under her breath.

The phone rang again. It was him calling back but Marelle ignored it however she suddenly noticed the time on the phone. Five to eight. She stood up quickly, panic already fluttering in her chest. Jacob had been in the bath for two hours! She had been talking to Bella for ages then Seb – Jacob hadn't shown himself and she was suddenly scared.

Her frantic footsteps up the stairs were enough to wake the dead but she stopped outside the bathroom door which was closed and paused. She put her ear to the door and listened.

Silence.

"Jacob!" she called. "Jacob!"

There was no lock on the door.

"Jacob!" She turned the handle slowly until it released amd very gently pushed the door open.

Her hands were shaking and her heart was jumping. People did not just drown in the river or the ocean – they drowned themselves in a bath and she felt a rise of tears in her eyes as the door slowly opened.

She pushed her head into the opening, looking in coyly as she didn't really want to disturb him in the bathroom. He was in the bath, his back to her. She looked at the back of his head – at the back of his neck where she had cut his dark hair so precisely that for a fleeting second she commended herself in amidst the panic that was beginning in her. She saw his head fallen slightly to the side and his beautiful square shoulders as his arms his arms supported himself in the bath tub.

"Jacob." She said, quickly opening the door a little more, relieved that he had not drowned himself! However, on opening the door fully a whole new scene greeted her.

All across the floor was a rusty red stain, smeared and splattered across from the bath towards the the wall. Marelle heard herself gasp as she moved forwards and into the room, looking down at Jacob in the bath. There was a strange sweet smell in the air. The bathwater was red – there was no other way to describe it – a deep, dark, dirty bloody red.

Marelle flew into the room, skidding in the sticky mess on the floor and crunching her knee into the side of the bath. She may have screamed – she could not quite remember what she did – but shouted his name in desperation.

"Jacob!" she yelled, grabbing at his arm and pulling it out of the water, looking for the source of the bleeding. She shook him, quite violently, shouting right into his face.

"Jacob!"

He came to. Suddenly and violently – panicking at her screaming right into his face, thrashing around in the bath, slipping. Marelle grabbed his arm and tried to help him up, but he was flailing around, grabbing at her, panicking and gasping himself. Eventually he got onto his knees in the bath and bent himself over the rim of it, gasping and still clutching at a handful of her top – right over he left breast. He exhaled noisily.

"Shit!"

Marelle's hands were on him. "Jacob you're bleeding, whats happened ...what have you done?"

He still had hold of her but turned his head breathing heavily, looking at his hands and the red bath water, confused and ultimately as scared as she was.

"Jacob, let me see ..."

He looked up at her, realised he had a tight grip on her left breast and let it go.

"I'm not." He said quietly. "Shit, I thought I was drowning."

"Jacob ..." she was scrabbling for him, grabbing his hands, his face, trying to examine him to see where the blood was coming from. "Jacob, let me see."

He sat up on his knees. "I'm not bleeding."

She stared at him. There were tears running down her cheeks, her mouth slightly open, her bottom lip trembling.

"I'm not bleeding." He said again, breathing heavily. "Fucking hell. I fell asleep and get woken up by you screaming in my face. I realised I was in water and thought I was drowning."

"You're not drowning." She said, "Whats all this blood then? What happened?"

"Nothing." He said. "Its this." He handed her a black bottle that was on the side of the bath. "I spilled it and was going to wipe it up when I got out – smell it, it stinks ..."

Marelle looked at the bottle. "Vampire Rose." She said. "Vivid bath soak." She looked at him. "What the fuck is this?"

"I don't knw. It was on the shelf and I used it. A bit alarming when the water went red but ..."

Marelle was still breathing heavily. She sat down on her knees on the floor beside the bath.

"Its not mine."

"Well its not mine ..." he echoed.

"Bella!" She exclaimed. "I thought you'd ..."

He looked at her then hung his head with a sigh.

"I'm sorry." She apologized, looking at the bottle again. "I bet this is Bella's. I'll fucking kill her!"

"Did you really think I'd slashed my wrists?" He asked.

"Well, you were in the bath for over two hours! In was on the phone to Bella and then Seb called – which I stupidly answered – then I realized what the time was and came up here to make sure you were ok ... and this ..."

"Its bubble bath."

"I know that now!" She exclaimed. "It scared me."

He sighed.

"I told you I should have done this alone. "He said very quietly, averting his eyes from her.

"What difference would it have made?" She asked, slightly surprised that he was still taking this tack.

"Because I could have found him then covered him up again – because police wouldn't have been called – because his body would still be there and because you wouldn't be so on edge thinking I'm going to top myself every five minutes." Marelle straightened her spine, kneeling on the bathroom floor in a smeared puddle of fake blood bubble bath and Jacob naked, kneeling in the bath tub of cold, blood red water.

"So you would have just covered the body up and left it there?"

He nodded, even if a little sheepishly.

"That was my intention. I only wanted to know where he was – I would have preferred to leave him there – now they're going to take him away. She sighed in exasperation. "You could not Jacob!"
"I could have – I could have just carried on along the ditch with no palava or mess and no-one would have been the wiser."
"So you would have just carried on … 'oh yes, theres Frankie' … and just carried on. You wouldn't have dissolved into the quivering mess you did?"
He raised his eyes to her this time. "Is that what I am? A quivering mess?"
"No!" she explained. "You know what I mean – you could not have just *carried on*! You just couldnt, you care too much about Frankie – the same that I care about you and that's why I worry about you doing something stupid!"
He was glaring at her in an odd way. She didn't like it.
"I should never have told you." He said quietly. "You think I'm an idiot. Just like everyone else."
"No, I don't. But theres a right and a wrong – and to just leave him there was wrong. What about his family? Don't they have a right to know what happened to him – in the same way that you know what happened to your brother? What if he had just disappeared all of a sudden and you never found out what happened to him?"
"And that's something else I should never have told you either!" He said. "And as for Frankie's family – what do they care? They moved on and moved away!"
"Of course they care Jacob but sometimes you just have to move on …"
She looked to his eyes but he looked away.
"You cant do this on your own. No one should have to do something like this on their own. I'm not letting you do this on your own; I'm not letting it eat into you and harm you – or us …"
"It would all be over now."
"No, it wouldn't." She shook her head. "What if in a few months they decided to build something in their garden? What if someone else moved in there and dug everything up. It would *not* be over. We knew this would be difficult and this day would be hard – especially for you … but we will get through it and we will come out the other side…"
He was staring at the floor, kneeling in the bath, his head bowed slightly forwards.
"You don't know how much you mean to me Jacob." She said, staring at him.
He lifted his eyes from the floor and looked into hers. For a moment they just stared at each other them almost as if an invisible force was in

action, she leant forward to him and him into her. By the time he wrapped his arms tightly around her he was sobbing bitterly and clutching onto her as if his life depended upon it.

It took a while to calm him down and a while to clean up the mess in the bathroom, Marelle was now covered in dried mud and fake blood. Once she was sure Jacob was settled, she jumped into the shower herself and washed away the events of that day. It was probably the quickest shower she had ever taken due to her worry of leaving him alone downstairs. Her hair was still dripping wet when she returned to find him standing in the living room looking out of the window.
"I might walk over there …"
"No Jacob, don't. It'll look weird …"
"I need to check that the digger is secure."
"No, you don't." She said in reply, it'll be fine."
"They might take him away … I'd like to be there when they take him away."
"I don't think that's a good idea."
He sighed.
"We could take a drive past."
"You wouldn't be able to see anything." She replied but she knew he would not settle until they had. "But we can have a look if you want."
Marelle drove. He directed her round the other way, so they approached from a different angle. The road they drove down was on a slight hill so you could, in fact, see the back of his old house clearly. It was just starting to get dark but there were obviously still vehicles there and the floodlights. The small tent they had erected over the hole was illuminated from the inside. There were still two police cars at the bottom in the lay-by where her car had been parked and a white van halfway up the field. The digger was exactly where it had been left. She drove down the road slowly, round a bend where the road was lower and then along past the lay by with the police cars in. There was now 'do not enter' tape across the entrance.
"Stop." Jacob said.
Marelle turned her head to him but stopped the car anyway.
He began to open the door.
"Where are you going?" she asked as he had one leg out already.
"I want to get something out of the digger …"
"Jacob you cant …"
"Its ok." He climbed out of the car and walked up to the tape.
She watched as he spoke to the policeman sitting in one of the police cars. Jacob hovered while they had a conversation. Then he got out of

the car and lifted the tape up for Jacob to duck under before they both walked up towards the digger – which was half silhouetted like a huge monster in the dim light. Marelle sighed to herself in both exasperation and fear. Darkness was falling and she struggled to see them as they moved up close to the digger and the small tent. She watched the clock. Eight minutes later he came back with the policeman, ducked under the tape and got back into the car. He had the digger keys.

"He thinks they'll move his body tomorrow." Jacob reported. "But he says to check in the morning if I can move the digger."

There seemed to be other thoughts in his head which he was not expressing but he gazed back at the tent as Marelle pulled slowly away. He didn't sleep that night. Marelle had dreaded what nightmares he may encounter or what he may do but he lay in bed beside her, awake all night. Admittedly she did sleep a bit but whenever she opened her eyes, she could see him on his back beside her; silhouetted in the room with moonlight casting shadows. She looked across at the profile of his face and the outline of his hair just a shadow in the moonlight. His eyes were open and staring at the ceiling, but he was silent and unmoving.

She followed him down when he got up at six o clock in the morning. He was dressed, clean, tidy and about to go out of the back door.

"Where are you going?"

"To work, I'm going to walk over and see if they'll let me move the digger. If not, I'll walk up to the farm."

"What!" she said. "Have some breakfast first then I'll take you up there."

"No, its ok, I'll walk over there." He said with a smile.

"No, have breakfast. The press were about yesterday."

"Press?"

She nodded. "That's why Seb called me last night – apparently he caught a glimpse of my car on some news story as we drove away."

"On the tv?"

She nodded. "Made national news apparently – chances are they've moved on to bigger stories today – but they may be there again …"

He looked a little disturbed by that and shuffled a little bit before he finally sat down at the table. Marelle didn't tell him anything more. While she was piling washing up in the sink and grabbing her cars keys, he went up stairs again and came back down wearing a black hoodie. It wasn't particularly cold and she did a double take as they went out of the front door.

"You cold?" She asked.

"No." he replied, following her out.

It took literally two minutes to drive around the corner to the lay-by. There were still police cars there, although one was different according to Jacob, and the tape was still across the entrance to the field. As Marelle pulled alongside Jacob turned and looked up towards the tent. The white van was still there but there was now a dark grey one also parked alongside it.

Jacob had his hand on the door handle but paused before a second before getting out.

He sat there looking, then took sunglasses out of a pocket and put them on followed by the hood of the black top. He looked like he was about to rob a bank as he walked up to the tape. Marelle sat and watched. He could look so casual and matter of fact if he wanted to; so as if he didn't care a toss about the body in the ditch while she knew, inside he was in pieces.

He spoke to the policeman who came forward at his approach. Jacob exchanged words with the policeman at the tape and pointed to the digger. The policeman pointed to the van and then to the entrance to the field. Jacob nodded putting his fingers in the front pockets of his jeans and rounding his shoulders. With a nod and a wave of acknowledgement he stepped a step backwards then came to the car and got in.

"They're taking his body away in a minute." He said. "He's already in the grey van – if you move over to the side they can get out."

She pulled the car along a little and into the side of the road out of the field entrance. "What about the digger?"

"No, they don't want it moved until forensics have finished … don't want it to disturb the ground." He went to get out of the car.

"Where are you going?".

"I want to watch the van go." He said quietly. "Pay my respects as he leaves."

Marelle felt a little bad for actually asking, but followed him out of the car. He placed himself at the rear of it, leaning against the back door. Marelle joined him and stood there, close. The grey van reversed onto the stubble field to turn around and after completing that manoeuvre began its journey down the side of the field towards the entrance. Marelle watched as the policeman had wound the tape back for it to pass through. Beside her Jacob pulled the hood off his head and run his hand through his hair; she felt him shift his position slightly against her so that his body was closer to hers. Then he reached up and removed his sunglasses. He drew himself upright and she followed, standing shoulder to shoulder with him at the back of her car as the grey van passed slowly through the entrance to the field and begin to turn away from them to start its journey past the house – Frankie's old house – out through the village and away.

Briefly she glanced up to him, unnoticed as he watched. Just a grey van. To anyone else it was just a dark grey van – could have been a builder, a plumber, an electrician. Its precious cargo unknown to the onlookers. Jacob watched it. Marelle looked back to the vehicle in the full knowledge of its contents; Frankie's body on its final journey from its resting place of the last thirty plus years and with it travelled all of Jacob's feelings and emotions from all that time; all of the days and the nights; all of the memories he shared with Frankie; all of the days in the sun with him.

Jacob stepped one stride away and watched the van move away until it turned the bend and disappeared. He remained staring at that spot for a few silent seconds. Still a stride in front of her, his back facing her, he replaced the sunglasses. Slowly he turned back to her.

"He's gone." He said and she could see a tear running down one cheek, catching the early morning sunlight.

Marelle raised her arms and let him move into them. Hugging in to her he placed his head on her shoulder and his hands against her back. She didn't say anything, just held him. Standing there behind her car he was clutching at her tightly but silently and remained in that embrace for a couple of minutes until he eventually stood up again, sniffed and looked down to the ground.

"I'll go down the yard then." He said.

"Ok, I'll take you there – may as well I've got to drive back anyway."

"No, its ok …"

"Sssh, get in." She nodded.

As he turned to duck into the car their attention was grabbed by someone calling.

"Hello!" A woman's voice. "Hi there!"

Marelle stood up to see Patricia walking briskly towards them from along the road. She was dressed in bright clothes and looked as though she may have been jogging.

"Morning!" She greeted, walking right up to the car and standing in front of Marelle, her hands on her hips and a smile on her face.

"Hi." Marelle said.

Jacob was hovering on the other side of the car, he'd put the sunglasses back on a while ago but a quick glance in his direction caught him pulling the hood up again too.

"Everybody ok?" Patricia asked.

"As can be expected." Marelle replied. "They've just removed the body."

"Oh." She said. Looking over them towards her garden. "Oh, I see." She focussed on Jacob. "Are you ok now? Derek said you were pretty upset by all of this?"

Jacob looked in her direction but there was no visible expression of emotion behind the glasses and hood. He nodded. "I'm ok."
"Good!" She smiled and turned back to Marelle. "Well this is exciting isn't it? Not what we expected!"
Marelle stared at her. She could feel Jacob's tension across the roof of the car.
"Well, I wouldn't quite describe it as that." Marelle said. "Someone has died here."
"It was years ago though, wasn't it? I was speaking to Forensics and they said the body is from a good few years back."
Marelle wanted to say a lot to her but was aware of prolonging this conversation with Jacob by her side together with the fact that she didn't want to make enemies of anyone here at the moment.
"Well I'd better get Jacob to work – we just came to see if he could move the digger yet." She also went to duck into the car.
"Ok!" Patricia smiled. "You can both always drop round for a coffee you know – when you're free." She waved at them in the car and walked briskly off.
"Jesus fucking Christ!" Marelle sighed and looked over at Jacob. He was staring out of the passenger window at the scene where forensics still had the tent. She reached across and gripped his thigh. "You ok?"
"Yeah." He sighed but obviously wasn't.
"Do you want to go home?" She asked.
"No, no ... take me to the yard."
When she pulled into the farmyard it seemed deserted.
"Quiet here?" She commented.
"Yeah, Adam took Sam and Skid to a trade fair – they're not back until Friday. Ryan should be here – and me. I'm meant to be digging ditches but obviously I cant ..."
"A trade show? What for, tractors!" She grinned.
"Yeah." He stated. "New broom and all that. Adam thinks he's got all these wonderful new ideas, but we'll see." He went to open the door. "I'll go and find one of those old lorries to work on – God knows there are enough of them!"
"You got the phone?"
He nodded, taking the hood down now.
"Well be careful. Call me if you want me to pick you up. See you tonight."
"Yeah." He said with a sigh.
"Are you sure you are ok?"
He nodded. "Just thinking about him in the back of that van?" He looked down at his knees. "His tiny body zipped into a body bag."
She touched his thigh. "Jacob, don't." She said softly.

With that he got out, leaned back in. "I'll see you later ..."

She leant right across the car to kiss him. He patted the top of the car as he closed the door and she watched him walk away across the yard. He walked slowly, tiredly – no – wearily like there was a great weight across his shoulders. She watched him go into the building before she started the car and drove home again.

FOURTEEN

He hadn't turned up by a quarter to six – she wondered if he wanted a lift home. Half of her was worried why he wasn't already here so she called him. He answered quickly.
"Hi." He sounded as if he was walking.
"Do you want a lift?" she asked.
"No. I'm nearly there. Be there in two minutes …"
"Oh, ok. Good." She smiled. "See you in two minutes."
He literally came through the door two minutes later. He'd still got the sunglasses on but his hair looked wet and was pulled back onto his head.
"Your hair is wet!" She commented.
"Yeah, I've been for a swim."
"What, up at the weir?" She turned to him, slightly astonished.
"Well not in the weir, but in the calm pool." He replied.
Marelle felt her stomach drop.
"Why?"
"I needed to." He said. "Too much going round in my head."
She wished he had told her; she wished he'd asked her to go with him. But he hadn't, he'd taken himself off without a word.
"Was it cold?" She asked.
"Its always cold, that's part of the attraction – numbs the mind."
Marelle wanted to say she was worried because he hadn't turned up exactly when she had expected him to and because she had just found out he'd been swimming in the river. However, his words from the night before still rang within her and she didn't want to add anymore evidence to his reasoning.

"Much happened today then?"
He shook his head. "Just Ryan. Asking questions about the body …"
She sighed. "Oh no."
He shrugged. "Its ok. He's pretty easy going, he doesn't push a point if I don't give him an answer."
She walked up to him and gave him a kiss, running her fingers through his hair and making it spiky again. He gave her a small smile.
"What do you want for tea?" She asked. "I haven't planned anything so we will have to improvise!"
"Well …" He began. "I was going to ask you if you wanted to come up to the caravan – I'll make *you* something instead. You can stay the night."
She smiled. He had all the awkwardness of a geeky thirteen year old sometimes.
"I'd love to Jacob!" She said.
He almost looked pleased with himself when she said that.
"What do I need to bring?" She asked,
"Nothing." He replied. "Just you!"
From what Marelle thought would be a very tortured and morose evening there sprang one which looked to be turning out very special and sweet. She walked up to the caravan with him arm in arm. He was quiet but seemed content and she hoped in the wildest of hopes that maybe with Frankie's body safely away from the scene that this denoted at least some burden having been lifted from him.
"So – are you actually cooking?" She asked, sitting down in his caravan with the door open in the early evening warmth of the late summer day.
"I'm cooking." He said.
She looked around. There wasn't any evidence of preparation.
"What?" She asked, smiling.
"Wait and see. Its special. I haven't done it for years but its probably my favourite thing – "
"Ok." She settled into the seat at the table. "Shall I do anything?"
"No." He said.
She watched him switch on the grill, put fish fingers under it. He then took a frying pan, emptied something into it which she couldn't see without standing up, and put that on one of the gas rings.
"Jacob?" She asked.
"Yes?"
"I thought you didn't like fish?"
He grinned. "I don't like fish, fish. I dont like bones in things and when you have whole fish it has bones. I like fish fingers!"
She smiled to herself at his remark. "So, what else have you been up to today except for swimming in the river?"

"Not a lot. No-one there – tinkered with one of the old lorries most of the day – at least until Ryan managed to flood the toilet."
He moved around the kitchen, checking the grill and the frying pan.
"How did he do that?"
"Knocked a hose off the tap just inside the door and didn't realise." He took a sliced white loaf and gave it to her, followed by plates, a knife and butter.
"Butter four slices." He said. 'Thickly!"
She made a face of unsureness as he turned his back again but nonetheless did as he asked.
He turned the fish fingers over.
"Did you clear it up then?" She questioned, buttering.
"No – made him do it!" He replied, placing salt, pepper and tomato sauce on the table.
"Two slices on each plate." He said.
"Yes Chef!" Marelle laughed and did as he asked.
"Right. Time to assemble!" He said with a smile.
He brought the grill pan to the table and placed four fish fingers on each slice of bread on each plate. Then he turned and took the frying pan, scooping a spatula full of fried mashed potato on top of the fish fingers.
Marelle laughed.
"Wait!" he held a finger up then took the knife she'd buttered the bread with and spread the potato flat until it formed a perfect one inch thick layer of potato. Then she squirted tomato sauce on top of each.
Marelle watched him with a grin on her face, turning her eyes to him as he finally placed the last slice of bread on top of each.
"My signature dish!" He said.
"Its carb overload!" She commented.
"Its wonderful!" He grinned. "Hang on!" He took two bottles of beer from a cupboard nearby, flicked the tops off and stood them on the table. He sat down opposite her, still smiling.
"Tuck in!"
"Are you serious!?" she laughed. "How am I even supposed to eat this?"
"Oh, ok, sorry. I forgot you're a lady!" He mocked, taking a knife and cutting hers in half.
"Go on. Try it. You'll love it. I guarantee!" Jacob picked his up and bit into the whole square of bread.
"Oh Jees!" He grinned. "I'd forgotten how good this is!"
Marelle laughed, picked up one half and took a bite. It was greasy, stodgy, salty, buttery and crunchy – all in one bite. It *was* wonderful.
Jacob winked at her and took a swig from one of the bottles.

Marelle looked at him and could not believe his mood. She'd never seen him like this with so much mirth and enthusiasm. Was the discovery of Frankie's body truly behind this? Had he finally snapped out of it?
"Oh my God Jacob! Where did this concoction come from?"
"Used to make it all of the time when we were ..." He changed his words mid sentence *almost* seamlessly " – at Uni!"
"So you just thought you would do it tonight?"
"Yeah ..." He said. "I wanted you to try it."
"Well, yes, its lovely but I doubt I'll be able to move much after I've eaten it!"
"We'll go for a walk." He suggested. "It's a lovely evening."
Marelle shook her head, amazed at him. Was this the 'real' Jacob; the one that had been cowering under the weight of Frankie's absence for all these years? Was she witnessing his first steps into the bright sunlight of his new world?
They drank beer and they ate the massive fish finger and mashed potato sandwiches. Marelle didn't feel the need to constantly hug or kiss him as tonight he didn't seem to need that assurance.
Afterwards they walked out across the airfield. The evening sunshine was mellow and warm. They walked hand in hand alongside the long grass and the wild flowers in the golden light. Halfway up the runway he stopped, turned to her and stared right into her eyes. Held her gaze but stared right into her soul with his deep brown eyes that she fell into. There was still a languid sadness in them; a painful depth of sorrow and utter despair deep, deep within them. Jacob stared at her intensely at that moment. The sun caught the tips of his hair, highlighting it red. He had that lopsided grin on his face which, juxtaposed against what she could see in his eyes brought a shiver to her. She smiled as she didn't know what else to do.
"Jacob ..."
"Ssshh." He said and leant forward to kiss her on the lips. He wrapped his arms around her tightly and held her to him in a vice-like embrace. Then he backed away from her but still holding her hands in his, leading her into the long grass and wild flowers.
Jacob kissed her again, sweetly, with a warmth that felt like it could break her heart. He sat down gently in the flowers and grass and pulled her down with him.
With the warmth of the evening sun on her back she sat astride him and in the golden hour of the sunset they made love in the most gentle and the most beautiful way she could have imagined. Finally collapsing on him she laid her head next to his as he lay back in the grass, Marelle just

wanted to touch him, to feel his skin against hers, to run her fingers through his hair and to just stay here forever with him.

They looked up at the sky, hazy and pale blue as the end of the day was beginning to oust the light. The barn owl silently meandered by – no doubt one eye on them but without watching.

"In whatever shit storm comes – whenever in your life ..." He said, quietly, precisely. "I want you to remember this evening."

She clutched her hand around his arm as they lay there between the grasses, the cornflowers, poppies and buttercups.

"I will never forget it!" She smiled and nestled her head into him.

Eventually, they rose out of the grass. He stood up and held out a hand for her, keeping hold of it as she stood up and they walked slowly back to his caravan with the light beginning to fade.

Climbing into bed in the caravan, she cuddled close. He had never before even mentioned her staying here with him. She felt strangely honoured as it felt like he had allowed her to enter the very heart if his life; the very centre of his unique and guarded world. If anyone had ever suggested she would be sleeping in a caravan she may have laughed at them. But in reality it was the most special night of her life and one which finally led her to believe he truly trusted her and one which meant their relationship was now set in stone. Marelle was pleased by that and felt they were about to turn a corner and head towards what she really desired. Marelle wanted to look into his eyes and actually tell him she loved him but held back; worried that such a bold statement may be a step too far. There would be a time and a place.

"I've never slept in a caravan before!" She's stated, laying in his arms.

"Neither had I until about ten years ago." He replied. "But its been my home since then ..."

"Its cosy."

"Its hot in the summer and cold in the winter." He remarked.

"Well you can come and stay in my house for the winter." Marelle smiled.

Jacob had his chin against her head and she felt him clench his jaw. "Mmmm". Was all he said.

She slept in his arms all night long. He seemed settled and did not wake during the night. In the morning, he got up and went to the kitchen to make tea; she could see him standing there with his back to her. She got up and dressed and joined him a few steps away, wrapping her arms around him from behind. He allowed it but continued making the tea.

"What are you doing today?" she asked, brightly.

"I don't know yet." He said quietly. "I guess I will have to see if they'll let me move the digger at some point. Apart from that I guess I'll just see what happens."

"I'll take you over there first, if you want …"

"No, its ok. I'll leave it for now." He said without the emotion of previous days.

He finished the tea and they sat at the table. Today he seemed distant yet strangely focussed on something. He had that intensity about him which was thinking of only one thing. From her experience it usually meant he was worrying about something.

"Whats wrong?" She asked,

He raised his eyes to her momentarily.

" – Nothing –" He said with a small, tight smile.

When they left, he locked the caravan with him heading one way and Marelle the other. He'd hugged her tightly, kissed her once on the forehead and then on the lips, lingering slightly until he moved away.

"Be careful." He said.

She smiled. "I normally say that to you!"

He smiled and nodded.

"Well be careful." She said.

Jacob gave a small smile, and they parted company. Marelle walked a few steps then turned to watch him walking away. He didn't look back at her.

Marelle walked back. She was still a little overwhelmed by the change in him last night – although he seemed to have slipped back to his old self a bit more this morning. There was a smile on her face as she walked into the house and she thought about just what could be. The happiness, warmth and spirit of him the night before had thrilled her. After all this time she had finally seen a full glimpse of him in full fleeting colour with all of the switches up to eleven! She laughed and sat herself down at the computer with a mug of coffee. Seb had sent an email. He had started if off with 'I hope you are ok. You know where I am if you need me.' Which she glossed over and read down to what he really wanted. Today she decided to get her head down and get this done, now that she had no reason to be distracted by looking for Frankie.

It was well after lunch when her phone rang. The number was withheld and she thought for a moment or two before answering. Finally she did.

"Hello?"

"Oh, hello. I was looking to speak to Jacob Frost?"

"Oh he's not here right now? Who's calling?" Marelle though it was the guy about saving the airfield and she tried to sound enthusiastic, hanging on to his next words.

"Ok, its DCI Catchpole – we met at the scene where the body was found at Parfield Groveham, a few days ago."

"Oh, yes, hi." She replied, a little disappointed. "I can take a message for him?"

"I'd like to speak to him in person if possible. Is there another number I can get him on?"

"Erm, no." she said. She didn't want the inspector calling Jacob on her phone when he was on his own. "I may be able to find him and get him to call you in a little while. He's probably at the farm – I can pop down and ask him. Is there a number?"

"Yes, its on the card I gave you – do you still have it?"

She did, it was wedged in her phone case. "Yes." She replied. "Its here."

"Ok, I'll wait to hear from him."

"Whats it about?" She asked.

"Just an update on the case – I'd like to give it to him personally."

"Oh, ok." She replied, a little dejectedly. "I'll get him to call you."

An update on the case? Was that good or bad? And why wouldn't he tell her? She dialled her mobile number and waited. It rang and rang but there was no answer. She sighed. Left it for five minutes then rang again. Still no answer. She wasn't unduly worried – there were pockets around here where there was no phone signal, she knew that. Or he was using some equipment and did not hear the phone. Fifteen minutes later she tried again but it just rang and rang. Marelle sighed, sat for a moment then picked up her car keys and headed for the farm.

The place still looked deserted. There was one car in the yard – an elderly looking Volkswagen but no other vehicles. The workshop door was open and she walked through it.

"Hello." She called as the place looked as deserted too but a scuffle immediately to her left drew her attention to Ryan who had been sitting on the workbench reading a magazine and was now in a heap on the floor looking sheepish. He threw down a cigarette and stomped it out.

"Is Jacob here?" She asked.

"No, he went out this morning, in the van." Ryan replied as if he was being the most helpful person in the world.

"Did he say when he would be back?"

He shook his head.

"Do you know where he went?"

He shook his head again.

She sighed. "I've been ringing him but he's not answering."

"Probably no signal?" He offered.

She gave him a little smile. "Ok. If he comes back can you ask him to call me?"

She realised she'd said 'if' and not 'when' and it disturbed her but she did not correct herself.

Once back at her car she got in and sat there for a moment. It was a quarter to three – Ryan had said he'd gone out 'this morning'. She had tried calling him for the past hour to no avail. She desperately wanted to worry but his words from the other night came back to her once more. She dialled the number again. Before she had not left a voicemail but this time she let it go through. The message on there was still hers – nonetheless he may pick it up.

"Jacob!" she said, trying to sound bright. "Its Marelle. I've been trying to call you – please call me back." She though she should have sounded more distressed, maybe even crying and he may have called back. Ten minutes later she had still heard nothing. In that time, she had driven home and was now sitting in her car on the drive to her house. Now she *was* worried; now a million thoughts were flying round in her head. She had no idea where he was.

She took a deep breath and dialled again. It rang once, twice, three times, four times. Marelle closed her eyes.

"Hi." He suddenly said.

"Jacob!" She exclaimed. "Where are you? I've been ringing for ages!"

"East of Ipswich." He said in a flat, tired voice.

"Where?"

"I'm under the Orwell Bridge."

"Is that far away?"

"No – an hour maybe, forty-five minutes." His voice sounded a bit odd, a bit waivering.

"Whats wrong?" She asked, biting her tongue.

He paused. "Nothing." He said with a sigh. "Its beautiful here. I'm in a layby beside the river, looking up at the bridge."

"Why?"

"Just stopped for a moment. You ought to come here – have you ever seen the Orwell Bridge?"

"No." She replied. "Jacob, I ..."

He interrupted. "Its massive; about a hundred and fifty feet high – a huge concrete structure spanning the river – its so high they have to close it in high winds ..."

"Why is it so high? Its pretty flat around here, isn't it?" Somehow, she was getting dragged into this strange conversation about a bridge.

"To let tall ships go through. "He said. "When they are on their way to the docks at Ipswich …"
"Oh. "She replied. "What are you doing?"
"Just stopped here in the sun. Looking at the water."
"Well where have you been?"
"Picked up some stuff for the old lorries – had to come from Germany. Stuck at the docks …"
So he did have a reasonable explanation.
"Oh, I see." She said, still a bit bemused by him at this moment and by the conversation they were having.
"It's a real feat of engineering …" He continued.
"You'll have to take me there." She answered. "You can show it to me."
He gave a little laugh. "What did you want? Whats wrong?"
Marelle had almost forgotten why she had called him but suddenly snapped herself to.
"Oh, yes – that Inspector who took your statement the other day called. He wouldn't speak to me – wouldn't tell me why …"
"What does he want?" He asked and she could feel the tension in his voice.
"Said its an update on the case." She reported. "Can you call him – maybe when you get back here? I've got his number."
He inhaled noisily. "I'll call him."
"Are you coming back now?"
"Yeah." He stated with a finality.
"If you call me, I'll come and pick you up from the farm."
"No, no, its ok. I'll walk."
"Ok, I'll see you in a bit then.'
"Yeah." He said, "you'll see me in a bit."
That had been weird beyond weird, his mood, his infatuation with the bridge – him not answering the phone when she sensed he'd been there for a while and there were no signal issues by the sound of it. After last night he had taken her on yet another roller coaster ride to the bottom of a curve.
Once inside, and out of pure curiosity she sat at the computer and typed in 'the Orwell Bridge'. She was presented with an image of said bridge; grey concrete against an azure blue sky; a series of high arches spanning a wide river across the flat Suffolk landscape. A groundbreaking design, erected in the 1980s. She looked at the picture, lorries on the bridge looked tiny and just visible above the parapet of concrete. Cars were obviously not visible from that angle. She read a bit of the narrative about it. Boring but it obviously fascinated Jacob for some reason. Maybe she would have read further and seen the news

stories below further down the page had Bella not called her at that point.

"Hi Bella."

"Hi babe!" She laughed. "What are you doing?"

"Just looking at pictures of a bridge." Marelle said, with a dry laugh.

"Ok, fascinating – you dabbling in civil engineering as well now?"

"No. but it seems that this particular bridge is one of Jacob's fascinations! I've just had a full description of it on the phone from him – thought I'd look it up just to see for myself!"

"Wow! Dedication!" Bella said. "Look babe, I'm checking – are you up for a weekender?"

"No Bella, you know I'm not into that."

"Its near you – an old holiday camp in Felixstowe just up the road from you. 80s stuff – Jacob would love it – if we got him pissed!"

"No Bella." She stated.

"Oh go on. I'm booking tickets …"

"No!" She repeated.

"Oh well, just me and Freya then. That'll be boring." She quipped. "Are you sure? I thought you were well into that 80s stuff – everyone will look like Jacob!"

"Sssh Bella! We are so over that now!"

She laughed. "You're so over nothing!" But then lessened the mirth and asked. "So how is he?"

"Well …" Marelle began. "He's really well – last night he was so sweet and funny and just so *perfect*! I actually think finding the body has had a very positive effect on him. Last night I could see the true Jacob shining through!"

"I'm so glad!" Bella smiled. "He is such a nice guy – despite the hair and the penchant for very tight jeans!"

They chatted and laughed for a bit more before Bella signed off but not without reminding Marelle that she could always come if she changed her mind.

Marelle was still smiling about that when she remembered the bubble bath and the strict telling off she had anticipated giving Bella. Should she call her back? She was debating on it when Jacob walked in through the back door. He had the black hoodie on again with the sunglasses but no hood up today. He opened the door and stepped in looking as if he was carrying the burden of an entire world on his shoulders. He pushed the sunglasses up onto his head once in the kitchen and Marelle could see a tiredness residing in his eyes.

"Ok?" she asked.

"Mmm." He sighed.

He looked despondent. No; he looked sad.
"I'd better call that guy." He said with another sigh. "Have you got his number?"
Marelle handed him her phone and pulled out the card to pass to him. He sat down at the table and dialled, staring at the table's surface as the phone rang.
"Put it on speaker." Marelle whispered, pointing at the phone.
He shook his head.
"Hi." He finally said. "Its Jacob Frost. I've got a message to call you."
Marelle sat down opposite him, staring at his face, but he did not make eye contact, and listened to half of the conversation. Jacob didn't say much just 'ok', 'yeah. 'I see' etc in reply to quite long passages that the inspector was saying. When the call ended Marelle looked expectantly into his face. Jacob sighed and looked at the floor. Eventually, he raised his eyes to meet hers.
"They've identified the body. Its Frankie." He said. Marelle drew a breath. Thirty odd years of his life had culminated in that statement.
"Dental records and clothing." He added.
He drew in a shaky breath, averted his eyes away from her. She was sure he shivered.
"Forensics are shipping out tomorrow – I can move the digger."
He swallowed, slumping on the chair, staring at nothing for a good few seconds. Then he nodded his head out of acknowledgement to himself. Marelle reached across and put her hand over his. He felt cold.
For a moment he looked to her, his dark eyes languid and wet. "His sister wants to visit the place where he was found. They're bringing her here on Saturday. Would like to meet me too ..." He lowered his eyes again.
"Frankie's sister?"
He nodded.
"Do you know her?"
He shook his head. "She was only a baby when he disappeared."
"Are you ok with that?"
"I suppose so." Jacob replied, staring at the floor. "He thanked me for telling him I thought it was Frankie." Jacob commented. "Said it had speeded up identification so his family could be informed as soon as possible."
"Well, that's good." She said, with a smile, squeezing his hand gently across the table.
He didn't answer.
Conversation that night was difficult. It was proving hard to break through the wall he'd hidden himself behind today. After last night

Marelle was still amazed at how much he could change in twenty-four hours. But, as she knew, this was Jacob, and this was what she was signed up to. Within her there was a hope that one day he would revert to how he had been yesterday, all day – every day – but till then she was chipping gently away at that wall, piece by piece.

To try and snap him out of it she brought up the subject of the bridge. Smiling she had told him she'd looked it up on the internet and as he had said it was a true feat of engineering and that she would like to see it – if he'd take her there.

He'd given one of those smiles with no happiness in it and just said "Mmmm." Flicked his eyes away and then added. "I've had enough of the bridge today."

Finally she had sat down close to him on the settee and cuddled close with a mug of tea in her hands, drawing her knees up and resting her head against him. The tv was on and he was looking at it but not watching.

"Oh I know what I forgot to tell you." She began. "That woman in the restaurant the other night. She left a message with them – asked me to call her ..."

"Did you?"

"Yes, I did." Marelle smiled. He didn't say anything as she continued. "She had the cheek to leave a message – they called me and gave me her number. I called her. She *was* staring at you ..."

"At me?"

"Yes, at you. I told you she was. Comes on all apologetic for being presumptuous then asks if you are Ezra's brother!" Marelle laughed. Jacob shifted his weight on the settee. "I told her you didn't have a brother – anyway she didn't need to know – and his name wasn't Ezra anyway ... I told you she was staring at you. Why she couldn't have just come over and asked I have no idea." Marelle went on.

"Why did she ask that?"

"Said you looked a lot like Ezra – said her brother used to work with Ezra and she knew he had a brother from round this area ..."

"Ezra?"

"Yes. Ezra. You're not called Ezra and neither was your brother so I told her she'd got it wrong."

"Who was she?"

"Er, I cant remember her name. She was in the restaurant – tried to get into the toilet the same time as you ..."

"Yes, I didn't look at her ..."

"Well it doesn't matter – she was obviously wrong or trying it on. I told her. End of conversation."

247

Jacob stayed that night but didn't sleep. Several times Marelle woke too and sensed him laying there, wide awake but silent.
In the morning he was pre-occupied with getting the digger back and eventually did so later afternoon. Returning to her again she could still not crack the exterior he was sporting – he wanted to be with her, but she could not raise a smile or laugh from him. He hugged her and kissed her if she made the first move, but his response was more from need than passion.
The day after he'd walked through the door at half five. Gave her a look which stopped her in her tracks then sat down at her kitchen table.
"What?' she asked, touching his shoulder and sliding onto a chair next to him.
He screwed his mouth tight. Averted his eyes to his fingers clasped together in front of himself. Took a breath.
"The rumour mill is starting to turn." He said.
'What?"
He raised his eyes to her. "Im being accused of being the son of a child murderer and concealing this from the police!"
"By who?"
"Sam."
"Well that's Sam. We all know what his game is."
'Yes, but ... shit sticks. They were all back today. Sam's father knows the place where Frankie was found was where I used to live. He knows the boy would have been buried there when my father lived there ..."
"How does he know?"
"He's lived here most of his life too ..."
"But he didn't *murder* him."
"No. But in all likelihood, he did *kill* him."
"It was an accident!"
"He was drunk."
"But it was an *accident* – it was your *father* – it wasn't you!"
"These facts don't matter."
"Its just them. Its just rumour – and them trying to be clever!" She exclaimed.
"Its probably all round the village by now ..."
"But people will know you were just a child how could you have known? You *didn't* know!"
"Gossip is a big animal." He said. "It needs a lot of feeding."
"But its not true Jacob." She said. "You know its not true!"
"I know, you know but people believe what they want to. Shit sticks ..."
"Tell the police what you know. Tell them what really happened."

He stared at his fingers. "Then it makes me look as if I've known all along ...and it drops my father in it."

"But he's dead Joacob ... if it takes the heat off you ..."

"It'll put the heat on me ... I don't know ..."

Neither did Marelle. Sam could physically do what he wanted to Jacob and he shrugged it off but this was worse. This was an opportunity that Sam had waited a long time for, and Marelle could see how this could break Jacob's already fractured relationship with everyone and everything.

"Well maybe ignore it and they get bored. If they don't get a reaction from you then they might get fed up and move on ..."

"If they don't get a reaction from me then they'll get one from everyone else – what if they tell the police – or the press?"

She swallowed. "But it doesnt matter because it's a lie!"

"Maybe but it's a nice story, isn't it? It's a nice little scenario. Village recluse uncovers a body of missing child buried in the back garden of the home he used to live in with his alcoholic father?"

"I think you should tell the police. There may be a bit of shit to go through but it will be the truth."

He shook his head.

She stood and held him in her arms. "Lets think about it for a bit."

Jacob woke up screaming in the night and frightened Marelle more than he had for a while. He had literally gone from silent sleep to bolt upright, screaming. She had woken with a jump, shouted to him then tried to grab him as he threw himself from the bed to the window. For a second she had panicked but soon realised he was wide awake. She took his arm as he leant on the window sill. He was shaking quite violently and immediately folded her into his arms.

"Its ok. "She whispered, one hand on the back of his head, looking him to her. "Its ok."

"No – its not." He cried. "No, its not. What if ..." He didn't finish his sentence but dissolved into sobbing again.

"What?" She asked.

"What if he wasn't dead when he buried him?"

Marelle froze against him. "Ssshh!" She said.

"But what if? What if he had still been alive?"

"He wasn't Jacob. He wasn't ..."

"You don't know." He cried. "What if he was buried alive. What if he could have been saved? I stood there, I looked at the body in the blanket and he could still have been alive then, right then. I could have saved him but he may have been buried alive!"

"Sssh. Jacob don't!" She said. "You don't know. You can't even begin to think like that."
"I should have looked. I could have saved him." He sobbed.
"Its gone Jacob. You cant change it … not now. If it happened, it happened."
"But I could have saved him!" Jacob cried.
"You don't know Jacob. Don't spend your life wishing on what ifs or could bes …"
"Why didn't I just look inside the blanket that night? Why was I such a coward?"
"Because you were a child – because your father was cruel to you and was threatening you then – you said so. You were scared of him. You – or anyone else – can't blame you for what happened that night."
"But I should have looked. I should have *known*."
"With hindsight we would all say the same." She hugged his naked body to hers. "But in the heat of the moment we only react how we think best. Its not your fault Jacob …"
He sobbed and she could feel him shivering even though it was not cold.
"Jacob, listen to me." She said, pushing him away and looking into his face. "Whatever happened in the past happened *around* you – you were not responsible for any of it. The past is gone; there's just today and tomorrow. And tomorrow depends on today …"
Marelle didn't know if he listened to her but she dragged him back to bed and wrapped herself around him until eventually they both slept.
Saturday morning was grey, cold and windy which was a vast change from the weather that had been in charge for so long. Marelle uncoiled herself from Jacob, climbed out of bed and reached for her fluffy dressing gown as she shivered. He stirred with her movement, stretching then opening his eyes. She looked over her shoulder at him – for a few seconds his eyes exhibited a glassy bewilderment then he blinked once and pushed himself up in the bed into a sitting position.
"Looks a bit blustery out there today." She commented.
He sighed, sat with his knees apart but the sheet draped over them. He scratched the back of his head.
"What time is Frankie's sister coming?" Marelle questioned.
Jacob yawned. "Said they would bring her to the site around midday. I'm not sure I want to go …"
She turned to him. "I think you should – I thought you were ok with it?"
"It seems a bit pointless."
"Its probably important to her."
"So what's she going to say? Have a look at the hole then thank me for digging up her brother!"

"Its obviously something she feels she needs to do. Will she know you?"
"I don't think so. She was a baby. No one from that family ever spoke to me again after he disappeared." He said with a melancholic tone.
Marelle sat there for a moment. She couldnt quite gauge his mood today but there was an apathy about it.
"Do you want me to come with you?"
He shrugged. "If you want."

FIFTEEN

At a quarter to twelve they went out of the house and to her car. The wind was strong. She had been watching it barrelling across the airfield all morning, blowing the long grass flat and pushing the trees in one direction. It was also colder, and she pulled out her padded jacket for the first time in months and slipped it on. Jacob was slightly less inert, but she could still see the clouds forming inside his head and following him like a trailing weight.

"Do you want to drive?" She asked, turning before she went to the driver's door. It was stupid and childish, but she thought maybe letting him drive would lift his mood.

He didn't say anything but took the keys from her and sat himself in the driving seat. Two minutes later he pulled the Mercedes into the lay-by at the back of Jacob's old house. The police tape had gone, the tent had gone – now it was just a field and a ditch – just as it had always been. It didn't appear that anyone had turned up yet, so they sat in the car. Jacob lay his head back in the seat and put sunglasses on. It was grey and cloudy but Marelle let him be if it made him happier.

She stared out across the fields, all now stubble or already ploughed. The weather changed the scene so dramatically – where was used to seeing the bright blue sky, rich brown earth and green verges and trees today it was muted into a rustic pallette of gray, taupe and olive green with the wind pushing a lean on everything. White bulbous clouds scudded across the icy grey sky, chased by the wind with no sun gracing them with an appearance. She turned her head back and looked at Jacob, laid back in the driver's seat. His head against the head rest, expressionless, slack-faced. The mirrored sunglasses were in place, but she suspected his eyes were closed. He'd showered and his hair was clean and shiny even in the dull light. It was standing up of its own accord as usual but Marelle resisted the urge to reach up and run her fingers through it. She smiled to herself and looked back up the side of the field towards the freshly dug ditch and where it had all stopped a few days ago.

There were a group of people there. She squinted and focussed. They were in Derek and Patricia's garden – Derek and Patricia plus two other people, both female.

"Jacob." She said.

He didn't respond straight away.

"Jacob!" she tapped his arm.

"What?"

"Theres someone over there …"

He sat upright, looked towards the group.

"They're in the garden. Shall we walk up there?"

"No, wait." He said.

Marelle looked towards them, just as Patricia noticed the car. She stepped towards the edge of the ditch and waved.

"Too late, she's seen us." Marelle commented.

Patricia said something to the other people then waved again, gesturing for them to go over.

Once out of the car at her behest, Jacob walked slowly, Marelle held his arm and herself close to him. He looked tall and gaunt, a long figure dressed all in black today – the hoody, skinny black jeans and his black work boots – unlaced of course. He hadn't put the hood on but still wore the sunglasses.

They walked up and stood on the spot opposite the place where he had uncovered Frankie's body. Jacob rested one foot on a clod of earth on the edge of the ditch. Marelle stood alongside him and brought both of her feet together close to his.

"Hello." Marelle greeted.

"Hello!" Patricia returned with her usual gusto. "We were hoping you would be able to come."

Marelle studied the group. Patricia in bright orange and pink with a turquoise blue scarf loose around her neck; Derek in grey; a slightly unkempt woman of about Marelle's age, scruffy blonde hair in a loose pony tail, dark grey suit jacket and black trousers – neither of which fitted particularly well. Then the fourth woman, dark short hair, sharp features, piercing ice blue eyes – probably older than Marelle. She wore a long smart blue woollen coat but had on what looked to be a brand new pair of wellington boots.

"Good morning." The blonde woman greeted. "Although its probably afternoon by now! Are you the digger driver?"

Marelle felt a shot of fleeting anger or something pass through her. Was Jacob '*the digger driver*?' – an inconsequential passer by caught up in this whole sorry mess.

Jacob nodded. "Er, yes." He said, quietly.

"I'm Michelle Tarney – family liaison officer – Mr. Catchpole sends his apologies he wasn't able to come this morning …"

The dark haired woman had raised her eyes to Jacob.

"This is Elizabeth Lee-Makin – she is the deceased's sister."

Marelle looked to Elizabeth Lee-Makin and felt her eyes fixed on Jacob. Briefly Jacob raised his head and his eyes to hers from behind the sunglasses, but he did not linger there.

"Pleased to meet you." He said quietly then looked away again.

"How did you find him?" Elizabeth asked.

"I … er …" Jacob began. "I was cleaning the ditch." He held out a hand towards said ditch. Marelle didn't look at him but he said it in a voice that was stuttering and unsure.

Elizabeth looked directly at him, almost unblinking.

"But from what I've seen my brother's body was found in this garden – not in the ditch."

Jacob lifted his eyes off the ground. "He was, yes." He said. "About there …" He pointed.

"I don't understand." Elizabeth said, shaking her head.

Jacob sighed.

"Erm, excuse me…" Marelle held up a finger. "Do we have to make him re-live this? He was pretty traumatised by it – in fact he's still having nightmares …"

"My family has been traumatised by the disappearance of my brother for over thirty years." Elizabeth said to her, bluntly.

"Erm, you don't have to answer if you don't want to." Michelle Tarney interrupted. "But it is a fair question and Mrs Lee-Makin does have a right to ask."

"Its ok." Jocob said. "I was clearing the ditch, but we had asked the people who lived here – Derek and Patricia – if we could clear the ditch and that it may mean digging into their garden a little to form a drainage route – they asked if I would be able to dig out a bit of ground as a vegetable patch at the same time. I started that but went back to the drain and scraped some soil away and there was something buried there … wrapped in a blanket."

Marelle turned her eyes to the deep swathe of earth, still dragged into a haphazard heap.

"So what did you do then?"

"I stopped digging. I got into the ditch to look." Jacob was looking off to the right as he spoke, not at Elizabeth anymore. "I was expecting it to be someone's pet buried there ... I didn't want to damage it or just pull it out – I wanted to show some respect."

"So you touched it?"

Jacob nodded. "I unwrapped the blanket." He seemed upset, albeit composed. Marelle tightened her grip on his arm.

"And ..?"

"And it was human remains." Jacob said, his voice breaking.

There was silence over the group as the wind blew around them. Marelle's attention was suddenly taken by the red kite circling above them, and she raised her eyes to it.

"Then what did you do?" Elizabeth asked.

"I cant remember. It's a blur after that point."

"He tried to bury it again." Derek chipped in.

"Did you?" Elizabeth asked, staring at Jacob but not getting any eye contact with him.

"I don't remember."

"He did – got in the digger and did that ..." Derek added, pointing to the heap of earth.

"Why?" Elizabeth asked.

"I don't know." Jacob sighed. "I don't remember."

"He was in shock!" Marelle exclaimed. "I told you, he was deeply traumatized by this ..."

Elizabeth looked up and down Jacob and then Marelle.

"For over thirty years he has been missing – his disappearance took my mother's life and no doubt has contributed to my father's demise too – I believe you told the police you thought it was my brother?"

Jacob nodded.

"How did you know that?"

"I've lived in the village all my life – I was here when he disappeared. I heard all of the stories – I knew he had never been found – it had to be him."

Elizabeth raised her chin, drew a breath of the cold air. "Thank you." She eventually said "at least that helped to identify him quickly so we could at least have closure on that."

"Why not come round into the garden?" Patricia said with a smile. "I can make a pot of tea."

"No, its ok." Jacob said.

"You've still got to put the garden straight ..." Derek stated.

"I know. I will." Jacob replied, quietly. He pushed his hands into the pockets of his jeans and sighed. "Is there anything else?"

"No." Elizabeth answered. "No, thank you."

"Erm …" Marelle asked. "What about the funeral?"

She heard Jacob take a sharp breath beside her.

"We'd like to come." She added.

"We cant arrange that until the coroner has completed the inquiry."

"I know, but will you let us know – so we can come?"

"There will be an investigation." Michelle said. "It's a suspicious death …"

There was a cold laboured pause where everything fell silent, even the wind. Marelle felt Jacob move inside her hand; she gripped at a handful of his hoodie and held him there.

Elizabeth fished in her pocket, took out a phone. "Whats your number?"

Marelle reeled her number off while Elizabeth keyed it into her phone. Seconds later Marelle's phone rang in her pocket.

"There. You have my number. "She said. "I will let you know, once his body has been released to us."

"Ok, thank you." Marelle said, Jacob was already beginning to move away – she held on to his arm, but he was pulling her. Once they got back to the car he stopped, leant on the roof and stared into space, taking a deep breath.

"I don't like her." Marelle stated. She looked to him but there was a blankness in his eyes; he was miles away. "Come on, I'll drive…"

They drove back in an uneasy silence. Not just the silence that she was used to with Jacob – that was an easy quiet silence – this was an intense, ringing silence that had the capacity to consume any noise in the universe and muffle it eternally.

They went back into the house and he sauntered quietly through, almost looking at everything as if he'd never seen it before. Marelle followed him, through and into the kitchen. He'd stopped and was staring out of the kitchen window towards the airfield. She walked up behind him, slid her arms through his and hugged him, her head against his back.

"I'm sorry." She said – not sure what for but it just seemed the right thing to say right now.

She felt him sigh, felt his ribcage expand within her embrace. Then he turned towards her, hugged her in to him but did not say a word. She cuddled close and then looked up into his face. His eyes were cold and his face expressionless.

"I'm going up the caravan for a bit." He said.

"Oh, ok … I'll come with you." Marelle smiled, squeezing him gently.

"No, I want to go on my own ... just need to be up there, on my own, for a bit ..."

She sighed, looking up at him.

"Its ok. I'll be back later ..." He replied. "I'll just walk up there ..." And he made space between them.

"Shall I pop up in a little while?" She asked.

"In a while. Give me some space for a bit ..."

Marelle didn't like this; she didn't like it at all, and she liked it even less watching him walk all of the way up the airfield, alone. She didn't know what to do – despite any assurances he made to her she still felt the thread that she held him by was gossamer thin and right now stretched extensively. She wanted to call Bella and just talk this through, but Bella would probably be into an afternoon of partying by now and her response would not be what Marelle wanted at this moment.

How long was 'a while'? Should she leave it for an hour, three hours? The wind had died somewhat but the sky was still a steely grey with no sunshine visible. The grey and muted tones over the airfield reflected this. She looked at the clock for the hundredth time. It was a quarter to four. Once again, she walked to the kitchen window and peered out and across the open field. There was smoke near his caravan. A winding column of dirty grey fumes reaching into the sky. She watched it and tried to ascertain its exact position and concluded it was close to his caravan. For a few seconds she watched it until it began to gather in intensity.

Marelle pulled her coat from the back of a chair and slipped into it, flicking her hair out of the collar she went out of the back door. Walking quickly today she held her coat around her. It was cold and her ears were starting to ache. His caravan was ahead of her and the smoke seemed to be coming from behind it. There was no sign of Jacob, but the top half of the caravan door was open. Tentatively she walked around it to the other side.

Jacob was there. He was sitting on a pile of breeze blocks with a small but fierce bonfire crackling away on front of him. She stopped and stood for a second, watching him. There was an acrid smell of smoke and she wondered what he was burning. Then he sensed her and turned to her, moving his gaze away from the flames.

She looked to him and smiled. He returned a small smile to her and she walked forwards. Without a word he pulled a wooden box alongside him and gestured for her to take a seat there. She did and they both stared into the flames.

She didn't speak and neither did he for a while but eventually he said

"I just don't understand how I spend my life trying to do the right thing only to be constantly impaled upon it."

"You've done nothing wrong Jacob. You should hold your head high and rise above the critics."

He gave a laugh. "I don't understand people ... I don't think I ever have, or ever will. I don't understand where I belong anymore ..."

Marelle felt tears prick her eyes. This was his, all his; his world; his universe – now he was saying he didn't belong here anymore.

"We could move away. I can sell the house. I still have my share of the money from the house with Chris – we could buy somewhere away from here." He stared into the flames as she spoke. "We could hitch the caravan up to my car and just go – anywhere. We could live in the caravan – I don't mind!"

He laughed and looked at her. Today he reminded her of the first night she'd knocked on his caravan door in the dark.

"Sweet, innocent Marelle." He said *"Search your pockets for the stars I left there for a rainy day, and if you place then in the sky their loving light will guide your way."*

Marelle stared at him. Blinked once.

"Whats that?" she asked.

"Its from a song." He replied.

"What song?"

"I don't remember. I just heard it." He turned and delved into a plastic box he had beside him and pulled out an old CD Walkman that looked pretty battered.

"Here ..." he said, placing one ear phone in his ear and passing her the other one. She obliged him and put it into her ear. Then he pressed play. Marelle didn't listen to much music. If she did it was loud and in the car – driving music she could sing along and bang the steering wheel to but as he pressed play and the music came to her through the earphone she was immediately touched by the simplicity of and the emotion in the instruments. There was a melancholic chord to it as she listened, holding her finger against her other ear to keep the music in her head. And when the vocals started, they soared with a feeling that hit her hard in the chest. She looked to Jacob; he was staring at the fire. The words he'd just said to her came into the song and the singer sang every word like a dagger to her heart. This was beautiful – she had never heard it before or recognized the voice. Marelle listened, taken along with the passion in the instruments and hanging on to every word sung. A song about love, loss and grief – it brought a lump to her throat as the last notes of a single guitar played out.

Jacob stopped it.

She took the earphone from her ear.

"That's beautiful." She said. "Who is it?"

He shrugged. "I don't know."

"He has a lovely voice – doesn't it say on the CD?"

"No, its blank." He said and popped open the Walkman. The silver CD inside was indeed blank.

"I've never heard that before." She said, just as her phone rang in her pocket.

Marelle fumbled, found it in the inside pocket of her jacket and took it out. "Shit Seb. I'm not answering." She exclaimed just as Jacob took the CD out of the Walkman and tossed it into the fire.

"Jacob! No!" She yelled, grabbing his arm but too late. She stared at him. "What did you do that for?"

"It means nothing." He said, looking at her.

"It was beautiful. I wanted to hear it again!"

"Its gone." He said.

"We don't even know who it was." Marelle sighed.

"You can probably find out. If you really want to … if you look …" He commented.

"But you already had it!"

"Yeah." He said.

She sat there, staring at the fire as the plastic of the CD made a puff of black smoke rise. Marelle sighed.

"Are you coming back now?"

Her phone rang again. She turned it in her hand and looked. "Fucks sake Seb, just leave a message." She said to herself.

Jacob stood up. He started to kick earth around the fire, smothering it. Finally, he picked up a plastic water container and poured it onto the fire with a hiss. The flames died with a curl of smoke. He kicked earth on it some more as he replaced the cap on the water container and stood it down beside the caravan.

He walked forward. Placed a hand on her should then slid his arm along them.

"Lets go back." He said.

For an afternoon at this time of the year it was unusually cold but he sat himself on the wooden bench in her garden when they got back. He was in a bit of a strange mood that Marelle could not completely gauge. His eyes had lost that fire, that spark she could often see in their depths – even in his darkest moments. Today they seemed flat, like sad dead eyes of fish on the fishmonger's slab. The wind had dropped now so the air was quieter, stiller. Marelle's stomach rumbled as she sat beside him.

"Shall i go a get fish and chips?" She asked, staring out towards whatever he seemed to be staring at but seeing nothing.
"I don't like fish." He said.
"No, I know you don't but – well you know what I mean …"
He shrugged.
"Sausage?" She asked.
"Yeah, ok."
Marelle gave herself a small smile. "You coming?"
"No, I'll wait here." He replied. "But, hang on …"
He pulled out a wallet and passed her money.
"No, its ok." She laughed. "You don't have to pay."
He wiggled it at her again. "I don't pay for anything here – I live here most of the time, but I don't make any contribution."
"You dont have to!" She laughed.
"Take it." He said, holding it out to her between index and middle finger. "I'll wait here."
Marelle smiled and took the money. "Ok." She stood up. "I'll drive, its quicker."
"I'll go in, its getting cold." He remarked and stood up too.
"Back in a tick." She smiled and gave him a quick peck on the cheek.
She'd caught the chip shop just right. There was no-one waiting so she nipped in and ordered, three minutes later she was done and was about to head home. She climbed into the car and placed the packages on the passenger seat and was just about to turn the key when the illuminated sign of the village shop gave her an idea. Smiling she climbed out of the car again and jogged along to the shop. That too was empty. Jill was behind the counter and looked her up and down when she went in.
"Hi." Marelle said. "Have you got any Bud or Becks or something similar?"
Jill turned. The alcohol was behind the counter and not self service like the rest of the shop. Marelle doubted anyone would get past Jill!
"No – not at the moment by the looks of it. "She reported turning back.
Marelle looked down at the shelf herself. "I'll take four cans of Red Stripe then." She nodded.
Jill picked the pack up and put it on the counter.
"Bit of a to-do over there, wasn't it?" She asked.
"What?"
"Finding that body, who would have thought?"
Marelle stared at her; her expression blank.
"People tell me he went missing years and years ago …"
"Yes." Marelle nodded.

"I didn't know the story but there are people in the village who do – said your friend was involved – so I hear?"
"He found the body. He was digging out a ditch."
"Oh ..." Jill mused, which which said a lot more than the single word should have. "Used to be his house though, didn't it – at the time the boy went missing – when he was buried there?"
"Jacob lived there with his father, yes. He was a small child when that happened."
"I guess he must have been ..." Jill replied. "But theres talk that his father murdered the boy, you know – buried him in the back garden ..."
"Yes, I've heard that rumour too!" Marelle exclaimed sharply. "People should be ashamed of themselves – making stories up and speaking on things they know nothing about."
"Well some people *do* know, there are people here in the village who remember it – cant believe that your friend wasn't involved – or at least knew about it! All those years, that poor child's parents didn't know what had happened ..."
"And what do you know about it? What do you know apart from the rants of the vicious hot bed of gossip that has been going on in here, hey? Jacob was a child when it happened – he was living with his father who was an alcoholic and beating Jacob day in day out – how the hell can a small boy be implicated in this?"
Jill took the money Marelle had laid on the counter and stood back..."
"Well I'd say there's all the more reason to suspect he murdered that child – if he was already a child abuser."
"You don't know Jack Shit!" Marelle exclaimed, angrily, to Jill.
Jill was taken aback a bit, she stared at Marelle and narrowed her eyes. "Oh I know enough. You should watch yourself with that one – I always guessed there was something going on with him. John says he doesn't want him in the shop, told me not to serve him if he comes in."
"You're fucking joking!" Marelle laughed.
"No need to swear at me young lady. You've made your bed, you've got to lie in it."
"Oh, I will!" Marelle hissed. "Because he's a better person than anyone else in this entire village – he's above all of your petty, evil gossip and you're all so far up your own arsed way of looking at the world – you are all a load of dirty, gossiping, conniving wankers who deserve each other! And we don't want to come in to your fucking stupid shop anyway – you can stick it up your podgy arse – and you can all rot in fucking hell!"
With that she took the four cans and walked out. When she threw herself into the car she was crying.

When she walked back in Jacob was sitting in an armchair in the living room, his legs over the arm, his feet bare. He had the tv on and was flicking through with the remote control. She walked past in the hallway and through to the kitchen, dumped everything on the table then walked back.

Jacob moved his eyes to meet hers, remote control poised as he stared at her. She stood in the doorway, took a deep breath and smiled.

"Shall we have it in here, on our knees?"

Marelle felt bad; she felt bad because of the gossip and the stupidity that this was bringing out in people, and she felt bad for mouthing off in the shop making herself look stupid and for adding fuel to their fire. How could they? How could they even think such stupid, horrible thoughts? All poised with their stabby little knives – waiting to make their cuts, add their pain. And why should he be banned from the shop? What had he done except find the long lost body of a child and hand it over to the police so the family could finally have peace.

She sat opposite him, watching him. The fish and chips tasted bland and every mouthful was a struggle to get down. She wanted to hug him but if she did she would cry; if she cried he would want to know why and she didn't want to tell him why.

He finished eating, squashed the paper into a ball and sat back with a can of the beer. He stared at her, his bare feet hanging over the arm of the armchair still. Marelle folded the half unfinished fish and chips into the paper and put it to one side. Sensing him staring at he she looked towards him. He looked so sweet, so true and so innocent – she smiled. He raised an eyebrow and patted the cushion in front of him which was exposed due to the way he was sitting across the chair.

She smiled, got up and placed herself on the space in the chair in front of him, folded her body against his then stretched her legs out across the arm with his. Marelle closed her eyes and rested her head on his chest. She could hear his heart beating, strong and steady.

As she sat there she imagined cold winter evenings in here, curled up with him; she imagined him laughing and joking with her; she imagined spending Christmas with him – of spending the next summer and the summer after – and all the summers she would ever be afforded. She imagined growing old with him and standing hand in hand in their twilight years laughing about how foolish they had been. That moment was nothing but emotional jetsom unless they held together by that bond of love. She imagined that right now and realized she had nothing, only that moment and however long it lasted. But she loved him, and she wanted him and wanted to tell him that, but fear of his reaction stopped her. She had everything to lose and the thought of that loss was enough to stop her turning her head to him right now and saying "I love you Jacob."

Instead, she forced herself upon him again; wanting him deep within her; wanting him to hurt her and she tried – God she tried. Her anger building at *them* and her want for *him*. Her hands on his naked body in the darkening of the evening, her fingers tracing his collarbone and then running through his hair. She wanted to take his pain and make him take it out on her; she wrapped herself around him, fingernails against his bare skin. He kissed her with eyes open and she stared right into them but only saw darkness.

And then they held each other in a hold that had the urgency of one final embrace. Marelle cried, sobbed against is shoulder until he stroked her back and told her

"Ssshh. Everything will be ok."

But the next day dawned and that night was over. The sun rose and she watched Jacob standing in her kitchen drinking coffee with those cold, dead eyes, his hair flopping over his forehead in the worn ripped jeans and an old faded blue t-shirt. It had a logo or something printed on it – faded and washed out but she could read it and decided it said "Yellow Son". She'd not seen it before but it looked old – or had just been made to look that way. A week ago, he had stood here in the same way, contemplating his task the next day. Now he stood here thinking about what he had done last week. He looked lost, and scared, and confused; sometimes he looked like a child; sometimes he looked older than his years. He could put a smile on his face that meant nothing and continue with the utter despair but either way she would be there for him.

The doorbell rang. She looked to him, he turned to look at her. It was barely ten o' clock on a Sunday morning – she walked through to the front door with some trepidation. She peered out of the window on the way through to see if there was a car in the drive; there wasn't. Reaching up she undid the latch and opened the door.

"Good morning!" Greeted Patricia, leaning in slightly, grinning.

"Hi." Marelle replied.

"Is erm Jacob, isn't it? Is Jacob in?"

"Yes, what is it?"

"Well I wanted to have a word …"

Marelle sighed, turned her head and called, "Jacob!"

Moments later he appeared, sauntering along the hallway, mug in hand.

"Patricia *wants a word*." Marelle said.

He walked up behind Marelle.

"Oh hello!" Patricia smiled. "Derek is fretting about the garden – do you know when you can put it straight? He wanted to make a start on the

vegetable patch and there is that big piece of turf that has been scraped up. We're not moaning of course but ... it is still a bit of a mess ..."
"I'll do it." Jacob said.
"Do you know when?" She questioned with a smile which she obviously believed would ameliorate any situation.
"I'll do it. Tomorrow." He said.
"Oh that would be excellent!" She replied. "Such a sad affair. That poor girl, losing her brother like that ... I suppose we'll need to wait for the coroner to come back with a verdict of the cause of his death and then the investigation can begin – who on earth would do something like that.?" She looked solemnly thoughtful but soon grinned again. "Any way, at least he can be re-united with his family now – and that's all that really matters, isn't it?"
Marelle could *feel* Jacob behind her.
"So I'll tell Derek it will all be sorted tomorrow then, ok?" Patricia continued.
"Yes. I'll be there." Jacob stated.
"Great!" She smiled again, turning and scurrying away down the path with a quick wave.
Marelle closed the door and turned to him. She sighed. He looked down at her and she watched his jaw tighten. She picked the car keys up from the table in the hallway.
"Get in the car!' She exclaimed.
"Why?"
She shook her head. "Just get in the car."
Jacob obliged as she ushered him out of the house and into the car. He looked at her oddly but sat himself in the passenger seat and pulled the seatbelt around his body. She jumped into the driver's side and sighed a long exasperated sigh.
"Whats happening?" He asked.
"We are just going to get away from here for a few hours!" She explained. "People are winding me up and I don't think the both of us staying in here, all day looking at each other is going to help."
"Its ok. I'm fine ..."
"No, your not. Lets just get away from her for a bit. I'm just going to – drive –"
He resigned himself to it, settled into the passenger seat. Marelle drove. She knew he would not make conversation of his own accord – she wanted to tell him what had happened in the shop last night but it would just just seem like she was piling it on him. He didn't need that right now, but she just had to get away from the toxic stupidity of the village even if only for an hour or two. After a while he did ask

"Where are we going?"
"To the coast."
"Why?"
"Just to get *somewhere*."
"But the coast is closer if you'd have gone the other way …"
"I'm going this way." Marelle replied.

She drove north east, towards the coast where Suffolk just nudged Norfolk and the shingle beaches from east Suffolk borrowed the sandy gold from Norfolk. She did not know that but just drove until she found what looked like a quiet and unassuming area. They parked in a tree lined lay-by and walked through the trees where there was a public footpath sign, across a well worn track across a rough grassy area. You could hear the sea and as the grass gave way to dunes they walked through a cleft in the sandy banks and there it was.

The sun was shining, the sky was blue. There was a slightly blustery breeze as the sand became soft, white and fine. Marelle stopped and stared at the sea with the sunlight glinting off it in a million fractioned facets. She took a deep breath and reached for his hand to clutch it in hers.

"That's better." She smiled. "I know what you mean when you say you need space. Sometimes I do to …"

He looked along the beach to his left. In the distance there were two people – then a bit closer one with a dog. Out on the horizon a container ship was passing slowly.

"Lets walk up the beach." She said.

They walked hand in hand, quite slowly, close to the water but not enough to get wet. Now and again, Jacob stopped and stared out to sea in the same way that he would stare out over the airfield. It wasn't long before the place, the sights and the sounds of it began to tug at their inner children and the urge to run and throw pebbles into the sea took over.

He aimed and threw harder and further than she could. Marelle laughed as it turned into a competition – which he won every time until he started skimming stones instead on a flatter area of water.

"Cheat." She said.
"Watch." He replied. "How many bounces?"
"Three." Marelle answered.
"No four." He flicked the pebble and it skimmed the surface of the water once, twice, three and four times.
"Do it again!"

He did and the stone gracefully danced across the water until it disappeared beneath the surface.

"We could live here." Marelle said.
"Why would we want to live here?" He asked, skimming another stone.
"Just to get away from *there* – I could sell my half of the house and I've still got my half of the house with Chris. I am sure we could find something."
"I thought you liked living in the village."
"I do. I love the village but I feel like we're in the middle of a circle and everyone has a spear pointed at us."
"It would be the same anywhere ..."
"We could live here." She repeated. "I could still work for Seb and I am sure you would be able to find something – something better than what you do now."
"I like what I'm doing now. I like the mind numbing senseless nature of it."
Somehow, she believed him with that statement.
"I like living there. I'be always lived there. Well, mostly ..."
"But what about then the airfield has gone? What when its all bulldozed and built on and we're looking out at grey concrete walls – we could start anew somewhere like this."
He shook his head. "I don't want to leave."
"But if I bought another house, would you come and live in it with me?"
"Whats wrong with the house you've got?"
"Nothing.' She said, sensing this was going nowhere; "Never mind, it was just a thought."
He spun another stone across the sea and counted out loud as it bounced seven times.
She pushed at him quite hard and laughed when he nearly lost his balance; he grinned and grabbed at her but she ran off, across the sand, laughing with Jacob in pursuit.
He was way faster than she was, and he soon grabbed her around the waist, swinging her off her feet and down on top of him in the soft sand. Marelle laughed breathlessly, fighting with her hair in the wind. He pulled her towards him and kissed her gently.
"Its good here." He said. "But I want to stay where I am."
The got back up and walked up the beach, turned around and walked back. They spoke about the sea, birds, the sky. They watched boats in the in the distance and a small motor launch just skimming the coast. Finally, they sat on a prominent dune which jutted out over the beach and watched the sea. It too was gentle today, rising and falling like the breaths of a giant sleeping monster.
"Did your brother drown in the sea?" She asked.

He took a moment to answer but eventually said. "Not sure. He he was found in the mouth of a tidal river so it could have been the sea or the river ..."

"Why did he kill himself?"

"I don't know. Nobody does really ..."

"Tell me about him ..." She asked.

"I don't want to talk about my brother." Jacob said, staring at the sea. "I hardly knew him. He was a different person." He paused, then continued, "tell me about *your* brother!"

"You know how I feel about my brother!" She replied.

"What about parents?"

"Fathers dead. Died years ago – left my mother and took up with some Malaysian woman – caught some strange disease out there and died – years ago now ... we weren't close." She squinted and looked out to sea. "Mum's still alive but lives with a toy boy in Spain. Brought us up knowing not to be tied to her apron strings – to be independent and strong – so now she's reaping the benefits out there – pretending she's twenty years younger than she is!"

He grinned.

"Seb has always looked out for me, and he finds it hard to stop doing it ... his wife is a bitch who he dotes upon. Whatever she says is automatically right! She's changed him ... anyway, I don't want to talk about my brother either!" She finished.

Marelle laid back in the coarse grass. He sat up above her, his head turned to the sea. A plane crossed the sky above them.

"We could go on one of those."

He looked up.

"Nah." He said.

"Have you ever been on a plane?" She asked.

"Of course I have!"

"Where to?"

He paused. "A few places ..."

"I went to New York with Seb – he took me for my twenty-first." She replied. "And I've been to Spain, and Italy."

"I've been to New York." Jacob said. "Long time ago."

She sat up. "You – in New York!" She smiled. "I find that hard to imagine!"

"Do you?"

She nodded. "Why did you go to New York?"

He shrugged. "I cant remember."

"You cant remember!" She exclaimed. "Did you go alone?"

"No, there was a group of us."

"From Uni?"
"Yeah." He replied.
She drilled her eyes into the side of his head, but he didn't look at her, just stared at the sea and played with a blade of grass.
"I suppose we had better go back." She said.

The drive home was less tense than the journey out. Getting away had relaxed her and relaxed him. They went back into the house still laughing and smiling to themselves. Marelle made beans on toast and later they went for a walk around the perimeter of the airfield. It was like it had been a few weeks ago except for the blue portakabins near the entrance.
"I'll get going early in the morning. Get there and sort their garden out. If I have time, I'll finish the ditch as well."
"Do you want me to come?"
"No." He said, a little surprised she had asked. "I'll be ok, I should be done by lunchtime."
In the morning he had gone by half past six. Took the bike and disappeared across the airfield leaving Marelle to read the three emails she had received from Seb yesterday. She'd seen them last night but had chosen not to read them then. All three were pleading with her to call him but the third did contain work for her. Almost as if he'd given up and just sent the work anyway. She did afford him a reply saying she saw no reason to speak with him and that everything was ok. It surprised her to get a reply from him virtually straight away.
"Marelle." It said. "I need to speak to you. A contact of mine reckons this body that's been found is a murder case."
She replied. "Yes I know".
He replied. "I want to make sure you were ok?"
"I'm fine Seb." She sent and left it at that.
Mid morning she toyed with driving up to the lay-by – just to make sure it was all going okay but eventually decided against it. He had said she didn't need to be there, and he was only smoothing their garden out. The only issue could be Patricia, but Marelle knew Jacob would have the sense to keep out of her way!
Therefore, she was surprised to hear the bike at just after two in the afternoon. She walked through to the kitchen, a little surprised as he rode the bike to the fence, pushed it over and came into the garden. Smiling, she opened the door. He had the helmet on still as he turned to her and parked the bike.
"Hi." She said, "All done?"

He took the helmet off, his hair flopped out and he ran his hand through it. Beneath his left eye was a dark red bruise – a couple of inches long and an inch wide. Above that eyebrow and on his forehead was a large graze, still oozing blood.

"What have you done?" She exclaimed, reaching a hand out to him. "Whats happened?"

"I've been suspended." He said, standing staring at her.

"Suspended, from what?"

"From working at the farm. Sam is refusing to work if I am there – pulled in a couple of the others in too – its nothing, its stupid but Adam can't deal with it so he has 'suspended' me until his father returns."

He started forwards, walked up the steps to the back door. She stepped aside and let him walk in.

"Why?"

"Because I'm the son of a murderer – and I might just be one too!" He said, sitting down at the table.

"What!" She laughed.

"They're refusing to work if I'm there, so I've been sent home …"

She sighed. "What happened to your eye?"

"Well Sam had to have a go – just to prove a point."

"He hit you!"

"He had a go." Jacob replied. "Swiped me once and I ducked out of the way for the second but smacked my head into the doorpost …"

"They can't suspend you – you've done nothing wrong." Marelle protested.

"Oh I was born!" He stated. "That's enough."

Marelle sat down on the other chair.

"When is Mr Wright back?"

He shook his head. "Another week, or so. He went to a relation's in Australia."

They sat for a couple of minutes, silence between them.

"Did you get the garden done?"

"Yes, I got that done then took the digger back. There was a welcoming party."

"Why can't you just work in the workshop?"

"Because they're being stupid – Adam included. He can't cope with Sam – he's already got him wound round his finger. It'll be ok when his father gets back but they're trying it on with Adam – and I'm suspended!"

"But you haven't done anything wrong!" She reiterated.

He sat there, legs splayed out in front of him like he'd been dropped onto the chair from a height, face blank, eyes staring down at the floor.
"Are you being paid?" Marelle asked.
He made a little face. "Whether I'm being paid is neither here nor there ..."
"If they suspend you then they should pay you."
"I'm being paid." He said, quietly as a full stop to the question.
"Do you want me to speak to Adam?"
"No." He replied. "Leave it. They'll be fine until something breaks down. No-one in there has a clue how to fix anything."
Right at this moment neither did Marelle.
He sat in the kitchen, staring into space for the best part of an hour. Marelle stayed in there but washed up, or looked in the fridge or swept the floor while he just sat there, not saying a word. Eventually he stood up with a sigh, kicked his boots off and went upstairs. Marelle looked briefly to the helmet on the table, the chair where he had been sitting and his empty boots on the floor. It didn't please her.
Jacob wandered back down and padded into the kitchen in his socks.
"Have you got any toilet paper?" he asked.
"There should be some on top of the cistern?"
"No, theres none there." He replied.
"Hang on." She looked in the cupboard under the sink. "Nope.' She said. "Is it completely out?"
He nodded.
"Shit!" She exclaimed. "Then no." She gave a small smile. "Sorry, are you desperate?"
"No, its ok. I'll go over the shop and get some ..."
He stepped forward and started putting his boots back on.
"Erm, its ok – I'll pop up to the garage – I need to get some diesel anyway ..." Marelle offered.
"I'll just run over there." He nodded towards the front door.
"No, no, I'll go to the garage – I was going anyway ..."
"I'll go over there – no need to drive somewhere." He insisted and began to walk down the hallway. "Wont be a tick ..."
Marelle ran after him. "Jacob?' She called. "Hang on."
"What?"
"I'll go to the garage, you can come with me ... we can chat ..."
"I only want to go and get toilet paper! I'll be two minutes!" He sighed. "Whats the matter?"
She swallowed. Marelle didn't want to say it – she smiled at him, but her eyes were wide and pleading.
"You can't go into the shop."

"What?"
"They won't serve you in the shop – and they probably wont serve me now either!"
"Why?"
"Why do you think?"
He stared at her in the hallway, for a second there was anger in his eyes. He screwed his mouth to one side and bobbed his head.
"When I went in there on Saturday to get the cans of beer – that stupid, fat blonde woman was in there – started on about '*such a to do*' then started saying that the owner didn't want you in the shop, she said she'd been told not to serve you! I mouthed off big time, so I'm probably banned as well now."
"Banned!' he said. "Banned from the village shop!"
"Well, they can refuse to serve us!"
"You're fucking joking!" He exclaimed.
"No, I'm not."
"Why didn't you tell me?"
"I didn't want to upset you." She apologised.
"But it would have been ok for me to just walk in there and make a fool of myself?"
"No – it was just at the end of a bad day. I didn't want to make things worse ..."
He sighed, ran a hand through his hair. Then he started forwards, past her and towards the front door.
"Jacob – where are you going?" She ran after him, placing a hand on his back.
"To the shop. I want them to tell me that to my face."
"Jacob, no – its not worth it ..."
"It is to me!" He exclaimed, opening the front door and going out.
"Jacob!" She called, following him.
"Fucking lunatics!" He mumbled, striding down the garden path.
"Jacob!' Marelle grabbed at him, her hand at his waist to try and stop him.
"Its only going to make things worse!"
He turned, slightly to her. She'd not seen him angry before.
"They're telling me I cant go into a village shop where I've lived all my life – just because of some hoo-doo fucking gossip!"
"Jacob, sshhh." She pleaded.
She stood with her hands flat against him in the drive, right down near the road.
"No!" He exclaimed. "No!"

"Jacob just come back inside – I'll go to the garage." She took hold of a handful of his black fleece he had on and pulled gently.
"Come on."
He shrugged her off and took a step away before he pivoted on one foot and turned back to her "Its fucking madness ..."
She took his arm, pulling him to her as out of the corner of her eye she saw Patricia and Derek coming home in their dark grey four wheel drive, slowing down to glare at them, scuffling in the driveway.
Jacob stopped and stared at her, seemed to take stock of himself then sighed.
"Come on." she said. "Come in the car with me, we'll go up to the garage."
He sat in the car beside her; tense and silent. The garage was about four miles away; she had been to it a couple of times – knew it had a shop. Marelle parked her car to the side, deciding she couldn't really be bothered to get fuel anyway – she had enough, and it was cheaper at the supermarket. So, she left Jacob sitting in the car staring at a brick wall while she went into the shop. She walked through it, found the toilet rolls and paid for them at the counter. She was walking out, rounded the shelves in the last aisle and there was Sam.
He stopped, right in front of her, didn't say anything but stared at her. Marelle averted her eyes and walked past him. Alongside she thought he was going to say something but instead he turned his head and spat at her. Marelle stopped, she had a black t-shirt on and there was a sheen of his spit across her left shoulder. He'd turned away and was walking towards the till. Marelle stared at him for a moment then wiped away the spit with the back of her hand. It took every ounce of resolve she had not to shout at him, not to call him out in the shop and say all of the things she wanted to but she swallowed it all down and walked out of the automatic doors, into the sunlight, past the white transit van parked at the pumps.
Jacob hadn't moved or changed his expression when she got back into the car. She handed the pack of toilet rolls to him, pulled on her seatbelt and started the engine. She reversed carefully and turned the car round; her hands were shaking on the wheel out of the sheer anger coursing through her. As she drove by the pumps towards the exit Sam came out of the shop. She kept her eyes straight ahead but knew Jacob was staring at him as he shouted
"Fucking murderer!! Fucking Scum!" at the car.
She pulled out on to the road and accelerated too quickly, losing the back of the car slightly for a second or two but she soon straightened it. Marelle glanced across at Jacob, he had his head tilted forwards, chin

pointed down, eyes fixed on his knees. He looked so child-like and vulnerable.

"Jacob." She said quietly, "Jacob I think we need to tell the police how you think this happened ..."

Not another word was uttered between them all of the way home. They walked into the house, Jacob carrying the toilet rolls and went through to the kitchen. He put the toilet rolls on the worktop then stood with his back to it. He stared blankly into space as Marelle went to the freezer to look for something for dinner.

"Did he say something to you in the shop?" He finally asked.

"No." Marelle replied. Her head behind the door of the freezer. "Not a word."

There was silence. She closed the freezer door and turned to Jacob. He had his back to the worktop, his head bowed forward and his hands to his forehead, his face twisted in agony at this unfounded persecution.

Marelle went to him. Wrapped herself around his hard, tense form.

"Remember what you said before." She said to him. "You said it didn't matter what everyone else thought because you knew you were right and they're wrong ... you need to tell the police what you think happened ..."

He was crying. He drew a shaky breath. "Its not just that ... its .... *everything.*"

She sighed, held him. "But if you tell the police it will stop their vicious rumours."

"But he still murdered him."

"He didn't *murder* him – it was an accident."

"I don't think that will make any difference to people's perception of it ..."

"I think you need to tell them what you think happened ..."

He had his eyes closed, his hand still to his forehead. "I can't go through with this." He muttered.

Marelle held onto his arm, held herself to him. "I'll be with you – I think it s what you've got to do."

"People keep throwing the word 'investigation' about."

"If you don't tell them then there is bound to be an investigation – they'll find out who lived there, and you'll be drawn in. If you tell them that you remember this happening then it may make this a less drawn out affair – take any investigation off you. We can't get away from the fact that it happened but we can try to deflect this away from you ..."

He shook his head. "I cant ..."

"You can. You *have* to."

"I should have done this on my own – should have left him there."

"But we didn't. We did the right thing – and telling the police what you think happened is the right thing too."

He swallowed. "I cant."

"You can. I've got his number. He said to call him about anything …" She looked up into his face, but he maintained that same stance. "Just tell him it's been playing on your mind and you remembered that night … your father coming in and saying he'd run a dog over and he was going to bury it in the garden. You were just a kid Jacob – no-one can blame you for this. Just tell the truth and everything will be fine."

He sobbed quietly.

"Come on." She cuddled herself to him. "Call him now. Get it over and done. Stop their stupid and vicious gossip." She looked into his face, but he did not move. She turned into him, pushed her arms beneath his and around him. "Come here. Its ok. It will be ok …"

It took a while. It took half an hour to compose him again; to sit him on a chair and get him to agree to speak to the inspector. Jacob's eyes were all over the place and would not look at her, his mouth was tight and clamped shut – just about as far from a smile as he could get. His head was bowed, his shoulders stooped over the table top.

"I'll dial then I'll give you the phone, ok?" She asked.

He nodded.

Marelle picked the phone up but just as she did it rang in her hand – looking at the screen she sighed.

"Bella. Not now!" She sighed but answered it anyway.

"Hi Bella."

"Hi – Seb's been trying to call me I think. Not sure how he got my number but …"

"Bell … can I call you back. Its not a good time …" Marelle interrupted her.

"Oh, ok, yeah." She stuttered. "Are you ok?"

"Yes Bell, I'm fine but just in the middle of something – I'll call you back …" she cut the call and raised her eyes to Jacob again. He was staring through the table top. Marelle found the number and dialled it. It was ringing when she passed it to him.

It rang and he stared at the table. The phone was not on speaker, but she heard when someone answered.

"Could I speak to DCI Catchpole?" Jacob said in a a reasonably calm and measured voice.

The other person spoke in return, more than a couple of words, more like a couple of paragraphs.

"Erm, no. I would prefer to speak to him. My name is Jacob Frost. Its regarding the body that was found in a garden in Groveham."

There was a pause.
"Yes, that's fine ..."
Eventually he said "Ok, bye" and handed her the phone back.
"He's not on duty. They are going to ask him to call when he's there tomorrow."

SIXTEEN

The evenings were starting to noticeably pull in. Dusk had already fallen before she cooked food then watched Jacob's complete lack of enthusiasm for it. He was still sat at the table staring into space while she was clearing everything away and the kitchen was starting to get dark. Then her phone rang again.
"Shit! Bella!" She exclaimed in realization. It wasn't Bella, it was a witheld number. She answered.
"Good evening. This is DCI Catchpole – I have a message to call Jacob."
"Yes, he's here. Just one moment." Marelle blocked the sound hole with her finger and turned to Jacob.
"Jacob, its Catchpole."
He took the phone but his eyes or blank expression did not change.
"Hello." He said.
Marelle sat and watched him and his side of the conversation. He said what she had told him to say – said it had been on his mind, said that he used to live in that house with his father and said he remembered his father coming home one night with something wrapped in a blanket which he had buried in the garden …"
There was a pause while Catchpole spoke.
"No. I'd rather stay here." Jacob stated.
After that he said "yeah" a few more times then the call ended and he handed her phone back.
"He'll be here in half an hour."
"He's coming here?"
He nodded. "Wanted me to go down there but I don't want to."

It wasn't what she had expected. She'd thought they would tell him and he would say 'thank you very much' and go off to do whatever he had to do. But in half an hour he was at their door and Marelle felt a small stab of panic over what could happen now.

Jacob was in a state. He was nervous as hell and was holding on to every cell in his body when they all wanted to take off in different directions. He paced up and down for ten minutes in the kitchen. With the graze on his forehead and the rapidly expanding bruise around his left eye he looked less than presentable in such a situation; he'd run his hand through his hair so many times it could have passed for a Halloween wig but Marelle didn't want to throw any more stones into the already troubled water so she left him to it.

As soon as Catchpole came into the room however Jacob drew himself together, put on the hard shell and strictly guarded eye contact from the very first second.

They all sat at the kitchen table. Marelle had offered the living room but Jacob said he would prefer to stay there, Marelle sat beside him. A hand on his thigh beneath the table.

Catchpole went through his story word by word, writing it all in a notebook. His questions were focussed and did not appear to be loaded; he showed no surprise or expression in anything Jacob said. Once all of the words had been said and now documented he finished by saying he would get that typed up so Jacob could verify and sign it. He thanked Jacob again and said he understood it hadn't been easy for Jacob to tell him all of this. Also, he said that they expected the coroner's report in the next day or so after which Frankie's remains would finally be released to his family. Any investigation of *how* he came to be there would then take place.

"What did you do to your face?" he had asked, getting up to leave.

"Walked into a door." Jacob replied before Marelle had the chance to say anything more.

Marelle saw Catchpole out and walked back through to Jacob. He stood, both hands gripping the back of a kitchen chair, shoulders stooped, head bowed. His knuckles were white.

So here it was. Over thirty years of his life laid bare in a thirty minute conversation with a detective chief inspector. Now it was out there; now there were no secrets, no guarded conversations, no plots or plans. Now that knowledge had been released, set free to try and soar wherever it chose to go.

"You ok?" She asked.

He took an age to answer. "No." He stated. For the very first time since she'd known him he'd admitted he was not ok.

"Its done now.' she said. "That weight is off your mind – its someone else's to sort out now …"
He lifted his head. For all too brief a moment he raised his eyes to her, he shook his head slowly and moved his eyes away from her gaze. She went to him, she pulled him away from the chair, into her arms and she held him; one hand on his back, one on the back of his head, pulling him into her. He was shaking and his skin felt cold and clammy. Marelle hugged him and rocked him and told him it would all be ok now.
"You've told them what you know; its out there; there's nothing they can use against you now – and when they have the investigation, and they prove that what you are saying is right then they can't hurt you with their vicious lies …"
He pushed her away from him, stood tall in front of her with his hands on her shoulders and stared right into her eyes.
"You think?" He said with a blank expression.
She nodded. "They can't hurt you because anything they say will be lies. Its done Jacob …"
He hugged her again, briefly, quickly then still holding her he turned his head to look out into the darkness across the airfield.
"Can I have a shower?"
She smiled. "Of course you can! You don't have to ask!"
He gave a little smile and walked slowly from her, heading upstairs.
She sat herself down at the table. The kitchen was warm, but she felt cold. Placing her head in her hands she closed her eyes a took a couple of deep breaths. Her phone began to ring on the worktop over the other side of the room.
"Bella." She said when she answered it.
"You didn't call me back babe! I'm worried about you …" Bella exclaimed and strangely didn't sound like Bella.
"I'm sorry. I'm fine – just a few things … going on."
There was a very pregnant pause.
"*Are* you ok Marelle?"
"Yeah, yeah." She shook her head to herself. "Yes! I'm fine!"
"Seb called me – I don't know how he got my number but said he'd been trying to call you – said he was worried about you and wanted to check you were ok. I called just to let you know but now I'm worried too …"
Marelle gave a little laugh. "Well as usual he's being an idiot and as you can hear I am absolutely fine!"
"You've never not called me straight back before – you sound like there *is* something wrong. Seb mentioned a murder investigation …"

Marelle took a deep breath and felt hot tears begin to prick at her eyes. She leant against the worktop, her legs crossed, her phone to her ear, her other arm wrapped around herself. She sighed.
"Marelle, what is it?"
"Its just that!" She exclaimed. "Rumours – people jumping to conclusions!"
"Im not jumping to anything ... its what Seb said. I'm just worried about you. Where's Jacob?"
"He's in the shower." She replied and suddenly remembered the incident with the bubble bath. "Hey, I've got a bone to pick with you – did you leave that fake blood bubble bath here last time?"
"Erm ... I may have done ..." Bella said.
"Well it scared me to fucking death Bella!" Marelle gasped. "I found Jacob asleep in the bath and I thought he'd slashed his wrists!"
Bella went to laugh but stopped herself short. "Sorry – but I didn't realise I'd left it there ... Marelle if you are thinking these kind of things then all is not well, is it?"
"Its everyone else Bella. If they'd just leave us – leave Jacob – alone, it would be fine!"
Bella sighed. "Can I do anything to help?"
"No." Marelle replied with a sigh. "It'll be ok. It'll pass ... its just pushed Jacob way out of his comfort zone ... he just needs to keep calm and let this blow over ... we'll be fine."
"But you just said you thought he'd slashed his wrists!"
"Well, I found him asleep in what looked like a bath full of blood!"
"But it's the *'why'* Marelle."
"Because he dug a body up – because he knew that child and they were best friends – because he's really upset about it and because everyone is accusing *him* of being a murderer ... he's told the police the truth of what he knows – he'd done *nothing* wong but ..." She paused. "... but today I got spat at in the shop!"
"Oh God Marelle." Bella said. "Why didn't you call me?"
"What can you do? I don't know what to do! I'm just worried about Jacob. Everyone in the village believes those stupid rumours about him being the murderer ... it doesn't seem to matter if ..."
Bella interrupted her mid flow. "Who! Whoa!" she exclaimed. "How is Jacob being accused of being a murderer?"
"He's not being accused; he's told the police the truth – it's the locals ..."
"But how Marelle?"
She stopped and let herself think about what she as saying; about how much Jacob had said himself – and decided to continue.

"The body he found, of the child – Frankie Lee – who had been his best friend at school ..." She began.

"Yes?" Bella encouraged.

"Well, where he found the body was in the garden of the house where he used to live with his father and Frankie disappeared while he was living there."

"You're joking?"

"No, I'm not. Jacob thinks he can remember his father coming home one night with something wrapped in a blanket saying he'd run over a dog. He buried it in their garden. Jacob is sure this is how the body came to be there. He only realized this recently when he was thinking about it, and he remembered that night. He was only a child when it happened, and he hadn't thought anything of it until now. The trouble is there are some people in the village who know he lived there and they're calling his father a murderer and subjecting Jacob to it too. He's been suspended from working at the farm because the other guys are refusing to work with him; they won't serve him in the village shop either. So, you can see it's a bit shit. We've literally just had the DCI here taking Jacob's side of the story..."

"Shit Marelle!" Bella said. "You should have called me – maybe you should talk to Seb?"

"Over my dead body! I'm not getting the 'I told you so's' from him even though he has no grounds for that. Jacob has told the police everything he knows – I made him do that to try and squash these stupid rumours and keep his nose clean."

"What about the kid's family?"

"His mother is dead; father very frail by what I'm told. They moved away a long time ago. His sister came up on Saturday to see where he had been found and asked to meet Jacob. She wasn't what we were expecting – seemed a nasty piece of work if you ask me ..."

Bella sighed. "Deep shit!" She said.

"No, its not. Jacob is completely innocent in this but as I said – everyone is jumping to the wrong conclusions."

"I'm coming down at the weekend!" Bella stated. "I'd come right now but I can't."

"No – its fine." Marelle protested – she was not sure Jacob would want anyone there.

"I'm not taking no for an answer Marelle – this must be hell for Jacob and you. I can just be someone to talk to if nothing else ..."

Marelle sighed. "We're not partying."

"No, we'll just chill – nothing else and I'm there as a fresh pair of ears if either of you want to talk. How is Jacob taking all of this – it must be hell for him?"

"Probably better than I thought he would." Marelle imparted. "Sometimes he seems fine but sometimes he loses it for a bit ..."

Bella sighed. "Has he said anything about harming himself?"

"God no! He even had a go at me for panicking when I found him in the bath – got angry with me for '*thinking he was going to top himself every five minutes*'!"

"Well maybe you can keep him that way ..."

Marelle smiled to herself. "I'm trying Bell!" She looked up as she heard him coming down the stairs. He wandered in, no top again and in a pair of jeans with no belt which were hanging very low on his hips.

"And here comes Mr sexy himself, half dressed!" Marelle commented to Bella. "I cant keep talking to you Bella, I'm far too distracted now!"

He walked across, reaching for the kettle.

"Hey Jacob, you don't mind if Bella comes for the weekend?"

"Don't ask him!" Bella exclaimed in her ear. "He gets no choice in this – and neither do you!"

Jacob shrugged and nodded, Marelle gave him a smile.

"Ok Bella. See you on Saturday then – but we're just chillin', no partying!"

"Scouts honour!" Bella laughed. "You take care ... both of you!"

She put the phone down, walked shoulder to shoulder with him. His hair was wet and he'd combed it flat again. Made him look older.

"Ok?" She asked.

He nodded.

Marelle turned and hugged him. He finished fiddling with the kettle and the tea bags before he reciprocated the hug, folding her tightly into him and resting his head on top of hers. He was warm from the shower and his skin felt baby soft. Marelle closed her eyes and breathed in the smell of him and the lavender shower gel he'd just used.

The disturbed night she had expected did not materialize. He slept soundly, quietly, beside her. When he awoke in the morning, he seemed completely level headed. Marelle guessed he'd pulled on that mask of indifference of which she was now aware he could summon at will. It meant he was holding everything inwards but at least he was coping. It was almost like he had re-set himself and at breakfast he even seemed happy.

During the morning he was out in the garden, he started tinkering with the bike. By lunchtime he had it in pieces – all spread out neatly. Marelle didn't question him; he was content. She made him a sandwich and a mug of tea when she had her lunch and they both sat out on the bench to eat it.

"Better go for a walk around the perimeter in a bit ..." He said. "Just to make sure no-one is crawling under fences or anything." There was a slight sarcasm in his voice.

He was doing just that when Catchpole called Marelle.

"Does Mr. Frost have his own phone?" He'd asked when she had answered.

"No, he uses mine." She replied. "He's not here at the moment."

He sighed. "I need to go through a couple of points on the statement I took and for Mr. Frost to sign it. Can he come to the police station today?"

"The police station?"

"Yes."

"Erm, can't you come here?"

"Not today ... we've also got an update on the coroner's report." He explained.

Marelle sighed. "What time do you need him there?"

"Anytime this afternoon. I'm here till about seven or eight."

"Ok. "She said. "Er, Mr Catchpole?"

"Yes?"

Marelle was about to tell him about Sam and Jacob's suspension but suddenly thought better.

"Its ok, its nothing.' She said.

"Are you sure?"

"Yes." She stated. "I'll tell Jacob to come down."

Marelle called him. He took ages to answer but eventually she heard his voice.

"Hi."

"Hi Jacob, Catchpole just called. Says can you go down the police station this afternoon? Says he wants to go over a couple of things in your statement ..."

"I don't really want to go down there."

"I know. I told him that but he's insisting; says he has an update on the coroner's report too."

Jacob sighed.

"I'll take you – as long as you know where to go because I've got no idea!

"Ok." he finally said in a quiet voice.

"Where are you?"

"Near the Thor site." He replied.

"What are you doing?"

"Nothing. Just looking and thinking ..."

"About what?"
"Me." He answered.
She was about to question that when he continued.
"I'll be back in about half an hour."
He moaned that he had intended to get the bike back together when he got back but went ahead and donned hoodie and sunglasses and said he was ready to go. She drove the twelve or so miles into town under his direction and parked in a car park behind a large, grand sandstone building.
"Wow! It's a big building." She remarked.
"Yeah, it used to be the old crown court building – and the old cells. Was local HQ at one point ..."
"You speak as if you're familiar with it!" she smiled.
"Only for a seven day ticket once." Jacob got out, adjusted the sunglasses and hood. Considering where he was and what he was about to do he was pretty calm, but she could see the beads of sweat on his top lip.
"Why don't you wait here?" He suggested.
"I want to come in with you!"
"You dont want to be waiting in there, do you? Wait here, hopefully, it wont take long."
Two and a half hours she sat there. Two and a half hours of worrying what may happen to him in there which only became a stronger feeling as time passed. She'd nearly called him or Catchpole to ask what was going on but managed to resist. Two and a half hours later Jacob returned to the car.
He sat himself in the passenger seat and stared straight ahead, still wearing the hood and sunglasses.
"He died of '*blunt trauma injury*'. His neck was broken. He would have died instantly."
The silence in the car was palpable. Marelle didn't know how to respond. She wanted to acknowledge it as being good news – if any good news could come out of this – but it was not the correct thing to say. Instead, she placed a hand on his thigh.
He was fighting with his emotions, twisting his mouth to stop his lip from trembling, just about managing to hold on.
'They're releasing his body – to his family – but there is likely to be an inquest to determine how. My statement is pretty much all they have."
"So what happens now?"
"The funeral. Then the inquest. He doesn't think I'll be called – then they'll decide if there was any criminal activity."
She gripped his thigh.
"It'll probably drag on for months ..." He commented.

"What about the funeral?" Marelle asked.
He shrugged. "Its his family's jurisdiction. I'm only a witness – wouldn't even be that if I hadn't told them what I knew. His body has been – or will be – released to his sister and his father."
"I asked her to let me know about the funeral." Marelle said quietly.
She took him home and he immediately went outside and continued doing whatever her was doing with the bike. It was into that quiet inertness that he fell and spent the next few days. He was functioning but half switched off – as if half his mind was dedicated to some background task while the other half kept up enough of a front to look normal. It was back to the layers that she had so wanted to peel away only this time. She felt he had added a few more.
She was still wondering why agreed to Bella coming at the weekend. While she had always been the best friend any girl could wish for throughout Marelle's life, coupled with the fact that she had a heart of gold – she always struggled to keep her wild side under control. That was not what she nor Jacob needed right now.

Bella arrived on Saturday. There was not the familiar clink of bottles as she walked into the house with a couple of holdalls which Marelle was comforted by. Maybe she had taken heed. She came in with a smile, in white jeans and a baby pink baggy sweater.
"Hey!" She laughed, falling into a hug with Marelle. "Hows it going?"
"Ok." Marelle replied. "He's coping, in his own way. Not heard from work yet though … his boss, well the farm owner, isn't back until next week … but, between police interviews, stupid people and everyone in the village accusing him of being a murderer I think he's doing ok!"
"And you?" Bella raised an eyebrow, denoting that was what she had really meant in the first place.
"Oh, I'm just jogging along, keeping an eye on him twenty four hours a day." She laughed but was serious.
"Where is he?"
"Outside. Spends most of his time messing about with that motorbike. I think he's taken it apart and put it back together at least three times …"
Bella walked through to the kitchen with her, peering out into the garden. There he was, standing there, dressed all in black, a rip in the knee of one leg of his jeans, turning some component of the bike over and over in his hands.
Marelle pushed past Bella and headed for the door.
"He's lost weight Marelle." Bella commented. "His face looks really thin."
"A bit, maybe." She agreed, opening the door. "Jacob?"

He looked up.

"So hows my best friend's favourite boyfriend then?" Bella laughed, going out to him. "Come on, give me a hug!"

It was awkward but he obliged, holding the part of the bike out and away to the side. He gave a tight little smile when she finally released him.

Marelle grinned; somehow, she found that adorable.

"What are you doing?" Bella asked him.

He shrugged. "Just sorting the bike out." He said, holding up whatever he had in his hand.

"Oh, I see." She smiled. "Gonna take me for a ride again?"

He laughed in response to humour her. "We'll see, I've got to get it going again first."

"Well I'll leave you to it."

Bella returned to Marelle standing in the kitchen watching them.

"Aaahh" Bella grinned. "He is so sweet!"

She was like a cat on a hot tin roof but Bella held on to it for their sakes; staying in the house, talking and laughing with Marelle. Jacob remained in the garden fiddling with the bike or watching birds – or staring into space. After a bit of a makeshift lunch, he announced he was going around the airfield. He probably wasn't amenable to it but Marelle suggested that she and Bella go too. So, the three of them wandered around the perimeter, Jacob in front with the two of them trailing behind, laughing and joking like two schoolgirls.

"What do you want to do tonight?" Marelle asked, pushing through the long grass – more used to it than Bella was.

"I didn't think you wanted to do *anything*."

"Well shall we all cook a meal together – or get fish and chips – if they'll serve me ... or what?"

"Barbecue?" Bella grinned.

"No, not again! I'd need to go shopping ..."

Bella shrugged, thought about it for a second then asked. "Is there a takeaway around here? Indian or Chinese?"

"Don't know. Jacob!" She called.

He was a few yards ahead of them, he had a stick in his hand that he'd picked up. He stopped and turned. His eye looked blacker today.

"Is there a takeaway around here?"

"There are a few in town, nothing in the village." He stopped and waited for them to catch up.

"We could get a takeaway? One big order?" Bella asked.

"Do you like Indian or Chinese Jacob?" Marelle asked.

He nodded. "Probably Indian, but either."

"Well treats on me!" Bella smiled. "We'll get a massive takeaway – God, haven't done this for ages!"

They continued round the airfield. Marelle pointed out a "red kite" to Bella only to have Jacob shout back "it's a buzzard, not a red kite!" She told Bella about the airfield, about the imminent development and the Thor site. For some reason Jacob did not venture up towards that today. As they walked Bella had picked wild flowers and tucked them behind her ear in her hair.

"Right I'm ready for a festival!" She laughed as they went back to the house.

Jacob turned and looked at her. "They're Dandelions." He said with a wry smile. "You'll piss the bed if you pick those!"

"What!?" Bella laughed.

"Its an old wive's tale." Jacob explained. "I don't think its true!"

"He knows all of the old wives tales." Marelle laughed. "He even says Good Morning to magpies!"

Bella looked at them both and shook her head. "You two! This Suffolk air must turn everyone crazy in the end!"

Marelle put the kettle on and Jacob went off into the garden. Bella stood in there with her.

"He seems ok." She remarked.

"Yeah, but he's not on 'full power' if you know what I mean? Yeah – he seems ok but I know how much better he can be … I know its all going round and round in his mind all of the time."

"Well distract him from it then."

"How? This is Jacob! Not much distracts him from his train of thought once he gets onto it."

"Well … you!"

"Ok, ha-ha …. No. I can't keep that up for twenty four hours a day."

"No, I mean dress up for him, put some make up on, flirt with him! Keep him *occupied* …"

"Bella. I spend my whole life trying to keep him 'occupied'."

"No you don't. You just let him take the lead and his lead is to go off and do his own thing – on his own – while you stand and watch him."

"Oh Bella!" She scoffed. "Don't be absurd! This is Jacob! I've spent most of my time trying to get him to notice me – chipping away at his hard shell. Now he accepts me – treats me like I am part of his life – despite having rebuilt some of his layers lately – which is exactly what I want. Yes, I want to spend the rest of my life with him and yes, I do truly love him more than I have ever loved anyone else in my life. But where I've got to is enough for now. Keeping him there is the challenge!

"Huh!" Bella laughed. "You've got to grab it while you can Marelle!" And she raised her eyebrows to her.
"In my own time Bella." She replied. "You want tea or coffee?"
The discussion later on was over food. They'd settled on Indian as Jacob had expressed that preference – the next question was what and how much? Bella had pen poised and paper in her hand.
"So, what do we want?"
Marelle shrugged. "Erm ... dunno. Its been a long time since I've had a curry – I've forgotten what I like!"
"You don't like Korma as you don't like it all creamy!" Bella stated, then laughed at what she'd said. Marelle hit her playfully.
"Oh, I don't know – anything – I'll just muck in ..."
Bella sighed. "Jacob?"
He was standing in the doorway. Summoned in from the garden to take part in the ordering. He had one hand high on the door frame, with his head leaning against it.
"Madras, pilau rice."
Bella pointed the pen at him. "I like a man who knows his mind!" She wrote it down. "What kind?"
"Anything but fish."
"Ok, so why don't I get that and a selection of others? We can all dive in?"
Marelle nodded. "Ok, sounds good. Are you going?"
"Yeah, I'll go but I don't know where I'm going!"
"Jacob?" Marelle asked.
"You'll have to go into town there are two or three ..."
"Why don't you go with Bella?" Marelle suggested.
"No, its ok. I can give directions."
"Go on, go and give her a hand." Marelle smiled. "Its no good me going, I don't know where it is either!"
He gave a little smile and looked to the side. "Its ok, I'd rather stay here."
"Its ok." Bella said, "tell me where to go I'll find my way!"
Jacob obliged and gave very detailed instructions, told her where to park and how long it would take her.
"You can take my car if you want." Marelle suggested.
"I'm not taking that bus!" She replied with a grin. "And it probably needs fuel too!!"
Marelle smiled knowingly in return as Bella set off.
Marelle walked across to Jacob and took his hands.
"You can trust Bella you know. She's a bit in your face but you can totally trust her in the same way you can trust me. She would never hurt me and for that reason she would never do anything to hurt you either."

"I know." He replied.

"Why wouldn't you go with her" Marelle turned to Jacob and asked with a quiet smile.

"I don't fancy a trip into town I'll keep my head down here." He replied with a smile in return.

"Oh – and I thought it was because you wanted to be alone with me!"

He turned his head to face her and gave her a full, warm smile for a change. "Maybe I did!"

Bella returned just over an hour later. She breezed in, takeaway bags in hand a clinking noise coming from her shoulder bag.

"Bonus!" She smiled. "You didn't tell me about the great little pub right next door – had a swift one while waiting for the order – brought a couple of take outs too." She turned her face to them as she dumped everything, including six bottles of Becks onto the kitchen table. Her smile turned into a cheeky grin. "Oh, I see you two have used the time wisely!"

Marelle looked to Jacob with a glint in her eye.

"Is it that obvious?"

Bella laughed. "Of course it is! Its written all over your faces!" She replied. "And you've both got changed and smartened up – makes me look a bit cazh …"

"Bella you look immaculate! You always do!" Marelle answered winking at Jacob.

"Right, ok!" Bella remarked, taking everything out of the bags and placing each container on the table. "So, I've got a selection – theres a Jalfrezi, a Rogan Josh, a vegetable birayani, a Madras, a vindaloo … and "she held the last container aloft. "… a free sample cos I sweet talked the guy taking the order – one of their special *very, very* hot Chef's special something or the other!" She grinned. "Try it if you dare! Oh, and poppadoms rice etc … "

"Bella! There are three of us not thirty-three!" Marelle exclaimed.

"Well. I'm hungry. Jacob looks hungry and I'm sure you can pack some of it away once you get started!"

Marelle grabbed plates and cutlery as Bella took the lids off.

"Dig in!" She gestured.

It started civilized, everyone helping themselves, chatting, drinking Becks.

"I got chatted up by a young guy in the pub next to the takeaway – and he said that theres quite a club scene in town and that there are a couple of decent nightclubs and a couple of pubs that have live bands at weekends – I might have to come and try them out sometime?"

"So in that space of time you chatted up the guy in the Indian takeaway, had a drink and also got chatted up in the pub?" Marelle asked.
"*Carpe diem* Marelle!" She laughed, scooping up a forkful of curry. "If its good, take it!"
Marelle shook her head, looked to Jacob who was eating with his usual focussed veracity – this pleased her as he'd only picked at food for ages. He wasn't looking at either of them, but Marelle stifled a little smile as he made a face after helping himself to one of the more 'devious' looking ones.
"If I come back down are you two up for a night out in the home town?"
"I don't think so."
"It would be great – we could get a taxi – come back here afterwards – it would only be in the local town … what do you reckon, hey Jacob?"
He raised one eye. "Maybe." He said and continued eating.
"Well hold that!" Bella exclaimed. "Jacob said maybe. I'll hold you to that!"
"We'll see …" He added.
"Don't you just want to take him to a club Marelle? Can you dance Jacob?"
"No." He answered.
"Bet you can. You're a dark horse, I know!" Bella laughed as she spooned some of the 'redder' curries onto her place with some more rice. "How come you don't have such a thick Suffolk accent Jacob? The guy in the pub was a bit of a 'Suffolk boy'!?"
"I unlearned it." Jacob said. "I stopped speaking like that when I was at Uni."
"So you used to speak like most of everyone around here? Like the guy I was speaking to in the pub?"
He nodded.
"Buh oi can still duet if I wannoo!" He imparted with a serious face.
Bella laughed. Marelle choked on the mouthful of curry she had.
"Fuck Jacob!" Bella laughed. "You really knock that accent out, all of the time?"
"No. I can kick it in if I want to º its gone, unless I want it back."
"Why?"
He shrugged. "It sounds better."
"To whom?"
"Anyone …"
Bella laughed. Marelle stared at him with a warm smile on her face. She reached across and ruffled his hair affectionately. Bella was still laughing to herself as she began to inspect what was left.
"No-one's touched the two hot boys then. Who's up for it?"

"I did have some of the vindaloo." Jacob commented.

"Yeah about a teaspoon full!"

"I'm not touching either of those." Marelle sat back and held her hand up.

"You up for it Jacob?" Bella asked. "I'm game if you're game?" She winked.

"Not sure." He mused. "I'm pretty full."

"You're pretty cowardly!" Bella pointed. "Come on, you're not going to let me eat you under the table, are you?" Then she realised what she's said and clapped a hand across her mouth – comedically! "I mean, come on. I'll challenge you – little old me – a girl – against you, a big tough guy …"

"What? To eat some of that?"

"No, to eat *all* of that!" She ordered. "No, I've got a better idea. Mix the vindaloo and that bad boy together – divide it in half – first one to finish!"

"For what?"

"For the honour of it!" She raised the bottle of Becks to him that she was drinking. "You won't beat me Jacob."

"Jacob, no." Marelle warned. "She once ate a pound of uncooked sausage meat and two raw eggs to prove a point!"

Bella laughed. "Oh God, yes! Do dare, double dare with my cousin who always had to go one better!"

Jacob was staring at them.

"How hot is it?"

"Find out." Bella grinned.

"Come on …" She took both containers, tipped it all into one, mixed it up with a spoon then dished out two equal portions. She pushed one towards Jacob and handed him a fork.

"Only a clean plate counts."

He stared at her. She grinned at him.

"Stop it!" Marelle said. "If either of you are sick – or otherwise – I'm not cleaning up after you!"

"Ssshh Marelle. Stop being a prefect. Nobody is going to get ill!"

"You did from the sausage meat and eggs."

"That was because they were raw." She gave Jacob a smile. He took the fork.

"Go." Bella said.

Marelle watched. It was like two six year olds egging each other on. She knew Bella and she knew how determined she could be. Always the tom-boy, always goading the boys into challenges they would never win against her. Marelle was surprised Jacob was even considering playing her game but at the same time it was good to see him relaxing a little and to see a playful side.

Neither acknowledged the food was too spicy for them – at least not for the first few minutes. After that she could see Bella's eyes begin to tear up and red patches started to bloom on her neck. Jacob was pretty composed but there was sweat running from his hairline down the side of his forehead. Bella stopped, shook her head and took a long drink of water. Jacob popped another forkful into his mouth.

"I'm not done!" Bella warned but her voice was saying otherwise.

"Just call it a day you two!" Marelle suggested.

Bella shook her head again then began to cough.

"Oh shit." She gasped, drinking water again.

"Bella!"

"I'm ok. I'm not done yet." She took another mouthful but immediately began coughing and struggled to swallow it.

Jacob took a breath through his nose, sat back and ate another mouthful.

"Stop!" Marelle ordered, pushing the food away from Bella.

She coughed and spluttered, laughed and pointed at Jacob. "Ok ... you win!"

He put down the fork, drew a breath then put his forehead down on the table.

"Shit." He said, taking deep breaths through his nose and exhaling slowly through his mouth.

Marelle shook her head. Only Bella could turn a quiet night in with a takeaway into this! It took a few minutes, a lot of water and a couple of bottles of lager to get some composure back from either of them.

"Whats next then?" Marelle asked. "Truth or consequences!"

"Hey now, that's an idea!" Bella laughed.

"No it's not." Marelle replied. "I should make you clear up for that."

Bella laughed. "Nice one Jacob. Count that as a bonus. You won't beat me next time!"

"I'm going for a walk outside." He said, getting up.

"If you're going to chuck up then I'm claiming victory." Bella warned.

"I'm not. I'm just going to get some air." He replied.

It was dark outside. The light above the back door illuminated the garden near the house but down towards the perimeter fence it was dark. Marelle started to tidy up, happy that most of it could go straight into the bin. She kept looking up to make sure she could still see Jacob out there. She could.

Bella stood up beside her. "Whats he doing?"

"Just getting some air. Like he said."

"He's such a good guy." Bella smiled. "You could see that all along, couldn't you?"

Marelle smiled."He makes me happy."

Bella grinned knowingly at her and walked out of the door herself, wandering into the garden and sitting herself on the old wooden bench. She'd picked up her handbag from the side as she'd gone out and began rummaging in it.

"Even if he's so sad ..." Marelle finished her sentence to herself in the kitchen.

Bella called Jacob over, patted the bench beside her. He wandered over and sat down.

"I want a word Jacob." she said. "I'll be quick because Marelle will wander out in a minute or two no doubt ..." She half turned to him. He had his elbows on his knees leaning forwards.

"She is obsessed by you. She eats, sleeps and breaths you Jacob – you know that. She would go to the ends of the earth for you. She wants to spend the rest of her life with you. I can see why and you two light each other up; she glows when she's with you. She loves you Jacob."

He was looking straight ahead. Bella turned her head to him. He smiled a bit then looked at her.

"Does she?"

"Of course she does!"

"But she's a lot younger than me. She could have the pick of whoever she wants."

"She wants *you* Jacob. Only you." Bella stated. "Make an honest woman of her Jacob."

He laughed. 'What?"

"Ask her to marry you."

He shook his head in disbelief of Bella. "I think she'd run a mile."

"She would not. Believe me, its all she wants."

He shuffled beside her and said nothing.

Bella waited for an answer but did not get one. She fumbled in her bag and pulled out a cigarette packet.

"Don't tell Marelle." she whispered, took one out and lit it. She took a few drags, closed her eyes and sat there.

"Oh, hey sorry – do you want one?" She suddenly opened her eyes, asking him.

He looked at her. "Go on then ..."

Bella was taken aback a little but passed him the packet, he took one, she lit it. Bella grinned and sat back.

As predicted, a couple of minutes later Marelle wandered out.

"Budge up." She said squeezing onto the end of the bench. "No ill effects yet then?" She asked, smiling.

"No, we're just fine." Bella grinned.

"Are you smoking again?!" Marelle suddenly asked. "I thought you'd given up?"

"Well, no – just around you mostly but I've been such a good girl I thought I would just have one very sneaky one out here."

"Oh Bella!"

"Sshh!" She said. Then giggled, nudging Jacob.

Marelle looked along at Jacob and was utterly taken aback to see him sitting there with a cigarette in his hand too.

"Jacob! You don't even smoke. What are you doing?"

"He just fancied one." Bella explained for him. "Leave him be …"

"But you don't smoke Jacob – I've never seen you smoke …"

"I used to." He said sheepishly. "Its just not a regular habit anymore."

Marelle tutted to herself. Sat there a little angrily and stared at Bella as she now blatantly drew on the cigarette.

"Bella?" Marelle asked. "Can I just show you something?"

She got up, Bella followed her into the house, leaving the burning cigarette on the window sill.

"What?"

"What are you doing?" Marelle sounded angry.

"I was just sitting out there with Jacob, having a smoke after whats been a pretty fun evening."

"But *what* are you smoking?"

"Marlborough King Size!"

"No you're not. They're not proper cigarettes, are they?"

"What do you mean?"

"You made then, didn't you?"

Bella laughed. "Marelle you use such funny words for things sometimes. Yes, I *rolled* them …"

"Whats in them?"

"Nothing." She shook her head and winked her eye.

"Bella!"

"Oh well just a smidgeon – its just hash – its fine."

"You've given Jacob one of those?"

"They're all I have."

"He doesn't smoke."

"Well looks to me like he's a quick learner then." She grinned. "He knew what it was when he took it. Just chill out. The only side effect will be to relax him." She replied. "Stop worrying!"

She smiled at Marelle, placed a hand on her arm. "Trust him. He's as good as gold. Now, I'm just going to the loo – I may be some time!"
Marelle went outside and sat next to Jacob. She cuddled close and lay her head against him.
"I didn't know you smoked."
"Used to, in my youth – didn't everyone?"
"I didn't."
"Well you're so pure, and perfect, and innocent." He whispered to her. "And I mean that as a compliment." He brushed his lips against her ear. She could smell what he was smoking. "Its ok, I've put it out now. He slid his arm around her and she turned into him.
When Bella came back they were in an embrace on the bench; seemingly oblivious to her or anything else in the world at that moment. Bella smiled to herself and ducked back into the kitchen.
He finally went to bed with her – chilled, warm and with a full stomach. She cuddled up to him in her bed with Bella in the back bedroom. Jacob was tired, content and happy for once and she closed her eyes thinking that once again Bella had been right and tonight had been a good idea.

SEVENTEEN

The bed suddenly shook and the headboard banged against the wall behind her. Marelle awoke from deep black sleep to conscious bewilderment and saw Jacob running naked across the room from the bed he'd left with some considerable force. Without warning or stopping he ran straight into the wall opposite between the door and the wardrobe. Marelle gasped in the moonlit darkness of the room as she sat up. Jacob hit the wall with a degree of momentum, rocking the wardrobe so it rattled against the same wall while at the same time and a result of his impact he was catapulted sideways, glancing off the wardrobe and ending up on his hands and knees on the floor.
"Shit Jacob!" She said, getting up herself to go to him. "Are you ok?"
But before she got to him he scrambled up and was off again, charging blindly towards the door which was closed. He hit the door shoulder first, lumping it violently on its hinges.
"Jacob!" She shouted. "What are you doing?"
He continued to throw himself into the door on, two, three more times.
"Jacob!" Marelle got up and went over to him, half scared but half used to this. She reached out a hand to him, taking hold of his arm as he threw himself towards the door again.
He shrugged her off, gasping and lurching himself away from her like she was some demon trying to drag him to his death. He made some kind of weird agonised sound and ran into the door again, crying to himself now.
"Jacob, its ok!" She said but was more scared by his reaction to her now.
He sobbed and began feeling along the wall frantically, hitting them with the palms of his hands.

"Hey, its ok ..." She wondered if she should open the door for him but worried that he would then have the whole house to rampage through. "Come on, come back to bed. You're dreaming ..."

Again, she reached out to him as he moved along the wall towards the window. Her hand just touched his back but it animated him and he leapt along the wall to the window, turning to her and holding one hand out as if to ward her off. His nose appeared to be trickling blood, probably from the first crash into the wall. Then he found the window, climbing onto his knee on the sill. Reaching up he suddenly located the window latch in the same split second that Marelle realised his intention and she ran forwards, grabbing for his hand as he made an attempt to open it.

"No!" She shouted, grappling for his hand as he fought her off, naked and crouched on the window sill, his bare form against the cold glass. He was crying and sobbing and flailing at her with his hands and she was struck with the fear that it was only a matter of time before he won and got the window open.

"Jacob no!" She shouted.

He lumped himself against the glass.

"Shit" She said to herself.

He was trying to push her away with one hand and open the window with the other. If he opened the window it would be impossible for her to stop him going through it. If he fell from there at best it would on top of her car, at worst onto the concrete drive.

"Jacob please!" She yelled.

"No, no, no." He yelled back. "No!"

She pulled his arm with one hand while the other was firmly holding the window's handle down, but he was scrabbling at her with his hand.

"Jacob!"

"No!"

"Jacob!"

"No!"

Then there was a knock at the door.

"Marelle, is everything ok?" Bella asked from behind the closed door being diplomatic enough not to barge in.

"Erm, no, there is a slight problem." She shouted back. "Come in but we're both ..." Bella came in. "... naked." She completed her sentence.

"Whats the matter?" Bella asked, "Oh God, what's he doing?"

"He's trying to get the window open. He jumped up and ran into the wall – he's been trying to force the door open now he's got up here ..." Her voice was scared as she struggled to hold the window closed with him pushing at her and trying to open it.

"Is he asleep?"

"I'm not sure."

At that point he began holding on to Marelle's wrist, grabbing at it and pulling her hand away from him, crashing his back into the window pane.

"Let me go." He choked, crying again, pushing away at her and succeeding this time; she staggered back a step or two but immediately shot forwards as he went for the window again.

"He's asleep." Bella said. "Slap him and wake him up."

"You can't – you shouldn't wake people up if they're sleepwalking – it may kill them …"

"Don't be stupid. Slap him! If he wakes up he'll realise what he's doing …"

Marelle looked at her, at least Bella had been sensible enough to sleep in a t-shirt.

"I'm not slapping him!" Marelle replied. "Come here and see if we can get him off the window sill."

Bella came forwards, reached out to his arm "Wow! He's hot!" She commented but as she held on to him, he began to fight again, flailing and turning himself to the window.

It all happened so quickly Marelle wasnt prepared for either but when he started to fight Bella – without hesitation – raised her hand and slapped him hard, right across the right cheek. For a split second his head snapped backwards in recoil but in an equally totally reflex reaction to the slap he had just received he struck out with his right hand and caught Marelle square on the jaw. It knocked her off her feet and onto her bottom as at the same time the forces being equal and opposite he tumbled from the window sill as well.

Marelle found herself on her backside on the floor, a million dots of light playing in front of her eyes and her head swimming. The whole side of her face was throbbing and she thought she could taste blood. Dazed, she shook her head and went to get up by herself, holding onto the bed. Bella had screamed and was instantly at her side.

"Oh God! Are you ok? He hit you full on …"

"I'm ok." Marelle sighed, struggling with the dizziness that was now coming in waves. "Is he ok?"

Jacob was on the floor, knees up, ankles crossed, his head in his hands. She went to get up but was unbalanced so she crawled over to him.

"Jacob." She said.

"Marelle!" Bella warned. "Be careful, he hit you!"

"He hit me because you hit him!" She hissed. "What do you expect? If you're half asleep and someone suddenly hits you? You're going to react, aren't you?" Marelle heard Bella sigh as she reached out to Jacob. Jacob was still coming to. She touched him and he reached out to her like an infant, scrabbling around and wrapping himself into her arms. She lay her head against his hair, her face in his hair. For a few seconds he held her then pushed her away. "Where did I hit you?" He asked. "Bella said I hit you?"
"You did but it was an accident ..."
"Where?"
"Here." She pointed to her face. "Its ok."
"No, its not ok. Its never ok." He held her again. She could feel him trembling.
Bella was standing there staring.
"I'm sorry Jacob." She said. "I thought it was the right thing to do."
He sighed, holding Marelle to him. "Maybe it was ... its ok."
She remained standing there, not really knowing what to do. "Are you two ok now? Shall I leave you to it?" She eventually asked.
"Well I'm wide awake now, Jacob's nose is bleeding – maybe we'll lick our wounds and have a hot drink ..." Marelle replied, pushing him away from her and looking right in his face.
"I'm ok." He whispered shaking his head.
"Ssshh." She smiled. "We'd better put some clothes on."
"Ill go down and be putting the kettle on ..." Bella excused herself almost as if she couldn't wait to get out of the room.
Marelle sighed and stared at him. "I thought you were going to jump out of that window – if Bella hadn't slapped you I think you might have so the punch in the face was worth it!"
"Are you ok?" He asked.
"I'll live." Marelle smiled. "I've never been hit before so I don't know how I'm supposed to feel."
He reached up and held her face with his hand.
"I would never, ever have raised a hand to you. Never ..."
"I know." She replied. "It was an accident. Please don't blame yourself." Marelle touched his nose gently with her finger. "Come on, put some clothes on."
There was a silence between them in the darkness. Jacob stood up, pulled on pants and a black t-shirt. Marelle stood there, she'd put on a pair of pants but was standing with her arms wrapped around herself. He walked over to her, crept his fingers onto her shoulder, tentatively as if he expected her to push him away. She didn't so he walked close behind her. He kissed the top of her head then gently placed a t-shirt –

his t-shirt – over her head. She found the arms in it and pulled it down. It smelled of him and for a second she lifted it to her face and breathed him in. He wrapped his arms around her, loosely.

"Are you ok?" She asked.

"Yeah, I'm fine."

They walked into the kitchen hand in hand. Bella was standing by the kettle, three mugs on the worktop. She looked quite shaken for Bella. Her eyes focussed on Marelle then moved up to Jacob. He did not make eye contact with her. It was a quarter to four.

Bella made hot chocolate. They all sat at the table drinking it. Marelle realised she was wearing the old faded blue t-shirt with 'Yellow Son' on it – the one he had been wearing the other day ... she looked down at it.

"I saw them a while back." Bella said.

"Who?" Marelle asked.

"Yellow Son." Bella said, at one of the weekenders ... "

"Oh." Marelle said. "Its Jacob's t-shirt."

"I can see that!" Bella replied.

Marelle looked to Jacob. He was sitting sideways on to them, one hand on the table, head bowed, looking down at the floor, his hair falling forwards into a spiky quiff. Marelle stared at him; there was silent tear running down his cheek.

Bella was desperately trying to get her attention when she said she was going back to bed and guided Jacob in that direction too. Bella followed her up the stairs, close behind, waiting for an opportunity to get her on her own. Marelle didn't afford her that; she followed Jacob into the bedroom, turned to close the door to find Bella standing there. She gestured, open empty hands in a shrug.

"Its ok. Night Bella." Marelle smiled and closed the door.

She heard Bella stirring in the morning but didn't take a lot of notice. Jacob was sound asleep beside her his eyelids flickering gently, his face relaxed and youthful. Marelle didn't want to wake him when he looked so peaceful so she closed he eyes again and tried to dispel the throbbing pain in her jaw.

Last night she'd glossed over it but now a few hours later she was aware she was probably no going to get away with pretending it hadn't happened. She had tasted blood last night and she could feel a row of raised abrasions inside hr cheek where her teeth had cut into it; he could also feel a slight firm roundness on her jawbone. Marelle wanted him to forget it and for Bella to forget it but when she presented this morning, she doubted it would be possible.

A while later she must have drifted off to sleep again and was woken by Jacob kissing her forehead as she still lay in the bed.

"Morning." She smiled, wrapping her legs round him as he turned and sat on the edge of the bed.
"Bella's in the kitchen." He said.
"Probably cooking breakfast because she feels guilty."
He sighed. "Not as guilty as I feel."
She sat up, touched his back, kissed his neck. "Its ok, it was an *accident*."
"Bella doesnt think so."
"It doesn't matter what Bella thinks, does it?"
He turned to her, she placed a kiss on his lips as he did.
"Don't fall out with Bella over this ..."
"I won't. Our friendship can stand a difference of opinion – it has – many times!" Marelle added. "Anyway, how about you? You ran into that wall pretty hard ..."
"I'm ok. I can feel it in my shoulder a bit but ... I'm okay ..." He sighed.
Bella was proudly cooking breakfast when they went downstairs together.
"I got up and went to the shop." She said. "Come on, sit down. Its ready I got some decent coffee as well."
She was smiling, acting normal.
Marelle sat down at her own table but felt for Jacob's hand beneath it. She took it and squeezed gently.
"Sorry about last night Bella." Jacob apologised with a sigh.
"Its ok. Don't worry I've seen a naked man before. I mean don't tell Marelle, but I've seen quite a few!" She winked. He gave a little smile. Bella had turned it into a joke – her way of getting over things.
"Three full English coming up!"
They ate breakfast, Bella chatted away, joked, laughed – didn't let the awkward silence that was brewing from enveloping the situation. At least until Jacob announced that he was going to sit outside in the sunshine and drink the mug of coffee. Marelle watched him wander down the garden, stand and look out over the airfield with his back to them.
Bella sighed.
"How many times has that happened?" She asked.
"What?"
"Him going off on one like that ... I sense its a regular occurrence ... you did warn me, so it has happened before."
"Not many times. Not that bad."
" ... and has he hit you before?"
"Christ no!" She exclaimed. "I told you – he only hit me because you slapped him. I happened to be in the way – "

"He still hit you. The circumstances don't matter – he didn't even know he'd done it. That makes it even worse!"
"Bella, can we just forget this happened? It was an accident and is unlikely to ever happen again."
"You face is swollen – and bruised."
"I know. I can't do anything about it, can I?"
"Doesn't he scare you when he's like that? It would sure scare me, especially if I was here on my own ..."
"It only scares me in that he might hurt himself."
Bella sighed. "Marelle, I'm not going to lecture you ..."
"Well you are because you've said exactly that!"
"I'm not. If you want to be with him then so be it – its up to you but ... well ... I'm always here. You know that."
"Hes not suddenly some monster Bella. Just because he did what he did last night doesn't mean anything. I mean you had him smoking hash who knows if that wasn't a mitigating factor?"
"He hardly smoked it. He put it out when he realised you didn't like it."
"See! And I'll say it again Bella he is the kindest, gentlest, sweetest person on this earth and what he did last night was an accident. He would never intentionally hurt me – I know he wouldn't. Christ he gets beaten up by the lunatics at work all of the time and he doesn't lift a finger against them – he sees the good in everyone."
When Bella had gone Jacob hugged Marelle tightly and apologised so profusely, blaming only himself. That night he slept like a baby with her in his arms.

When Marelle asked him if he was going to ring the farm about going back to work he said there was no point. Mr. Wright was not back for another week and speaking to Adam would just be wasting everybody's time. He went off over the airfield saying he had a few things to 'tidy up' but said he would come back and have lunch with her. Marelle worked but with one eye on the airfield. She saw him walking about with a large pole a few times. She had no idea what he was doing but he seemed to be suitably employed doing it. The bike was still in he garden – it looked a lot better than it had originally with his recent fiddling and cleaning. He'd remarked that it looked almost roadworthy the other day and she'd laughed along with him. As long as it stood there, she was relieved that he would not disappear on it.
That afternoon he said he was going to the caravan to 'have a sort out'. Marelle supposed that could mean him burning more stuff – but it was his stuff. Part of her was pleased that he seemed to be finding things to do and getting himself back into a routine; the other part didn't like him

going out of her line of sight. But he'd wandered back at about five and appeared content and she was happy that some kind of normal was spreading back into their lives.

Bella called in the morning 'just to check everyone was ok'. Marelle confirmed they were but kept the conversation neutral with Jacob sitting opposite her.

The day after he did the same. Going off in the morning and returning at lunchtime.

"What are you doing?" She'd asked, purely out of curiosity.

"Just tidying. Theres a good chance I'm going to have to move the caravan so I'm just making sure its mobile and clear around it. "He'd replied matter of factly without an ounce of emotion in his voice.

"Do you reckon?" She'd asked,

"Sooner or later it's going to have to me moved. Just making it a but easier."

"Move it into my garden."

"We'll see ..."

She'd made tea and a sandwich and was now standing leaning against the worktop. Someone suddenly banged on the front door down the hallway. Jacob turned his head and looked towards it, a slight concern on his face. Marelle tutted and walked away from the kitchen, along the hallway to answer it. She ws expecting Inspector Catchpole and opened the door just enough to poke he head around it and see who it was.

The very last person she expected to see standing on her doorstep stood there, a familiar smile on their face, eyes still warm and honest.

"What the fuck are you doing here!" She exclaimed.

Chris turned full on to face her; his cheeky, usual grin.

He gestured with an open hand "Hi Marelle!"

"Seriously! What are you doing here?"

"I just came to say hello and have a little chat."

She glared at him. Eight years of her life she had lived with him, shared a bed with him and he still annoyed her.

"How do you know where I live?" She asked. him. "You've spoken to Seb, haven't you? He's sent you down here just to try and sweet talk me ...well forget it Chris, you can't sweet talk me."

He sighed."I did see Seb and he did tell me your address but I'm not here to 'sweet talk' you. Far from it ..."

"I don't want you here Chris."

"I thought we were still friends, still *amicable* and all that." He did that little dodging movement that had always irked her.

"Amicable to a point yes. Turning up on my doorstep unannounced on a mission from Seb – no!"

"I hear you've got a new partner?" He asked, still smiling.
"That from Seb too?"
"I saw Bella too – a while ago. I was shopping with Heidi - *my* new partner..."
"How civilised."Marelle said.
"Can I come in, have a cup of tea?"
"No." Marelle stated. "Say what you've got to say on the doorstep."
He gave a little laugh.
Marelle heard movement behind her, she opened the door wider without looking behind herself. Jacob had obviously overheard the conversation and deemed it safe to come to her defence.
"Well ..." Chris began. "As I said, my new partner is called Heidi and was ..." His eyes moved to behind Marelle obviously at Jacob's height. "Oh hi!" He said.
Marelle looked around as she felt him close behind her. Jacob was there, one hand on her shoulder now but standing there in the doorway with his sunglasses on and the black hood of the hoodie on his head and pulled tight around his face.
"Hi." He said.
Marelle sighed as invisibly as she could then reached her hand up to gently pull the hood from his head while trying not to look too obvious about doing it. Jacob didn't resist but is hair – dirty from whatever he'd been doing that morning – popped out of the hood and stand straight up. She lowered her hand and placed it on his back.
"Jacob, this is Chris. You know who Chris is ..."
"Hi." Chris said again. "Pleased to meet you." And Chris, being Chris, couldn't help but add, "that's an interesting look!" In the politest way possible.
"He thought it was someone else!" Marelle excused him. "So, you and Heidi ...?"
"Oh yes. Well Heidi and myself are planning to get engaged and I wanted to tell you personally in advance – so you didn't hear it by rumour or second hand gossip."
"Well congratulations. Thank you for telling me." Marelle smiled.
"I wanted to do it face to face, you know, we go back a long way and as we are still friends. I didn't want it to be a shock to you." He smiled.
Marelle smiled in return. Jacob just stood there.
"So – I can see you two are happy here. Is the house ok? It seems like a nice village."
"Yep, all good." She said.
"Ok." Chris smiled, sensing he wasn't going to get any further and knowing Marelle as he did that it wasn't worth pushing a point. "So, I'll

head on home then – I would like you to come to the party of course – both of you ..." He laughed. "... and the wedding. Heidi wants to meet you."

Marelle smiled.

"Have you had a tooth out?" He suddenly asked.

"No, why?" Marelle questioned, quite perplexed at him asking.

"Your face, its swollen and a bit bruised." He pointed tentatively.

"Oh, that ....no!" She laughed. "You wouldn't believe it ..." She felt Jacob shuffle behind her. "I was pulling something out of a jammed drawer and my hand slipped off it and I ended up hitting myself in the face!"

"Really?" He laughed. "I thought maybe you two had been beating each other up!"

"I walked into a door." Jacob said from behind her.

"Aah I see!" Chris grinned. "Seems like you are as accident prone as each other – sounds like a good match! He was joking but Marelle shifted her weight uncomfortably.

"Well you will have to meet Heidi. She will love you ..."

"I'm sure she would." Marelle nodded.

"Well take care then – both of you." He pointed back at them still with a grin. "I'll let you know when the 'big day' is."

"Ok Chris." Marelle replied. "Have a safe journey home."

"Er, yeah, thanks." He nodded and began to walk away.

Marelle watched and waited until he was out of earshot then muttered "be sure to report it all to Seb. I'll wait for him to call."

She closed the door and turned to Jacob.

"Seb has sent him – how else would he know this address? Bloody cheek! I bet they thought that up pathetic excuse to come down and speak to me between them. So he drove two hours just to tell me that!"

"He seemed genuine. "Jacob said. "It was a nice gesture for him to let you know."

"Jacob!" She laughed. "As if I ever want to see him again."

She walked back into the kitchen. Jacob followed.

"Sorry." She said.

"What for?"

"For him."

Jacob shrugged. "You could have asked him in. I don't mind."

"I don't want him in here. He's nothing to me! He broke up with me – I kept it amicable to make my life easier. He was probably seeing this "Heidi' then if the truth is known." She ranted.

Jacob didn't say anything but stood staring off into the distance.

He went back over the airfield in the afternoon – Marelle had thought about going with him but decided to finish the work she was doing for Seb so she could forget all about him once it was done. She saw Jacob off with a quick kiss and a friendly hug. She buried her head into his chest and felt tears prick her eyes. She blinked them away before turning her face up to him.
"See you in a bit."
He nodded, smiled and was gone again.
Chris turning up at her door had been a bit of a surprise to say the least. He would have been the last person she would expect to turn up. It was obvious Seb was behind at least part of it but good old dependable Chris – who everyone loved – was the type of person to drive two hours just to let her know he was getting engaged. It was almost as if he was asking her permission! Well, she'd told him straight and honestly – she had moved on too. But she couldn't help but feel a tiny pang of jealousy pulling at her. In eight years, he had never mentioned getting engaged or married but in the six months with Heidi he'd made that commitment.
Now he was going to go back and report to Seb that she had definitely hooked up with a lunatic!
Jacob wandered back to her at lunchtime. As soon as she set eyes on him walking up her back garden path it brought a smile to her face as she opened the back door to greet him. He looked up to her as he approached; he'd got an olive green military style jacket on over the black fleece which he'd not had on earlier and which she'd not seen before. Just looking at him thrilled her. His hair, his face, the way he walked. Tall, unhurried, worn black jeans tucked into his unlaced boots, steady sure steps and gentle hands. Marelle stared right into his deep brown eyes. How could she even compare him to Chris or even let him cross her mind.
She reached out and hugged him in the entrance to the doorway.
"What?" He asked, sensing her need.
"Just wanted a hug." She smiled. "New jacket?" She asked when they parted and he walked right into the kitchen.
"No, I found it when I was sorting stuff out. I havent seen it myself for years!"
"Looks good." She remarked, turning to the worktop to prepare something to eat for both of them. They had just both st down to eat when her phone rang. She sighed, thinking and expecting it to be Seb – she was surprised he hadn't called already. She picked up the phone; it was Catchpole.
"It will be for you." She said, sliding her phone towards him.

He stared her in the eye as he took the phone.
It was a short conversation, but she got the just of it. He had been asked to go to the police station.
"What for?" She asked.
"Said he had a couple of questions and wanted to check a couple of points."
"I'll drive you down this afternoon."
He didn't say anything in reply for a moment or two but then said. "Can I take your car? No point in us both going."
"Erm, yes, if you want. I'm happy to take you though, I don't mind."
"You'll only end up sitting in the car for hours again."
She didn't reply. She didn't really want him going on his own, but she equally didn't want to insist she went. Jacob appeared to be coming to terms with everything and able to cope so maybe she should cut him loose a little.
"Its ok, I'll go on my own if you dont mind me taking your car. To be honest I quite fancy having a drive!"
There was however, something quite unnerving about watching him drive off in her car on his own. He wore the sunglasses and raised his hand with a small smile as he drove away.

Marelle contemplated wandering up the airfield to sneak a peak at what he'd done 'tidying up' around the caravan and was staring at his bike in the sunshine. It was cleaned up, polished and almost looked perfect standing there in her garden. She smiled to herself at his diligence and care for it. She turned her head to the airfield when there was suddenly a loud, two blast beep. At first, she thought it was a police siren but when it repeated she realised it sounded like a car horn – no, it sounded like a lorry's air horns. Marelle looked and listened, looking towards the sound. Two long blasts then a pause. Then a long one, punctuated at the end by a few short blasts. It took a few more before she realised it sounded like someone was trying to get in the gates to the airfield – and they sounded impatient.
"Shit." She sighed.
She couldn't drive round there as Jacob had the car – to walk would take a little while so they would just have to sit there blowing their horn until she could get there. As she walked, she tried to call Jacob but there was no reply.
Pulled into the recess at the front of the main gates was a huge, green lorry with a long trailer on the back of it. It was too long for the entrance so he had the cab at an angle with the trailer zig-zagged into the space available. Even so, the back of it hung on to the road a bit. On the trailer

was a massive piece of machinery which reminded Marelle of a tank! She had no idea what it was, but it was painted blue and white with "Devorah" diagonally on the side. As she approached someone came up against the wire of the gate, waving a piece of paper in the air. He was small and dark with olive skin.

"You open gate." He shouted in what she guessed was a mid European accent.

"I drive seven hours and gate is not open. You open gate – now!"

"I can't open the gate. I don't have the key – you will have to wait."

He seemed more than frustrated. "Open gate. Now!"

She shook her head. "I can't. I don't have the keys."

"Well where key then?" He had the strangest ice blue eyes.

"The person with them isn't here. I will call him."

"I was told I would be let in. Seven hours – I have to get back to depot …"

"I'll call him." She turned away to use the phone as he jabbered on angrily – even kicking the gate at one point.

She dialled again and waited. Still no answer. Jacob could well be a while; it had been a couple of hours last time. Turning back to the irate lorry driver she gestured with open hands.

"I can't raise him at the moment. You will have to wait …"

"I not wait! I wait too long now! Time is money – you know. You don't care."

Just at that moment the phone rang in her hand.

"Hang on, hang on!" She said to him as he rattled the gate violently. "Jacob?"

"Yeah, he said breathlessly. "You've called a couple of times – ok?"

"Theres a really irate lorry driver trying to get in the gate on the airfield …"

He sighed.

"Been blowing his horn for God knows how long before I walked up there. He has a huge lorry with some gigantic piece of machinery on the back …"

"Fucking shit hole!" He shouted behind her.

"Is that him?" Jacob asked.

"That's him; he's kicking the gate and everything."

"Ok, well I'm now leaving. I'll be half an hour at best – just walk away of he's being abusive."

"Ok, I'll let him know. Or are the keys here? I can let him in?"

"No, I've got them." He replied. "Ok, I'll be there shortly."

"How was it?" She asked. "At the police station – what did Catchpole want?"

"Oh – nothing." He replied dismissively. "Just the same shit over again."
"Oh." She said. "Are you alright?"
"Yeah, yeah" He answered. "I'll be back in a tick. I'll go to the main gate."
"Ok."
She turned back to the lorry driver. "He's now coming. He'll be about half an hour."
"No – I will not wait any longer. I go and you have to pay for this. I not wait half an hour!"
"Its up to you." She shrugged.
"Fucking bitch." He spat and strode back round to the cab to get back inside, still going ahead to himself.
Marelle shrugged. He didn't start the lorry and didn't go as he had threatened. She just hoped that Jacob turned up inside half an hour.
While she waited Marelle looked over to his caravan to her right. Maybe she might take a wander over there just because she was here anyway. No doubt under the close attention of the lorry driver she walked away. He had pretty much cleared everything from around the caravan. It was completely bare around it and looked ready to tow away at a moment's notice. Marelle walked right up to it with the intention of peering in the large front window but he had pulled the curtains. For a second, she stood staring at the caravan in its denuded state with all of the curtains closed. It looked cold and closed now, standing there waiting to be shipped away. It was just a caravan, but it represented so much and seeing it like this filled her with a melancholy that laid deep within her chest.
She began to walk back slowly, past the portacabins that had been left there a while ago. Where, she wondered, would this new lump end up? The lorry driver got out of his cab and began shouting again which alerted her to Jacob's arrival by the gate. She quickened her pace and walked up to the wire as Jacob rounded the cab of the lorry with the lorry driver in his face.
"The gate must be open. I not wait, I not wait – this costs me money – I drive seven hours."
"Devorah have keys." Jacob said. "I'll open the gate now. Where are you putting this?"
"How do I know? Just bring to site – I drive seven hours and end up waiting here for you – you should have gate open!"
"No, I should have the gate locked at all times ..." Jacob stated.
Marelle giggled to herself. How could he be some calm and patient with someone like this?
"This is a shit hole. I put in complaint – you are rude to me. I tell them!"

"You can tell them what you want." Jacob replied, unlocking the gate and letting it swing open. "You know, I don't care." He turned back to the lorry driver who was a good few inches shorter than him. "There you go ..."

"You tell me where it goes. I only driver. I don't have no plans for site."

"Over there." Jacob pointed, walking over to open the other gate.

The lorry driver walked off, still moaning to himself. He shunted about in the lorry a bit until he eventually had it straight. Jacob had walked over to the side of the gates with Marelle.

"All ok?" She asked.

He nodded but his jaw was tight. Be better when he gets out of the way – has he been rude to you?"

She laughed. "Not really. Just generally being a tosser!"

The lorry moved through the open gates and onto the airfield. He pulled straight, cut the engine then got out again with his piece of paper.

"You unload quickly – I need to get away ..."

Jacob stood upright. "I'm not unloading it! I only open the gates."

"You unload it now! Says on paper – operator to unload ..."

"Well I'm not the operator. If they want someone to unload it then then will have to send someone with you."

"You fucking unload machine – I waste too much time at this shit hole." He pointed quite threateningly at Jacob.

"I can't. I can't operate one of those. I don't know how to. Its probably worth the best part of a million quid so I'm not inclined to touch it." Jacob explained staring right at him.

The driver stared back at Jacob with such an intense anger that Marelle thought he was going to hit him. Jacob kept his cool and stared right back at him from behind his sunglasses.

"So' what I do now hey? So' what I do? Seven hours I drive here and now you say you wont unload machine? What I do now?"

"You can take it back to where it came from or you can call Devorah and ask them to send an operator to unload it."

"You call fucking people! Not my problem."

"Not my problem either. I'm only here to open the gates. I don't touch plant."

The driver threw his arms up. Marelle flinched as she thought he was about to throw a punch. Jacob maintained his position. Still, except for a tiny twitch of his right cheek. He shrugged when the lorry driver turned back to him.

"You fucking arsehole." He exclaimed. "You fucking arsehole and I put in a complaint about you ... you pay for second delivery – you pay for my lost time in this shit hole."

"If you make you way out, I will close the gate behind you." Jacob said, extending an arm to show him the way.

"Fucking arsehole!" He exclaimed again and spat as he walked off.

Jacob turned briefly to Marelle as the driver got back into the cab. He gave her a little smile and twitched his cheek again.

"What is that thing anyway?" She asked, nodding to the back of the lorry.

"It's a concrete crusher." He replied.

They both stood and watched as the lorry started up again and he noisily and violently turned it around in his anger, crunching gears and running it onto the grass. He put his foot down as he left but managed to shout

"Fucking arsehole."

Out of the window at Jacob before he left, way too fast and with his hand on the horn for most of the first mile of his return journey.

"Wow! I don't want to be here when he comes back!" Marelle said, raising her eyebrows.

"Don't worry. You won't have to be!" Jacob replied, pulling the gates closed. "Are you coming back with me?"

"Yeah" She nodded and ran through the gap he had left for her.

He drove back and once in the house he handed her the car keys.

"I got some fuel." He said. "You were a bit low."

"Oh thanks! I forgot." She replied. "Did they say anything about the funeral?"

"No." He replied. "Were you expecting them to?" He pushed the sunglasses up onto his head and she looked up and into his eyes at last.

"No, but, well I thought they might have heard. I did ask Elizabeth to let me know – maybe nothing has been arranged yet. I will give her a call tomorrow." She replied, smiling at him – his right eye and cheek twitched again as she did so.

"Whats wrong with your eye?" She asked.

"Nothing."

"You keep twitching it like theres something in it – let me see …"

"No, no. Its fine." He said. "It does that sometimes."

"Does it. I've not noticed it until today?"

"Yeah, its some nerve thing I guess. It's happened before – its just like an involuntary movement … theres nothing wrong."

"Oh." She said, totally unconvinced. "Ok."

He wouldnt say much about what they had asked at the police station so she left it.

"I see you've tidied around the caravan?" She remarked. "It looks really neat."

"Yeah, it had to be done sooner or later. Ten years of crap soon mounts up. Its ready to move when I have to."
"Are you going to put it in my garden?"
"Don't know yet. If we put it in the back, we wont be able to get it out again once they start working on the airfield –and I wouldnt wnt to put it your drive at the front."
"It would be ok in the front. I don't mind it being in the back either."
He gave a small laugh. "Its not entirely your house is it? And what if you want to move or sell the house?"
"I wont. I'll buy Seb out – I told you." Marelle replied. "Anyway, you can move in here with me – properly – cant you?"
"Well. I'm happy to stay here with you but I'd like to hold on to the caravan … you know …" He said. "I may be able to put it somewhere down the farm?"
"No! Jacob! You cant put it down there – put it here. In the front if its easier, I don't mind – I just want you to be close to me." He smiled one of those small innate smiles that he did to placate her. His right eye twitched again.

Marelle took the opportunity to call Frankie's sister the following morning. Jacob had wandered off across the airfield again. He was quiet – not an odd thing to ever think about Jacob – but there was just a kind of anxious silence about him which was different. She'd also noticed the twitching was still there. The frequency appeared to be increasing. Jacob however did not seem bothered by it and that it 'happened sometimes'. Marelle *was* a little worried about it.
Elizabeth's phone rang and rang. Marelle didn't leave a message but decided to call again later.
Marelle thought about calling Jacob and suggesting that she took lunch out to him on the airfield – the weather wasn't brilliant but it was good enough to sit somewhere sheltered and have a mini picnic. Her plans were scuppered however when he walked in her back door earlier than expected. He looked tired but gave a gentle smile to her.
"I was going to bring a picnic out." She said, still making sandwiches.
'Sorry – I just wandered this way so I thought I'd come back."
"No matter." She answered. "We can eat outside anyway – just in case that lorry comes back!"
"He won't be back today. It'll take them at least a week to sort that out."
They sat outside on the bench with sandwiches on their knees. Jacob didn't say a lot but suddenly sat up straight, took a deep breath and then turned to her as if he as going to say something. Then his eyes went blank, he screwed his mouth as if thinking about it then looked down

and away again. Marelle stared at him expectantly – he didn't say anything but she watched his right eye twitch again. She left it for a few seconds then asked
"Are you sure that twitching isn't anything you should be worried about?"
"Its nothing. It's done it before. It'll last a week or two then go. I don't like it either."
She pursed her lips to herself. That was telling her to shut up about it.
After a few minutes silence he looked across the airfield. It was cooler today. There was a breeze which took any residual summer heat out of the the air. He had the olive green jacket on again. He pointed to the sky.
"See the clouds." He said, "they look like mountains."
She looked and nodded.
"When I was a kid I used to pretend the clouds were mountains in the distance – and all of this land was a vast wilderness in a big country!" He told her.
She smiled and pushed her leg close to his. He continued looking at the clouds.
"Shall we stay in the caravan tonight?" She asked him.
He didn't move his head or look at her. "Why do you want to stay in the caravan?"
"I thought you might want to. You know, if we have to move it soon – I thought you might want to for "old times sake!" She leant into him playfully with her shoulder as she said it.
He gave a little laugh and turned to look at her. " – if you want."
She smiled and ignored the fact his right eye was twitching again.
The caravan looked bare and incredibly tidy. Before it had been neat and tidy but now it was minimalist. Marelle had no idea where he had put everything but suspected it had been binned or burnt. She longed to look in the wardrobe as she seriously hoped he hadn't had a clothes cull as well. Climbing into the cold sheets in the bed and cuddling up to him she giggled.
"We could still sleep in here sometimes if it was at my house." She laughed.
He didn't reply but slid his arm around her shoulders and hugged her in to him.
"We'll see." He said eventually, kissing her gently on the top her head then laying his head against hers. And that was how they slept, in each other's arms, in the caravan, in the darkness, in the middle of a disused airfield.
In the morning she lay on the bed and watched him walk through to the kitchen. He'd pulled on a t-shirt and a pair of pants. She smiled.

"I haven't got much in the line of breakfast – I've got tomato soup, a pot noodle and beans with pork sausages – I don't have any bread or milk ..."

"Ooh, I don't mind."She replied. "I haven't had beans and sausages in a tin for years – I'm game if you're game!"

He took the tin out of the cupboard with his back to her. Marelle thought of the night she had strode across, banged on the door of this caravan and the gaunt face in woolly hat had poked out. What if she had gone the other way – to the house over the road instead – Patricia and Derek's; or what if she had just stayed in her house that night? Would their paths and lives have ever crossed subsequently?

Now he she was here with him as he heated beans and sausages in that same caravan. Marelle rolled off the bed and walked through to join him, wrapping her arms around him from behind and hugging him.

"You eat much better with me!"She laughed.

"I think I survived by myself. I didn't do too bad!"

"No, I like the results!" She laughed, laying her head against his back as he attended to the cooker.

So with a mug of black tea and half a tin of beans and sausages each they sat in caravan, looking out over the airfield. As they ate a lone hare loped across in front of the caravan. Slowly, checking the ground – unsure of them.

"Look" She pointed.

He nodded.

"Do they turn white in winter?"Marelle asked.

Jacob grinned. "No!"

"But I saw it on the telly, I thought hares turned white in winter – for camouflage?"

"Not these ones. Some hares do but these are just normal Suffolk hares – they don't turn white."

She smiled at him for not mocking her.

"I tried to call Elizabeth yesterday but there was no reply. I'll call her again today." Marelle told him but he didn't say anything in response.

EIGHTEEN

They walked back to her house after breakfast, Marelle had declined a cold shower in the caravan although Jacob had partaken. He'd said his intention was just to hang around on the airfield today in case the lorry came back.
"Why don't you call the farm?" She suggested as they went through her back door and into the kitchen.
"He's not back until the beginning of next week. Nothing is going to change until then." He replied.
"Its stupid." She remarked.
Jacob shrugged.
"Right – I'm going to have a hot shower!" She said, heading for the hallway but stealing a kiss from him on the way. "I'll be ten minutes. Wait for me to come back down, won't you?"
He nodded and walked back to stare out of the window.
Marelle walked happily into the hallway and was about to go up the stairs with her hand already on the newel post at the end when she noticed what looked like something hanging over the panel of glass at the top of the front door. She stepped down from the first step and walked back along towards the door. There were what looked like three blue ribbons on the glass. Puzzled, she lifted a hand and opened the door.
There was nothing hanging down so she poked her head out and looked back at the door. She drew a sharp breath as she realised what she was looking at were not ribbons but a scrawl of aerosol paint right across the front door including the glass. There were two words. Murderer Scum.

Her first thought was how could she hide this from Jacob; then realised she could not. As she turned her eyes also settled on the word SCUM scrawled across the windscreen of her car in red aerosol.

She gasped. Her hand to her mouth, walking out and looking back at the house. Over the front door it said 'Murderer Scum'; across the living room window it said 'Murderer' and as she looked closer at her car she saw the foot high writing along the side in blue saying 'murderer'. She stared. Her knees felt weak and she could hear her heart slamming in her chest. Then she turned and ran back through the open door.

"Jacob!" she shouted. "Jacob!"

There must have been frantic panic in her voice as he appeared in the hallway before she got to the kitchen door.

"Jacob, look …" She pointed and he followed her outside.

Both of them stood looking back at the house; she gestured to the car, almost crying.

"*Look.*" She said, tearfully.

He looked; at the house; at her car. Jacob drew a short sharp breath.

"Its ok." He said. "I'll get it off …"

"No – we should tell the police!" She exclaimed. " … they cant do this!"

"We can tell them if you want but I don't think they'll be bothered by this. Its not a threat; its just opportunist sabre rattling …"

"But who would do this?"

"Almost anybody in the village according to recent events." He said quietly. "Go in."

They both went in and he closed the door.

"I'll have to go and get some stuff to clean it off …"

"Will it come off? What if it won't come off?"

"I'll get it all off, but I need to go and get stuff to clean it …"

"Well you can't go in the car – not with it like that!" Marelle exclaimed.

"It'll be ok."

"No, it wont. You're not driving around I it like that – you can't see out of the windscreen!"

He sighed. "I'll go on the bike."

"But its not roadworthy, is it?"

"It'll be ok … if I keep sensible … and keep my eyes open."

"No Jacob you can't. What if you get stopped? It hasn't even got a number plate on it!"

"I'll be careful …" He said. "I'll not attract attention to myself – I wont be long …"

She sighed but as he put the crash helmet on and set off on the bike, she realised she was shaking. Marelle walked around the house for a bit then decided to go and have the shower she had been on her way to in the first place.

When she came back downstairs with damp hair there was still no sign of Jacob. Telling herself not to start worrying she picked up her phone and dialled Elizabeth's number again. It rang several times then went to voicemail once more. This time Marelle left a message.

"Hello Elizabeth – its Marelle Buckleigh – Jacob Frost's parter. I hope you are ok. I was just calling to see if there are any arrangements for Frankie's funeral yet? If you could give me a call back that would be lovely. Many thanks. Bye bye."

She put down the phone and stood looking out of the window, her arms wrapped around herself when she heard Jacob returning. He came across the airfield and into her back garden.

"Right." He said. "You stay inside. I'll sort it out – it'll be as good as new."

"I'll help."

"No, I'll do it, its ok. You stay in here."

For most of the day he cleaned paint off the house and her car. Marelle had often looked out on him and almost been absorbed by his quiet and stoic determination; his apparent contentment at having something to focus his mind on. Even so she was also watching the twitching which looked to her to be getting worse and not subsiding as he had implied it would. But as he had said to her – he didn't like it either – so she would keep quiet about it.

By the end of the day every trace of paint was gone, and her car was far cleaner and shinier than she had ever seen it. He came in, late afternoon and sat himself tiredly on a kitchen chair. He sighed.

"What if they do it again?" She asked.

"Then I'll clean it off again." He replied, quietly.

Marelle walked past him and playfully ruffled his hair with a smile. She reached for the kettle but as she did her phone rang in her pocket. Fumbling, she pulled it out.

"No number." She said, putting it to her ear "It might be Elizabeth – hello?"

"Oh hi, this is Leah from East Archaeology – I was hoping to speak to Jacob Frost?"

"Oh, yes..." Marelle said, a bit taken aback. "Hold on for a moment."

She put her finger over the hole in the phone and turned to him.

"Someone called Leah from some archaeology thing – asking for you ..."

He raised his eyebrows but took the phone from her.

After a series of 'oh's" and 'yeahs' and a final 'I'll be there in five minutes' he ended the call and handed the phone back.

"Archaeology – just passing and wondered if she could come onto the site for a quick recce …"
"What, now?"
"Yeah, said she was just down the road – I'll go and let her in."
"How did she get my number?"
"Oh, I put a note on the gate – to call if there was no-one around …"
Marelle looked slightly annoyed by that, but he added
"I'm, normally with you if I'm not here so I thought that was sensible."
Which she agreed with.
"I'll come with you …"
"No, its ok. I'm only opening the gate. She said she wouldn't take long so I'll hang around and close it again afterwards …" He said, standing up.
Marelle sighed to herself as he walked off up the airfield. Elizabeth hadn't called back – she had thought this call was her. She checked the time, twenty to five. Marelle dialled her number again. It rang and rang, going through to voicemail again. Marelle did not leave a message.
An hour later Jacob had still not returned. Marelle slipped on her trainers and headed off in the same direction he had gone in an hour ago; half worried; half jealous that the woman on the phone had sounded very young and confident.
She could see him as she approached. Standing near the entrance, just by the portacabins. He had his back to her and was pointing towards the far side of the airfield. Beside him stood a petite female figure; slim and tiny, long blonde hair in a pony tail out the back of a baseball cap. As Marelle got closer, she could hear her laughing. The girl saw Marelle before Jacob did but when he saw her eyes looking behind him, he turned. Marelle walked up with a smile and wrapped her fingers around Jacob's arm, pulling close to him. He had sunglasses on but had taken the hood off.
"Hi." Marelle smiled.
"Hi." The young blonde woman replied then continued her conversation with Jacob.
" – yeah my parent's parents lived around here in the fifties or sixties so I'm pretty excited to have lead on this one …" she nodded. "We're planning on next week but I can give you a call when we turn up?"
Jacob nodded.
"It's a very nice site." She commented.
"Pity its going to be raised to the ground." Jacob said. "It's a beautiful place. Been my home for the last ten years – but I've lived in the village all my life you see – it's a shame it cant be saved."

"Well that's why we're here – to document and make sure anything of interest is saved ..." She smiled.

"Interest to whom?" Jacob asked but in a non aggressive tone but nonetheless got his point across.

"Well different things meant different to other people." She said. "We can't save everything – but ..." She gave a sympathetic smile.

Jacob nodded, knowingly.

"So – thank you for letting me in and showing me round. Its always good to have someone around with local knowledge." She began to walk towards the gate. "I'll be back, next week hopefully!"

"Ok, bye." Jaconb answered, walking behind her to close the gate and slipping out of Marelle's grasp as he did so. The girl climbed into a small white van with a red and brown logo of 'East Archeaology' on the side. She gave a little wave as she drove away.

Jacob walked back to Marelle and slid his arm around her shoulders as they strode on.

"Nice to actually speak to someone who is polite and happy – who is *interested* in this site and actually cares ..."

Marelle smiled. "You're such a sucker for a pretty face!"

He squeezed her shoulders. "Yes, I am." He replied.

A few days passed uneventfully. Jacob seemed bored and listless. Marelle had the feeling that he was in limbo – waiting to get his job back – waiting for everything to be resolved – waiting to move on. It frustrated her that she had heard nothing at all about Frankie's funeral either as that would afford him some closure at least. While he was outside, over the airfield she took her phone and called Catchpole.

"Hello, this is Marelle Buckleigh – Jacob Frost's partner." She said when she eventually got put through to him. He paused for a second as if he explanation of who she was had thrown him but after a second or two he answered.

"Oh yes. Hello. How can I help?"

"Well, I don't know if you can, but do you know if any arrangements have been made for the funeral of Frankie Lee? I've been trying to get in touch with his sister to no avail ..."

"Oh, er ... yes, hold on." He put the phone on hold for a short while. Marelle waited.

"Yes." He said when he returned. "I can't go but two of my colleagues will be attending. Its Wednesday 25th at 11 o clock at ..." He audibly fumbled with a piece of paper. "St Leonard's Church, Chidworth, Hampshire."

Marelle was silent for a little too long as she'd scribbled it down and was staring at it.

"Did you get that?" He asked.

"Yes ..." She replied. "That's next week ... Hampshire?"

"Yes, we will be attending too ..."

"Ok ..." Marelle said, still pondering on it. "Ok, thank you – I'll let Jacob know."

Marelle stared at the paper she'd written on. The 25th, next Wednesday. Less than a week away, in Hampshire! Where the hell was that? For some reason she had expected it to be here; she didn't know why but she was shocked it was somewhere else. She was shocked the date was so near and she was shocked that Elizabeth had not returned her calls. Marelle walked through to the kitchen and looked out. Jacob was over on the airfield poking around in the grass with a long stick. She looked at the paper and she looked up at him. He hadn't seen her, so she went back through to her computer.

Chidworth was on the edge of the New Forest – it was four hour journey from there. The funeral was at eleven so it would mean an early start – or an overnight stay. She sighed. Nothing about this was going to be easy.

She waited until Jacob came in then walked through as he was kicking his boots off just inside the back door.

"I know when the funeral is." She stated, starting the conversation.

"Oh, right." He said.

"Its next Wednesday, at eleven o clock."

He looked up and nodded.

"But its not round here." Marelle explained.

"Oh, ok. Where is it?" He asked, standing and staring at her.

"Its in a place called Chidworth." She continued. "Its in Hampshire. Its about a four hour drive from here."

He stared at her, went to say something then didn't. His eyes looked dark and troubled, no sun in them to bring out the gold that they were flecked with.

"Where?" He asked.

"Chidworth, St. Leonard's Church, Chidworth."

He wrung his hands together in front of himself, looked back outside, looked back to her. His right eye twitched once, twice, three times.

"Why not here? He lived *here*?"

"Its probably where they live now ... where his father lives ... where his mother is buried ... I don't know why but that's where it is ..."

"I thought he would be buried here …." He said. "Where he lived, where he died." The words were coming out, but his mind was already heading in another direction.

"I know, but its not. Its there … we need to think about getting there."

"I can drive." He said.

"Its ok, I can drive." Marelle added. "But we will need to leave early – or we can book into a hotel – do you want to send flowers?"

He just stood there staring through her as if she wasn't there.

"Jacob!" She called. "Do you want to send flowers?""No." he replied. "No flowers – flowers are wrong."

"Ok." She nodded, a little surprised. "So do you want to drive down early or stay in a hotel the night before – or stay in a hotel after the funeral and drive back the next day?"

"No." he said, "no."

"No to what?" She asked.

"I don't care." He said suddenly but quietly. Then he turned, shoved his boots back on and went out of the back door, up her garden and across the airfield again.

Marelle watched him go, striding quickly now, almost as if he was headed somewhere. Putting the piece of paper down, she pulled on her own shoes and went after him. Marelle had to run to catch him up and did so reaching out to his arm and pulling herself to him as he walked briskly with a purpose.

"Jacob, where are you going?" She asked breathlessly. "Jacob!"

He stopped suddenly, so suddenly that she carried on a stride but pulled to a halt a step ahead of him.

"This is what happens!" he said, angrily. "This is what happens … when you … when I …" he shook his head in disbelief. "Its taken me …"

Marelle stared at him; he looked pale, his eye was twitching like crazy. She didnt understand a single word he had just uttered.

"It makes no difference. We can go down there – I can take you anytime you want to go."

"I don't want to go there." He suddenly shouted. "Im not … its not …" he threw his jacket off and cast it onto the floor. With an odd, angry, empty glance in her direction he pulled the fleece over his head and threw that on the floor as well; followed by the t-shirt he had on beneath. His top half bare he walked around in a small circle; then stopped, undid his jeans and began to take them off.

"Jacob!"

He ignored her and continued stripping off until he was naked in front of her, in the middle of the airfield.

Marelle glared into his eyes. It took her back in her own life, to a time when she was about four – when she'd done the same thing in a toy shop when her mother had refused to buy her a doll she so much wanted and demanded. In sheer frustration she had stood in the middle of the shop and taken every piece of clothing off in an act to exercise the last vestige of control she had on that day.

Her mother had refused to buy the doll; in fact her mother had just walked away from her; picked up all of her clothes and then just walked away. Leaving her to cool off and come to her senses.

Everyone had laughed at her then, pointed and called her cheeky and naughty. But she'd been a four year old child with no concept of retribution, salvation or anything else which was fuelling Jacob's actions here. But nonetheless, she followed her mother's lead – not saying a word she picked up his clothes as he strode off to the long grass that the breeze was ruffling over the far side of the airfield.

Marelle was pretty wired by the time he came back to the house. She had gone against every cell in her body and walked back with his clothes, back here to wait. A couple of times she'd looked round to see his naked body walking off in the opposite direction and at her final glance he had sat down in the long grass. Now, an hour and a half later he'd walked up the garden path and into her kitchen. In that time, she had drunk three of four mugs of very strong black coffee and tried not to constantly watch out of the window. It had been a leap of faith but now he was here.

He came in through the door, his eyes on the floor.

"Sorry." He said as he stood there.

"Its ok. I did the same when I was four years old. Unfortunately, it was in the middle of a toy shop!"

He didn't smile.

"Your clothes are there." She pointed to the pile on the table. His boots on the floor below.

He nodded, took a couple of steps forward and began to re-dress himself, garment by garment. Once complete, he raised his eyes to her. "We'll drive down in the morning, maybe stay that night somewhere and drive back the next day. It might be an emotional and tiring journey to drive back on the same day ..."

Marelle smiled sympathetically. "Ok, I'll find somewhere." She replied looking deep into his eyes but seeing a fear still there.

Over the next couple of days Marelle had an overwhelming sense of treading on eggshells. While Jacob was 'normal' there was a brittleness to him that she felt would shatter at any moment. He was loving, he was kind, and he was as sweet as ever but it all seemed like a veneer glossing over the real turbulence beneath. She understood why he had been so upset over Frankie's funeral not being here but at the end of the day it was not an unreasonable thing to expect to happen. It had, however, happened to be a major sword in his side that was provoking the homunculus to be fighting so violently inside.

As he had instructed, she found a nearby hotel. She had chosen carefully, not sure what he would be like in that situation especially with a spike in is emotions following the funeral. It had to be somewhere quiet – but no so quiet that the owner was watching your every move! It had to be somewhere large enough for your presence not to matter – with preferable no children around, just in case his actions were misconstrued again; it had to be an inert place where they would be left alone. She thought she had found just that ina a chain of bland, commuter hotels and booked a room. She told Jacob but he wasn't particularly interested – just offered to pay for it.

Sitting close to him on the settee on Sunday evening, her back against him, legs stretched out along the seat, she asked

"Do you think you should give the farm a call in the morning?"

He sniffed behind her. "No, they'll contact me – "

"How?"

He didn't reply. "He should be back, shouldn't he?" Ring him – if they are going to ask you to go in then you need to tell them about the funeral – you won't be available for a couple of days ..."

"Its ok."

"Its not ok Jacob, if you don't call then I will!"

He sighed. She felt him take a couple more breaths against her. "Ok, I'll call them in the morning."

The tv was on; there was a documentary on about pollution. Neither of them were particularly taking any of it in.

"Have you got a shirt for the funeral? Do you need anything ironed or washed?"

"Its sorted." He replied.

"I don't know what to wear – I'm not very good at formal wear."

"Wear whatever you want." He replied. "Frankie wouldn't mind ..."

Jacob wasn't sleeping particularly well – but at the same time he wasn't having nightmares or sleep walking. Instead he just lay in bed, awake, beside her, staring at the ceiling with unmoving eyes.

In the morning, iun the kitchen, she passed him her phone.

"Ring the farm." She said.

Jacob looked tired and he seemed too weary to make an excuse, so he took it and hit the 'call' button. Marelle stood over the side of the

kitchen, watching. No-one answered but he hung on, keeping his eyes on the floor. Eventually he spoke.
"Hello Adam. Its Jacob, I was just checking in to see when you want me back at the farm."
She could hear a meandering, whiny voice in reply but it was far too quiet to make out words.
"Ok." Jacob said.
She watched him stare at the floor again until he offered "Yeah, ok. I'll wait to hear from him then."
She gestured to Jacob but he refused to see her as he cut the call.
"You didn't say about the funeral." She said.
"No need." Jacob sighed. 'He's really sorry but he 'forgot' to let me know his father has extended his stay in Australia by another ten days. He won't be back for well over another week."
Marelle sighed.
"But he has told his father and they are quite happy to carry on as we are at the moment and he will sort it out when he gets back."
He shrugged, passing the phone across the table to he then went to get up. "I'm going over to the gates and the caravan."
She watched him go. He was slouching his feet, and his right eye was definitely twitching more too. Marelle stood at the kitchen window and watched him disappear in a straight line up the concrete runway – away with his thoughts.
He didn't come back at lunchtime. She called him but he didn't answer and it rung off. Marelle gathered herself, walked around the house for five minutes then called him again. It rang five times, but he answered.
"Yeah." He said, Jacob never answered by saying 'yeah' and it seemed a little odd but she let it go. He sounded distracted.
"I thought you would be back for lunch." She asked.
"Oh, er probably not. They've just turned up with the concrete crusher again – I'm just letting them in. God knows how long this will take …"
"Is it the same lorry driver?"
"No, this one seems more civil. There's a guy in a van to unload it as well…" Jacob replied.
"Shall I come up there?"
"Why?!"
Fair enough question, she thought. "What about lunch then?" She continued.
"I'll get something later …" He replied, dismissively.
"What time are you coming back?"

He sighed. "Not sure. I'll try to be earlier than usual – I'd better go as he is just about to drive over a manhole and I'm not sure it will stand the weight ..." He said quickly and rang off.

He was literally five minutes away and she wanted to go up there and fought every muscle in her body to remain here. But he sounded a little hassled and she didn't want to be on the receiving end of the 'too many questions' conversation again and definitely not today.

Jacob finally walked into her kitchen just before six o clock. He wasn't any earlier than he normally was, but he came in carrying a suit in a protective cover over his shoulder. There was a tenseness about his face and it looked gaunt, slightly grimy in the closing light of the day.

"Hi." She smiled, moving straight over to him and placing a kiss on his lips with her hands flat against his chest. He kissed her back then tilted his head back to look at her.

"You been drinking?" She asked, noticing the smell of beer on his breath.

"Just had a bottle in the caravan, while I was sorting this out ..." He lifted the suit a little to acknowledge it.

"Everything alright up there?"

"Hmm?" He questioned, a little vaguely.

"With the concrete crusher ... and the lorry? Marelle reminded him.

"Oh yes. Got that in then another lorry turns up with a load of metal fencing to drop off." He said as they parted, he walked over to the door and hung the suit on the back of it. He walked back and slumped down on a chair.

"It's a mess over there now." He sighed. "It's gone now."

Marelle turned to him from the oven. He had his head resting on one hand, his eyes to the floor.

"Ring your guy?" She suggested.

He shook his head. "He won't stop this – he may get a delay but they'll still keep bringing stuff in – at best it will just be the actual Thor site that's preserved. Pretty soon they'll fence the whole thing off. We won't be able to wander on and off like we do ..."

Marelle hadn't thought about that, she paused for a second.

"We'll have to talk to each other through the wire like prisoners!" He said, dryly.

"Don't be daft! You'll still be here anyway ..." She answered. "Do you need to get the caravan out then?"

"Not yet." He replied. "But it looks kind of like I feel up there at the moment."

"What do you mean?"

"Like a tiny island in a raging, boiling sea – just about to get washed away forever."

Marelle couldn't lift his mood and knew that to try would be some task with the events of the next few days looming large. He was obviously more troubled by the stuff being dropped off on the airfield than he was truly expressing and Marelle totally understood his feelings. His mention of it being fenced off had opened a realisation in her that very soon it would be neither his nor hers to walk about on. Eventually it *would* be gone forever.

He ate everything she put in front of him which surprised her – even though conversation was sparse. Then he went up to shower. While he was gone Marelle took a peek inside the suit bag. She didn't remember seeing this in his wardrobe – a perfect black suit – it looked brand new or freshly laundered. Hanging on the hanger with a crisp white shirt and black tie. She smiled as she fingered the tie; it was black but had a subtle diagonal stripe where the material alternated between matte and satin. It was one of those little touches that made Jacob stand out from Mr. Average!

He came down the stairs looking cleaner and much fresher than he had earlier. It looked liken he had towel dried his hair and just left it how it had ended up. Marelle gave a little grin to herself simply because he looked so adorable like that. He gave her a complacent smile as his eye twitched and he sat down with a pair of pointed toe leather shoes in his hand.

"Do you have any shoe polish?" He asked.

NINETEEN

Marelle had wanted to discuss the time they were leaving for the funeral and the general logistics of the journey but he was off the next morning before she had time to broach the subject. It was just starting to spit with rain when he went out and he pulled the hood on the hoodie up onto his head as he strode off. She watched him and hoped that after tomorrow things would relax a little.
Just after lunch her phone rang. She had expected it to be Jacob, but it wasn't.
"Oh hi! A slightly formal voice said. "This is Leah from East Archaeology – is Jacob there?"
Marelle pursed her lips. "No, sorry, not right now."
"Oh dear. I'm on my way to the site and there is also an excavator coming – will he be there?"
"Well he is probably over there right now – I'll pop across and let him know."
"Oh, are you sure that's ok?" Leah asked.
"'Yes, its fine, I was going over there anyway." Marelle lied but an excuse was an excuse.
She found him up near the gate. He appeared to be closing it. The rain was still spitting, she had pulled her hood on too. With a sigh she looked around at the scattered machinery, equipment and portacabins that had all been dumped haphazardly just inside the gate. It looked like a scrap yard. Since she had last been up here there was the addition of the concrete crusher, a pile of metal fence panels and what looked like a toilet block. It *was* a mess. Jacob looked to her.

"That Leah the archaeologist just called. She's on her way with an excavator."

His facial expression didn't change but he glared with angry eyes.

"Anybody else?" He asked.

"Not that I'm aware of ..." Marelle replied, turning to follow him as he tramped back towards the caravan. He'd just got there when the small white van pulled up at the gate. Marelle turned to look at the same time he did just as the heavens opened.

Jacob walked back, Marelle behind him as the rain blew across. Leah had got out, dressed in less feminine waterproofs today. She waved. Jacob did not return the gesture.

"Hi, is it ok if I come onto the site. There's an excavator just behind me. We're bringing it here today with the hope of starting tomorrow – as long as the weather is better!" She laughed.

Jacob looked at her. Didn't say anything. Unlocked the gates again and slid the chain through, putting the padlock in his pocket. He pushed the gate wide open, secured it with a breeze block. He then turned to the second gate and pushed it wide open too. It snagged against the ground at one point and he angrily shook it to release it. With both gates propped wide open he walked to the centre of the entrance.

"Thank you." Leah smiled.

"All yours!" He said. "I'll not close them again. Theres no point now."

And he placed a hand on Marelle's shoulder as he passed and guided her in the direction he was heading – back towards the house.

"Aren't you going to come back and close the gates?" She asked, worriedly looking back at them standing wide open as he strode on.

"No." He said as he walked on for a bit with her jogging beside him. "I'm not here tomorrow – they can do as they please. I'm finished with it, its their's now."

He strode the rest of the way back without a word between them. Marelle was upset to hear him say that but, she knew it was true as well as he did. It just could have been a little more gentle.

"I'm going to wear a little black dress with that three quarter jacket." Marelle said. "I've got it all ready ..." After dinner when he still hadn't relaxed.

He nodded.

"Have you got everything ready?" She asked, looking up at him.

He looked to the side but nodded. "I need you to cut my hair – if you would?"

She smiled. "Yes, of course I will. It is a bit long on top I suppose – but I do kind of like it!" She commented. "Go and wash it and I'll get my stuff out."

She heard him in the shower as she got out her bag of tricks. She'd be losing her touch – only ever cutting Jacob's hair and into the same style she thought to herself – but she liked it so it didn't matter! Jacob took longer than she expected, and she had gone off to find her iron to take a couple of creases out of her dress when he came down. Naked from the waist up but with a towel around his shoulders.

"Here." She said, getting up from the cupboard she was searching in. "It won't take long. It just needs a tidy up."

He sat down on a chair. "Take it all off." He said.

"No, no, no – I'm not going through that again – you're simply too adorable with this haircut – I"ll trim it."

"Take it all off." He stated.

"Uh-uh." She said. "I like it the way it is."

"So you only like me for my haircut?"

"No!" She laughed. "Of course not ..."

"Then take it all off."

"Jacob, no." She said, realising he was serious. "It wont suit you."

"Its my hair."

"I know, but – it looks so good."

"So, if I told you to cut off all of your hair because I liked it that way you would, would you?"

She paused. "Yes, I would – for you."

"You should never let anyone tell you how you should look."

She sighed. "I'll just trim it, make the top shorter ..."

"No. take it all off. Number one, all over." He insisted.

"Number one my arse. No Jacob." She protested.

"Well if you wont then I will – and it wont look very pretty then ..."

She sighed. This time he sounded as if he actually would.

"Why?" She asked.

"I just don't want it like this at the moment. It'll grow back – you can cut it like this again when it grows back. Just take it all off for now."

Marelle sighed, she felt like she wanted to cry.

"Well let me just ... make it short ... all over .... It doesn't have to be down to a number one." She said, quietly, dejectedly. "At least let me cut it into some sort of style – if you really hate it then I'll give you the clippers ..."

He sighed. "Ok, go on then."

It very nearly broke her heart as she put the guard on the clippers and ran them through the top of his hair. It was almost as if she worried that changing his hair would change him; almost as if she had created him from nothing with that first haircut and now it was going her creation would be going with it. She was as silent and solemn as he was while she worked.

Marelle finished and ran her hand across it. There was barely enough length to run her fingers through now. Out of habit she pushed the front up, just a little.

"There." She said with a sorrowful little smile. "If you hate it then the clippers are all yours." She told him and laid them on the table but sincerely hoped he would not pick them up. He took the mirror she handed him and there was a vanity about him when he looked in it and examined her handiwork from all angles.

"Oh." He said. "Its not what I wanted but I can live with that."

He raised his eyes to her and gave a warm smile – even though it wasn't as genuine as she would have liked.

It hardened his features, made his jaw look squarer, his cheekbones more prominent – his eyes darker.

She smiled in return but felt her eyes begin to tear up. For as long as she could she held the smile, but her lip began to tremble and she could not stop a tear escaping down her cheek.

"Oh what! You're crying over my hair!" He exclaimed. "Come here!" he stood up and she went to him, wrapping her arms around him and burying her head in his chest. He laughed and gently rocked her to and fro.

"Thank you." He said. "It looks perfect."

He may have said he was happy with it but she wasn't. Sweeping up the hair from the floor and throwing it away hurt her more than it should have. All through the evening she found herself staring at him in snatched opportunities. He looked so different, but he wasn't different; it made him look older, harder at the edges but at the same time child-like an vulnerable. It was a good haircut and in a way she had pulled victory from the jaws of defeat but it still made her sad that the lopsided grin and warm smile he could give on occasions would not be the same with that haircut.

At the end of the day Jacob had done what he felt he had to do – for whatever reason. And at the moment that was the meandering path she was allowing him to tread upon. Once all of this was over, she would see her way to getting him on the straight and narrow again.

They'd talked briefly, decided to leave at six in the morning to give themselves a chance should there be traffic issues. Getting up early was not a problem for Jacob and consequently not for Marelle anymore. In the morning when they were both up and getting ready there was a mournful silence about the whole process.

Jacob was much more organised; he'd already got a bag packed and didn't panic over what he had forgotten. Marelle was flustered – not least by the hour of the day and the fact that they were going to be stuck in the car for four or five hours. She had debated on bringing her clothes and changing when they got there but sods law said they would be late and she wouldn't have time. She was straightening her hair in the hallway mirror when Jacob walked downstairs in the suit. She turned her head slightly and looked at him. Even with the new haircut he looked stunning – the suit was a perfect cut – fitted his slim frame without drowning him – a precise little detail on the jacket was just nipping it in at the waist a little to give shape to the profile. It was *not* an off the peg suit! Teamed with the fitted white shirt and that beautifully stylish tie he took her breath away. Even the black, shiny, pointed shoes screamed at her. She sighed – if he looked this good for a funeral then what would he look like for a wedding? His wedding? Their wedding!?

"I'll not wear the jacket in the car." He said. "It shouldn't crease but I don't want to look like a sack of shit."

"*You wont look like a sack of shit*!" She exclaimed. "Leave that to me ..." She added under her breath.

"You look good." He said, quietly into her ear with a hand on her shoulder as he walked by. She watched him; smiled a little smile in awe of how good he looked in a funeral suit. He picked up his sunglasses and placed them on his head. His right eye twitched faintly.

"We'd better go – as soon as you are ready." He said.

"I'll drive." Marelle remarked, as they walked out of the door. Jacob had loaded up the car while she had finished her hair.

"No, I'll drive." He replied.

"You can't, not all that way ... you're not insured."

"It'll be fine. If theres any damage to anything I'll pay for it." He said. "I'd rather drive. It'll keep my mind off the upcoming day."

There wasn't much she could say to that so she handed him the keys and sat herself in the passenger seat.

A long car journey with Jacob was always going to be difficult. He drove and didn't mke much conversation unless she did. The radio was on but neither of them were really listening to it. She liked watching him drive; he was steady and sure, methodical and she always felt safe with him behind the wheel. A bit like she did with Seb driving! Bella was a nightmare and Marelle always drove them if she could – Bella's driving scared her and it was an incidental operation usually carried out as quickly as possible between singing, checking make-up, eating or changing a CD. Jacob was steady and sure, completely in control of the car although not a slow driver once he got onto the larger roads.

"I'm surprised you don't have a car." Marelle commented, half out of an excuse to look at him – no *gaze* at him – despite the new haircut. She was, admittedly, warming to it.

"Never really needed one over the past few years."

"So, you used to have one?"

"Oh yes ... a few over the years. My last one was stolen ..."

"Stolen?"

"Yeah." He replied. "Never did get it back."

"And you haven't had one since?"

"No ... used the farm van – never had any cause to go anywhere much so ..." He shrugged as he drove.

"What sort of car was it?" Marelle asked.

"What?"

"The one that was stolen."

"Oh ... "He answered at length. "I was a rather nice little black Mercedes SLK ... I'd had it from new – but it got stolen from me."

"How come?"

"Long story." He replied. "My fault I suppose. I kind of left it somewhere and someone decided it was in need of a good home ..."

"And you couldn't get it back?"

"No. There were a few mitigating circumstances."

"Oh." She said, a little puzzled.

"Didn't get another one, just started using the farm van but as I said – I didn't have any need to go far."

"My first car was a Ford Fiesta." she smiled. "A red one. I loved that car – but Seb said it was getting old, had too many miles on the clock. I sold it to a friend and you know what? That car is still going today!"She smiled but Jacob did not pick up or carry on the conversation.

The miles and the hours passed snd she turned to thinking about the funeral ahead. Marelle hadn't attended many funerals in her life – her father's and an aunt whom she hardly knew. She had no idea what to expect at Frankie's or what would be expected of her – or Jacob. Her role was to be there for him – and that was what she would do.

"Do you want me to drive for a bit?" She'd asked about two hours in.

"No, I'm fine." He replied.

"Ok." She smiled, staring at him for a moment but he didn't turn to look at her. His right eye did not seem to be twitching so much today, she thought.

They made good time until they hit traffic just before leaving the motorway. The traffic came to a complete standstill and after twenty minutes sitting there Marelle started looking at her watch. Jacob remained totally calm, one hand on the wheel, one up against the window-sill in the car with his head resting on his arm. It was nine thirty and by Marelle's reckoning they had the best part of an hour to go.

Jacob didn't say much, just sat there, infinitely patiently waiting until the cars and the lorries began slowly moving again and he replaced both hands on the wheel. They'd lost a little over half an hour but if all else went well they would be there before eleven.

Eventually they travelled through the small village of Chidworth. It was more built up than Groveham, with pretty, thatched, chocolate box cottages lining the roads with less open space between them but nonetheless it was still another small English village. Jacob drove down the street slowly, looking at the houses and heading towards the grey stone church they could see the prominent steeple of.

It did not appear to have its own car park and there were cars parked nose to tail all along both sides of the road around the plot of the church. There were people already heading for the lych gate in ones and twos, walking around the shiny hearse that was parked right in front of the gate. Marelle felt Jacob tense suddenly at the sight of the long black car and she looked at the coffin the back as they drove by.

He didn't say a word, just pulled into a space behind what looked like a delivery van. There was no less tension but there was a resigned reluctance as he got out of the car and slid his jacket on. Marelle walked round to him, stepped up the kerb and for a solitary moment touched his arm in solace. Then she noticed he had Frankie's badge pinned to his lapel. The slightly tarnished silver wings that he had salvaged from the ditch. Her eyes fell to it, probably stared at it too long but she eventually raised her eyes to his and took his hand in hers. Today he had no sunglasses, no hoodie – just him in the suit, hair short and dark, jaw tense. Somehow, she felt his exposure but understood why he had chosen to lay himself bare right now.

She gripped his hand in hers as they walked along the pavement to the church. Alongside a stone wall surrounded the large graveyard bounding the church on three sides. He did not look at the hearse as they passed it and walked through the lych gate then along the yew lined flagstone path to the main door of the church. They stepped into the inner vestibule together with Marelle's heels clicking on the floor. It was quite dark once you were in there, but the rest of the church opened up before them through a second door with a black and white gothic tiled floor and the bright colours from the stained windows looking more inviting.

Then there was Elizabeth, dressed in a sharp dark grey skirt suit, neat black shoes clamped tightly together. She raised her chin and waited until they were closer to her before she spoke.

"How can you have the audacity to show your face here!" She stated angrily but oh so quietly. "You were *not* invited."

"We wanted to come. I told you we wanted to come." Marelle said.

"His father is responsible for the death of my brother!" She hissed, pointing a finger like a gun at the centre of Jacob's chest. "And you think you have the right to walk in here and expect to be welcomed. Your father murdered my brother and you *knew* – you knew all along but chose to subject my family to decades of torment to save yourself." She was breathing heavily and almost spitting as she spoke.

Marelle went to protest but Elizabeth raised a hand.

"I'm not going to make a scene – not here, not now but you are not wanted here. I won't stop you but I don't want you anywhere near any of my family or friends – they do not need to know who you are. And as soon as this is over, I don't want to see you ever again." She walked past them, out through the main door into the light and towards the hearse.

Marelle gripped Jacob's hand. She could feel him trembling. She didn't know what to say; she didn't know what to do.

"Do you want to go?" She finally asked him.

He shook his head, took a lead and walked through the door into the church.

In the main area it was surprisingly light and airy inside. It was almost full, an array of heads in front of them, none looking round. At the front was the dais, awaiting the coffin. Marelle felt lost and uncomfortable, wanted to say what she really felt like saying to Elizabeth but was sensible enough to realise this was not the time nor the place. Jacob pulled her slightly to the side and led to a small cold pew at the back – obviously reserved for village pariahs or lepers in medieval times. He sat down there and she sat down next to him. The two of them alone at the very back of the church. He would not look at her, but his eyes were full of uncried tears. She squeezed his hand which was still in hers, but he did not respond.

"Its ok." she whispered. "You're here. That's all that matters."

But the organ started up over her words and heralded the entrance of the coffin into the church.

Marelle turned her head and watched. It was a small coffin, obviously that of a child; pale wood with gold handles. There were four pall bearers who carried it down the centre of the building; it looked like it contained no weight at all. On the top of it was a spray of wax-like white lillies. Jacob's eyes followed it once it had passed them but then focussed back on the floor in front of him.

Elzabeth walked behind the coffin, slowly and then took he seat in the front row of pews.

The vicar began the ceremony his words bearing no relevance to Frankie or the life he had led alongside Jacob. Marelle was not truly listening to his words; to Elizabeth's words or to anyone else who had chosen to speak of this child they did not, nor ever had known. Instead, she focussed on Jacob, cold and trembling beside her, head bowed, silent. He did the right thing at the right times – he stood up when they sang the hymns – although Marelle did not hear him sing – and he bowed his head when they prayed. It was forty minutes of her life she would not ever want to re-live but eventually it ended with a prayer and at the very end she did hear Jacob repeat "Amen" as a stoic statement.

Afterwards, the congregation filed out behind the coffin. Marelle stood and watched, clutching Jacob's hand as he remained staring at the floor. He hadn't cried; he hadn't sobbed – he hadn't allowed any of the emotions she had expected him to go through today, but she got the sense of a cold and shattered soul beside her.

Marelle watched Elizabeth behind the coffin, arm in arm with a tall, elderly man who was struggling to walk. Was that Frankie's father? She wanted to ask Jacob but didn't want to speak in this vacuous silence that she felt was penetrating right through to her bones. She watched the procession filing out, in twos and threes, dark tones, muted colours. People with heads bowed, gentle smiles to one another – who knew who all of these people were? But not one of them – not a single one of them had ever known Frankie in the way that Jacob had.

And Jacob remained sitting there, staring at the floor; long after the coffin and everyone else had filed out. The church was silent. Marelle turned to him.

"What shall we do?" She asked in a whisper.

"I want to go to his grave." Jacob said.

Marelle shuffled. "Well maybe we go off for a bit and come back in a little while – when they've all gone?"

He nodded.

She squeezed his hand. "Come on then we'll go back to the car. See if we can find somewhere to get a cup of tea and come back when they have all gone."

She stood up, still holding his hand. Eventually he stood too but was a little unsteady for a moment.

"Hey, you ok?" Marelle asked, clutching at him.

"I'm fine." He replied.

They walked out, back along the flagstone path, away from where everyone else had gone into the graveyard. Neither of them looked back as they made their way back to her car.

"I'll drive." She said. Holding out a hand for the keys.

Jacob never said a word as he sat in the passenger seat. He didn't cry; he didn't mention a single word Elizabeth had said; he said nothing. Marelle didn't know where she was or where she was going but she pulled the car out of the space and just drove out through the village; turned right at a t-junction and headed along that road. It soon became tree lined as the road passed through a forested area. The sun had started to shine was was filtering through the early autumn leaves above them. Pretty soon she saw a car park up ahead – obviously for people to pull into when they walked in the woods here. Without a word she pulled into it and was pleased to see a small kiosk which appeared to be selling drinks and snacks, surrounded by picnic tables. It wasn't busy as she parked, switched off the engine and turned to him.

"What do you want? Tea? Anything to eat?"

"No – I'm fine." He answered in a very quiet voice.

"Have something or you will be fainting on me!" She suggested.

"Tea then." He said.

"Ok," she smiled. "Be back in a tick."

She got out, took the keys with her and went to th kiosk. It was 'manned' by a pleasant young woman, smartly dressed in a pink and white striped uniform that said "Carole's Kitchen' on it. Marelle ordered two teas and two sausage sandwiches – which were in fact a sausage in a mini French stick. The person in front had ordered one and it looked good!

"On business?" The girl asked, smiling as she made small talk.

"Oh – no ..." Marelle smiled. "We are at a funeral actually."

"Oh, I'm sorry. I didn't realise ..."

Marelle smiled in return. "That's ok."

"Not from round here then?"

"No, we're from Suffolk."

"Ooh that's a long way." She said. "I used to go to an aunt's in Suffolk, when I was little. It was always sunny!"

Marelle laughed. "Its not always sunny! I've only lived there a little while anyway."

"Is that your husband then?" She asked, nodding towards the car park.

Marelle whipped her head round. He had got out of the car and was walking across the car park.

"Jacob!" Marelle shouted to him. "Jacob, where are you going?"

He heard her, stopped and pointed towards the trees.

"Shit!" She said to herself, turned back to the girl. "I'll be back in a minute!"

She strode across the car park as quickly as her heels would allow.

"Jacob! She grabbed his arm. "Where are you going?"

"Toilet." He said, staring at her.

She stared back at him, right into his eyes and questioned him, gripped his arm. Remembered what he had said to her that night in the bath and then let go of him.

"Don't be long. I've just got to pick the tea up."

He nodded and walked off into the trees. With a sigh she returned to the kiosk and fumbled for her purse to pay.

"Is he ok? He looks a bit pale?" The girl asked.

"Yes – he's just .... he's fine. It was a close friend's funeral and he's a bit upset."

Marelle paid, took both teas and both sausage sandwiches and went back to the car. She was standing beside it when he appeared out of the woods and began to walk back. He looked out of place in the smart suit walking out from between the trees but nonetheless she breathed a sigh of relief as he approached her.

He refused to eat. He did drink some of the tea if not much.

"You'll faint if you don't eat." She warned.

"I can't eat." He said. "My insides are in too much of a knot for anything solid to get through."

She sighed.

"We'll go back in a bit. You know you can come down here anytime you want; they can't stop us ... I'll bring you down whenever you want to come."

"No, its ok. I'll say my goodbyes today and that'll be it." He stated, which chilled her more than it probably should have.

When they returned to the church most of the cars were gone. The church door was closed and the only evidence that anything had taken place was the freshly opened grave in the middle row of headstones behind the church itself. They walked towards it in isolation now and finally stopped where the flowers began. There were many wreaths, sprays of flowers – all beautiful – all pointless.

Jacob stood staring at them.

"Hang on." He said, turning away from her and walking off.

She went to call after him but held her words as she watched him walk back to the car. She observed as he leant into it then came back behind behind the stone wall, along the flagstone path then up between the graves.

In his hand he had flowers.

But it wasn't a shop bought wreath or bouquet. It wasn't artificially arranged or decorated. Her eyes fell to the three magenta rose heads, bound together into a spray with strands of the long grass from the airfield. The same as the roses he had brough to her.

Jacob crouched and placed the roses on the grave, in the centre, at the front.

"They're from the airfield." He said.

"I know." Marelle tried to say but her voice eluded her and she felt a tear run from her eye. She sniffed. "That's beautiful Jacob."

He crouched in front of her, just staring. Having a silent conversation with Frankie. Marelle stood with the mild autumn sunshine on her back, looking down at Jacob, the back of his head, bowed in his own thoughts. It was hard to believe this was the same sun that touched them at home as here it seemed different in a strange way. She watched him; a grown man but somehow still a child before her right now; she wondered what he was thinking; what he was saying.

Then, still crouching, he fished in his pocket and took out a penknife. Marelle stared at him as he exposed the blade. For some reason she could not move, her breath stopped in her throat.

"Jacob." She wanted to say but nothing came out.

Then he reached up to his lapel and took off the badge he was wearing. Marelle watched as he carefully dug a small hole in the fresh soil of the grave between the flowers and pushed the badge down into the ground. Gently, he re-covered it and patted the soil. Marelle sniffed, snivelled to herself as tears rolled down her cheeks and she felt her legs weaken.

He remained there, staring at the grave, at the flowers, at the earth of the freshly opened grave which Marelle could only assume was Frankie's mother's. She looked down at Jacob and she hardly recognised him as he crouched there. He looked too small, like a child in a man's suit but his taught face lined with sadness and despair. She wanted to touch him, to hold him – but right now, at this moment, she felt he needed to be alone.

"I've asked you once, I'm telling you now – I don't want you here – if you don't go immediately, I will call the police and report you for harassment!"

Marelle's head snapped round to Elizabeth striding across the graveyard. She had left two people standing by the lych gate – one the man Marelle assumed to be Frankie's father. The other a male in an ill fitting black suit, lending an arm to the older man.

"What do you think you're doing?" She spat.

"Paying my respects ..." Jacob said quietly, although he did not move from his crouched position.

"You have no right to pay respect to any member of my family – your father killed my brother in cold blood – killed him and buried him in *your* garden without telling anyone." She exclaimed, an anger bristling her. "For all those years! It killed my mother and it's killing my father – and its ruined my life – how can you show your pathetic face here?"

For a second Marelle actually thought she was going to aim a kick at Jacob as he crouched there.

"Get away from there – its my mother's grave too." She stated loudly. "Get away!"

Jacob stood up in a single movement, rising to his full height. He kept both eyes on the grave as he stood then turned himself until he faced Elizabeth. He was taller than her but for once he looked her in her ice blue eyes.

Marelle took a step to the side, took his hand in hers as he looked down at Elizabeth contemptuously.

"My father has spoken of you at times. "She said in a quietly angry voice. "By all accounts you were just some delinquent child from the village who hung around Frankie, leeching off him whatever you could. Leading him astray, probably led him to his death. You've no right to be here." She stated, staring him straight in the eyes.

Marelle felt no response from him, no tensing, no verbal response, nothing. She gripped his hand, but it was inert within hers. She stared at Elizabeth herself, felt cold air exhale through her own nostrils. Truly, Marelle felt her body tense and adrenalin flow into her – she wanted to raise a hand and knock that cold hard face into oblivion.

Jacob stared into Elizabeth, just stared, expressionless – lost for words or choosing not to say any. With a lingering look to her he stepped away, holding Marelle's hand and walked towards the lych gate.

He walked slowly, deliberately – along the flagstone path and line of yew trees. Frankie's father and the other male were at the gateway. His father looked thin and pale, his features stretched thin by time, his skin almost transparent, beyond frail as the other person in the ill fitting suit clutched his arm in support.

Marelle glanced quietly at him, but Jacob did not. He kept his head down and walked on. In Frankie's father's eyes Marelle though she saw recognition and pity – somewhere in there among the rheumy confusion and fatigue. He almost opened his mouth to say something – but nothing came in the few seconds it took for Jacob to pass, with her one step behind, clutching his hand.

They walked down the road to her car, parted ways as they approached. Marelle went to the driver's side and Jacob to the passenger without question. She couild sense his head spinning from there and was glad he had not insisted on driving.

"Ignore what she says. We can come here whenever you want to – I'll bring you whenever you want to. You can come every weekend if you want – I don't mind." Marelle said quietly as he stared straight ahead of himself.

"Its ok." He replied. "I don't want to come back here."

She held the keys in her hand, waiting, looking at him, wondering. There were no tears; there was no emotion on his face. She stared at his profile; it was mask-like, inert, empty.

"We can go to the hotel." She suggested.

"No, I'd rather go back."

"Back?" She asked. "Home?"

"Back." He nodded.

"Ok." Marelle replied, still sitting there and holding the keys. "Why don't we go and find somewhere to have a coffee or something and we can talk for a bit?" Marelle herself, didn't actually feel ready to drive for four or five hours.

He shook his head. "I've no words. "He said. "Too much in here …" he pointed to his head, almost like a gun, Marelle winced internally.

"I know." She said, putting the keys into the ignition with a sigh. "Well let's get home – we can start to sort everything out now – at least this is behind us …"

Jacob was silent, sat stiffly in the seat, staring out of the front screen at nothing. Breathing quietly beside her. She had put the radio on quietly but was not listening to it. She drove but could not get Elizabeth out of her head. Marelle felt that she should have defended Jacob to each and everyone; she should have stood up and said what he couldn't bring himself to; she felt like she was as bad as they were for just walking away.

By late afternoon she was tiring. They hit traffic on the motorway and came to a halt. She sighed.

"Damn." She said.

Jacob was still unmoving and not responding to her.

"Look I'm going to come off here when I get a chance. I need to find a loo and to be honest I need a coffee … "She looked to him. "Are you ok with that?"

He nodded. "Yeah." He replied succinctly and softly.

It was half an hour crawling at a snail's pace in three lanes of traffic before she got the chance to exit. She had no idea where she as heading as she took the car off the motorway and up the incline of an exit slip road to a t-junction at the top. She stopped and wondered which way to go. Turning left felt ike she was going back on herself, so she turned right and started along a quiet, tree lined rural road.

It was half five, she doubted she was going to find a café along this route that was still open at this time and she didn't really want to head into a town. Then up ahead she noticed a half timbered building, set close to the road with a welcoming sign at the front whch said 'The Keystone Arms welcomes you'. She slowed.

"Shall we have a look in here?" She asked, "looks quite nice."

He didn't reply but she pulled into the large car park at the side. It did not look busy – but then, it was early evening on a Wednesday so she would not have expected a pub on a rural route like this to be heaving.

It looked well kept, clean and tidy on the outside, lots of signs – all saying 'welcome' or how great the place was. Hanging baskets adorned the walls and around the front entrance. She stopped the car.

"I'm going in to get a coffee at least and go to the loo …" She said. "Are you coming in or waiting here?"

To her relief he said. "Yep, okay" and got out with his hands in his front pockets, looking around himself. Halfway across the car park he donned the sunglasses and kept them on as they entered through the large dark, oak front door.

The place was big and open plan inside. It had probably been a number of smaller rooms but had been opened up into one large space. It was relatively dark within, done out in red carpets and dark wood – but tastefully so. Everything looked sparkling clean. Over to the right were a line of tables alongside a bank of windows. Two were fully occupied – one by an elderly couple quietly eating a meal and the other by a family with kids standing on the seats. Immediately in front of them was a large, brightly lit, well stocked bar. Behind it stood a man with grey, short hair, in a pink checked shirt, smiling in greeting and ready to serve. To his left was a slight, young blonde girl in a black polo shirt, wiping glasses.

"Good afternoon." The landlord greeted. "Welcome to the Keystone Arms."

"Hello." Marelle smiled, moving up to the bar.

"How can I help?"

It seemed strange to have someone in front of her actually being friendly!

"Erm – could I possibly have a coffee?" She asked, "Jacob?"

"Yeah …" He said.

'Two coffees!' Marelle smiled.

"I'll get them." Jacob offered.
She turned to him. "Oh, ok ..." He'd stunned her slightly and actually seemed to be acting like a human being. "In that case I'm popping to the loo ..." She whispered. "Shall we sit over there?" She nodded to a booth to their left, well out of the way and pretty secluded.
Jacob looked. "Ok." He said.
She pecked his cheek as she headed for the ladies. "Be back in a minute." The toilets were warm, carpeted and hospitable. There were fresh flowers, fresh toilet rolls and plenty of freebie toiletries. She went to the loo, washed her hands, preened her hair then took out her bag to touch up her make up. She didn't look half as bad a she actually felt and commended herself for scrubbing up so well despite everything! With a final look at herself in the mirror she returned to the main area and looked across to Jacob who was still standing at the bar. He turned and gestured to the two coffees on the table that she had suggested sitting at. With a smile Marelle sat down there and took a sip of black coffee as she waited for him to join her. When he rounded the wing of the booth, she looked up to him with a smile. He didn't reciprocate and still wore the sunglasses – in his right hand he had two whisky tumblers stacked one on top of the other. Both had a decent measure of alcohol in them, with ice. Her eyes fell to them as he sat down and placed them on the surface of the table.
"Jacob, I'm not drinking, I'm driving!" she laughed.
"I know." He said. They're for me."
She stared at him. He removed the sunglasses.
"You need coffee, I need a stiff drink." He said.
"You've got more than a stiff drink there!" she remarked.
He fished in one glass with his fingers and took out the ice.
"What is it?" She asked.
"Whisky." He said. "Can't you smell it?"
She shook her head. "I'm not a whisky drinker – I wouldn't know what it smells like – is that a double?"
He nodded and downed one glass.
She felt uncomfortable; she was surprised by his actions – "Jacob." She said quietly, shifting in her seat a little. "You don't drink ... is this wise?"
He fished the ice out of the second and left it on the clean, shiny table surface.
"Its fine." He replied, sipping the second.
She sipped her coffee. He had the glass against his forehead, stared at her with it between his eyes.
"You can have my coffee." He said, "I didn't want it anyway."

"Do you want something to eat?" she asked. "You've had nothing and now you're drinking on an empty stomach."
He shook his head.
"Don't you go being sick in the car ..." She warned.
"I wont be sick in the car." He repeated her words.
She watched him drink the second.
"I reckon we've still got a couple of hours drive left – once I get back on the motorway." She commented, wondering if she wanted the second coffee; she needed it but didn't know if she could last two hours without another toilet stop if she did.
Jacob turned his head, looked over his shoulder then in one movement his body followed and he got up. She watched him walk to the bar.
"Jacob!" She called after him. He rolled to the bar, ignoring her and approached the slight blonde girl.
She smiled sweetly at him, maintained that warm welcome throughout and he returned to the booth with two more tumblers.
"Jacob!" Marelle said sternly.
Behind him she watched the blonde girl speak to the landlord with both of their eyes on Jacob.
"You know." He said, lining up a third ice cube on the table before sliding it up and down with one finger. "You know, I understand why my father drank like he did ..."
She sighed.
"Because when you're thinking about drinking then you're not thinking about anything else – and when she wraps that warm blanket around your shoulders and holds you in to her perfection you don't want to be anywhere else."
"Its just been a shit day Jacob." Marelle said. "Its gone now. You don't have to do this."
He grinned. "Don't lecture me."
She stared into his eyes as he drank the double measure in the glass. She could smell it now.
"Jacob stop!" She exclaimed. "This is not you – stop it!"
He gave a hollow laugh. "How do you know? How do you know which one is really me? How?"
"You're talking silly now!" she said quietly to him, without any aggression. "Come on, we'd better get going."
He shook his head. "I'm not finished."
"I think maybe you are Jacob."
He stared at her and raised his eyebrows as he drank from the second glass, ice and all. Then he placed the glass back down, a little too heavily, pushed against the table with his hands and straightened his arms,

taking him up to a standing position. She could see the start of a glaze in his eyes, the slackness of his face, the tilt of his head ... strangely he'd lost the twitch in his right eye. He stood upright, wobbled a little but picked up the glass again and drained it, banged it down on the table, loudly. She looked up at him and tried – God she *tried*, to keep the look of distaste from her face but he leaned forward and kissed her roughly, inappropriately for here with one hand groping at her chest – then stood up again with a grin which with his hair that short looked almost sinister.

"Piss." He said and leaned off to fall into a turning stride towards the toilet. He wasn't happy drunk like he had been with Bella – he was angry drunk and in a way, it was so out of character for him. She heard the toilet door bang and hoped to God there was no-one else in there. Shaking her head, she stood up, picked up all of the ice and put it in one tumbler, then tucking her bag under her arm she carried what she could back to the bar.

"Everything ok?" The landlord asked.

She smiled, almost with a relieved sigh that someone cared enough to ask. "Yes, yes – we've been to a funeral. It was difficult ..."

He gave a little sympathetic smile.

"He doesn't usually drink ..." she explained, her voice failing as she began to wonder why she was telling him.

"Have you got far to go?" He asked.

She made a face. "Probably a couple more hours drive as yet."

"Don't stop anywhere else." He advised with a solemn wink.

"I'm not intending to."

He stared at her with one eyebrow raised. "And you're ok – with him ...?"

Marelle's eyes widened. "With Jacob!? Yes, of course." She laughed. "He's just had a bad day."

At that moment he burst out of the toilet door, took three strides then tripped on the metal runner at the edge of the carpet. He went flying, Marelle grabbed for him, but he made it to the bar before he hit the floor.

"Hey, steady on." She smiled, taking his arm.

He ignored it as if it had never happened but leaned over the bar.

"Could I have a double Scotch please, with ice?" He said and fumbled unsteadily in his pocket for change.

"I'm sorry Sir. I think you've had enough for today – I suggest you let this young lady take you home." The landlord told him, quietly but firmly.

Jacob laughed softly. "I don't have a home – I exist in the space between everyone else." Grinning he held on the the edge of the bar. "Can I have that Scotch?"
"Sorry Sir, not today …"
"Jacob, lets go. We've still got a few hours to drive." Marelle smiled, taking his hand and squeezing it.
"I'll get a cab." He said. "Can I have a double Scotch, please." He held up a twenty pound note.
The landlord shook his head. Marelle sensed that everyone was staring at them.
"Jacob." She called, keeping it light, taking his arm and gently pushing towards the door.
"No." He said. "No, no, no – I'm not done …"
"We need to go Jacob."
He staggered as she pushed him. "Whats wrong? My money not good enough? I'm not good enough …" He slurred to her, staggering backwards, away from the direction she was trying to guide him in.
"Its not that Jacob. Come on!"
"Fuckers!" He spat at the landlord, at the blonde girl and at the rest of the customers who were staring.
"Jacob. Come on!" She tapped and turned his shoulder towards her, took his hand and pulled him like a six foot reticent child.
"Out." She said, pushing him gently with her hand in one steady push in the centre of his back. "Out."
She didn't want to get aggressive with him because she felt he could get aggressive back right now.
"Fuckers!" He exclaimed again. "You don't know who I am!"
She pulled his sleeve, turned him to her and he stumbled as he neared the entrance – so much so that he crashed face first into the partition at the side of the main door.
She placed a hand around his back and protectively guided him to the doorway but instead he decided to fight against her, holding on to her wrists and forcibly holding her hands up in front of herself, pushing her against the wall.
"Ow! Jacob!" She exclaimed, pushing back into him with her body as he let go of her wrists and the both of them almost fell through the door in a bundle.
Outside Marelle took a breath and twisted upright again. Somehow, he had made it down the steps and staggered into the gravel car park.
"This isnt you Jacob!" She exclaimed. "Just calm the fuck down." She pushed him towards her car and this time he obliged, standing by the passenger door.

She tutted and opened the door for him. He stood and stared at her; a look on his face that was halfway between a grin and breaking into a sob of utter despair.

"Get in." She sighed, pushing at his shoulder. He resisted and she pushed harder. In that split second, he raised a hand but stopped short in mid air.

"Just get in." She told him, her voice quaivering now.

He folded himself inside. By the time she climbed in she was crying.

"For fuck's sake Jacob! You always have to prove them right, don't you?" She sobbed. "What did you do that for?"

He turned to face her in the seat, his face pressed into the back of the seat like he was in bed.

"Finished." He said.

She sighed shakily. "Yes, I'm finished." She started the engine. "Put your seatbelt on."

He pulled it around himself but was in such a strange position in the seat it was impossible to get it around himself properly and plugged into the clip. He tried once then decided to just hold it.

With a shaky, cadent breath to herself she reversed the car out of the space, turned it around and pulled back onto the road.

"I've got no idea where I am." She said to herself.

He didn't answer but lay on his side in the seat, staring at her. She could feel his gaze, she could hear his breathing. Marelle drove – looking out for road signs to take her back to the motorway towards somewhere she recognised – not driving particularly quickly and talking to herself because he didn't seem to be responding.

"How come it takes so long to get back on a motorway when I only just came off it?" She said, driving on a bit further. A couple of minutes on she saw a welcome blue sign pointing her in the right direction. "Oh here we go …" She remarked. "Hallelujah!"

Then her eyes moved to the rear view mirror and she saw the police car close behind, its blue lights twisted into life.

"Oh shit!" She whispered, not really knowing what to do – she'd never been pulled over by the police before and this was not a good time.

"Shit." She repeated, dithering whether she should stop here or carry on to a lay-by she could see up ahead. Gripping the wheel tightly and slowing down she headed for the layby and pulled into it. The police car pulled in behind her. She stopped and glanced at Jacob. He was asleep.

"Jacob!" She called. He didn't respond. "Jacob!" But the police officer was by her door already. She put the window down.

"Good evening madam. Can you just turn the engine off please?"

She obliged then lifted her head to him.

"Good evening officer – I'm sorry – I'm a bit lost – but I can see the way to the motorway now …"

"Is everything alright?" He asked, leaning and looking in.

"Yes, I'm ok now I know where I've got to go. Sorry I was driving a bit slowly …"

He looked to Jacob. "And what about him?"

"He's asleep." She smiled. "I'm sorry he's a bit drunk, I'm taking him home …"

"Can you get out of the car for me?" The police officer asked and he opened her door.

Her legs were shaking as she got out and stood up. He gestured for her to go to the back of the car with him and he positioned himself at the back of the lay-by.

"Do you have your driver's licence?"

"Not with me." She said. "Sorry."

"And your name is?"

"Marelle Buckleigh."

"And this is your car?"

She nodded. "Whats the matter? What have I done?"

He stopped, looked at her. "We had a call from the landlord of the Keystone Arms – said he was concerned for your welfare due to the behaviour of the – g*entleman* – with you."

She gave a hollow laugh. "I'm fine; he's just drunk – honestly – we've been to a funeral and it was quite difficult for him – he doesn't usually drink but for some reason he decided to go a little over the top."

"The landlord said he was both physically and sexually abusive to you …"

"No!" She exclaimed. "No! Its Jacob – he wouldn't hurt a fly!" She felt upset at what he'd said – was that what it actually looked like to a total stranger? So much so that they had called the police?

"And his name is?"

"Jacob Frost." She said, now feeling quite upset and realising she probably had streaks of tears on her face from the struggle getting him into the car.

"I'll need to speak to him." The police officer said.

"He's asleep. …"

"If you would like to sit in the back of my car for a couple of minutes."

"No, not really." She replied. "I really need to be with Jacob if you are going to speak to him – he's had a bad day – he's a bit fragile …"

"It won't take me a moment." He reiterated, opening the door of the panda car for her. "You're not under arrest. I'll just speak to him and make sure I am happy and you can be on your way."

Reluctantly, she sat in the car, pulled her legs inside and he closed the door.

Her heart was racing and her head was spinning. She had probably had too much caffeine and not enough food. Now he was opening her car door and shaking Jacob by the shoulder.

Marelle opened the door and got out again.

"Officer?" She called.

He looked towards her.

She beckoned to him. With a look at Jacob, he walked over to her.

"Officer." She said, "he has mental health problems – I really need to be there – he may freak out otherwise ..."

"Oh I am sure I can cope with someone as inebriated as he is ..."

"Officer, please!" She pleaded. "Just let me come and stand over there. If he can see me he'll be ok ..."

He looked between her and the car, with the passenger door open.

"Its not what it looks like." She added. "He's not dangerous – he's ... he's just depressed and he's scared ... please ..."

He sighed. "Come over here then."

Marelle stood behind her own car as he tapped Jacob on the shoulder.

"Mr. Frost." He announced. "Can you get out of the car for me?"

Marelle was aware this could go one of two ways. Jacob could be "Jacob" and get out slowly and stoically or he could be the drunk he had turned into earlier and come out screaming and fighting. She crossed her fingers, mentally, behind her back.

Jacob got out. One leg first, one hand groping for the side of her car until he stood with both feet on the floor and straightened himself up – albeit slightly unsteadily. The suit was still pristine and fell into perfect form around him as he pulled himself up to his full height. He still had the sunglasses on his head but he did not pull them down.

"Can you confirm your full name sir?"

"Jacob Wiliam Frost." He replied in a quiet voice which confirmed to Marelle he was falling back into character.

" – and date of birth."

Jacob thought, got the first part right then struggled. The policeman looked at him strangely – Marelle piped up Jacob's correct date of birth to assist. The police man turned to her.

"I'd rather it came from him."

The he turned back to Jacob. "Is that correct Sir?"

Jacob nodded, he was swaying.

He asked a few more questions – why, where, what – which Jacob answered, sometimes with his eyes closed but nonetheless politely. Then he walked to the back of the car talking on his radio.

"Can I sit down?" Jacob asked.

"No, I'll be two minutes – just stay there where I can see you."

Jacob stood there. Marelle looked to him but he didn't look tp her. The officer communicated on his radio for a while before he returned to them. When he did he walked right up to Jacob.

"Looks like you've got a clean ticket – lets keep it that way? Hey?" He said. "What was going on at the pub?"

Jacob shrugged.

"The landlord reported that you were being abusive to this young lady?"

"I wasn't." Jacob replied, swallowing.

"Well it didn't look like that to everyone else." He explained, looking right into Jacob's face but Jacob did not return eye contact.

The policeman turned to Marelle. "Are you happy to continue your journey with him and that there is no danger of physical violence to yourself."

Marelle laughed. "Yes, of course!"

"Well in that case I suggest you go straight home, sober up and get yourself a good night's sleep." He advised Jacob. "And be thankful you have such an understanding partner." He gave a look to Marelle and then a glance back to Jacob. "On your way." He finally said.

Marelle moved closer to Jacob. He went to say something to the police officer, formed his mouth into the start of a word and then stopped abruptly, leaning his back against the top of the open door.

She touched his arm. He was shaking.

"Maybe you'll remember my face, you'll be fishing it out of the river soon." He said quietly.

Marelle gripped his arm and looked up to his face. The policeman looked around on hearing him say something.

"Jacob!" She whispered back to him. "Its ok." she called to the officer.

"Come on Jacob get in the car."

He gave a sigh then got back in with Marelle hovering over him. She closed the door and walked round to the driver's side. As she got in Jacob opened the door again and began to get out.

"Jacob ... where ..." She exclaimed as he rolled out of the car.

She extracted herself again and walked round the front of the car just as he threw himself towards the undergrowth, his hand on his knees as he wretched violently. She sighed walked up and placed a hand on his back. The police car was still behind them. He wretched until there were tears streaming down his face. When he stood upright again he was unsteady and swayed. She took his arm.

"Lets get you in the car." She said. "Come on lets go home."

Marelle walked him to the car, put him in the passenger seat then leant in and fastened his seatbelt. She closed the passenger door and walked around the back of her car. As she passed, she paused and made eye contact with the police officer still sitting there in his car. He watched her as she got in.

She sighed, turned the key, pulled her own seat belt around herself and drove carefully away from the lay-by.

Jacob did not say anything and at that moment she could not find the right words. Soon he had closed his eyes and looked to be asleep again. She wanted to stop and hug him; touch him – pull together the edges of the chasm she could feel opening up beneath her feet. She hated this; she hated the way the world was turning around him and she wanted it to go away. She wanted it to just be her and Jacob and everything would be perfect. Marelle was tired and angry, hungry and teary eyed. This day was finally ending and it was starting to get dark. She drove the remainder of the journey on autopilot with her head thumping and Jacob asleep beside her.

TWENTY

The village sign was welcome sight as she finally passed it, drove down the main street, past the farm, past the shop and finally to her house. With a warm feeling of relief, she slowed and pulled the car nose first into the drive, right up to the house so that the headlights washed across the front of it.
"Oh shit!" She exclaimed, bringing the car to a halt. "Oh no ..." She sighed. "Oh God!"
They'd been back. Across the front of the house in three foot high black letters were the words 'Murderer Scum' again. Bigger than before and spanning the whole width. Across the front door it said 'killer' and across the living room window the word 'scum' was emblazoned.
She sighed. They did not need this – not ever, but especially not now. Without thinking she let her foot off the clutch and stalled the car with a jolt. It woke Jacob. He stirred in the seat, stretched himself a bit and then sat up stiffly. He sighed.
"Are we back?"
She nodded " – but it looks like someone has been busy in our absence ..."
She looked to the house and he followed her eyes too. There was a moment of silence then he burst out of the car, walking up and looking at it in the pool of the headlights.
"I'll get it off." He said quietly as Marelle followed him out.
"No, leave it – we're too tired." She said.
"No, I'll get it off now. They're not defeating me so I leave it here ..."
"Jacob, its nearly ten o clock!" She protested.
He began to walk off.

"Jacob, I'm tired, cold and hungry – please – leave it."
'Then go to bed. I'll clean it off.'
She sighed. "I'm not going to bed if you're messing about out here ..."
He went to walk off along the side of the house.
"Jacob, come in first at least ..." She pleaded.
He ignored her and carried on.
So, for the next three hours she stood out there wrapped in her coat, drinking hot chocolate and barely able to keep herself awake standing up as he worked like a madman cleaning off the callous words which had been displayed across the front of the house. She'd long since stopped asking him to leave it and come in – he was on a mission and nothing would stop him – although he seemed driven on by something much deeper than the humiliation of the words being there. He had not even changed out of the suit and still had the black tie perfectly knotted. Marelle had leant against the wall and watched him, closing her eyes for a second or two and flirting with sleep as he worked on.
Eventually he completed the task, took everything back behind the house then walked back to her as she leant against the wall, hugging a mug.
"You could have gone to bed." He said.
She shook her head – "with you out here, doing this? I don't think so."
He walked past her and up to the front door. Marelle followed him and they went inside.
In the cold light of the kitchen he seemed completely shattered, completely wretched. For a moment he just stood there, hands and arms loose at his sides, eyes on the floor.
"What if they come back again?" She asked.
"Oh, they will and I'll clean it off again, and again, and again ..."
"We need to make it crystal clear to everyone Jacob – we need to get across that any of this is not your fault."
"We can't ... we will never be able to. People see what they want to see – we can't change that, ever."
"But its nothing to do with you!" She cried, quietly.
"But it is. I'm the son of someone who has killed – in their eyes – *murdered* – a child. That's close enough – that's someone to hang the blame on at least ..."
She shook her head.
"I've lived like this here for over ten years – been able to just get on with being – me – no-one has bothered me particularly. No-one likes me or makes the effort to speak to me, or include me but ... that's fine ... that was what I wanted, what I *intended*. Then one day I opened the door ... just a chink ... just a tiny chink and suddenly everybody has run in,

destroying my world, pulling down my bricks one by one and crushing them to dust …"

Marelle stared at him as he stood there in the kitchen, still in the suit she had admired so much earlier in the day, still with the shadow of a black eye and a scuff on his forehead, still with the curtain of his drinking today hanging on him. She stared at him with tears of frustration and pity in her eyes. There was a cold hand gripping the back of her neck in realisation of what he had said.

"So you blame me?" She uttered, quietly.

"No, I blame myself." He said quickly. "I set rules and I broke them. I don't hold anyone else responsible for my actions, any of them, *ever*." He stared at the floor. "Now I don't know what to do."

Marelle gathered herself, drew a breath and walked up to him. She stopped a couple of inches in front of him, took his lapels gently in her hands and looked up to him.

"Its late Jacob. We've had a pretty vile day – lets just go to bed and see what the morning brings … "

She led a weary and deflated Jacob up the stairs and into her bedroom. He went through the motions, but Marelle had no idea what was actually on his mind or what he had really meant by what he had said. He'd broken the rules by letting someone into his life and that *someone* was her. And with her had come all of the baggage, hostility and disparagement that he had successfully eluded for the past ten years.

She'd melted his heart and taken his soul into her hands without truly knowing what she held or how to handle it. Jacob was unique – she knew that; he was both strong but wholly fragile; there were things she did not know about him and which he would not voluntarily tell her. They'd shared so much and nothing all at the same time. He was a bright and colourful butterfly who had briefly settled on her in the sunshine of a summer day. He was but a moment – a passage of time in her life – a very small passage of time in her life but oh! How she wanted those wings to flutter against her heart, for the sunshine to last forever and for him to be here, with her, eternally.

Marelle lay against him, huddled against his side, her head on his chest. He was warm, and vital and living but she felt strangely remote from him as he slept beside her.

The morning dawned before either of them woke. When she finally opened her eyes Jacob was still fast asleep in a silent slumber beside her. She'd learned that if he was in that deep a sleep you did not wake him – you let him sleep when he was finally asleep. She looked at her watch and was astounded to see it was a quarter to ten. Almost swearing at such slothiness she slid herself out of bed and grabbed clothes to put on. There was a definite chill in the air today and she climbed into a warm shower to wash away the remains of yesterday. Once dried and dressed she combed her hair straight and left it to dry for now. Before going downstairs, she went back into the bedroom to find a pair of socks. Jacob hadn't stirred. She stopped and stared at him; today would be better; today they had it all behind them. Today they would start again.

Walking over to the chest of drawers by the window she was distracted by blue flashing lights passing outside. She stopped and walked right up to the window. A police car drove past with its blue lights flashing but no siren. It slowed past theirs but continued for another hundred metres along the road and pulled up alongside the kerb behind another police car that was already there. Marelle leaned inwards, pressed her face into the glass to see better. She held her breath to stop it from steaming up and from the fact that they were parked in the road right outside the house where Patricia and Derek lived. A policeman and woman got out of the car which had just arrived and began to walk up the garden path to their front door.

As she watched Marelle solemnly turned her eyes to the grey van that was also gliding slowly past their driveway as well. It too stopped behind the police car.

Marelle stood for a moment, ringing her hands together. She looked to Jacob, but he was still soundly asleep. She looked to the window again. Her hair was still wet as she wrapped her coat around herself and jogged up the road. Behind her she had closed and locked the door silently and was now here, running up the street with both back and front door keys in her pocket. It was colder and she wished for sun. There were the two police cars parked in the road; the grey van had now gone but there was a dark blue saloon there that looked like DCI Catchpole's car from before. Marelle rounded the hedge, strode up to the door and knocked.

Patrica answered, looking particularly pale for her.

"I saw the police cars ..." Marelle said. "Is everything alright?"

Patricia's eyes were wide. "There's another body." She said.

"Where?"

"In the garden. Derek made a start on the vegetable patch – he was moving the rose bush beside it and .... there was another body ..."

Marelle stared at her; she didn't know what to say.

"Come through ..." Patricia said, moving aside. "The DCI is here from before ..."

"No." Marelle took a strep backwards and shifted her weight. "No, I don't want to come through … its ok …" she backed away. "I'll be with Jacob." She said, feeling weirdly faint as she turned.

"It's a child." Patricia called. "It's a tiny child."

Marelle ran back, suddenly not feeling the cold until she fumbled to find the key and open the door. There was no covert unlocking of the door as there had been when she had just left when she had turned the key oh so carefully and silently so as not to awaken Jacob. This time the key finally thrust into the lock, she flung the door open then banged it closed as she headed straight up the stairs.

Her entrance had obviously woken Jacob. He was sitting up, rubbing his face when she ran in. He looked to her, took in her face as white as a sheet, her mouth open, her eyes wide.

"Whats wrong?" He asked.

Right now, right now in front of him she did not want to impart the news. Marelle didn't want to let that demon scurry in through the crack in the door as well, but she had no choice. This time she had no choice.

"They've found another body." She gasped.

"Where?"

"In the garden … in the garden where Frankie was."

He stared at her, one hand on his head, his eyes filled with confusion.

"There were police cars going by when I got up – they were all parked up here …" She nodded. "I went over there, and Patricia said they had found another body – near a rose bush – a child's body."

Jacob shook his head a little. "No?"

"It seems there is. The police are there."

He continued shaking his head. His right eye twitched – he needed a shave; she had not seen him look this unkempt before.

"Well, if there is another body down there then they know as much as me about it …. I remembered what happened with Frankie but there is nothing else …" He said in a quiet, gruff voice. "I'm going to have a shower."

He got out of bed and walked off slowly, scratching the back of his head. Marelle pulled the bed straight, stared out of the window some more but nothing seemed to be happening – at least as far as she could see. The activity would be round by the lay-by she guessed – where they had been before.

She heard the shower start up as she went along the landing and downstairs. Stopping in the kitchen doorway she felt her mind finally filter all of the thoughts that had been dancing in her head since she'd spoken to Patricia.

A second body! Why the hell was there a second body? Who was it? Indeed, did Jacob really know? He'd been quite dismissive about it. She shook her head to chase these thoughts away but her mind kept turning. Was there something he really knew that no-one else did? Had he 'allowed' Frankie to come to light hoping others would remain buried? Did he really know anything about this?

"No, no, no" She said to herself, shaking the thoughts away – *why* was she even entertaining them? She'd seen the look on his face when she had told him; he'd been as shocked as she was. But, she knew he was a master at disguising his true feelings. She stopped, reprimanded herself again but, nonetheless, the thoughts were still there. She flicked on the kettle and put bread in the toaster.

When Jacob wandered into the kitchen he'd smartened himself up but wore an old faded t-shirt that had obviously seen many better days. The sleeves looked big and for once his arms looked skinny hanging from them. It was untucked in the ripped blue jeans he had also put on with it. He had washed his hair and one side of it was pushed up where he had rubbed it with a towel. It reminded her momentarily of how it used to be and she felt a melancholy emotion rise within her – almost making her wish she could return to that first night when she had knocked on his caravan door. How differently she would play it a second time.

He sat himself down on the same chair he always favoured. It was strange how she thought about that now – he always sat on the same chair in the kitchen; always the same armchair in the living room; always the same side of the bed. Little things but nevertheless little things that had integrated him so intrinsically into her life. Marelle placed a pile of toast in the middle of the table. She had buttered and spread most with lime marmalade – didn't say anything – just left him to pick and eat. Eventually she too sat opposite him. He looked to her, made eye contact for a second then flicked his eyes away. Marelle smiled, something inside was urging her to capture this butterfly while she still had the chance. But there was a distinct panic inside her as she looked at him and a sense that he was fading away. Marelle had always said there would be a time and a place and right now, she knew she was approaching it.

He had just started eating when the doorbell rang. Marelle got up and walked through to the front door. Jacob ignored it.

She was not surprised to see DCI Catchpole on the doorstep.

"Good morning." He greeted. "Is it possible to speak to Jacob?"

She sighed. "He's just having breakfast ..."

Almost sarcastically Catchpole looked at his watch. "It's a quarter past eleven!"

"Yeah, well, we went to Frankie Lee's funeral yesterday. It was a long drive and an awful day. We were going to stay down there last night but Jacob was so upset he wanted to come home. So, we drove back the same day – got home late only to find someone had spray painted 'murderer' all over the front of the house – again. Jacob insisted on cleaning it all off before we went to bed. I think he's entitled to be having his breakfast at a quarter past eleven." She imparted.

Catchpole was a bit taken aback by her breathless soliloquy, but he replied

"Oh, I see. I can speak to him now or he can come down the station later …"

She sighed again, stood aside slightly. "You'd better come in."

Jacob was eating toast and staring into space when she walked back in with Catchpole in tow.

"Its DCI Catchpole." She announced. "He wants to have a word."

Jacob briefly moved his eyes to him, then away again. He chewed a few more times. "Morning." He eventually said.

Marelle pulled out another chair – one that neither of them ever sat on and gestured to Catchpole. He sat.

"Do you want tea?" She asked.

"No, no thank you. I've had plenty of tea already."

Marelle looked at Jacob. He did not make eye contact with her, just carried on chewing. He didn't look worried or disturbed at Catchpole being there at least.

"I gather that you both already know that there has been another body discovered over the road?"

"Yes." Marelle replied. "I spoke to Patricia."

"Well. Jacob, you were obviously aware of Frankie Lee's disappearance – can you shed any light on this one?"

"No." Jacob said. "I knew about Frankie because he was my friend; because he went missing one day and was never found and because I always thought that one day he would turn up. If there is anything else buried there I have no knowledge of it."

"But you lived there?"

He nodded.

"How long did you live there?"

"Since I was born."

"Until when?" Catchpole fired questions at Jacob.

"Till about ten or eleven years ago – officially. I suppose I was there, with my father until I was eighteen, went to University then was just 'around' for probably twenty years but didnt 'live' there as such. I came back when my father was too ill to carry on – just before he died but up until that point I had filled in for him a lot on the farm ... when I could ..."

Catchpole stared at Jacob. "Where did you live, when you were 'around?'.

Jacob shrugged. "With friends, I rented a flat for a while, came back here for the odd few days now and again ..."

"Where did you rent a flat?"

"Not round here."

"Where?"

"North London."

Catchpole stared at him. "What about your mother?"

"She died."

"When?"

Jacob spewed information like a well rehearsed speech. "When I was a baby?"

"How did she die?"

"Complications of childbirth."

Catchpole continued to study him as he questioned, "your child birth?"

Jacob nodded.

"So who brought you up?"

"My father." Jacob replied.

"You've said before that he was an alcoholic?"

Jacob nodded again. "Started drinking when my mother died. I never knew him any different."

"And he brought you up?"

"Well ..." Jacob said with a wry laugh.

"What about siblings?"

Jacob suddenly raised his eyes to Catchpole and actually made eye contact. He paused, took a piece of toast and bit off one corner.

"Brother." He finally said.

"And where is he?"

"Dead." Jacob answered.

"How did he die?"

"He killed himself – ten years ago."

"Oh, I'm sorry." Catchpole said. He paused for a moment. "Do you know why?"

Jacob shook his head.

"So you weren't close then?"

"No, I hardly ever saw him or knew him. He was brought up by my grandparents when my mother died. Then he went his own separate way. We hardly ever saw him."

Catchpole sighed. "What did he do?"

"Who?"

"Your brother."

Jacob looked to Catchpole with a perplexed look. "What does it atter what he did?"

"Just background. Just trying to establish who we can eliminate from any enquiries ... its ok, we can find out if we need to anyway ... what was his full name?"

"Nathaniel Ezekiel Frost." Jacob stated, staring at the toast on the table. He shuffled in his seat slightly then raised his eyes to Marelle as he spoke again. "He worked for a record company. He travelled around a lot. He never really came here. You can forget him." There was disdain in Jacob's voice.

"We are not going to 'forget' about anybody Jacob – not until we've got to the bottom of this ..." Catchpole warned.

"How do you know the second body isn't ancient?" Jacob asked. "Maybe its just a coincidence?"

"Maybe it is." Cathcpole replied. "That's what we are going to find out."

Jacob kept his gaze on the table and there were a good few seconds of awkward silence.

"How much older than you was he?"

"Three years."

"And he committed suicide?"

Jacob nodded.

"Where?"

"Down south, Bristol, area ..." Jacob replied.

"If you don't mind, how did he ...?"

"Drowned himself." Jacob stated cutting into the end of Catchpole's sentence.

He nodded. "Drowning is usually an accident – why was it considered suicide?"

"Because he was pissed out of his head and high as a fucking kite when he disappeared – because for the previous three weeks he'd completely lost the plot and been severely depressed – then he was discovered dead, in a river – it was deemed suicide."

Marelle felt she was listening to something she was not supposed to hear. It made her feel less than comfortable, but Catchpole was undeterred.

"Did you identify the body?"

"No!" Jacob exclaimed. "What has any of this to do with a body found in the garden over there?"

"Background info." He said.

Jacob sighed. Catchpole left it at that for a few seconds but then asked.

"Was your father a violent man?"

"No!" Jacob answered. "He wasn't a trouble maker – he didn't look for a fight but he was an alcoholic – he used to take it out on me because I was there, in the way, wanting food or clothes or money when he came home and just wanted to sleep ... but I wouldn't have said he was violent – he may have made bad decisions and he may not have had the capacity to understand some of his actions but he was not a violent man." Jacob stated. "I believe he was once a loving and gentle man."

"Are your parents buried in the churchyard here?" Catchpole questioned.

Jacob nodded.

"And your brother?"

"No."

"Where is he buried?"

"He's not." Jacob replied. "He was cremated and his ashes scattered."

"And you have absolutely no recollection or knowledge of anything else being buried in that garden ...?" Catchpole asked.

"No, I told you. I know about Frankie disappearing and thats why I suspected it was him when I found the remains in the garden. I know of nothing else."

"And there are no other family members – aunts, uncles, cousins?"

"No. None that I am aware of ..."

"So, you are the very last surviving member of your family?"

Jacob nodded.

"As there have now been two bodies discovered we are likely to search the whole area. What will we find, Jacob?"

"I have no idea. In all likelihood you will find nothing." Jacob replied succinctly.

Catchpole nodded. "Jacob you seem like a very educated person, articulate when you speak – how come you're here – working on the farm and living on a disused airfield?"

"I think that's my business." Jacob said. "Maybe I like it here. Maybe I like being on my own, being left alone – just doing mind numbing things so I don't have to *think*."

Catchpole sat and stared at him, a strange half smile on his face. "You're an interesting character Jacob. Far more interesting I think that most people give you credit for."

Jacob did not acknowledge his comment nor raise his eyes to him, so catchpole continued.

"I'll be in touch if I have any more questions – I'm sorry if they don't seem relevant but you are the only person around here who has much knowledge of the past here."

Marelle looked to Catchpole, then Jacob, then back to the DCI.
"I'll ask the patrol to keep an eye on things around here for a bit – just in case there are any more issues with the spray paint on the house."
Jacob wasn't responding, he was sitting there seething like a petulant child, flicking one finger repeatedly against the handle on his mug.
"Well I'll leave you two to your – breakfast." He said, getting up.
Marelle got up and saw him out. When she returned to the kitchen Jacob was still sitting tapping the mug. She stood for a moment staring at him but when he did not move she sat down. Waiting a moment more, she then reached out her hand and clasped the one tapping the mug in hers. He stopped tapping but did not move his eyes and his mouth remained tight and closed.
"I think he was a bit harsh with you." She said.
"Just joining in with everyone else I guess." He answered in a straight, quiet voice.
"I didn't know some of those things about your brother … "Marelle told him, quietly, holding his hand. "Did he …"
Jacob interrupted her, lifted his hand up and shook hers off his. "Why does everyone get a fucking fixation on my brother? My brother, my brother – I don't want to talk about my fucking brother, ever again, to anybody." He raised his voice way above his normal tone and spoke angrily.
"I'm sorry." Marelle apologised, feeling reprimanded. "Lets talk about you then."
"No – " he said quietly. "I'm out of talking, about anyone or anything." He got up. "I'm going outside."
He went out into the back garden and sat himself on the wooden bench. Sitting stiffly as though in a dentist's waiting room before treatment he did not look relaxed or even comfortable. Even out there, with no one in front of him his eyes darted from one place to another; she'd also noticed earlier that the twitching was back.
Marelle cleared away breakfast and hovered in the kitchen while keeping an eye on him. He remained there, getting up at one point to look at something on the bike, then sat down again. Today he didn't even seem interested in going across the airfield to see what had happened in his absence and with the gates wide open. Today he was someone else and just about as far away as he could be.
Marelle watched him from the kitchen. She watched his chest rise and fall quite visibly as he sat there contemplating. The shorter hair made him look older, made the lines on hs face harsher. Today there was a past visible in him – a journey he'd been on; the road he'd travelled – a history she knew little of but was suddenly aware of. And when she

looked at him out there now a million thoughts poured into the funnel in her head; voices calling to her; telling her that she may soon hear "I told you so" echoing in her brain. She wrestled with that thought, with the sudden blocking of other thoughts in her head – for sure there was something she did not know; maybe other people had seen it long ago and she, blinded by the light, had not.

Don't turn against him. Her mind ran in and scared away those thoughts. How could she even let them enter her consciousness? The words floated around inside her head – alcoholic, junkie, druggie, paedophile, weirdo ...There had been glimpses of certain behaviours in him now and again – moments when something seemed to mean something to him, and he reverted to type. Marelle looked at him and felt complete guilt that she could even entertain these thoughts when she knew she had seen the real him day in and day out; when she knew how sweet he could be and how vulnerable he really was.

She wanted him. She wanted to free him from all of this, take him away somewhere safe – somewhere new where they could start over and he could be his own true self.

Marelle wanted to go to him but feared his reaction if she did. She debated with herself, about whether it would hurt more to have him push her away today or stand here and keep watching him in agony on that bench. She stepped forward and turned the handle to the back door.

He didn't move when she sat down beside him, sat close to him and gently placed a hand on his thigh.

"Ooh Jacob, its quite cold out here."She commented."Do you want a jumper."

"I'm ok." He said, leaning forwards and resting his elbows on his knees. Bella had said he'd lost weight – today he did look thin. She sat next to him, gently sliding her hand up and down his thigh.

"Jacob." She suddenly said. "I'll sell this house. I'll tell Seb I want out – we'll go somewhere else – start again ..."

He shook his head. "No – you can't do that." He said quietly with a strange, slight smile on his face.

"I can and I will – I'll do it right away – "

He shook his head again."You can't." He laughed. "I don't want you too."

"But Jacob, listen ... "She said, breathlessly, took another lungful of air and turned to him. "Jacob, you know how much I've fallen for you, you mean the absolute world to me – I just want to be with you – it doesn't matter where. Jacob, I just want to be with you come hell or high water, Jacob for God's sake, I love you!"

She looked to his face, his eyes flickered momentarily at her words but otherwise there was no reaction or acknowledgement – which was exactly what she had expected.

"Ok." He said after a fashion."So I'm sitting here and I don't know what to do but I have two options. Whichever one I choose there will be no going back and both will change my life forever."

Marelle was not following him.

"Do I figure in either of those options?" She asked, nervously yet stung with emotion.

He nodded. "Maybe." And raised his head to look out over the airfield. Marelle sat sideways on, staring at him until she could contain herself no longer. She threw her arms around him and hugged him so tightly she felt his bones beneath her hands.

"Jacob you've got to confide in me. You can tell me ..." She pleaded with her head against his shoulder. She felt him sigh; she felt him tense but he did not turn and hug her in return.

"I know." He said quietly, staring across the airfield and bouncing one knee up and down.

He said he '*knew*' but did not make any attempt to say anything. She took his hand in hers. His hands were surprisingly smooth and his fingers long and slender. She wrapped hers around his and looked at his hand as he looked across the airfield.

"Theres more stuff on there." He said, distantly. "Theres a digger over here, probably the archaeologists but it looks like they've broken ground ..."

"Don't you want to go over there – we could go for a walk?" She suggested.

"No, I'll go later ... when they've all gone." He replied, flatly.

Marelle sat there, close to him, holding his hand like they were a pair of love-struck teenagers. It felt awkward but she did not want to let go. Today he seemed so lost and distant that she feared he would just float away into the atmosphere if she released his hand. Usually, she could guess what he was thinking – or dwelling so wholly upon; today she had no idea but knew it was deeper than that – much deeper – and she could simply not reach him.

Finally, she reached up and kissed him on the cheek. He turned his face to her and gave a warm smile, full of humility – unexpected when he was so distant. But then he turned his head away and again, slightly away from her this time and looked back across the airfield.

She sat there with him for as long as she could and eventually tried to coax him back into the house.

"I'm going to make a cuppa – are you coming in?" She asked, patting his thigh.

"In a minute." He replied, still looking away from her.

Marelle went in, still watching him from the kitchen window. He was restless; shifting position when she left to rest his elbows on his knees again, he dropped his head down to stare at the floor. After five minutes he stood up, took one more lingering look over the landscape before he turned to walk in. He looked so tall and thin today – lanky – gangly as he stepped up the steps, opened the door and came into the kitchen. Marelle held out a packet of chocolate digestive biscuits to him, but he shook his head.

He drank the tea but didn't make much conversation. The he pulled on the black fleece and went back outside. This time he started tinkering with the bike and eventually started it up. Its roar into life made Marelle jump and she rushed to the window in fear he was about to take off, but he was just sitting astride it in her garden. He let it run for a short while the cut it, got off and parked it again.

She made dinner but he picked hopelessly at it. Marelle watched him and felt her stomach lurch inside her at what she was watching.

"I'm going for a wander over there." He'd announced shortly after the meal.

"I'll come with you!" Marelle exclaimed, grabbing her coat and slipping trainers on. Outside she hooked a hand into his arm and huddled close to him as he strode out of her garden and onto the runway.

There seemed to be a couple more portacabins up near the gate – which was still wide open. The archaeologists had dug a couple of shallow trenches in the grass and there was a random pile of metal fencing and old empty oil drums which was new as well. Jacob stopped and observed it all as a breeze blew an empty fast food package past his feet. He sighed.

His caravan still stood in its place, all of the curtains pulled, completely cleared around it. Somehow it stood out more today amongst everything else.

"Shall we hitch it up and tow it to my house?" She'd asked. He'd shook his head.

"No. Not till I *have* to."

She gave a little smile but felt concerned for its vulnerability here.

"Lets go to the Thor site." He said.

They'd rounded the trees and were approaching the three runways when there was suddenly a sharp whistle from behind them. Jacob stopped and turned, Marelle clutching his arm and mirroring his movements.

About thirty metres behind them were two figures. They were walking with a purpose; one of them had a pronounced limp but it didn't appear to be impeding their progress. Marelle recognised one figure and her eyes instantly dropped to what he had in his hand.

"Looks like we hit the jackpot tonight." Sam said, pointing the baseball bat he had in his right hand at them. "Fucking dirty paedophile murderer and his scheming little fucking accomplice."

The other figure laughed and Marelle realised he was an older duplicate of Sam. His father. Jacob stopped, faced them. He did not appear scared. Sam walked right up until the four of them stood face to face, three feet apart.

"You can run now. I'll give you both a head start and we'll destroy the caravan instead or you can let me rearrange your face so you wont forget what happened every time you look in the mirror – scum!" He said.

"You dont scare me Sam." Jacob stated. "You never have – and you never will. You can't hurt me anymore."

Involuntarily, Marelle tugged at his arm. She would willingly take the coward's option.

"Jacob. "She whispered, pulling at him.

"No." he said. "Lets see what he's made of ..."

Marelle gripped his arm with both hands and took a step backwards.

For a few seconds they faced each other, staring. Jacob was taller but Sam was considerably heavier and much younger – and he held a weapon. He swung the bat in a slack figure eight in front of them. Marelle winced. Sam rised the bat and poked Jacob in the chest with it, making him take a backwards step towards the low wall of the first missile runway. Jacob shrugged her from him and gently pushed her to the side. She raised her hands to her head as Sam took a second swing. Jacob grabbed at the bat, stopped it hitting him but did not get purchase on it. He staggered back as Sam advanced, bat at shoulder height ready to swing again. For a split second Jacob glanced over his shoulder to see exactly where the wall was behind him and at that moment Sam took the swing.

If Jacob had been facing forward the bat would have caught him straight in the face but as he had his head turned it caught him on his right shoulder and although he staggered at the impact, he was still upright and ready with his hands to defend himself when the next swing came.

"No!" Marelle screamed and ran at Sam, threw herself against him which helped deflect that strike away and caused her to rebound and stumble towards Sam's father who grabbed her arm and pulled her towards him.

"Go on son." He encouraged. "I've got this one." As he folded his arms around her with a crushing force that became tighter as she struggled. Sam took another swing which Jacob did not get to – it was slowed, but cracked against his jaw which sent him sprawling against the concrete wall of the missile site.

Marelle screamed, kicked, struggled but she could not escape his vice-like grip as he laughed behind her.

Sam went in for a second swing at Jacob's head which was now against the wall; Jacob saw it coming and managed to get his head out of the way but as he rolled the bat hit into his ribs and obviously winded him for a second or two. He was awake enough to raise a foot against Sam and push him away forcefully; away enough to give him space to sit up against the wall but Sam, recovering from being pushed away by Jacob discarded the bat and went in with his fists, cracking Jacob in the side of his head and sending him head first into the wall.

"Jacob!" Maerelle yelled, trying to kick at Sam's father as he held her in front of him.

Sam had one knee on the wall, above Jacob, he hammered punches down onto him until all Marelle could see were Jacob's legs over the top of the wall, his back arched over the edge.

"Stop!" She yelled. "Stop, you're going to kill him!"

"No we're not – we're just going to teach him a lesson." Sam's father said. "Just teaching him that he's not wanted round here – just teaching him that maybe he should leave ..."

"Leave him alone!" She screamed at Sam until her voice ended in hoarseness and her throat hurt as he grabbed a handful of Jacob's fleece to lift him up and smack his head down onto the concrete wall.

Marelle aimed a backwards kick at Sam's father's shin – it connected, and he swore at her. She tried to turn her head to look at Jacob, but her eyes settled on something laying in the grass by the low wall. Then something Bella had once said to her in one of their random conversations popped into her head. *Drop* – Bella had said; if someone had you in a hold they expected you to fight to get free from – if you just suddenly dropped down it would be a surprise and may give you a chance to break free. Marelle remembered the drunken conversation they'd been having while watching a fight outside a nightclub. Marelle had one chance and she had to be quick.

There was blood on Jacob's face, but he aimed a punch back at Sam however with Sam on top of him on the wall there was little more he could do. Sam was half his age and twice his weight and he used that advantage to smack Jacob's head into the hard surface again.

Marelle took a breath, expanded her ribcage then exhaled and at the same time just dropped to the ground She felt his hands grab at air above her head as she crawled as fast as she could towards the bodies flailing on the wall.

Her fingers wrapped around the long cold neck of the bottle of pink fizz that she'd left there that night, ages ago. She was aware of Sam's father moving towards her and concentrated on making a single movement where she lifted and swung the bottle to bring it down accurately and forcefully right into Sam's left temple.

It hit hard and she saw his head snap back instantly. She grabbed Jacob by the fleece as Sam fell away and dragged him away on shaky legs.

"Run!" she shouted, pushing him.

Sam rolled into the grass and his father went to him instead of her.

"Run!" she exclaimed to Jacob, taking his arm and pulling at him, not entirely sure how capable he was of actually moving, let alone running. She dragged him, stumbling and flailing until he found his feet and did not question it but ran with her.

TWENTY-ONE

Marelle didn't know how they made it back, but they crashed through her back door and landed in each other's arms against the worktop. She clung tightly to him, both gasping for breath, she sobbed; he held her.

"Are you hurt?" He whispered.

She shook her head but pushed his face away from her with her hands cupping it.

"Oh God Jacob!" She sobbed. "Look at you!"

His nose was streaming blood down his face and there was matted blood in his hair on the side of his head where it had been repeatedly bashed into the concrete. A bruise was beginning to darken along his jawline.

"We need to get you to a hospital." She cried, looking right into his face. "And call the police."

"No." He said, 'I'm ok, leave it."

As he spoke, she suddenly noticed a gap in his teeth that hadn't been there before and let out a little yelp as she turned him to her.

"Jacob!" She lifted his lip with her finger and exposed the gap, on his right side. That, or the impact which broke it, had also cut the inside of his mouth.

"You've broken a tooth!" She gasped.

"I know." He replied. "I can feel it."

She cried and hugged him to her, sobbing bitterly against his chest.

"I'm ok." He stated, quietly.

"You're not, you really need to go to the hospital – do you have a dentist?"

"No." He answered. "I didn't lose consciousness – I'm fine. Just a bit cut and bruised."
"I thought he was going to kill you."
"He wouldn't do that – his intentions were to hurt, not to kill …"
She pushed herself away from him again.
"What if they come here?"
"They won't come here." He said.
She sighed, wiping her eyes with the back of her hand. "Sit down, let me look at you."
Jacob sat down on a chair which she pulled out for him. He closed his eyes and rested his face against the outstretched fingers of his hand.
"Are you in pain?"
"My neck hurts but nothing else – yet."
Marelle sighed. "I don't believe you … look at me …" She bent down and looked into his face. He opened his eyes and stared right back into hers. For those few seconds he gave her the most intense stare she had ever seen from him. The depth in his dark eyes was unfathomable; his expression was blank but his eyes pleaded with her, asked her questions and told her things his lips would never utter. There was sadness in its many folds, twisting and turning on itself, painfully squeezing the very last ounce out of him. It was the gaze of a soul lost. He flicked them away and the connection was gone.
His nose was encrusted with dried and congealing blood, he had a deep graze on the side of his head, his lip was swollen and he had a tooth missing. That was what she could see. She had seen the baseball bat connect several times to different areas of his body so there would be more beneath his clothes, not to mention the abrasions and bruises from the wall that he had been bent backwards over.
She stood up and cradled his head against her. "Why don't I run you a hot bath, you can get in and I can inspect all of the damage?"
He agreed so she found herself a while later in the bathroom with him sitting in the bath tub while she gently washed his hair and his back, noting bruises appearing along his collar bone and ribs. He never winced or complained, or said anything, just sat there and let her wash away the blood and the mess.
"Is that Sam's father?" She eventually asked.
He nodded slowly. "He's been inside for GBH. Was ten times worse than Sam until he got stabbed in the back in a fight in a pub. Now he plays the disability card but he's still a nasty piece of work. I remember him being a teenager when I was a kid. Everyone was scared of him."
She held the warm flannel on the back of his neck and he closed his eyes. Marelle looked at him and thought of what she'd seen in his eyes. She

felt tears rise and she tightened her mouth, swallowing them away – took a breath and managed to recompose herself.
"We can't carry on like this Jacob." She said, softly.
He remained, with his eyes closed and her hand pressing the warm flannel against the back of his neck. There was a pale trickle of bloody water running out of his hair and down the side of his neck.
"I know." He finally replied in a voice that seemed to have accepted defeat.
He was a broken man in more ways than one when he climbed into her bed that night. Marelle lay against him, stretched against his side, just touching his skin against hers, her hands flat and gentle on his arm. Marelle vowed that this would be the last time, that tomorrow, no matter what he said she was finding that somewhere new to go.
Somewhere in the night she felt him stir. She asked him where he was going, her voice cutting through the darkness like part of a dream.
"To the toilet." He had yawned.
'Ok," She said, nestling her head into the pillow. "Hurry back ..."
It was one of those sleepy, not really awake conversations that you sometimes half remembered in the morning. The bed was warm as she turned onto her isde and instantly returned to a deep fulfilling sleep.

She awoke in sunlight, blinked and turned over, reached out her feet to touch his legs but found the bed empty. Marelle sat up confused and looked about herself. The bed was cold.
"Jacob!" She called.
She pushed herself up properly in the bed, recalling the events of yesterday evening.
"Shit!" she gasped to herself, throwing the covers off and putting her feet on the floor. She remembered him getting up and going to the toilet – what if he was concussed – or worse and had passed out in the bathroom. Her heart was in her mouth as she ran along the landing.
The bathroom door was half closed, she pushed at it, looking around its edge – ready to find him on the floor. The room was empty, pristine – the toilet seat was down.
"Jacob?" She called again, walking back along the landing, looking in the back bedroom, the spare room. "Jacob!"
Panic was fluttering into her voice. She ran along the landing – down the stairs, through the living room and into the kitchen. Her wildest hope prayed to see him standing there waiting for the kettle to boil, tapping a spoon on the worktop.
He was not there.

"Jacob?" She called – walking up to the back door and peering outside. The bench was empty. It was a lovey still, bright, sunny day but he was not in the garden. Marelle turned the handle on the door; the key was in the lock, but the handle turned and the door opened. She had locked it last night; she *knew* she had locked it because she had stood there looking at Jacob and wondering how black and blue his face would be in the morning. She *knew* she had locked it – she'd checked it twice because there had been a fear in her that Sam and his father may turn up. The back door was unlocked now. She opened it and went outside, standing barefoot on the step. Jacob must have gone out through the back door.

Marelle stood on the step, a soft breeze tousling her hair across her forehead. Why had he gone out? Maybe he had gone up to the caravan to check it was ok? Maybe he would? Maybe he had gone to search out Sam – early in the morning, catch him with an element of surprise.

"Shit no!" She said to herself. He wouldn't, would he?

"Fuck!" She said to herself, imagining Jacob finally setting about Sam and wreaking revenge for all the years of abuse. Marelle spun on the step, was heading back into the bedroom to find clothes and take herself in search of him when she noticed what was laying on the kitchen table.

Marelle stopped and stared. She felt weak, she felt her knees buckling and her head spinning as she reached forwards.

On the table was an A4 sheet of paper, covered in writing. On top of it was Jacob's phone – her phone. She drew a breath and felt the silence in the house – the clock ticked but there was no sound. The house was empty; he was not here. Her fingers touched the sheet of paper, gripped the edge, pulled it towards herself.

It was written in black biro. Neat handwriting with a slight slant to the right, upper and lower case, considered punctuation. Marelle read the words as cold fingers walked down her spine.

"I'm sorry but I need to go. I need time and space to decide what the future holds for me. I don't yet know how much time or how much space.

I know I can never be the person you think I am or who you want me to be. I am not that person – I can try to find that person, but I am not sure he even exists anymore.

You brought light and love into my world, and you changed me. But I cannot stand in that light and I am not deserving of that love. My life is a lie and I have flown too close to the flame.

Decisions will be difficult. It is a one way road. I may go down it and never come back but I will try.

I'm sorry. I do not want to hurt you but do not follow me. I will be long gone.
And yes, I do love you, Marelle. I hope I will be able to come back to you, but I have to make decisions as to what the future holds for me.
All my love, J."

Marelle held her hand to her mouth. She read it again and again. He had gone; he'd slipped out while she slept – he'd written this note – he had sat here and written it – while she slept – he'd unlocked the door and gone – while she slept. Suddenly she turned and flew to the door again, ripped it open and stepped out into the garden, barely dressed and barefoot. Turning in a circle she looked about herself. The bike had gone. He must have pushed it away as the sound of that would have woken her without a doubt. He'd walked away with the bike.

Marelle sobbed, she clutched the paper to her; she picked up the phone from the table and stood in the kitchen.

"No Jacob!" she cried. "You can't do this!"

She cried; she stood in the middle of the floor and cried. She didn't want to be here; she didn't want to be in this house without him here with her.

Amd where was he going to go? He had nowhere – his whole life was here. The bike was not roadworthy – if he was on the road then surely he would get stopped straight away? They were near the coast – what if he'd gone and got on a ferry – did he even have a passport? As she stood there with tears streaming down her cheeks, every thought that came into her head brought a million more questions. Where was he? Where was he going? Why had he gone? Why had he slipped out when she was asleep? Why hadn't he spoken to her about this? How could she contact him? What if something terrible happened to him? Marelle sobbed and collapsed onto a chair. Why had she let him go – *why* hadn't she realised and stopped him. Marelle cried, covered her eyes with her hands. She overwhelmingly wanted to speak to him; she wanted to hear his voice – she wanted to just pick up her phone and call him – like she always did. But his phone was laying on her table – it told her he did not want to be contacted.

Where would he go? She thought of all the places The weir, the pool, Frankie's grave, the beach she had taken him to? Why would he go to the weir? It was too close and he knew she would look there. He had said he never wanted to go back to Frankie's grave and she couldn't see why he would at the moment. Or the beach – he'd liked it but had no obvious longing for it. The only other place he had shown interest in was the bridge – but it was a bridge. Why the hell would he go there?

No, he'd taken off – she had always feared he had the capacity to do it but thought she could keep him here. How long had he been gone? She didn't know. What time had he got up to go to the toilet? She couldnt remember. How long had he sat down here writing this note? She had no idea. How far could he have got by now?

She closed her eyes and was instantly confronted with that awful image of him in a morgue – from her dream she'd had. Marelle gasped, sobbed – what if that was coming true? What if they knocked on her door and said they had found a body. But how would they know to contact her if they did find him? She had no connection to him – he'd be an unknown person – no-one would know who he was or to contact her. Jacob was out there, alone – unconnected and with no-one to look for him. He could be dead now and she may never know.

Through new, hot tears she looked at the note again. He said he needed time and space; he said he would try to return – he did not say he was going to do anything to harm himself and he had berated her for even suggesting that before. He had always come back to her – why would this be any different? He said he would come back.

But that didn't help. Right now, that did not help. He was not here and she had no idea where he was among the eight billion or so people on the planet.

For a moment she sat there, staring into space. She picked up her phone and her finger hovered over Bella's number. No; she would not call her – not yet. He'd said he would come back; he had always come back. Give him an hour or two and he would pull that lanky frame of his into her kitchen, say he was sorry and then take her into his arms. Jacob was infinitely sensible – he would not do anything stupid.

Marelle finally dressed and walked over the perimeter fence and onto the airfield. She headed for his caravan. It was the weekend so there was nothing going on despite there being diggers and various items machinery scattered about. The gates were closed. For a moment she stood and wondered if Jacob had closed them on his way off? Marelle stood staring at the gates – even they looked static and lifeless today. She turned towards the caravan. Thankfully it appeared to have escaped any revenge onslaught from the events the night before and remained exactly how he had left it the last time he had come up here with her.

Tentatively she walked right up to it. Placed a hand on the door where she had first knocked on that dark, cold night. When he had just been the weirdo on the airfield wearing a woolly hat in the cold caravan. She smiled. And the door where Bella had drawn a heart in pink lipstick –

Marelle almost laughed but her throat constricted on her and she lowered her head to the keysafe.

Maybe he had changed the combination – her fingers dialled in 1008 and the cover sprang open. There inside was the key with a red enamelled number '1' as the keyring. She pushed the key into the lock then paused. Somehow this felt wrong; she felt like she was violating any trust he had placed in her, but he knew she would do this! He could have changed the combination or taken the key. He had done neither. She turned the key and opened the door.

It was dark inside because all of the curtains were closed. She opened some of them and let the sunshine in.

Marelle could smell Jacob in here. Just a sense of him, just the scent of his newly laundered clothes; the scent of any deodorant he wore. Marelle stood in the caravan and took it in. For over ten years he had lived in this space. She had not even known he existed. This tiny space had been the centre of his universe – then she had knocked on his door. Now he'd gone.

The caravan was virtually empty. Everything had been put away, tidied up. It was pristine and clean – and empty. Marelle went into the bedroom; the wardrobe where she had sneaked a look that day after Sam had clouted Jacob in the pub car park. She opened the door again and was surprised to find it virtually empty. Had he taken the clothes with him? All that was left was a dinner suit and a dark grey fleece. She picked up the sleeve of the fleece and sniffed it. The photo in the red leather frame of his brother and his parents had gone too. She wondered where and sincerely hoped he hadn't burned all of this stuff when he had sat up here with a fire. She looked briefly at the dinner suit; he'd obviously decided he would not be needing that wherever he was. But she nonetheless imagined him in it, and he looked good. She hoped one day she would see it for herself.

Finally, she noticed a small bundle of white material stuffed down behind one corner of the shelf. It looked old and had a hole in the neck – she unscrunched it and held it up. It was a plain white tee but on the back in red, what looked like red permanent marker pen, someone had written "Ezza you cunt" in scruffy capital letters. Ezza? Ezrah? He had denied all knowledge of that name. She stared at it, maybe it was just a coincidence? She folded it carefully and put it back on the shelf.

Then she looked in all of the cupboards and all of the drawers. There was nothing; it was as if everything had been cleared out, thrown away – or burned. He had said he was tidying up; he'd said he was putting things straight – but he'd been clearing it out as if he had known all along what he planned to do.

She left the caravan, locked it and began to walk back. After a couple of strides she stopped and turned to look back at it. It was cold and empty and alone here. It looked as bereft as she felt. With a sigh she turned and began walking back.

A small part of her expected him to be there when she got back – along with a small part of her which spent the rest of the day and evening just expecting him to walk in through her back door, hug her and say sorry. But by the time she decided to turn in for bed that had not happened. Marelle was worried; she was scared and felt like her insides were ripping themselves asunder but she maintained composure by the single overwhelming feeling that he *would* return. He had always come back – when he'd disappeared unexpectedly – when he'd been gone for longer than she had thought he would be, when he was angry or upset or just completely off on one – he had *always* come back to her.

Marelle lay down in the cold bed he'd left at some point early that morning and resided with that one overwhelming thought. *He would come back to her.*

And as she lay her head on the pillow she wondered just where he was. Had he checked into a hotel? Was he sleeping out in the open somewhere – or was he still moving? He'd be cold and hungry. Was he sitting somewhere now thinking about her and wondering what she was doing?

The night took its toll; although she had slept here, alone, many times – even before she had hooked up with Jacob – but tonight she heard every noise the house made; she woke and sat up at every rustle; every tap; every car that went past just in case it stopped. One ear was constantly listening out for the bike in the distance. She had become so tuned in to the sound of that and the expectation that hearing it meant he was on his way back to home to her. But not tonight. Each sound was not him and he did not come home. Marelle remembered listening to his heartbeat and his breathing – vital signs of life that she had taken for granted – and that brought her right round to the image of him on the mortuary slab, cold and lifeless. She buried her face in the pillow and sobbed. What she would not do to just be able to call him right now. She remembered his gentleness, the softness of his hands and the clarity of his skin, the look of innocence in his eyes – of vulnerability – the way he portrayed that wide eyed look so perfectly. That day she had first cut his hair he had changed in such a way that delighted her. Jacob was a flawed genius – too perfect for this world – too pure to be tainted by life and too humble to knock it down when it attacked him. He was always quiet but said so much – and when he did speak, he spoke with an eloquence that denied his birth and upbringing. He was unique; he was special – he should not be out there on his own right now – unprotected, vulnerable, alone. He was too fragile for that. It kept her from sleeping as he filled every corner of her mind in a montage of images she had collected. Because right now, that was all she had.

The next day she was cold and tired. She wandered down hopeful, but nothing had changed. She checked her phone and checked it again. If he knew her number, he could at least contact her if he needed to. *If* he knew it; she had put it into contacts in the phone she had given him – he may have never even memorised it. She stared out of the window and could see a blue truck shunting around in the distance on the airfield. There would be no-one to save the airfield now.

Marelle wasn't hungry but made a slice of toast, she buttered it but left the lime marmalade off. There wasn't much left – if he came back he may want it. She ate, forcing each mouthful down as she stared out over a scene that felt so very different today.

There was something in her emails from Seb. She didn't want to work and knew she would not be able to concentrate. But, she wanted it to appear as if everything was 'normal' and not give him reasons to ask questions. She spent the morning working with one eye on her phone and one ear outside.

At lunchtime she filled the kettle and as she stood at the sink was aware of activity at the perimeter of the airfield. There were three guys in orange hi-vis vests erecting a line of metal fencing just inside where the perimeter fence was, or had been. It was almost up to her garden and appeared to be going round the entire perimeter. Soon the gap at the end her garden would be closed and she would no longer be able to get onto the airfield. Not knowing how this would go, she walked out, stepped over the fence and went up to them.

"Er ... hello." She smiled.

The one who seemed to be supervising turned to her.

"Oh, hi. Can I help?"

"Are you putting that all the way round?" She made a little circular gesture with her finger.

"Yes, we've been told to close the whole airfield off. There will be work starting on here next week and we don't want people wandering on to it anymore."

"I live there ..." She pointed. "Wont I be able to get on here anymore?"

He shook his head but seemed friendly enough. The other guys erected another fence panel and blocked off few more feet.

"No, it's a construction site. You shouldn't really be on here now."

"What about the caravan?" She pointed.

"Its ok at the moment. I will need to speak to its owner though."

"He's not here." She said. "I don't know when he will be back."
"We can always move it into the compound."
"But it's his home – he may come back at night and need to get in."
"Then he will have to contact the site foreman. When is he back?"
She looked into his blue gray eyes. He was young; younger than her, "I don't know. He lives with me, but he's gone – I don't know where he is ...."
The guy looked at her for a second then turned his attention to the others.
"Would you be able to help move it into my garden?"
'What?" He asked.
"The caravan. Its mobile – he made sure of that – could you help me move it into here?" She pointed to her garden. "Once you've put the fence up we wont be able to."
"Well ..." He said, looking puzzled about the whole situation.
"Please!" she pleaded.
He stopped, turned and sighed. "I don't know if we can."
"It won't take much, I can help – I can tow it with my car."
He gave a little smile. "I'll have to speak to my boss ..."
An hour later they were hitching Jacob's caravan to a four wheel drive pick up truck. She had been inside and secured everything she could. The guys had been more than helpful, and their boss had even come over to give directions as well. They moved off gently with the caravan in tow. It broke her heart to see it move from that spot and she felt one connection shatter inside her as it wobbled and bounced away. They had to cut away the remains of the chain link fence to get it through and its last few metres off the airfield were probably its roughest as it bounced through the long grass and lumpy turf.
They reversed it into her garden, at the end, quite close to the fence.
"Here?" He asked.
"I think that will be ok." Marelle replied.
The three of them then spent the next hour getting it level and stable. It looked so much bigger in her garden, but she smiled when it was there.
"I'll make you a cup of tea." She offered.
"No, no. Its ok, we still need to get this fencing up. Are you ok with that here now?"
"Yes." She smiled. "Yes, that fine." But it wasn't. "Thank you!"
So the fence continued and closed off the airfield as she watched. The caravan looked lost, out of place, worried. He'd kill her – he'd told her not to put it in the back garden as it would be stuck there forever. Right now, she didn't care. She wanted him to come back and moan at her.

Marelle was still staring out of the window when her phone rang on the table. Her heart lurched and she shot across the kitchen so quickly she sent a chair flying sideways and nearly spun her computer off the table.
"Hello." She said, not even having looked at the caller ID.
"Oh hello." She did not recognise the voice. "I was hoping to speak to Jacob."
"He's not here at the moment. Can I take a message?"
"Oh – erm, when will he be back?"
"I'm not sure. Who's calling?"
"Its Mike Nicholls, I was speaking to Jacob a while ago about the Thor site at Groveham Parfield."
"Oh, yes! Hello!" she smiled. "This is Marelle – I'm Jacob's ... partner ... he gave you my phone number."
"Oh, hello Marelle. Well, I was hoping to speak to him but well, its good news for now. They are looking at preserving the site as a heritage site …. It'll stop work for 6-8 weeks at least. In that time, I have got chance at to put a good case together – I may need his help."
"That's great news!" She smiled, feeling a lump in her throat. 'Thank you."
"He can call me when he's back …"
Marelle drew a breath. "I'm not sure when he will be. He left yesterday – slipped off when I was asleep – left me a note saying he needed time and space to think."
"Oh." He said. "Oh dear. Well I hope he's ok. I know all of this has upset him quite a bit … but well, theres good news now. Hopefully you can get it to him."
She smiled to herself. "I'll try."
"Well I hope he's back soon – but they should cease work now if they've started anything yet. Unfortunately, its only the actual Thor site they're looking at but in the circumstances this is the best possible outcome we can hope for."
"I'll tell him as soon as I can." She said. "But – well, if I can help at all let me know."
"Most appreciated. You take care."
Marelle put the phone down and was suddenly overwhelmed with tears. She flopped into a chair. Why now? Why now when he was not here to tell? After all this time – there was a glimmer of hope on the bright blue horizon but he was not here to see it. Marelle began to really cry for the first time since he'd slipped away. She allowed herself to cry for him, bitterly. She sat there and she cried. And the more she cried the more she cried. The tears would not stop and with each sob it took her deeper into the dark thoughts that she had been chasing away all day.

Jacob would be alright because he was ultimately *sensible* – he was straight and level and practical – unless he was not; unless he was embroiled in his own torment which she knew he was ninety nine percent of the time. When he wore his tormented sould like that she knew he was apt to wander into those dark corners where harm would seem inevitable. And it was that which she feared and reared its ugly snarling head right now and breathed fire right into her heart.

For twenty four hours she had managed to kid herself but now she had to face up to the fact that Jacob was probably as close to the edge as he could possibly be and it wouldn't take much to push him over. 'Time and space' was a phrase he used all of the time but it was an excuse for him being overwhelmed and not coping – an excuse for him to lose his head. What the fuck he was doing wherever he was – she had no idea but when she let her mind wander, she could not get away from the glaring fact that was not a good one. She had to find him, and she had to find him quickly.

Her first thought was to call the police – report him as a missing person – what what would that do? At best it would drag his name round every police force, maybe get mentioned in local press; local tv – everything he would despise and serve to drive him deeper and darker than he already was. At worst it would alert the police to the fact that he had done a runner just after the second body had been found. What would that look like? She could not risk dragging his name through the dirt on either count and anyway – doubted they could help much.

Marelle knew she could well drive around looking for him but unless she had some clue to where he had gone it would be akin to looking for a needle in a haystack. Plus, knowing Jacob, he was likely to be keeping himself less than visible. However, he was on the bike, and it would need fuel – maybe that was a good place to start. The second problem was that she had no photographs of him. He had never let her or anyone else take one. So, if she picked that course of action she would have to give a detailed description of him – which to be honest probably wouldn't stick in anyone's minds or make an impact on people.

Her next approach was to scan the news and the internet – every news site, local or otherwise – looking for something – *anything* that may be Jacob. It was a massive task with a double edge; if she found anything that could remotely be him then it was good news; if she found anything that looked like it was him then it was probably bad news. Marelle read all of the accidents and incidents over the whole country in as many news leads as she could find but nothing today looked like it could be him.

In the afternoon she got into her car and drove around. Truly, she did not know why as she did not expect to see him. Nonetheless it was a stone to turn so she turned it. But as expected, she uncovered nothing. Marelle did try to ask in a couple of petrol stations but after a rambling and somewhat desperate sounding description in each case which was met by blank and uncomprehending expressions by the attendants, she realised she was wasting her time.

After the third day of his absence she began to feel the ingress of thoughts that asked her was he really going to come back? If he was, as he said in the note to "try and come back" then surely it would have been within twenty four and at most forty eight hours. Once beyond that point she feared that another world would have eaten its fingers into him and he would soon be lost forever. Perhaps right now he wasn't even thinking about her – maybe now she was far from his mind?

What if he didn't come back? What would she do? Without Jacob she had no reason to stay here – and wasn't sure she wanted to. But what if she left then two, three years down the line he did return and she was not there?

There were no answers – only questions. Until he returned there were no answers to her questions. There were no answers to anything anymore – her whole life was suddenly an explosion, forever expanding outwards with every tiny part of it moving further and further away from each other. She could not gather it all up or try to put it all back inside her because the glue that would secure it was missing. She would forever watch those parts of her life drift away.

An unexpected knock at the front door the next morning brought on the same moment of panic, the same flutter in her chest and profusion of adrenalin coarse through her. She opened the door and was immediately confronted by Mr. Wright from the farm.

"Good morning." He greeted. He looked just like someone who had spent three weeks in the sun. "I was hoping to speak to Jacob."

She wanted to say 'so was I' but decided against sarcasm. "I'm afraid he's not here." She replied.

"Oh, ok ... shall I come back later or can you pass him a message?" He questioned.

That sounded like bad news and a coward's way out, she thought. Truly she wanted to push him for his first option but in the circumstances it would not be possible to tell him when to come back and she wanted to know what was going on.

"You can leave a message if you want."

Mr. Wright smiled. It was a sheepish smile. "Well, firstly I'm sorry that this has happened – obviously it was something Adam wasn't sure how to deal with but as I am sure you will agree, he did deal with it in a fair manner ..."

He raised his eyes to her for acknowledgement – she narrowed her eyes to him scornfully,

"Well – it was his only option unless he wanted everyone else to walk out on him!"

Because he was scared of them, Marelle thought to herself.

"But we need to resolve the situation." He continued.

She stared at him – yes?

"So I'm planning to get the workshop moved to another barn at the other side of the yard where I keep my lorries at the moment and this would be away from everyone else – I'm happy for Jacob to continue working for me but I may have to 'remove' him from the farm – at least until all of this has passed."

"And you think it will pass?" She asked, her voice no longer content to stay within.

"Oh I'm sure it will." He smiled.

"Well as far as I can see he has lived here all of his life and this deep seated persecution of him has not yet 'passed'."

He laughed a little. "I think persecution is quite a strong word ..."

"Do you?" She stated. "Well let's say hatred, derision, cruelty then?"

"Now, now ... its just a bit of banter – they're youngsters ..."

"Sam came close to killing Jacob the other night."

"Well if that's the case it looks as though Jacob got the better of him!"

"You haven't seen Jacob."

"How is he?"

"Black and blue all over." She said, surmising he was; hoping he was at least still conscious and had not succumbed to any of the injuries he had sustained. "Sam and his father attacked us on the airfield – wanted to '*teach him a lesson*'."

Mr Wright gave a laugh but soon changed it into a cough when he saw the expression on her face. "I am sure its only banter – he's a young lad – he likes to show his prowess – and it didn't happen on my property so its not really my responsibility."

She sighed and closed her eyes. "But you are responsible for the welfare of your employees?"

"Only when they are working for me." He added. "But I have just come here to try and sort things out. I will move the workshop and I will honour the offer I made to Jacob *but* it is going to take time – a month or two – and until that time I wont be able to offer Jacob any other work. I can't have him there with the other lads at the moment."

She stared at him, anger in her eyes.

"But once we have the workshop set up elsewhere then I will start him on a new contract of employment and he can come back. I will let him know as soon as it is ready." He continued.

"Tell me something." Marelle stated. "What has Jacob *ever* done to *anyone* in this village that makes everyone so sold on harming or hurting him any which way they can – just *what* has he done?"

Wright smiled. A half sympathetic smile. "Well you now what he's like – he can't socialise with anyone – he doesn't speak to anyone – he doesnt even make eye contact with anyone – he has always been seen as a bit of an outcast – he sets himself up for ridicule and derision – he's an easy target and they keep aiming for it."

"He's done nothing." She answered. "He is the most gentle, humble person I have ever met. He never retaliates – he never fights back or had a bad word to say but he is constantly being punished – *constantly*." She bit her lip and suddenly felt tears in he eyes and her lip tremble. "He can't keep taking that." She finally said in a tearful voice.

"Now ... now, Jacob is a good worker; a good man. I think he's strong enough to contend with what the world has to throw at him."

She sniffed. "Is that what you think?"

"Of course – he's hung on in there for a long time now – he's not going to let young Sam get to him."

Marelle sighed and felt like physically banging her head against the brick wall she stood next to. No-one understood. No-one. Marelle truly didn't understand Jacob, but she had a better idea than anyone else but right now there was too much distance between them for her to try and guide him out of this mess. Nobody in the whole wide world would give a fuck about him – except her. Not one other person on this earth knew him; knew his name or cared whether he lived or died; cared about what he had done in his life or where he was now. No-one; except her.

Mr. Wright left as soon as he could finish the conversation and get away. He'd said what he came to say but had received considerably more than he had expected. None of it however, she doubted, had made any impact on his own charmed life.

And as the next few days in his absence dawned she felt that gap become wider. Marelle felt the yawn of where he was and where she was opening up as each day, hour and second passed. He had said he would try to come back; she had expected it within twenty four to forty eight hours, or else she'd thought to herself, he was gone. Now well past that she still woke every morning with the hope in her heart that he would saunter down her garden path again.

TWENTY-TWO

A knock at her door mid afternoon made her slowly rise from in front of the computer. Stories were starting to break over the discovery of a second body in the garden, but they were scant and factual which suggested the press were only working from carefully worded press releases from the police. She'd read three accounts and all were identical. Marelle walked to the door and opened it to DCI Catchpole.
"Afternoon." He greeted. "Is Jacob there?"
"No, sorry he's not." She said.
"I have a few questions I'd like to ask him – can he come down to the police station later?"
Marelle shuffled. She didn't want to tell Catchpole that he'd gone – that would make Jacob look guilty and raise suspicion about any knowledge or involvement he had in it but, she could only string Catchpole along for so long.
"Erm ..." She leaned against the door post. "Why don't you come in – I've just made tea ..."
He walked into the kitchen behind her, she made him tea. Catchpole didn't sit down but him standing up annoyed her, so she gestured for him to sit.
"When will he be back?" He asked.
"I don't know."
"Can you call him?"
"No, he left his phone here – "She nodded towards it, still laying on the worktop.
"Where is he?"

383

"I don't know." She placed the mug in front of him. "Have you identified the second body yet?"

"No." he replied.

"I've seen the story on the news on line."

"They're still excavating the garden."

Marelle smiled to herself at this comment.

"How long has he been gone?" Catchpole asked, changing back to the subject of Jacob which she'd tried to steer off.

"Oh, a while."

He smiled knowingly but said nothing else.

"What do you want to ask him `– I might be able to help?"

"Just background questions, that's all ..."

"I think he'd told you all he knows." Marelle stated.

"I thought he may have *remembered* some more details ..."

"Is Jacob a suspect?" She questioned.

He shook his head. "No, not as it stands. As he said, he was a child – this body is believed to be slightly older that the other one."

"Older?"

"Been there longer.

"Well I don't see what Jacob can help you with if that's the case."

"You know about his brother? He asked.

Marelle nodded.

"Interesting case." He remarked.

"But he died ..."

He nodded. "Suicide, apparently. Interesting character but there are some strange circumstances around his death."

Marelle didn't comment. She did not plan to add to his information.

"He drowned in a tidal river ... not unheard of but not a usual method of suicide. By all accounts he disappeared for four or five days and then turns up washed up at the mouth of the estuary. Post mortem found a lot of alcohol and a cocktail of drugs but he died by asphyxiation due to drowning. From what I read I would have thought it would be deemed misadventure rather than sucide. Was identified by a 'close friend' who reported he had been suffering from severe depression and panic attacks for a while and had taken to drinking and that he courted a morbid fascination with water and drowning. He died a few days after his father – leaving Jacob as the only surviving member of the family."

"Jacob said they weren't close, he hardly saw him."

"No, I can see that, but he was older than Jacob – by about three years I think ..."

Marelle nodded.

"Funny thing is Jacob has always been under the radar – his brother pops up here, there and everywhere but Jacob ... " He made a face. "No trace – nothing– he was the only living relative so all of his brother's stuff went to him but it looks like he's managed to remain completely off the radar all his life. He was born, then nothing – until now."

Marelle gave him a wry smile. That pretty much summed up Jacob's life as far as she was concerned.

"Well that's Jacob, isn't it?" She commented.

"When did he leave?" Catchpole asked suddenly again.

"Early morning." She replied, which wasn't a lie; she just didn't say which day. "Was it a body of another child that was found?"

"We can't disclose details yet – there is still an investigation taking place."

"You said it was 'older'?"

"Buried a while before Frankie Lee we guess by the information from forensics."

She nodded. "Oh, I see ..."

"Jacob didn't attend his brother's funeral you know – seems it was organised by a group of 'friends'."

"I know. He told me that. I suppose his father had just died too and he had that to contend with."

"Maybe." Catchpole said. "I see you've got the caravan in your garden?"

"Yes." She answered. "They've closed the airfield off now so we had to move it."

"We?"

"Us and the developers."

"Surely if he is acting as 'caretaker' he could have left it there – or have they laid him off now?"

Marelle pursed her lips. "No, but he's kind of 'on-call' – they've just got through an investigation into making it into a heritage site so they've got to stop work ..."

"Really?" He asked.

"Yes, apparently. So, he will be needed for a while longer." She smiled with some sweet sarcasm.

"Has Jacob said anything to you about the discovery of the second body?"

"No." she laughed. "Only that he knew nothing about it."

"Ok, I just wondered if he had remembered anything – like he did with Frankie?"

"No." She said.

"When did you say he would be back?"

"I didn't. I'm not sure but I can ask him to ring you when he does ..."

"Ok, that would be good." He replied.
When he'd finished his tea he left, but as he stepped out of the front door he turned back to her,
"If he has disappeared you need to report him as a missing person – we can look for him…"
She smiled but those words hit her hard – that was what he was now – but she would not admit it to Catchpole.
"I don't need to do that!" She said with a grin as fake as his sincerity. "He'll be back later."
But she knew that in a day or so Catchpole would be back too.
Marelle walked back into the kitchen and stood staring out of the window at Jacob's caravan and the airfield beyond the new fence. Work seemed to have halted and there was little activity over there. She sighed.
"Where are you Jacob?" She whispered to herself.

The following day was warm and thankfully, sunny. She had propped the back door open and worked in the kitchen for a while. She did her usual trawl through the news stories that she had no interest in, except in looking for any trace of Jacob. There was nothing – which she held as no news at least being good news but wondered as she read emails what he was doing at that precise moment. She imagined he was sitting in the sunshine somewhere, thinking about coming back to her.
Walking out into the garden she was pleasantly surprised but the warmth of the sun and lack of a usual breeze. She walked up to the metal fencing and held on to it with her fingers, pressing her forehead on to it, looking up and down the airfield. There did not appear to be anything going on. The machinery was there but it was standing still and idle – like a herd of prehistoric monsters frozen in time. Marelle looked to the spot where his caravan had once stood. All of those times she had looked over to it, looked for lights on – or lights off – craned her neck to look across at that – the little white box that contained the prize – the present and the future. Now it was behind her but that space where it had been and the absence of it in its rightful place saddened her.
"What the hell did you put it there for?" He would ask when he came back and she laughed to herself at that.
Above her she was alerted to the mournful shriek of the red kite, circling overhead. She looked up, shielding her eyes against the sun, watching the dark silhouette of the bird on a thermal of air above her. Marelle stood and watched it, circling slowly and wondered if it had seen Jacob leave – if she had seen him go and where he went. Marelle

watched the bird until she suddenly swooped easily away and glided to the far side of the airfield. Marelle turned, pressed her fingers against the fence again and peered out, watching the bird now in the distance.

"Marelle." A voice suddenly said behind her.

She jumped and flew round, the fingers of one hand still wrapped around the wire of the fence. Seb was walking towards her.

She sighed.

"You could let me know when you are planning to turn up – at least out of common courtesy …"

"And how? When you won't answer the phone when I call."

"Email?" she suggested.

"Then you would go out and say you hadn't seen it." He retorted. "What are you doing?"

"Nothing, just looking over there …"

"Whats that thing doing here?" He nodded to the caravan.

"Nothing."

"Why is it even here?"

"Because they've started work on the airfield – we had to move it."

"Why is it in our back garden? You won't be able to get it out of here once they start building …"

"Yeah, Jacob said that too."

"Well why the fuck did you let him park it there!?"

She shrugged. "What are you here for?"

"See what state you are in."

"So, your minions have reported their far-fetched stories back to you then? I didn't really appreciate opening the door and finding Chris standing there!"

Seb grinned. "I didnt send him. He asked me if it was a good idea to let you know that he and his new girlfriend were planning to marry – he's *considerate* you see – didn't want you to find out via gossip."

"Wouldnt have bothered me anyway. We split up – remember? There *was* a reason for that!?"

"He met Jacob, I take it?"

She narrowed her eyes at him. "You *know* he met Jacob. He gave you the full debrief I take it?"

Seb grinned sarcastically. "Well he said you were very hostile; and Jacob was dressed like a drug dealer and also said that you had a bruise on your face and he looked like he'd been beaten up. You were a pretty pair by all means …"

"Fuck's sake Seb! Blow everything out of proportion why don't you? I explained it all to him – I didn't have to but I did – did he not relay that too?"

"Yes, he did, and I don't believe a word of it anymore than he does."
"So you *did* send him to spy then?"
"No. I didn't." He stated. "Why are you out here, pining at that fence, like you've lost something?"
"I haven't lost anything. It's a lovely day – I was out in the sunshine … you should try it sometime. You know, just switch off and enjoy whats around you."
He laughed. "What? What crap is that? You turning into a fucking hippy or something?"
"Fuck off Seb." She turned back to look over the airfield.
"I'm not convinced Marelle. Look at you – you're normally dressed properly. Your hair is a mess and you look like you haven't slept for weeks."
That hurt. True she had trackies on and one of Jacob's old t-shirts – maybe she had forgotten to brush her hair this morning, but that comment was unfounded.
"I'm sorry – I didn't know I was meant to be turned out first class at all times."
"You always used to be. You were always dressed neat and tidy – usually wore make up – now look at you. He's dragged you down to this – I warned you. Living in a fucking caravan like some drop-out. Can I come into the house, what state is that in or have you turned it into a fucking commune?"
"Its not in any state!" She raised her hands in frustration. "You've just caught me on an off day where I decided not to dress up, or put on make up, or do my hair – come on into the house, come on in. Theres nothing to hide – you can search it if you want – just in case you think theres a stash of crack or something in there." She stormed off towards the back door, up the steps and through it with Seb in tow.
"Any chance of a tea or coffe?" He asked once inside.
"Make it yourself. I don't want one."
He did so. Marelle folded her arms and stood with her back against the worktop.
"I might want to sell my share of the house." She said.
"Oh yes, why is that? I thought this was paradise on earth? Well, that fucking caravan will have to go before that happens."
She didn't reply for a moment, just maintained a sullen pout.
"Why?" He asked. "You seen sense and moving on from that outcast?"
"No – I'm going to marry him. We want to move away from here."
Seb laughed – at her. "What?! No, I'm not selling up so you can fund his lay about lifestyle. If you want to sell it you can buy me out first."
"Well I'll do that then." She said.

"At full market value." He added.

"Whatever."

There was an uneasy silence as Seb stood there drinking tea with her sulking beside him.

"So, where is he then?" He finally asked.

"Out."

"Clearly." He replied succinctly. "What about whats going on over the road ..." He nodded his head towards it.

"What about it? Its got nothing to do with me."

"But it has to do with him, doesn't it? Another dead body, dug up right near the first – whats going on over there, hey?"

"Don't know. There police are there ... that's all." She shrugged.

"Two bodies. Dug up in a garden where your dearly beloved used to live – both children, apparently? Doesn't bode well does it – not with his record ..."

"Record! What record? For fuck's sale Seb – its got *nothing* to do with him. He was a little fucking kid at the time!"

"Well you know what they say – like father, like son."

"Yeah and they also say you cant choose your fucking relations!"

Seb sighed. "Whats gone wrong Marelle?" You used to be such a sweet girl – happy – out for a laugh. He's changed you for the worse and you are going to commit yourself to that?"

"Yes!"

"Why Marelle? Why? You're young and pretty and clever. Why him? He must be fifteen years older than you."

"He's a ten years older than me." She interrupted.

"You could have your pick of someone "better" – someone with prospects – someone '*normal*' – he's a fucking farm labourer who lives in a caravan – it'll be a disaster. That's notwithstanding whatever 'afflictions' or 'addictions' he comes with."

"Because I *am* happy with him. He makes me happy. And you don't know what that is – you haven't been happy since you married Caroline – you would not know what I mean!"

"Oh shut up and stop acting like a spoiled little brat who has found a bit of rough. It doesn't suit you."

"You can't stop me doing what I want to do."

"No, I can't. But I can make it difficult for you. I can stop giving you work – and remember I pay you twice the going rate – which is only because you are my sister and I'm happy to help you. And I can insist on the full price for this place."

She shrugged. "Then I'll get another job."

"Doing what?"

"Hairdressing."

He laughed. "You really are a dreamer Marelle … and you can't expect any help from me for a wedding to *him*. Won't that be a seedy little affair … God forbid I can just imagine it."

"At least it won't be as pretentious as yours – trying to copy the Royal Wedding"! You make me sick!"

There was a second or two of silence, then she spoke again.

"Go!" she said. "I don't want you here. You just come down to have a go at me like I'm still your kid sister. I don't want it and I don't need it – go – go on!"

"Marelle, give this up – come back and live with me – we can sell this place and split it fifty fifty. Come and work for me properly – I'll put you through a Uni course – get a worthwhile qualification …"

"A *worthwhile* qualification!" She exclaimed. "Like everything I have ever done in my life is worthless! I don't want to come and live with you – I don't want to come and work 'properly' for you – I want to cary on what I'm doing here and be with Jacob."

Suddenly she was fighting to hold back tears as this was, at the moment, pure speculation. But she sure wasn't going to cry in front of Seb.

"I'll give you six months." He stated. "I'll give you six months to see sense – I doubt it will last much longer anyway – after that you're on your own on whichever path you choose to go with him and then you won't hear from me again."

And he pushed himself away from the worktop and made a move to go. She raised her tear filled eyes to him but thankfully he did not look at her.

"I'll prove you wrong." She said. "One day you will look at Jacob and regret you ever treated either of us like this!"

He gave a little laugh as he left. "As I said Marelle, you're a dreamer."

"At least I have dreams." She called after him.

"Bye Marelle." Seb said before he walked out of the front door and closed it behind himself.

She stood in the hallway looking at the closed door. She heard his car start up and drive away. Tears rolled down her cheeks – she'd held on to them this long but now they flowed in realisation that all of her dreams were based around Jacob and she had no idea where he was or even if he would return. A week had been and gone with no word or sight of him, where was he and what was he doing? Where was he sleeping – was he alone? Marelle could not imagine him alone out there, dealing with everyday things but on the other hand she could easily see him making a new universe for himself somewhere. In the same way he had done here – only she may not be part of that exclusive new universe. He may meet a new Marelle in that parallel world.

"Shit no!" She cried. "Shit no, Jacob …"

When she rose from a sleepless night the next day she did heed what Seb had said – but not for his benefit – for Jacob's should he come back. That day she showered, washed her hair, dressed smartly and put on make up – it didn't make her feel much better but at least she would look good for him – if he turned up.

Cathchpole rang. She watched it and let it ring. She had nothing new to tell him and didn't feel bothered to make excuses today. He didn't leave a message.

An hour later her phone rang again and she was expecting it to be him. It was not, it was Bella.

"Hi Bel." She said then instantly bit her tongue. Bella had once commented that she only ever called her 'Bel' when something was wrong.

"Hi." She greeted. "All ok?"

"Yeah, all good." She lied.

"Jacob ok?"

"Mmm, fine." Marelle hated lying to Bella because Bella always knew when she was lying.

"Oh, you sure about that?"

Marelle laughed. "Sure I'm sure!"

"Good." Bella said but seemed totally unconvinced.

"Look, we're coming up to this weekender thingy in Felixstowe this weekend – I'm travelling up with Freya on Friday – are you around – thought we could pop in and say hi on the way …"

"Eh, erm, Friday?" Marelle asked.

"Yeah – be about lunchtime."

"Well. I had promised Jacob I would drive him down to Frankie's grave on Friday. He wanted to go again …"

"Oh." Bella replied. "Oh, ok – so you won't be there then?"

"No, I doubt it. It's a four hour drive each way at least – we'll leave early and may not be back until late …" Where had that enormous white lie come from? It had been too easy.

"Oh, ok then. Probably won't catch you. Maybe on the way back on Sunday – but then, we may not have time unless we leave really early ,,, which we will if its shit!"

"Maybe. Let me know what time on Sunday if you want to drop in, we'll probably be here then."

"Ok. But as I said, if we stay till the end we'll probably be on a mad dash home! But look, I'll let you know."

"Ok!" Marelle chirped, a little too lightly.
"Marelle!" Bella laughed. "You sure you're ok?"
"Yes, why?"
"You sound odd. You been drinking?"
"Hell no Bella!" She exclaimed. "Probably too much coffee!"
Bella laughed. "As long as its all its too much of!"
"It is."
Marelle smiled. "So I'll see you if I see you on Sunday – otherwise give me a call, hey?"
"Yeah, will do …"
"And enjoy your weekend!"
"Oh, I will certainly try. Been good if you and Jacob could have come."
"Oh I don't think so. Its just not his thing – you know that! We'd be brewing up all kinds of trouble as I am sure you can imagine!"
"Maybe next time. He'd be fine!" Bella grinned. "Well take care. Lay off the coffee. Love to Jacob."
"Ok, see you soon." Marelle smiled, then sighed.
She took a long breath and laid the phone down. That was a whole lot of lies – to someone she trusted and who trusted her. Marelle didn't want to lie; she did not want the barrage of unfounded sympathy and implied 'told you so's' that telling the truth would bring.
Catchpole called another couple of times over the next day or so. Each time she resisted answering and he did not leave a message. Finally, on the Thursday afternoon, nearly three weeks after Jacob had disappeared Cathchpole turned up on her doorstep.
Marelle could have just not opened the door but she knew he would be persistent and did not know how far he would take it if she kept avoiding him. Again, today she had made sure she looked groomed and smart – she opened the front door and looked around it.
There was a tiny flicker in his eyes as he acknowledged the change in her appearance but that was all.
"Afternoon." He greeted, "Sorry, are you off out?"
"No." Marelle replied.
"Is Jacob there?" He still hasn't called me."
"Er, no. He's not here at the moment." She answered, suddenly flicking her eyes away from his narrowed grey ones. "Sorry, I thought he would have called you by now."
Catchpole sighed. He had his hands in his pockets, looked straight at her and tilted his head slightly.
"When did he go?"
"Pardon?"

"He's disappeared, hasn't he? When did you last see him?" He asked, he had the attitude of a friendly uncle – at the moment.
"No – he hasn't!" She lied, making a smile. "He's just not here right now …"
"When did he disappear, hey?"
Marelle looked at the floor then rised her eyes to him. This was the very last thing Jacob would have wanted and she felt like it was a betrayal of his trust he had placed in her, but it had also been nearly three weeks since he had left that morning.
"You'd better come in." She said, quietly, stepping aside.

"So, when did he go missing?" Catchpole asked again, once inside.
Marelle took a deep breath – told herself it was ok. "Nearly three weeks ago." She finally said.
"Three weeks!" Catchpole remarked. "And you've heard nothing from him?"
She shook her head.
"Did he say anything? Leave a note?"
"He left a note." She confirmed.
"What did it say?"
"Just that he 'needed time and space'; that had some hard decisions to make – that he couldn't be the person I wanted him to be – and that he would try to come back …"
"Can I see it?"
Marelle paused. She classified the note as personal and didn't really want to share it. However, she took it out of the drawer she had put it in with the phone. Carefully, she unfolded it and handed it to Catchpole. He read it slowly.
"It doesn't strike me as a suicide note." He said. "But you cannot guarantee what his intentions ultimately were …"
Marelle looked at him, pleading with her eyes for him not to say that.
"Looks more like a 'dear john' letter than anything else. So this was all he left?"
She nodded again, holding her hand out for the note's safe return to her. Catchpole hung on to it for a bit longer.
"Did he leave anything else?"
"Only my old phone, which I let him borrow. There's nothing on that."
"What time did he leave?"
"Somewhere between about 3 and 8 in the morning. I was asleep – when I woke up, he'd gone."
"On foot?"
"Probably on that old motorbike. It's gone too but I didn't hear it."

393

Catchpole sighed, handed the piece of paper back to her. 'Three weeks …. It's a long time, you should have told me earlier …"
"I expected him to come back." She sighed.
"I will put a call out to other forces to keep an eye out for him. He's an adult and has gone of his own accord – he can't really be classed as vulnerable and I wouldn't take this as a suicide note – we wont instigate an active search but I can put the word out. Do you have a photo?"
"No."
He made a face of surprise.
"I don't have a photo of him. He doesn't like having his photo taken."
"Description then – what is he, six foot?"
She nodded, "Probably."
"What does he weigh?" Then he realised that was a pretty absurd question. "Slim build I guess, brown eyes?"
She nodded.
"What was he wearing?"
"I'm not sure."
"What did he have om the last time you saw him?"
Marelle shook her head, searched her teeth with her tongue. He'd been naked.
"We were in bed …" she paused, drew a breath then continued. "He would probably be wearing a black fleece, black jeans – his workboots …" She sought for what was missing. "An olive green military style jacket …"
"Did he take any clothes with him?"
"Not that I know of but he kept a lot of stuff in the caravan. He'd cleared it out recently, most of his clothes had gone. I caught him burning some of it …"
"When?"
She shrugged again. "Couple of weeks before he went?"
Marelle stared at the floor for a second. "I thought he was just tidying things up because he knew he was going to have to move the caravan – bit now I think he was always planning to leave?"
"He has proven ability to slip below the radar – he may have planned this and carried it out to perfection."
"I know." She said. "That was why I was hoping he would come back."
"Most people come back within the first 48 hours if they intend to – does he have a passport?"
"I don't know, she replied blankly.
"Has he gone missing before?"

"Not since I've known him. He sometimes goes off unexpectedly and doesn't answer his phone, but he has never not come back or eventually replied to me."

"This is what his brother did, you know?"

"But Jacob is not his brother, is he?" She answered looking into Catchpole's eyes.

He left a while later, having reiterated he would put the word out about Jacob and that he would be in touch if they had any news. Marelle thanked him but doubted he could help. They didn't know Jacob.

TWENTY-THREE

She spent most of the day staring out of the kitchen window and worrying that she had totally betrayed Jacob. Catchpole had still not said why he wanted to speak to Jacob and now the police were looking for him. She had got caught up in the emotion of him being missing and the supposed extended hand of help and understanding that Catchpole had offered and caught her off guard enough in a moment of desperation and she had accepted it. This could have ruined any chances she had of him coming back to her.

Catchpole had asked for a photo but she had none. Not one single photograph of Jacob – only his image in her head which she conjured as often as possible for fear of it fading away and her forgetting that jawline, those cheekbones, those eyes. A cold reality hit Marelle that she had nothing of his – except for a couple of t-shirts and a practically empty caravan in her garden. There was very little trace of his life here anymore – he'd carefully planned and deconstructed it all – right in front of her and she had been too stupid to notice. All the signs had been there for weeks – signs she should have picked up and acted upon. It scared her, it terrified her that she alone had let him slip through her fingers so blindly.

Within her though was the eternal hope that he had said he would 'try' to come back. Jacob was a man of his word; she knew that but three weeks on she would have expected him to turn up by now. Marelle hoped against all hopes that he was still out there; still close by, agonising over his 'difficult decisions'; about coming back to her. She closed her eyes and imagined a swirling mist reaching out fingers and tendrils of her thoughts across the space between them to connect with

Jacob's thoughts; wrap their tiny fingers around each other for dear life and eventually pull him and her back together again. Deep within her she still felt that connection and that all was not yet lost.

Reality hit her in the morning when she opened the cupboard to find it completely empty. For the past three weeks she admittedly had been using up things that had been languishing here for months but today the tea bag box was empty; there was no coffee; no sugar – milk had run out a week ago. The freezer was like the Marie Celeste and she didn't have a single slice of bread or biscuit in the place. Normally she would have popped over to the village shop but that had ceased to be an option from the night she'd confronted Jill over Jacob's exclusion from there.
There was a bottle of sparkling wine in the fridge and for some reason a box with two after eights in right at the back. She had no idea how they came to be there as she hated mint and chocolate! They were her options for breakfast – it was time to make a trip to the supermarket. If Jacob did come back she would need food and tea bags in the house!
Marelle walked along the aisles thinking what Jacob would like. She put all the things into her trolley she knew he favoured – he'd never admitted to liking anything in particular but she had watched him and noticed things he chose over others or the items he showed most enthusiasm for. She imagined what she would cook for him when he walked through the door.
With two bags of shopping on the back seat of the car she set back, eating a chocolate bar as she drove as she had declined the breakfast choice at home. It was a beautiful sunny day and the village looked pretty beyond its vindictive undercurrents as she entered the edge of it. The early autumn sunshine dappled through the browning leaves on the trees and danced off the roofs of cars and slates on the houses. Up ahead the steeple of the church rose through the late foliage of the surrounding horse chestnut trees. Marelle looked towards it and suddenly felt the pull of the beautiful little churchyard and wanted to go there in that quiet solitude for a moment. There was frozen stuff in the back, but she indicated left and turned down the little lane to the church.
Her car was the only one in the car park and she pulled up against the low stone wall. A memory of Frankie's funeral suddenly haunted her for a moment as she sat in the car; that had been a terrible day that she longed to forget. She got out of the car, hoping the warmth of the sun may push thoughts of the funeral away. The birds were singing in the trees surrounding the churchyard, it still had that calm tranquility that it had before when she had sat on the bench and Jacob had turned up in

the van from the farm. She'd sat with him on that bench. She smiled and walked to it now, staring for a second before she turned and sat herself down on its sun warmed, smooth surface. Looking out at the graveyard her eyes moved to the headstones of Jacob's family. Marelle looked, blinked, focussed and felt her heart pound in her chest at what she saw. Getting to her feet she walked quickly over to the grave of Jacob's mother and father. When she finally stood in front of it, she placed a hand to her mouth and gasped.

The headstone had been smashed in half. It stood there like a broken tooth; the newly exposed surfaces of the broken stone lighter in colour and cleaner. The whole top half of the stone was broken completely off. Marelle's eyes read the inscription left – Jacob's mother with the break line just above her name – the half which proclaimed his father's name smashed and laying in the grass behind.

Standing in the neat grass of the graveyard with the sun shining on her back and the sound of birdsong in the quiet peaceful air the full impact of this violation wrapped its fingers around her throat and she felt a lump rising. Had Jacob seen this? Who had done this? Although she had a very good idea. It was a cowardly act of the utmost disrespect; it was not just a strike to Jacob's father but to his mother and his grandparents alongside who were innocent parties in this. It saddened her to think someone could be that ignorant and vindictive. The graves were bare and she wished she had flowers to put on them by way of an apology for other people's behaviour. Maybe later she should get some and bring them back here. As she stood with her head bowed in apology for this, she wondered about the act of placing flowers on a grave right now and it deepened her sadness at this whole sorry situation. Maybe she just couldn't bring herself to do it, not unless Jacob was at her side or she would wonder just who she was placing them for. Had Jacob seen this? Had this been the stone that had troubled the water enough to for him to go? She doubted it as he wasn't a frequent visitor anyway, but nonetheless she understood it could have been a seemingly small item in the grand scheme of things which proved to be the final straw.

And somebody had come prepared to do this – it wasn't something you could kick over with your foot. It would have taken brute force, ignorance and some kind of tool to break that stone like that.

In recompense, Marelle stopped and gently pushed the broken piece of the headstone around to the front of the remaining stump and leant it against it as best she could. That was all she could do.

With a gentle smile and a silent apology from her she turned and walked away, through the gap in the wall and back to her car.

That single act had irked her more than she would have expected. It plagued her all of the time she unpacked the shopping and put it away. Death was sacred and to disturb and violate those resting in peace was wrong; so wrong. Was it a criminal act? Was it criminal damage? She suspected it was – should she tell Catchpole?

She supposed she should, but it would probably makes things worse in the long run. She decided to sleep on it and make a decision before he contacted her again.

She had not slept well over the past three weeks; when she did it was very light sleep with one ear constantly listening for the door or his bike. Half the time she didn't go through the normal bedtime ritual and often laid down on the bed at three or four in the morning, when she as finally so dead beat that she would she knew she would fall asleep quickly. That night, however she had got into bed a bit earlier, fallen asleep reasonably quickly and opened the door for dreams to make an entrance.

Marelle was in the churchyard, by the graves just as she had been that day. The sun was shining, it was warm and the birds were singing sweetly. She noticed the headstone for Jacob's parents' grave had been repaired and looked perfect once more. In her hand she had a bunch of yellow roses interspersed with small white flowers like the ones that gew in the long grass on the airfield. There were already flowers placed on Jacob's parent's graves and she thought to herself in her dream they they still looked so fresh – she had put them there a week ago – but they still had their luminous colour and sheen on the leaves of fresh flowers. For a second Marelle stood and looked at their grave and silently thanked them for their son whom she had been so lucky to meet, and to know, and to love.

Then she stepped to the right, stooping and finally dropping to her knees in the warm, soft grass. She lifted he head and looked to the pale grey marble headstone in front of her. It was new and the turf around its was new. As Marelle reached out to place the flowers in the vase at the foot of the headstone and raised her eyes and read the words, carved black into the grey stone.

"Jacob William Frost." It gave his birth date and underneath it another date.

Marelle awoke suddenly, blinking her eyes with her face half in the pillow. Her thoughts were wild and unco-ordinated for as second as she wondered why it was dark and the sun had gone; as if the dream was reality and now she was cast into a dark nightmare. Then as her thoughts aligned themselves, she had the vision of the new headstone in the graveyard with Jacob's name inscribed on it. She felt the pain of grief overcome her and for a further moment she struggled with the living and the dead. Angrily she brushed tears away from her face and recalled the second date that had been on the marble. It was yesterday's date.

Marelle drew a breath, held back tears – it was her mind playing games with her; images and thoughts from the day randomly stitched together in a haphazard fashion. Jacob was not dead; he did not die yesterday. He was alive and he would come back to her.

After that she found it hard to sleep. When she closed here eyes she saw the headstone again. When she lay there staring into the darkness she thought of the other dream she'd had of Jacob in the morgue. That was still a clear and vivid vision that she felt she would never dispel and the sheer perfection of it haunted her right now. As her thoughts went deeper she was faced with a realisation she had not considered. If – and only if – something did befall Jacob, no-one would know it was her they should contact. He had no living documented next of kin as far as she was aware. He could die and she would never know.

Marelle swallowed and closed her eyes; reaching across and empty bed where he had once laid next to her. She stretched her feet out, feeling for his which were not there; imagining her hands wrapped around his warm body, feeling his lungs expanding and hearing his gentle heart beating within him.

As soon as it began to get light she was sliding out of the bed and sitting on the edge of it looking back at the place where he used to lay. She did not make the bed anymore; just got into it and got out of it. She'd done that since the day he 'd gone and gazed now at that side of the bed where he'd buried his head into the pillow beside her.

Marelle walked across the room and looked out of the window. She wore one of the old t-shirts Jacob had left behind. It draped on her coming to mid thigh and the sleeves were baggy. She looked to the sky outside. Marelle never pulled the curtains closed here and quite liked getting woken by the rising sun. Today however there was no sign of it. The sky was steel grey and angry, packed with clouds like dirty cotton wool, teased at the edges. It looked like there was going to be a storm. Like the one she'd got caught in over the airfield after they had been to the Thor site for the first time and they had sheltered in his caravan. The thunder and lightning had crashed so loudly around them on that day and lingered so long. They'd both been soaked to the skin and she had borrowed his clothes to wear. Marelle smiled. It had been on of the first times she'd felt really close to him. She remembered something he had said – was it that day? She couldn't remember but he had said *'if you travel high enough – up and above the clouds – the sky is always blue and the sun is always shining. Its always there but sometimes you cannot see it because there are clouds in the way.'* With a soft sigh to herself she dwelled on that thought as the storm clouds gathered above her.

The sky held the rain which surprised her. Outside it was very dark and threatening but so far not a single drop of rain had fallen. Today Marelle felt oddly sad. It was as if getting to the three week point was some kind of way marker or some corner she was now turning in the road which slightly obscure any view of Jacob she may have still had. That, coupled with the vision that had come to her last night filled her with a greyness that matched the sky. What could she do? She had been on a mission with Jacob to find Frankie – now she had a new mission – to find Jacob. He had always said that she was a 'a fresh pair of eyes' – maybe she also needed a different viewpoint as well. She stood pondering on it and wondering if it was time to confide in Bella and ask her for help?

A knock at the door took her attention and she carefully stood down the mug she was holding to her chest as she stared across the airfield from the kitchen and turned to go and answer it.

Patricia stood there, dressed in red with a red and white polka dot scarf around her neck.

"Hello." She said a little less chirpily than she usually did. "I'd like to speak to Jacob."

"He's not here at the moment." Marelle replied.

"When will he be back?"

Marelle shook her head. "I don't know."

"Well I need to speak to him." Patricia stated. "They told me none of this should be discussed but I need to speak to him – he's the only person who knows anything about this …"

Her voice did not sound so bold as usual and Marelle noticed she seemed to be wringing her hands around each other in front of herself as she spoke.

"He doesn't know anything about this …" Marelle imparted.

"Of course he does!" Patrcia snapped. "How can he have lived there in that house with his father and not known what was going on?"

"He was seven or eight years old! Even if he *had* seen anything he was a very young child – he would not have *known* anything."

"They have dug up the whole of our garden and we can't even start to put it straight yet. It's a total mess and making Derek very frustrated. I need to speak to Jacob – I need to know exactly what went on there." She stated, very angrily, pointing behind herself.

"He's not here."

"Well where is he? When will he be back?"

"I don't know."

"He's done a runner hasn't he?" Patricia continued narrowing her eyes. "Hasn't he?"

'No." Marelle said defiantly. "He just needs some time on his own. Its affected him very deeply as well."

"Well that's an admission of guilt if ever I saw one!" Patricia exclaimed. "Do the police know?"

"Yes!" She snapped. "They know and they are not bothered. He is not a suspect. He says he knows nothing. I believe him and *they* believe him."

"But there were two bodies buried in our garden – the bodies of *two children* – one was an *infant*. Somebody killed and then buried those two children in our garden!" She stated slowly and forcefully. 'They think there could be more – and they've dug the whole garden up."

"Well were there?"

"What?"

"Any more?"

"God forbid no!" Patricia gasped. "But his father killed two children and buried them in the garden ... his father was a cold blooded murderer and who was the second child, hey? Your friend needs to answer some of *our* questions."

"He's not here." Marell repeated defiantly.

"No, because he's run off, because he knows what went on there – he's hiding something."

"He's hiding nothing!" Marelle replied.

"But you don't know where he is and I take it the police don't know where he is?"

"He said he needed time; he said he would be back."

"Just like he's always done. I've spoken to a lot of people in the village about him and his weird ways." She pointed. "No-one has a good word to say about him, notwithstanding this – general opinion is he's a flaky fly-by-night – has a habit of disappearing and turning up again. He's hiding something – everybody says – he's hiding some dark secret and its something to do with whats going on in our garden." She pointed and almost seemed tearful – pointing back behind herself again.

Marelle stared at her. There were a thousand words in her head; a hundred things she could explain to Patricia and show her that she was talking absolute shit. Marelle just stared at her.

"Fuck off." She finally said and closed the door.

Marelle stormed back into the kitchen, threw herself down on a chair, placed her head in her hands and cried. She cried bitterly for everything, *just everything* and in that moment, she understood why he had slipped away.

The rain held off until mid afternoon then it started. Straight down and steady; grey rain from a grey sky; just falling. She watched it and wondered where he was – was he sheltering; was he warm and dry? Was he thinking about her?

Marelle truly did not know what to do. Three weeks was a long time and she felt the chasm of that time in every cell in her body and they ached with a passion. She had told Catchpole but he did not seem to be ready to treat Jacob as a missing person; she knew she should also tell Bella an at least get another pair of eyes involved. She knew also that this would eventually get back to Seb and his utterings of 'I told you so' would be intolerable.

But what should she do? Stay here – wait for day after day in the hope that he would return while in the meantime grieving for the person she may – or may not – have lost forever. Maybe she should start travelling around, asking questions – like it seemed everyone else did. Perhaps she should put together some posters and put them wherever she could. Like a lost dog.

Marelle sighed and felt her hope drop yet a level lower. The posters would only work if she had a photo – which she didn't because he didn't like anyone taking a picture of him. Once again, she was hit with the fact that she had nothing of him to really remind her of his face; his voice or that rare beautiful smile.

As the rain lashed against the window Marelle started to form an idea of a plan in her head. For a while she sat, thinking about it, then she sat at the kitchen table with a pen and a writing pad; then she put the computer on.

She would start with a circle around the village and ask in places around that circle where he may have crossed. If someone had seen him then she would know which direction he had gone and could make the next circle around that area. If no-one had seen him then she would make the circle bigger – and so on. At some point, someone, somewhere would have seen him. But she needed a picture.

Maybe if she did not have a picture, she could describe him to someone who had the skills to draw him. They used 'artists impressions' on the television all of the time, didn't they? Surely it would not be difficult for someone who could draw, or paint? She wracked her brains but could not immediately think of anyone. Right, tomorrow she would call Bella and ask if she knew anyone – failing that she would have to consult the Yellow Pages. God, it couldn't be difficult, could it?

Marelle smiled to herself. Happy to have a plan. She looked up at the clock and realised it was already dark outside, the rain was still falling and she was alone, in the darkness, working in the light from the laptop.

Her stomach rumbled. It was the first time she had felt hungry since Jacob had disappeared.
"I *will* find you Jacob." She said.

She cut two doorstep slices off a loaf of bread she had bought at the supermarket. It was a little past its best but would toast. She squeezed the two slices into the toaster and pushed it down then poured water from the just boiled kettle onto a teabag in a yellow mug. Once toasted she slathered it in butter and carried the tea and toast through to the living room and placed them on the floor next to the settee. She flicked on the tv then went back to the kitchen, she picked up her phone and the old one that Jacob had used together with his note which she had now placed in a stiff brown envelope for safekeeping. It was precious. She wanted to read it again, think of him saying the words he had written and maybe, just maybe, look for clues.
Marelle read it twice, making sure not to get butter on it as she ate the toast. Then she read it a third time. Each time it stabbed her in a different way. Eventually she returned it to the envelope and pondered on what he had said.
Then, sipping the tea, she picked up her old phone. She wanted to read the texts he had sent to her while he had used it. She flicked through it, it still had her name, her photo but his texts to her. There were not many, just a couple. They were brief and to the point. Like the note she read them two or three times, but they yielded nothing. She sighed and was about to put the phone down when she noticed a 'draft' text that had not been sent. She opened it and immediately gasped a small cry and clapped her open hand to her mouth.
The draft text was a picture of Jacob; a selfie taken on the airfield, before she'd cut his hair short. It was a sunny day and he had taken the picture at arm's length with the camera above him. It looked like it was at the Thor site. His hair looked great, his brown eyes warm and on his face was the most beautiful smile. Beneath the picture were the words "remember me like this."
Marelle sobbed as she looked into his eyes and cried; she saw in them warmth and the love he had for her; she saw that familiarity that she had cultured, and she saw the recognition of his true feelings for her. Why hadn't he sent this to her? Had he meant her to find it like this? Yes – that was exactly how she wanted to remember him – but in her arms, warm and vital beneath her hands. Marelle clutched the phone to her, embraced it as she wanted to embrace him; clutching onto that last moment he had left for her.

She touched his picture gently; she caressed his face. That lopsided smile. That tiny dimple in his cheek. Each time she looked into his eyes the tears came again. It was almost like grieving for someone then discovering they were not dead. At least that was how she felt right now.

Then, realising she now had the precious picture she had wished for she had a minor panic that something would go wrong with the phone and she would lose the picture before she had worked out a way to get a copy from the phone. Quickly she took her own phone and took a photo of Jacob's picture. Just to perpetuate it – just so there was not only a single copy in existence – just to be on the safe side. The picture came out better than she had expected and she sat for a moment or two staring at that one as well.

She now had a picture. Marelle could now start her plan – she could make posters; she could print out the picture and take it round with her; she would dilate in an ever increasing circle until she found him.

But the words in his note and the words in the draft text message began to combine in her head as she re-read the note and stared at his image. It was so similar to the one of his brother that he'd had in the caravan – they looked so alike – and she wistfully pondered on his words she felt an overwhelming fear that he had never meant to return.

Clutching the phone to her, she lay her head back and closed her eyes. Re-animated the image and saw him smiling at her in real time; the sun lighting up his face, a true warm happiness in his eyes; his arm sliding around her shoulders and him placing a kiss on the top of her head.

She awoke. It was those seconds where she did not know where she was or what she was doing but was suddenly confused and slightly shattered, fumbling for her phone which was ringing. She discovered the phone still in her hand and looked at it in puzzlement. It was not that one ringing – her own phone was blasting out its ringtone on the seat of the settee beside her. She half cursed to herself, picking it up. Reality was, she was dribbling and her heart was racing fast at the awakening by an unexpected call. She looked at the phone, wiping away the dribble from her face. It was twenty-one minutes past ten and it was Bella.

Marelle sighed. The last thing she wanted right now was one of Bella's drunken ramblings but she decided to humour her and answered it. Tomorrow she may need her help.

"Hi Bella." She said.

"Where are you!" Bella exclaimed.

"At home?"

"Where's Jacob?" Bella asked.

Marelle sighed to herself. She drew a breath through her nose. "I don't know."

Bella seemed a little taken aback at Marelle's reply. "You don't know?"

"No. He disappeared, three weeks ago. I haven't seen or heard from him ..."

"So you lied to me about not being there yesterday?"

"Yep." Marelle answered. There was no point in hiding the truth now. She had decided to tell Bella anyway.

Bella paused for a moment. She didn't give Marelle the bollicking she expected for lying to her. "Well, you're not going to believe this but, well ... we are at this weekender but its shit. It was shit last night and shit tonight so we decided to have a drive round and see if we could find somewhere better ..."

Marelle sighed. It sounded as if Bella was somewhere noisy – in a club or a pub. She could hear Bella well enough, but she could also hear people laughing and shouting in the background. There was loud music too.

"Well ... we had been out of own and back again and we came across this seedy little pub on the outskirts but it's got karaoke and its absolutely rammed. So we came in and its brilliant and well ... we're standing here and Jacob is up there singing karaoke!"

"What!" Marelle was suddenly fully awake and listening.

"He's actually very good!" Bella laughed. "I thought maybe you were here?"

"Bella where are you!" Marelle exclaimed, already standing up and and slipping on shoes.

"In Felixstowe ..."

"Yeah, but where? How far away?"

"I don't know ... about an hour from you?"

"Whats the name of the pub?" Marelle ran to the hallway and looked for her car keys, the phone to her ear.

"Erm, I'm not sure ..." Bella said, "Whats the name of this pub?" Marelle heard her ask someone.

"The King Billy ... the King William ..." She corrected having had a reply from some random person.

"Whats the address?" There was panic in Marelle's voice as seconds ticked away.

"I don't know! Why?"

"Because I'm coming up there!"

"Well if you get on the A14 and head for Felixstowe – go over the Orwell Bridge ... there were police all over it earlier, they made us stick to one lane ... said there was a police incident ongoing but they let us through

"... keep going towards the docks and the pub is down that road, right at the end. It's a tiny pub but its got a big car park beside it ..."

"Are you sure its Jacob?" Marelle asked. Bella didnt sound drunk but well, she may be.

"I'm pretty certain – but it looks like he's given himself a haircut – you won't like it!"

"I did it before he went ..." Marelle explained. "Has he got a tooth missing?"

"Erm, I don't know. He's got leather trousers on!" She giggled.

"Has he seen you?"

" – No. I don't think so."

"Well don't let him see you, he'll run. Who are you with?" Marelle was thinking on her feet, breathless and panicking.

"Just Freya."

"Ok, just keep him there ... don't let him go – if he goes then follow him and ring me!"

"Marelle, how can I keep him here without letting him see me?"

"Use Freya – she's a pretty little blonde thing – use your imagination!" Bella sighed.

"What time does it close?" Marelle asked, keys now in hand and shoes on feet.

"I don't know. Eleven? Twelve?"

"Bella, just keep him there!" Marelle stated. "I'll be there as quickly as I can."

The rain was still beating down when she went outside, car keys and phone in hand. She had no coat and bare feet in trainers but she did not have the time to worry about that. She fell into the driver's seat and put the key into the ignition. If she was honest, she had no idea where she was going but she started the car and pulled quickly out of the drive.

She didn't really know whether to go right or left out of the drive but figured if she at least got to an A-road she could find signage that would tell her which way to go. The signpost she eventually saw in front of her at a T-junction said "Ipswich" or "Norwich". She sat there, debating. She had turned towards Norwich when she had driven to a beach and Jacob had commented the coast was much nearer in the other direction. He had also said he was 'east of Ipswich' when he had been at the Orwell Bridge that time and Bella had said to go *over* the Orwell Bridge. Marelle sighed, indicated and turned in the direction that said "Ipswich". It could have been the most important decision of her life.

The roads were wet and quiet. She drove on as she passed through a couple of villages. Marelle panicked slightly, not sure if she was going the correct way and thought about turning round but she carried on, following an instinct she felt she had to trust. Eventually a large green road sign loomed up in front of her. It said "Ipswich A14" as the second exit and she smiled to herself taking the car around the roundabout and off up the slip road to pulled onto the dual carriageway. She glanced at the clock in the car – it said 10:45. She knew it was a few minutes fast but nonetheless she pressed the accelerator to the floor. The tyres cut through the puddles and the tracks made by the lorries on their daily journeys to the docks – faster than she should have been or wanted to be going in weather like this, heading for the coast.

With one eye on the clock she drove, wipers slapping across the window. Thankfully the road was relatively quiet. It felt like she had been driving for hours in the dark, but the time was just coming up to eleven. Marelle had no idea where she was nor recognized a single inch of the area; she was just in a car, on a road, speeding towards where she'd been told Jacob was.

She passed the exits to Ipswich, knowing at least she had to carry on – so she continued. Up ahead she saw blue lights and her heart began to sink. There was no slip road to get off but the traffic was very light. Instinctively, she slowed slightly, realising the police car was parked in a lay-by with its blue and red lights flashing. The road ahead looked clear as it snaked and began to rise in front of her. As she glanced at the police car, she saw the sign that said "Orwell Crossing" and she realised she was about to cross over the bridge where Jacob had called her from. The lanes over the bridge seemed clear and she sensed climbing upwards into the darkness. Despite it being dark it was still not possible to see over the concrete walls at the side of the bridge but in the distance she could see lights below whch told her she was at a significant height above the river that ran below. As she neared its apex there were police in fluorescent coats, walking along a narrow walkway behind the barrier and the parapet of the bridge. They had torches and were walking back towards the police car in the lay-by. Marelle watched them as she drove by but they were not taking much notice of her or the other traffic. She descended the bridge, feeling the fall away of the road as it it dropped down again, bumping over the metal join between bridge and road as it levelled out once more. The road sign said "Felixstowe" and "docks". Both were ahead but she began to panic as to whether she needed to go to Felixstowe or the docks. Bella had said to head for the docks so as the road slowed her and she came to a large roundabout, she drew a breath and took the second exit.

She drove into what seemed like an industrial area. It was street lit with business parks on each side of the road. It did not look like the type of location for a local pub with a banging karaoke. She sighed, staring, wondering whether to turn around or just carry on. Up ahead she could see a more lit area, so she continued, leaning over the steering wheel and looking up at the lights. It was a Macdonalds – that looked more hopeful. Surely a Macdonalds would be near a pub or at least a busier area. She indicated and turned left up a slight hill, past the Macdonalds and a supermarket. The businesses made way to what looked like a more residential area which filled her with hope. It had to be here, somewhere. Marelle slowed, looking left and right. There streets were deserted and there were row after row of houses. No pub. She drove on, beginning to wonder why she had turned left here – Bella had not said anything about turning left. She drove over a small crest of a hill but just found more houses, all the same, lined up in rows in front of her. The clock said 11:23. She slapped the steering wheel with her hand.

"Shit!" She exclaimed.

Then her phone rang. It was not what she wanted to hear. She'd told Bella to ring if he left.

"Bella?" she answered, as she drove slowly.

"Marelle – where are you?" Bella asked.

"I don't know. On a housing estate somewhere near Felixstowe ... I don't know which way to go!"

"Marelle, we can't stall him much longer – we are out in the car park – its raining – I've sabotaged Freya's car and pulled some wires off – she fluttered her eyelashes at him and is playing the damsel in distress – he's trying to get the car started but pretty soon he'll realise its not going to go and if he goes now we can't follow him!"

"Shit Bella!" Marelle exclaimed. "Where are you? Has he seen you?"

"No, I'm in an old phone box over the road – its stinks of piss."

"And its definitely him?"

"Yes! Its definitely Jacob – and yes, he has a tooth missing!"

Marelle felt a cry in her throat. "I must be so close. Oh God, I don't know where to go. I turned up by a Macdonalds and I don't think I should have!"

"Macdonalds!" Bella asked. "We went in there earlier – you shouldn't have turned up there!"

"Where do I go then?" She sobbed.

"Calm down!" Bella said. "Look, turn around, come back to the Macdonalds then turn left. Get on that road and just keep straight – don't turn off it. The pub will be on your right a little way along ... only its shut and its pretty much cleared out."

"Ok." Marelle replied. "Ok, I'm turning round. Can you see him?"

"Yes. He's under the bonnet – Freya's in the car."

"Just keep him there Bella. If he has to see you then let him see you – I don't care what you do to keep him there but just keep him there!"
"I'll do my best – hurry Marelle."
The road back to the Macdonalds seemed so much longer than it had when she had driven up it and there were tears running down her cheeks when she finally saw it again. She gasped a sigh of relief and pulled up at the junction. As instructed by Bella, she indicated left and pulled the car back onto the road, accelerating smoothly.

She drove constantly looking to her right. Bella had said the pub was on the right. Up ahead she could see traffic lights and Bella had not mentioned them – so it had to be between here and the traffic lights which meant she was now within a few hundred yards of Jacob.

Then she spotted it. A cream coloured, pebble dashed, small building. Small for a pub, right beside the road, a large car park to its right. Her eyes moved up to the sign – a picture of an old king in crown and ermine beneath which it said King William.

Marelle indicated and turned the car right, across the left hand carriageway and into the car park. As she had turned in she saw the telephone box set slightly back in a small area of unkempt foliage. The door to it was half open and Bella was stepping out. She was grinning and pointing into the car park.

It was dimly lit; illuminated only by a light on the side of the pub and what light reached into it from a street lamp out in the road. There were two or three cars parked sparsely in it. She squinted and tried to focus her eyes more quickly in the relative darkness compared to the road she had just turned off. It was still raining but she had not really noticed, focussed now on a white car towards the far end of the space; its bonnet up and a figure beneath it, delving into the engine bay with a torch.

Her breath caught jaggedly in her throat and her heart was banging in her ears. He was here; he was actually here. It was him, alive and breathing. She recognized his legs; his stance; his bottom – it was Jacob, right here in this dirty little car park behind the pub that the locals called the King Billy.

She pulled a little further into the car park but still a way back from where Jacob was with Freya's car. Her own breathing and heart beating were all she could hear as she sat there for a split second trying to make herself believe that he was really here; that she wasn't at home, in her bed, dreaming. Leaving the engine running and the lights on she opened the car door.

As soon as the cooler air and the splashes of rain began to hit her, she found the animation to launch herself from the car, running away from the open door and Bella who was walking up behind her. Marelle ran, no feel of the rain or her footsteps on the gravel; no feeling of anything as she focussed solely on Jacob.

Marelle ran into him from the side, arms outstretched to envelope him as her body touched into his. Her head found its place against his shoulder and her arms wrapped themselves around him with a hold that would never release again. He was taken by surprise and half turned, his own arms outstretched behind her back as she ran into them. There was a fight response in him at her sudden and unexpected contact, but he did not act upon it. Instead, he staggered back a step, turned slightly then recognizing the body between his arms he finally closed them around her and pressed his hands warmly into her back.

He gave a laugh, or a sob. She didn't know for sure. She felt it beneath her hands. Marelle hugged him so tightly; she screwed her eyes tight shut and just squeezed him to her in one, consuming, delicious embrace. He was wet, his clothes were wet and his hair was flat against his head.

Gently, she took his face in her hands, looked right into his eyes. He blinked rain away and smiled at her. Marelle leant into him, closed her eyes and kissed him with a passion that had no anger, only love. He responded as she wanted him to which ignited an exploding confidence in her which said this was right and the time was now.

What had been lost was found; what had died was alive again; the shattered pieces of glass reformed themselves into a beating, fragile heart and footsteps which bothered the face of the planet again.

"Jacob Frost!" She cried. "Will you marry me?"

EPILOGUE

"I can't." He shook his head as she held it in her hands and they stood in the car park with the rain falling and the bonnet on the car open. "I can't marry you."
"*Why?*"
He stared into her eyes. "It's a long story."
She stared back at him, she could see he didn't know whether to laugh or cry as her hands cradled his face. "Well, maybe you'd better tell it to me."

Printed in Great Britain
by Amazon